MABEL AND THE UNHOLY NIGHT

Mysteries of Medicine Spring

Book One: Mabel Gets the Ax
Book Two: Mabel Goes to the Dogs
Book Three: Mabel and the Little Green Men
Book Four: Mabel and the Unholy Night

MABEL AND
THE UNHOLY NIGHT

By

Susan Kimmel Wright

DEDICATION

To director Bob Vogel, members of the Ruthfred Lutheran Church Senior Choir—past, present, and future—and organist, Essi Efthimiou.

And to the memory of our extraordinary organist and friend, Fred Schell.

"…I will give thanks to him in song." (Psalm 28: 7(b) NIV)

ACKNOWLEDGEMENTS

Heartfelt thanks to the following:

My editor and publisher, Miralee Ferrell and the wonderful team at Mountain Brook Ink.

Dorothy ("Dot") Corbett, beloved and much missed friend from our Second Saturday writing group, who has gone home to be with Jesus. Dot christened this book *Mabel and the Unholy Night.*

Peggy Arelt, who suggested Mabel join the choir and discover her special gift.

Susan Reith Swan and Valerie Brendel, for plot consultation and beta reading.

Kika Wright, arts administrator and anti-racism educator, for serving as my sensitivity reader.

Lynnette Bonner, who designs my stunning covers.

My agent for this series, Jim Hart, now retired.

All my wonderful readers. If you've bought my books, read my books, shared them with others, recommended them to your book club, written a review, or rated them, thank you from the bottom of my heart. There would be no Mabel without you.

My family—human and animal—and all my dear friends, for their unfailing loyalty and support.

"Thanks be to God for his indescribable gift!" (2 Corinthians 9:15 NIV)—Christ who came down to us on that first Christmas Day.

Chapter One

BIG, LAZY SNOWFLAKES HIT MABEL'S CHEEKS, and she stuffed her damp mass of chestnut hair under the hood of her red parka. Days of cold, torrential December rains had given way to snow overnight. Just a light coating on the ground so far, but a front marching across the weather map from Canada suggested more was on the way.

Mabel's best friend Lisa sang *It's Beginning to Look a Lot Like Christmas* as they climbed the hill between stands of snow-frosted pines and spruces. Mabel felt a fleeting impulse to sing along, but kept her mouth shut. She'd had a lifelong dread of singing in public, stemming from an unfortunate incident in third grade.

Feeling a burst of Christmas spirit nonetheless, she risked a small, graceful leap over a fallen branch. Then, of course, her boots skidded. Her arms wind-milled frantically, and she laughed off her embarrassment as John caught and steadied her.

"Easy there." He laughed too. "This isn't the place to be dancing *The Nutcracker* without your toe shoes."

"Also too early." Lisa's fiancé Tim gestured around them. "This'll all be melted before then."

He was right, Mabel supposed. They hardly ever got snow for Christmas down here in the southwestern corner of Pennsylvania. Easter, maybe—that had happened a couple of times.

"It's beautiful, anyway. Enjoy it while it lasts." John grinned and tilted his face up into the swirling flakes. He grabbed Mabel's mittened hand and began towing her along the slope. "How about a spruce? They hold onto their needles pretty well."

Mabel had no preference. It was enough for her to be part of this magical snow globe scene with John. A few months ago, she'd been single, turning fifty, and recently fired from her long-time, dead-end job as a lawyer. The firm had claimed she'd been a bit brusque with a few clients—who, in her opinion, had certainly had it coming. Mabel had successfully challenged her firing, to the tune of a nice, fat wrongful-termination settlement. Since moving to her late grandma's house in the village of Medicine Spring, she'd passed the 5-0 mark and was still unemployed—but now, she had a boyfriend.

Private investigator John Bigelow was smart and kind and thought Mabel was wonderful. That she found him handsome was just a bonus.

Mabel stopped and looked around. A sudden whiteout blurred everything beyond the closest row of evergreens. "Where's Barnacle?"

Why had she listened when John said her dog would be okay off leash? The tree farm was all but deserted, and Barnacle had been romping a moment ago, delirious with joy, but he didn't always come when called. Even at a mature ten, the big mixed breed still had enough cattle dog in his DNA to make him rambunctious when he wanted to be.

"Barnacle!" Mabel yelled into the wind. She turned to Lisa and Tim. "Has anybody seen Barnacle?"

Both shook their heads. "Not since he ran up that way a bit ago." Lisa gestured toward the top of the slope, where woods once part of the old Jubilee Johnson property marked the edge of the tree farm.

Mabel's heart sank. Barnacle didn't know this area. If he started following a game trail, he might soon be lost—with more snow and cold blowing in.

"You pick something out for me," she told John. "Nothing tiny. But not too big either—my size." She measured her own five-foot-nine height with one hand. "I've got to go find Barnacle before he wanders too far off.”

If he hasn't already.

“Hey.” John caught her sleeve. “Not without me, you don't. I'm the idiot who told you to let him run a bit.”

Tim spoke up. “We'll all go—won't we, Lisa?”

Mabel's tiny, dark-haired friend nodded sturdily. She'd stood by Mabel since kindergarten, no matter what. “There's still lots of daylight left. We'll have plenty of time to pick our trees after you catch Barnacle.”

Mabel knew she should protest. She didn't want to be a party pooper, but it made sense to take enough people to fan out a bit.

She looked around at her friends. John, ruddy-cheeked, wore a red-striped watch cap covering the high-and-tight “winter haircut” now replacing his normal shave-down. Lisa rubbed her nose, already rosy from the cold. Snowflakes glistened in Tim's dark beard.

Mabel took a deep breath of cold, pine-scented air and blew it out. “Okay. You're right. Thanks, guys.”

While the men stashed their saws under a sheltering spruce, Mabel felt in the deep pockets of her parka for Barnacle's leash. Once they'd caught him, that leash was going on and staying on.

“Where was he headed when you saw him, Lis?”

Lisa pointed. “Through there. The big break in that row of pines.”

Inwardly, Mabel groaned. If he'd entered the wooded area, which sprawled over forty acres, they could be tramping around for a long time. Not to mention, Barnacle might no longer even be in the woods. If he decided to chase after a deer, he might follow it right out of the woods onto a road and get hit by a car.

A surge of anxiety drove Mabel forward.

Meanwhile, what was the likelihood of one of them stepping in a hole or tripping over a branch or rock obscured by fallen leaves? Given Mabel's track record, an accident was quite probable. She foresaw a sprained ankle in her immediate future, if not a full-out broken bone.

"Barnacle," she called again, as she and Lisa climbed the slope, feet slipping on the wet, matted grass.

"You know," Lisa said, "he may not even hear you over the wind."

"His hearing isn't that great anymore," Mabel admitted with a pang. "For that matter, if he's busy with something—like rolling in dead possum guts—his ears won't work at all."

Lisa squeezed Mabel's arm. "We'll find him."

The guys caught up to them. Putting fingers to his lips, John gave a shrill whistle.

To Mabel's relief, there came an answering bark, though with the wind, she wasn't sure of the direction.

Lisa caught her eye. "Well, he can't be too far."

"Is that him?" Tim pointed.

Mabel sighted along his extended arm and saw a dark-speckled rock move at the edge of the tree line above. Her heart leapt. "Yes."

She called again as she stumbled forward. Now, she saw him look up. He barked again, then went back to whatever unspeakable activity he was engaged in on the ground. *Ugh.*

"He's got something." John squinted.

"I know." Mabel grimly pulled out the leash.

"At least, he's right there." Lisa smiled. "And he sure isn't going anywhere."

"Leave it," Mabel called without much hope. The dog's head popped up, and he barked and grinned.

"Come here, boy." She stopped, afraid he might grab his treasure and carry it off if he suspected she planned to take it from him.

"Treats." Mabel dug a leftover packet of saltines out of her coat pocket. She ripped it open and held out her hand.

Unable to resist the food, the dog frolicked up to her and sat. While she fed him with her right hand, Mabel grabbed his collar with her left. "Gotcha."

Snow had begun to coat the ground, not to mention Mabel's clothing. She peered at the solid mass of dark clouds smudging the sky. "Looks like the storm's ahead of schedule. We better get our trees and hit the road."

"What *is* that?" Lisa wandered closer to Barnacle's find, leaning forward for a better look.

John frowned and held out an arm, keeping her a few steps back. "Better leave it right where it is."

Her dog now securely leashed, Mabel ventured nearer.

Barnacle made a lunge for his find, but she pulled him back. "What—?"

Tim stepped next to John and squinted through the snow. They exchanged a narrowed look. "Is that what I think I'm see-ing?"

John nodded. "If you think you're looking at a human skull, I'd have to agree."

Chapter Two

MABEL SWIPED SNOWFLAKES FROM HER EYES. "You'd better be kidding." This could not be happening again. Even before this occurred, she'd reached the point of having to stop and count every time another body cropped up.

John didn't smile. "I would *not* kid about something like this, Mabel."

She studied Barnacle's discovery and swallowed. The skull bore a camouflage of dirt and a greenish patina of what looked like algae. Moss grew in the deep, golf ball-sized depressions which had to be eye sockets, now fringed with snowflake lashes. Though it no longer had the smooth, gleaming white look of bone, the domelike skull shape and size were unmistakable.

"Oh, no. What are we supposed to do now?" Lisa crept as close as John would let her and peered down. "Are you sure it's real?"

John shrugged. "Of course not. But it sure looks real…and old."

"Could it be a Halloween decoration? Tim squinted.

"Way up here?" John arched an eyebrow.

Mabel brightened. "Even if it turns out to be real, it might've belonged to a fraternal organization. I read an article where someone found a skeleton under some floorboards a few years ago. It turned out to be an old prop for an Odd Fellows initiation."

Lisa made a disgusted face.

"Well, regardless," John said, "what's it doing out here in the woods? Real or fake, we better let the tree guy know—and the police."

Tim nodded. "I guess that scrubs our Christmas tree hunt for the day too. I'll catch up with you guys down at the sales shed. I'm going to grab the saws before they get buried in snow."

"I'll stick with you," Lisa said. "John and Mabel can head down."

Mabel didn't know whether to praise Barnacle for his discovery or complain. She sighed. "Come on, buddy. You've done it now."

The tree shed, bedecked with a strand of colored lights, sat by the edge of the parking lot at the bottom of the sprawling, tree-scattered hillside. Behind it, a selection of pre-cut trees stood in rows for the convenience of customers disinclined to tramp around in the cold and cut their own.

"I'll put Barnacle back in the car and meet you over there," Mabel said. "I can't believe we have to do this again." This skull was getting on her last nerve, not to mention dampening her Christmas cheer worse than a cup of curdled eggnog.

John handed her his keys and gave her arm an encouraging squeeze. "Don't worry yet. This isn't our problem, and it might be made of resin."

When Mabel returned from the car, John was no longer in sight. No other customers remained in the lot either, but the tree shed radiated warmth and welcome. A curl of smoke from the stovepipe in the roof wafted downward, mingling its scent with the smells of pine and spruce.

The after-hours cover hadn't yet been rolled down over the sales front, but the jovial young farmer who'd greeted them on arrival was no longer in evidence. Mabel looked toward the hill and saw Lisa and Tim approaching.

She waved. When Lisa rewarded her with an answering wave, she decided to wait.

The shed was painted Christmas stocking red and wore a sign in green over the awning—CUT YOUR OWN. Wreaths for sale hung down the sides and along the bottom of the wide front counter. While she waited, Mabel checked the price tag on a stunning spruce-and-pinecone beauty studded with tiny silver bells and a big red-and-silver bow.

She choked and dropped the tag. If she ever did manage to buy a tree, she'd just tie a few of the trimmings to a nail on her front door.

Mabel sniffed. Somewhere she'd noticed a sign for free hot chocolate and cider—she could use some fortification at this point.

"Mabes," Lisa called. "What's going on?"

"Hey." Mabel wiggled her cold toes inside her boots. "I don't know. I think John went inside while I was stowing Barnacle."

Lisa blew her nose. "Tim's putting both saws in our truck for now. Oh, here he comes."

"What's up?" he called.

Mabel shrugged. "Let's find the door."

As they trooped around the side, no door appeared, but Mabel detected the mingled aromas of spices and chocolate. "Must be all the way in the rear."

They rounded the back corner into the cut-tree lot, trudging over broken pine sprigs and fallen needles. Snow continued to drift down, still taking its time but starting to stick. Strings of clear lights glowed in the gathering dusk.

"There we go," Lisa announced.

The sign on the back door read, "Employees Only," but there were two windows facing the tree lot, and Mabel saw John inside. She knocked.

The young farmer they'd met earlier flung open the door. His shock of red hair stood in all directions and his brow was furrowed. "Yes?"

John's face lit. "These are my friends."

Tim stuck out a hand to shake. John introduced them each

before gesturing at the tree farmer. "And this is Barry. He owns this place."

"Hey." Barry made an apologetic gesture at two electric urns sitting on a rough-cut wooden counter along the wall. "You're all welcome to some cider or chocolate, but I'm afraid it won't be too warm. They've been unplugged a while."

"That's okay. Thanks." Mabel took a Styrofoam cup and stuck it under the spout labeled "Hot Chocolate" in black marker on a strip of masking tape.

Barry turned back to John. "You're sure it was a human skull?"

John shrugged. "As sure as we can be without going close enough to pick it up."

Barry ran a hand up through his wild brush of hair. Mabel could see how it had gotten that way. She sipped her chocolate and grimaced. It was lukewarm and fading fast. She strolled over to the glowing potbellied stove and held a hand over the rising warmth.

Lisa sidled up next to her and unzipped her parka. She smiled at the young farmer. "Feels good after being out."

Barry frowned as if he hadn't even heard her. "Maybe I oughta go take a better look with a good flashlight before I drag the police out here."

John shrugged. "Up to you. It's your place but I'd get a move on if I were you. That snow's going to be a problem before awful long."

"Darn it." Barry darted a glance at a metal cashbox sitting on the battered wooden table he seemed to be using as a desk.

Mabel guessed he wanted to count his receipts—and didn't feel comfortable leaving his money sitting there with a bunch of strangers.

"Hey," she said. "If you guys want to go back out there and lock this place up, it's okay. Lisa and I can wait in one of the cars."

There was no way Mabel was hiking back up that hill in the cold and snow. Plus, it felt like her cute new boots were starting to give birth to a blister on her right heel.

"Hate to run you gals out." Barry sounded sincere, but he was also grabbing his keys and jacket.

Lisa gave an almost imperceptible sigh and zipped up again.

"Was it just the skull you folks saw?" he asked.

"At that moment." John crammed his cap back over his ears. "Hard to see much with the snow."

When they stepped back outside, the wind had picked up. Mabel turned her back against it and hunched her shoulders. "Hey, John?"

He raised his eyebrows in question.

"I'm going to need your car key again."

"That's all right," Lisa dug a key fob out of her pocket. "I have one for the truck."

Of course. She and Tim would soon be married, and it would be her truck too. Mabel waved and turned to follow Lisa.

Lisa hit the unlock button on the big, dark green, late-model Ford. From John's classic muscle car—whose paint job was still a work in progress—came a heartrending wail.

Mabel hesitated. "Oh, poor Barnacle."

"It's okay," Lisa said. "Tim isn't fussy about his interior. Bring that sad boy over here with us."

"Well, if you're sure." Mabel cupped her hands and yelled for John again. He turned and jogged back across the parking lot.

His vintage Dodge Challenger didn't have a remote. She waited for him to unlock, then grabbed the eager dog's collar as he tried to launch himself out the door. "Whoa, there." She leashed Barnacle and mouthed, "Thank you" to John over the wind.

To her surprise, Barnacle continued to dance and pull. His eyes danced with eagerness. "I think he wants to go with you."

Mabel looked up at John, whose hazel eyes laughed back at the dog.

"Pass me the leash. He wants to go with the rest of the guys."

Speechless, Mabel watched them disappear into the swirling snowflakes. She shivered and rubbed her arms.

"Come on, girl. Shake a leg." Lisa hung out the driver window, and the big truck's throaty purr meant the engine—and, no doubt, the heater—were already running.

On the second try, Mabel clumsily pulled herself onto the high passenger seat. She was a sturdy 5'9" and only a tad out of shape, but the effort made her question her devotion to the irresistible universe of carbs.

"Barnacle wanted to go with John."

"I saw that."

"He never chose anybody else over me before."

"That's good—it means he's accepted John into his pack. Dogs are good judges of character."

Mabel kept her thoughts to herself. She wasn't jealous—not very. Barnacle's steadfast loyalty to her though, above anyone else on earth, had been something she could always count on.

Then the creases on her forehead cleared. "Oh, for Pete's sake, it's that skull. He wants to get back to his find."

"No doubt. I'd kind of like to be back up there and look around, myself." Lisa rubbed condensation from her window and squinted.

"I'm curious too, but we couldn't see much right now anyway. Besides, I'm chilled all the way through."

"They'll end up having to call the cops anyhow," Lisa said. "At the very least, that skull is such a professional-grade replica that they're going to have to take it in to be examined."

Mabel struggled to pull off her wet boots so she could thaw her feet under the blast of heat pouring down toward the floorboards. "Once the police come in, that whole hilltop is going to be taped off. I wonder if there are more bones up there."

"I imagine so, if the skull's genuine, don't you think?"

"Well, by the time the body's had time to skeletonize, wouldn't animals have dragged pieces far and wide? Plus, there may be layers and layers of leaves on top by now."

"Maybe. Maybe not." Lisa's dedication to true-crime programming had gifted her with a wealth of crime scene knowledge. "You'd be surprised how fast a human body can be reduced to bones."

Mabel shuddered. "They might bring cadaver dogs in to help search. I don't know how they'd react if a whole big area like that was strewn with bones though."

Lisa ran the wipers. "I hope the guys don't hang around up there too long. This snow's really coming down."

"It's going up near forty again tomorrow. Most of it'll melt by afternoon. I feel bad for Barry. Once the police and crime techs get here, he won't have a lot of room for customers."

"You don't think they'll shut him down, do you?" Lisa asked.

"Hope not. I wouldn't think the cut-tree lot, at least, would be considered part of the crime scene." Mabel groaned. "And I never did get my tree."

<h1 style="text-align:center">Chapter Three</h1>

IT WAS DARK BY THE TIME JOHN and Tim slogged down the hill again. Barry trailed them, talking into his cell phone.

John unlocked his car door and reached inside. A moment later, he backed out, holding a brush-scraper combination, which he waved at Mabel before starting to clear snow.

As Tim came up to them, swiping half an inch of snow from his parka hood, Mabel tugged her damp boots back on. Lisa climbed down to relinquish the driver seat, but Mabel wondered when they'd be allowed to leave.

Lisa tilted her head toward Barry, still on the phone as he reentered the tree shed. "Talking to the police, I'm guessing?"

Tim nodded. "Yeah. Unless there's been an accident or something, they ought to be here soon."

"Are we waiting?" Mabel asked, though she already knew the answer.

"Yep. Since we were the first to come upon the remains."

Mabel glanced over at Barnacle. John had looped his leash over a fence post while he worked, and the dog was frolicking and snapping at snowflakes like a puppy. "Technically, Barnacle was first."

Tim grinned.

"We're sure at this point the skull's authentic?" Mabel asked.

"Yeah. Since Barnacle also just located what looks like a collar bone."

Mabel threw her head back. She couldn't handle another

murder investigation—if that's what this was. Homicide had almost become a full-time job at this point. "Well, most likely this will turn out to be a hunter who was out alone and had a heart attack, right? Or a wandering dementia patient. Something like that."

"Maybe." Lisa tapped her lips. "Or a shallow burial that didn't stay buried."

Mabel scowled. "Less likely. I still think this will turn out to be from years ago."

"Weird it's only popping up now, if so," Lisa insisted.

"I guess we're going back inside?" Mabel gestured at the shed.

"Might as well. It's warmer in there, and we don't have to waste gas." Tim waved them ahead of him.

Mabel wandered over to John and Barnacle. The dog jumped at her and whined. Drool dripped onto her boot. "I know, buddy. It's past dinnertime. Soon, okay?"

John was putting his brush away. He straightened. "I take back any and all previous disparaging remarks. Barnacle's a born cadaver dog."

Mabel shook her head. "He's just a fan of bones."

"Did Tim tell you?"

"Yeah." She gestured at the car. "He said we're waiting for the police. Why did you bother cleaning off snow?"

"Figured I'd get a head start. I'm hoping this won't be too drawn out. Our part of it, anyway. All we know is we discovered human remains—which weren't deposited here recently, unless they were already reduced to bones at that point."

"Sizemore won't like this." The local police detective had already started commenting on Mabel's all-too-frequent appearances at crime scenes.

"She may not like it, but that can't be helped. Let's go warm up."

Mabel shoved her unhappy dog into the car. John had already thrown an old cover across the back seat when they'd set out earlier that afternoon. Barnacle began scraping it into a heap, managing to leave big, soggy pawprints on the upholstery as he dug at the blanket.

John cringed but shut the door on the mess in progress.

By late the next morning, the storm had blown its way eastward, dumping snow in the mountains and causing headaches for drivers and road crews on the Pennsylvania Turnpike. Here, the sun had ventured out, and shaggy patches of faded grass were already emerging from yesterday's fluffy white blanketing.

Mabel's friends had all gone back to work. Lisa taught kindergarten, and Tim was employed by a woodworking company. John was teaching criminology courses at the community college and subbing in the school district. He was marking time during a suspension of his PI license, imposed over a tough call he'd made in protecting a client.

Mabel stood back to admire the wraparound porch on the old Victorian she'd inherited from her namesake Grandma Mabel. Grandma's frugality, along with age-related dementia, had left Mabel with a houseful of clutter. On the bright side, it had also helped preserve a treasure trove of vintage Christmas decorations.

Granted, her mid-century gems were a bit timeworn, but Mabel loved them all the more for it. The ratty tinsel garland she'd finished winding around the porch railing was an outdated combo of silver, red, and green. With strands of lights and a bow or bell here and there, it would look much the way it had on Mabel's childhood Christmas visits.

The flocked poinsettia garland she'd strung on the inside staircase was much too fragile for outdoor use. If she received any Christmas cards, she'd hang them below the poinsettias, the way Grandma used to.

Mabel frowned. People didn't seem to send cards much anymore—herself included. Maybe if she sent a few, she'd get some back. She added cards to her unwieldy mental to-do list with a sense of despair.

From the living room, Barnacle gave a sharp bark. He and Koi the cat had been watching her from the window, but now, he seemed to have decided enough was enough.

Mabel was ready to come in anyway. Her inner lunch bell had already sounded a while ago, plus she'd promised to stop by the Medicine Spring PD and sign her statement describing their discovery of the skull. She gathered her box of decorations and supplies and headed for the back door.

By the time she'd shifted the load to her left arm so she could turn the doorknob, Barnacle's bark had become repetitive. Generally, that meant a sighting—like a strange person or animal in the yard.

Mabel turned to see her mail carrier's red SUV coming down the street. Barnacle could recognize the sound of that car when it was still blocks away. In nicer weather, Nancy parked up on the corner in front of the historical society headquarters, located in the old Sauer mansion, when she didn't have any cumbersome parcels to carry.

But today the slushy sidewalks and chilly gusts of wind weren't ideal for a sixty-something with an artificial hip to be hiking around with a heavy mail pouch full of cards, advertising, and Christmas packages on her back. Three other houses sat across the street from the Sauer house, but what would have been the remaining lots on their side were now just woods.

Mabel's house sat alone against the woods of Willow Creek

Park, at the dead end on the Sauer house side of the single long block that was Carteret Street. To deliver Mabel's mail on foot, Nancy would have had to walk all the way down from the mansion past Mabel's vacant field.

Nancy jerked to a stop and waved. After depositing Mabel's handful of mail in the box at the curb, she turned in the side driveway and headed back up the street to deliver to the houses on the other side.

Mabel hurried and dumped her Christmas decorations inside, shoving Barnacle out of her way as she slipped out again.

She hoped there weren't any big bills in the box. For the past eight months, she'd been managing on the small inheritance Grandma had left her, along with her severance package from the firm where she'd labored as a back-room lawyer for twenty-three thankless years. Now, Christmas was happening—on top of inflation, handyman expenses, car repairs, and vet bills.

Not for the first time, Mabel felt her stomach wrench with anxiety. She'd hoped to build a writing career, but that was proving harder than expected. At some point, she feared, she'd have to look for a job again, though her previous attempts on that front had led nowhere.

No. She wouldn't think about that now. After the holidays would be time enough to try to figure out a budget for the New Year.

With a deep breath, Mabel pried open the warped mailbox door. A colorful heap of Christmas advertising circulars lay folded over a few envelopes and a dental reminder postcard. A quick glance revealed two envelopes contained charity pleas. The third envelope, fat and red, appeared to be a Christmas card—the first for her hallway display. Clutching the mail to her chest, she hurried inside.

Mabel dumped everything in a heap on the cluttered kitchen

table and pulled off her coat. She had time for a quick lunch before heading to the police station to sign her statement, but first, she needed to satisfy her curiosity about the unexpected Christmas card.

Koi seemed to share her interest. The tortoiseshell cat had already leapt onto the table and, ignoring all the advertising and charitable solicitations, was sniffing the solitary red envelope.

Mabel plucked the card from under the cat's nose. "This is addressed to me, not you." She studied it…no return address, and the handwriting was unfamiliar. Perhaps masculine? The envelope was faded along one edge and had suffered a couple distinct creases.

"Looks like whoever sent this dug an old one out of the bottom of the drawer." Carefully, she ripped it open.

A nostalgic design showed a couple in a one-horse sleigh making their way under a starlit sky to a church in the valley. As Mabel opened it, a folded sheet of paper dropped into her lap. The card was unsigned. Puzzled, she unfolded the paper.

The handwritten letter was signed, but try though she might, Mabel couldn't make it out. The text of the letter was somewhat easier, but for a spot or two.

Dear Mabel,

Merry Christmas to you and yours. I'm sorry to [illegible], but I have a big favor to ask of you.

Mabel groaned inwardly. This was so typical of her life. She couldn't even figure out who this person was, and here they were, asking for favors right in the middle of the Christmas crunch.

I wouldn't be asking except it's so [illegible].

Oh, no—no, no, no. The last thing Mabel needed was to take responsibility for someone else's needs. She was already struggling to handle her own problems.

And I wouldn't ask for myself, but I'm hoping you'll do it for [illegible]. I know you girls are close, and maybe you'll put in a good word for me?

Mabel frowned and squinted again at the illegible name. Maybe Betty? She didn't know anyone by that name, let alone consider herself close to her.

"It *is* addressed to me, right?" she asked Koi, who looked as puzzled as Mabel felt. The cat ran her tiny nose over the letter, then turned her attention to the envelope before recoiling, lip curled, as if she'd smelled something offensive or distressing.

Barnacle shoved his face onto her lap, smiling up as if to ask if they were all having fun yet. Mabel gave his head an absent pat. "Well, this is a fine pickle," she told him. "I don't know any of these people."

She snatched the red envelope back from Koi, who'd started chewing on the corner by the stamp. Mabel smoothed down the damp paper and checked the address. *Yep.* It did say "Mabel Browne," and her address was correct.

Well, she guessed the address was correct as far as it went. Her mystery correspondent must not have known her zip code, because there wasn't any. *Huh.* Only the Christmas spirit could have induced the post office to deliver mail without the proper zip code.

Mabel laid the envelope down, but then grabbed it back up. That stamp Koi had almost ingested said, "4¢." Not even Christmas spirit could have persuaded the post office to deliver mail for four cents, in this day and age.

A mournful Abraham Lincoln gazed at her from the blue stamp, as if commiserating. "I must be catching Grandma's dementia." She grimaced at him in return. "None of this makes any sense."

Desperate for answers, Mabel fished the letter back out from the clutter on her tabletop.

I have feelings for [illegible]. She doesn't know. I doubt I've said ten words to her all these years. But maybe you heard I've got a good job now, and I can support a wife the way she ought to be supported. If you think she might have me once she gets to know me a bit better, I will be the happiest man in town. In the whole [illegible].

I promise you I will treat that woman like the princess she is. You know me, Mabel—

"No, I don't," Mabel whispered.

I'm a good Christian man and a hard worker. Please say you'll talk to her. All I'm asking right now is if she would be willing to go out with me. Thank you, Mabel.

Your friend, [illegible]

The truth washed over Mabel in a rush. This wasn't her mail at all. It had been intended for Grandma Mabel, and at this point, only the good Lord in heaven knew who had sent it.

Chapter Four

THINK, MABEL, THINK. SITTING HERE RUBBING her forehead wasn't helping. What was she supposed to do with mystery mail that belonged to somebody else—to her own dead grandma? It had to be too late to fulfill this unidentified person's request.

The cancellation date was too faint to read and somewhat marred by cat spit. When was the last time a card could be mailed for four cents? Mabel fiddled with her phone, and a moment later, found her answer, which at least narrowed down the timeframe. Four-cent first class postage had only been in effect between 1959 and 1962.

Yeah, Mabel was pretty sure it was too late to tell Betty—or whomever—that this guy had a crush on her. Realizing this gave Mabel a pang. She hoped at some point he'd worked up the nerve to do his own romancing.

"Why don't you speak for yourself, John?" she muttered, thinking of the famous Pilgrim love triangle of Miles Standish, John Alden, and Priscilla Mullins.

Surely, he'd soon have realized Grandma hadn't followed through and done something about it. Nevertheless, this unknown man had left Mabel with her own twenty-first-century quandary. Where had this letter been floating around for the past sixty or so years? And what should she do with it now that she had it?

Lunch first.

She propped the card up in front of her while she fixed a PBJ and glass of milk. One more thing to worry about, on top of Christmas stuff, money issues, plans for Lisa's upcoming bridal shower, and that skull they'd found at the tree farm. She frowned.

Not to mention, she was supposed to be volunteering someplace soon, so she could write about it for the book she planned to write for seniors with time on their hands. When she'd gotten this bright idea back in October, she'd been convinced she could put together a snappy little book that would help her launch a lucrative writing career in no time.

Two months later, she could say she'd done some volunteering, none of which had gone all that well. Her writing career was still sputtering—mostly because, as Mabel was now realizing, writing was harder than she'd anticipated. Maybe she should wait till after the first of the year to relaunch.

This thought brightened her mood. She opened one of her notebooks and headed a page: NEW YEAR'S RESOLUTIONS. Below that, she wrote her first entry, "Write volunteer book."

There, that felt better.

Mabel finished eating her sandwich and put the mysterious Christmas card in her bag. She'd stop in at the post office right after signing her police statement. She might not find out anything new about the bones Barnacle had discovered, but maybe at least she'd learn where this letter had emerged from.

Mabel shifted her feet as she stood in line at the tiny Medicine Spring post office, behind a husky older lady in a long brown woolen coat, fur-topped snow boots, and with an old-fashioned tie-on plastic bonnet protecting her curls. It seemed the woman was trying to find the cheapest way to ship a box of Christmas goodies to her sister in California.

Mabel pulled down her hood and unzipped her red parka. The heat was going full blast in here, and the transaction ahead of her didn't seem to be going anywhere. She studied the displays of padded envelopes, flattened shipping boxes, and commemorative stamps for the third time and checked her phone for messages.

The police station had taken no time at all. Her statement had been simple—"bare bones," in fact, like Barnacle's treasure. The closemouthed officer she'd spoken with hadn't had further information he was willing to share with Mabel. She hoped John might be able to wheedle more out of his contacts.

"Next."

Mabel jumped. She fished in her bag and brought out the card as she stepped up to the clerk.

"Hi, there." She laid the envelope on the counter. "I, uh, received this in this morning's mail, and I'm very puzzled."

The clerk picked up the card and her black eyes lit. "Oh, you got one of our blasts from the past." The woman seemed to study Mabel. "You aren't old enough to be the intended recipient. Sorry for the confusion, but all we could do was deliver by address."

The clerk, judging by her smooth dark cheeks, couldn't have been much over thirty herself. She moved to set the envelope aside, and Mabel realized she was about to take it from Mabel and not give it back.

Mabel opened her mouth to explain about Grandma, but then it dawned on her that federal postal regulations in all likelihood precluded giving mail to unauthorized third parties. In the eyes of the law, Mabel would be considered an unauthorized third party, even if the mail in question was sixty years old and the addressee was her own grandmother.

"Oh, but I *am* Mabel Browne." Mabel fished in her purse. She was about to pull out her driver's license when it occurred to her that her birthdate would give her away. *Ahh…* She held up her old photo badge from the law firm where she'd worked.

"Oh, my goodness." The clerk looked back and forth between Mabel and the ID badge. "You must have found the fountain of youth. I'd never have thought you were…" She frowned in confusion. "…Over seventy? Eighty?"

Mabel tried to appear modest as she snatched back the ID and averted her face. "Oh, just healthy living, I guess." Out of habit, she rubbed her nose. Grandma Mabel had always told her that her nose would grow like Pinocchio's if she told a lie.

As the clerk handed back the card, Mabel glanced behind her. A man had come through the door, but nobody else was in line. She reclaimed the card and slipped it in her bag. "I wondered where on earth this had been floating around all this time. You said it was one of your blasts from the past, like there were more. What happened?"

The clerk also glanced at the approaching customer. "Long story short, we found an old mail sack out by the loading dock yesterday. All the postage had already been cancelled, so we sent it on out with the carriers."

"But..." Mabel had so many questions.

The clerk gave a pointed look over Mabel's head at the next person in line, then back at Mabel. "We have no idea where it's been all these years or who brought it back. It's being looked into."

She raised a hand as if about to wave the next patron forward, but then leaned closer and whispered. "I don't mean to be nosy, but would you mind sharing what moisturizer you use?"

Mabel felt a blush rising up from her neck. "Oh, nothing special. Just good genes, you know."

The clerk leaned back and tilted her head to study Mabel's face. "You're amazing. I wouldn't have guessed you were any older than sixty, at the very most." Her voice dropped again to a conspiratorial whisper. "You look completely natural."

Mabel managed a weak smile and eased away from the counter.

The customer behind her made an exasperated noise and elbowed her out of the way. The man was perhaps in his seventies and dressed in an impeccable gray tweed dress coat that might have been cashmere, so perhaps he was used to good service. He glared at Mabel beneath bushy steel-gray brows.

"Merry Christmas!" the clerk chirped and waved Mabel off.

Completely natural. The woman could have been commenting on what fine work an undertaker had done.

Well, at least, Mabel now knew she looked exceptionally well for a sixty-year-old—or maybe, on the darker side, a dead body. Then, the truth struck. *She thinks I've had work done—like an eighty-year-old after extensive plastic surgery.*

Mabel forced her feet to keep walking. By trying to pass herself off as an octogenarian, she'd invited this, after all.

Once outside, she decided a pick-me-up was in order after that humiliation. A new little coffee shop had opened up a couple doors down from the post office, and she had yet to try it. Mabel checked the time—she'd have liked company, but Lisa would still be at work.

On an impulse, she dialed Nita. Decades had gone by since she and Shanita Bedford had played together during Mabel's summers with Grandma in Medicine Spring. Since they'd run into each other again recently, however, their old friendship had re-bloomed as if never interrupted.

"Hey, Nita."

"What's up?" Mabel heard voices in the background and hoped Nita's bookshop wasn't too busy for her to get away for a short break.

"I'm over by Demitasse—you know where I mean? I wondered if you might be able to shake free for a quick coffee."

"Love to. That's about the only benefit to owning your own place." Nita's voice grew muffled. "Hey, Zac, can you cover me for a bit? I need to run out."

Then she was back. "See you in ten, okay?'

Mabel found the tiny cafe nearly empty, but for one older

man in the back corner, reading a magazine and nursing a diner-style coffee mug. She ordered a Christmas Eve mocha latte with a crushed candy cane topping, along with a bear claw pastry, stifling the voice of her conscience. It had been rough back there at the post office, and she needed a caffeine and sugar boost.

While she waited for her order, and for Nita to arrive, Mabel claimed a little tile-topped table by the front windows. The center of each tile was decorated with a yellow-and-blue flowered demitasse cup that matched the striped wallpaper. She hung her jacket over the back of one of the two old, mismatched oak dining room chairs.

As she slid into her seat, Mabel found herself making eye contact with the customer in the corner. Embarrassed, she looked away and pulled out her phone. Stealing another peek through her lashes, she realized he was still looking her way, so she began scrolling.

The guy was what—seventies? Eighties? Was he eyeing her up—did he think she was in his dating range?

When she peeked again, he'd returned to his magazine—*The New Yorker*, she now saw. Apparently, she'd been flattering herself. She shook off her awkwardness. She had John. She didn't need men decades older than she was succumbing to her charms.

He was fit and handsome though—with a strong nose, which might once have been broken, the most prominent landmark in a rugged face topped by an unruly mop of hair the color of tarnished pewter. His casual quarter-zip ragg pullover, faded jeans, and worn boots gave him a youthful appearance. Wouldn't her older friends swoon?

No sooner had her order been called than the door opened again, and Nita swept in, propelled by her usual explosive energy. Her scarlet swing coat swirled around her full but shapely figure. A burst of crinkly, near-black curls threaded with glinting ribbons of honey gold added to Nita's already considerable height—any time she appeared it was an "entrance."

"Hey, Mabel." She threw her coat over the other chair and

called out, "Hey, Grace," to the barista as she headed to the counter, where Mabel was collecting her goodies.

"Hi, Nita. Glad you could make it."

"I was so glad to get out of there." She turned to the barista, a fresh-faced blonde in a Mennonite prayer cap and lilac-print cotton dress. "Could you make mine a cream Earl Grey tea? Big one, please, and maybe a toasted English muffin with some butter on the side?"

She paid for her order and returned to the table with Mabel. "That witch who lives out by you was giving us a hard time because she couldn't find the book she wanted. We said we'd be happy to try to locate and order it for her. Of course, she didn't know the title, the author, or anything about it except it was a blue cover with the word 'ocean' in the name and had something to do with a lost love." Nita rolled her expressive light-gray eyes that were so startling and beautiful in her dark golden face.

Mabel grinned. "I didn't realize you knew Linnea."

"I was happy enough not to. I mean, business is business, but since she moved here, we cringe every time she comes across the threshold."

"At least, you don't live next to her."

"Why's she gotta be so disagreeable?" Nita scowled. "Life's too short."

"Agreed."

Nita shuddered. "Shake it off, Nita. Shake it off."

Mabel sipped her latte. *Heaven.* "Hey, Nita. Um, how old do you think I look?"

Nita stared. "Fifty going on thirty, same as me."

"No—not how old I *am*. If we hadn't grown up together, how old would you think I am, if you saw me on the street?"

Nita smirked. "Some particular reason you're asking this right now?"

"Is there some particular reason you're avoiding the question?"

"Objection overruled, Mabel Browne, Esq." Nita chuckled. "There's no way I can ever forget that I've known you forever. I look at you and see a ten-year-old little white girl with banged-up knees and a puffy ponytail, who could say five words and crack me up. Or just give me one of those looks, and I'd start giggling."

Mabel delivered a side-eye.

Nita's grin erupted into a belly laugh. "That's the look right there. Hey, what's gotten into you? You never used to worry about how old you looked."

"I was never fifty before—or just convinced somebody I was over sixty."

"Girl, I've got no clue what you're talking about, but you look great. I don't know why you're so hard on yourself. If you don't trust me, look at John. Does he act like he thinks you're over the hill?"

"No-o-o… But—"

"Nita, your tea and muffin are ready."

"Hang on."

Mabel watched Nita collect her order. She seemed to know the barista, Grace. This was a nice, friendly place. Mabel would have to stop more often too.

When Nita returned, Mabel made a determined effort to stop thinking about how on earth she could've passed for decades older than she was. She cleared her throat. "You must be in here a lot."

Nita shrugged and pried the lid off her takeout cup. "A few times. They haven't been open long. Grace is my neighbor. Her family has the farm next to mine now."

Memories of swimming in the farm pond, climbing in the haymow of the old barn, and pretending to drive the old sleigh stored below the loft flooded Mabel's brain. "You still have the farm?"

"Yeah, but obviously I don't farm it. Live there alone now, since my divorce. My son grew up, and he and my brothers didn't want to deal with the farm. I don't mind—I like it peaceful. Grace's folks bought the old Miller farm after Clarence Miller died and Marie moved in with their daughter."

Mabel paused in the process of buttering a slice of warm

bear claw. This was the first time Nita had mentioned her divorce, but this wasn't the time to probe. She had no recollection of Nita's old neighbors, either. While she tried to bring up a mental image of the older couple, Nita went on.

"The Stoltzfuses have seven kids. Grace is one of the older ones. Most of the other kids are at home. They either help work the farm or take care of the house and kids. They bought a couple acres from me on that side for potatoes, right after they moved in. They're good neighbors—let's just say I have a lifetime supply of jam, pickles, and home-canned produce."

"That sounds nice." Mabel closed her eyes to savor the frosting and sliced almonds on her bear claw. "The only neighbor I've got is Linnea."

Nita shifted in her seat. "Listen, what about that skull you guys found? Do the police have any idea how old it is or who it belonged to?"

"If they do, they haven't told me."

"Where did you find it again?"

Mabel described the spot as best she could while Nita ate and nodded.

"Hmm," was all Nita said, brow creased as if she was thinking. Mabel waited for more, but Nita's mind seemed to have wandered.

Mabel cleared her throat. "Now, it's your turn to tell me how it's going with your new town supervisor gig."

Nita flung herself back in her chair. "Please don't make me think about it. I won't even get sworn in till after New Year's, and I want to resign already."

"Hey, it can't be that bad. You're a natural leader—you'll do great."

"I shouldn't have said I'd do it. I didn't even run—in most cases, that's a good sign someone doesn't want the job."

Mabel patted her friend's hand, noticing with a pang the contrast between her own stubby fingers and Nita's long, immaculate, French-tipped nails. "Well, you did say yes, once you got elected. The town needs you."

"I don't know the first thing about being a township supervisor…not to mention I got a business to run but…"

Mabel interrupted. "Otherwise, it was going to be one of those two yahoos who did run for the job. That's why people started the write-in campaign for you in the first place—and that's why you agreed to accept."

Nita brightened. "There's still the recount. I did only win by two votes."

"You'd be as upset as the rest of us if the vote got overturned."

"I guess so. I only agreed to serve for a year, you know, and see how it goes. Those guys and their supporters have already been badmouthing me though."

"You're a hero, Nita."

Nita snorted. "I'm a patsy, and you can quote me."

For a moment, they both concentrated on their snacks, and then the conversation shifted to Lisa's bridal shower, which was coming up after the holidays. Snow flurries danced aimlessly outside the window.

Nita looked at the round railway clock on the wall above the sugar and cream station. "Well, I need to be getting back." She gathered her plate and napkins and put the lid back on her cup.

After tossing her trash, she returned to shrug into her coat and collect her purse and leftover tea. "Thanks for calling—I needed this. If you find out any more about that skull, let me know. Don't forget. I'm kind of curious."

"Sure." As she watched her friend go, Mabel picked up her own trash. Too late, she realized she hadn't even told Nita about the weird card she'd received. *Oh, well. Next time.*

Chapter Five

It was nearly two when Mabel returned home. Her weekly copy of *The Shopper* lay in the driveway, where she could hardly avoid running over it. Fortunately, it was in a plastic sleeve, so while she'd flattened it, it hadn't gotten too wet.

She hung her coat over the back of a kitchen chair and peeled the wet, muddy plastic off her newspaper. Her animals crowded in, blocking her path to the waste can. "Glad to see you too. If you let me through, I'll get you a treat."

Hearing the magic word, Barnacle and Koi headed over to the fridge. Mabel grabbed a couple of pet snacks from the jars she kept on top and tossed one to each of them.

Koi settled to crunch her treat, nibble by delicate nibble. After slobbering all over Mabel's fingers, Barnacle swallowed his whole. He followed her back to the table, licking his chops as he went and sniffing the floor with a hopeful expression.

Ignoring him, Mabel shook open the paper. A banner at the top, "Good Neighbors, see page B1," caught her eye. She knew this referred to the feature page that appeared each week in the second section of the paper.

Her eyes widened at the teaser below—*The Rendlesham Forest Incident—Christmas UFOs?* The article was by Jackie Croft, a local sci-fi writer who'd invited Mabel to join her writers' group. Mabel had yet to take Jackie up on the invitation, but maybe after Christmas.

The article took up a mere half-page but reminded Mabel that Jackie had also encouraged her to submit one of her volunteer articles to the paper. A sidebar spelled out the paper's guidelines and how to submit.

Mabel sat back. Could she do this? She'd already written two volunteer articles, both of which now sat composting in her computer files. How hard would it be to cut one in half and email it in to *The Shopper* Good Neighbors page?

If the paper didn't take her offering, what did she have to lose? Sooner or later, she was going to have to be brave and try to publish something.

Mabel swallowed hard. On the other hand, if she couldn't even get a small article in *The Shopper,* what did that mean for her struggling writing career? At fifty, she didn't have decades to get it airborne.

If a little weekly newspaper rejected her, Mabel knew she would never write again.

Another voice in her head snorted. *It's not like you're writing all that much right now, is it?*

"It's the holidays." Mabel closed the paper on Jackie's article. She'd get around to submitting something soon. Like Grandma Mabel used to say, "Rome wasn't built in a day."

She sighed, knowing she should sit down right now and do some writing. Luckily, her phone rang. Though it was only two in the afternoon, the caller ID told her it was Lisa.

"Mabel. Did you sign your statement yet?"

"Yeah, I went this morning."

"I'm stopping after work. Do you know if John's found anything out?"

"No, but I doubt it. It sounded like the police planned to do some kind of grid search for more bones. I don't think they're anywhere near doing any kind of analysis. Where are your kids?"

"There's a safety program this afternoon. I got a break to set up snack time."

Mabel tapped her lip. "I wonder if the tree lot's off limits. I still need a tree."

"Maybe Tim knows. I could ask."

"I feel like I should be thinking of that poor dead person instead of Christmas decorating, but time's a wastin'."

"I know. The holidays are crazier than usual, with the wedding coming up."

Mabel held back a groan. As Lisa's best friend and only bridal attendant, she had a lot of responsibilities too, all of which she'd stuck on the back burner along with decluttering Grandma Mabel's overcrowded house or doing any writing. She cleared her throat.

"Look, why don't I try getting hold of John? If he has any news, I'll text you."

Mabel hastened to end the call before Lisa started asking about her progress on finding guava juice for the bridal shower punch. She promised herself she'd spend some time online and calling around this very evening, though she didn't know why Lisa couldn't be happy with another tropical nectar like mango or pineapple.

Her phone rang again. *Hot-Blooded.* She really needed to change John's ringtone before she embarrassed herself one more time.

"Hey," he said. "Did you sign your statement yet?"

"Yup. I guess you did too?"

"Early this morning. What are you up to right now?"

She was grateful John couldn't see her guilty flush. "Um, I just started decluttering some of the bags of paper in Grandma's spare room." As she said this, Mabel scooted to the front room and grabbed a bag.

"Aw, too bad. I handed back the last of the student papers a bit ago, and I'm done for the semester. I wondered if maybe you wanted to hit the tree lot early."

"I could do that." Mabel dropped the musty-smelling bag, and paper cascaded onto the floor. Immediately, Barnacle came to snuffle through the spillage, and Koi started batting at a crumpled receipt.

"I don't want to interfere with what you're doing. We can go later if you want."

"Really, I'd rather go now, before it gets crowded when people leave work. I can do this any time." *But so rarely do.*

"Ack!" Mabel jumped as a mouse ran over her foot, with Koi in hot pursuit.

"You okay?"

Mabel clutched her chest. "Yeah. A mouse must've been building a nest in that bag of paper. Koi's after it now."

Koi darted from one bag to another, then raced after the mouse as it scurried between the fridge and the wall. Barnacle barked encouragement, and his tongue lolled in obvious enjoyment of the fracas. What he lacked in prey drive, he more than made up in enthusiasm.

"Hang on." Mabel grabbed the frustrated cat and shut her in the tiny half-bath under the stairs. "Sorry. I can't cope with a murder in my own kitchen right now."

John was laughing when Mabel picked up the phone again. "From what I could hear, that was an epic chase."

"The mouse escaped, but I'm afraid I just postponed the inevitable. I can't bear watching her torture and dismember the poor thing."

"Do you want me to pick up some traps?"

Mabel shuddered. "Good grief, no. I mean—"

"Live traps, then? Catch and release in the park?"

"Um…" Mabel envisioned a cartoon mouse, shivering in a ragged coat as snow came down around him. As a young child, she'd been scarred by a picture book called *The Mouse Who Came for Christmas.*

"What? Are you worrying about that too?"

"No, of course not. It's just that it's getting awfully cold and…"

"Mabel. What you have is a field mouse. They get into houses in the fall, but they're very well equipped to live outside. If you're worried, stick him in what's left of your shed. That'll offer some protection. Or even find a deserted barn. There are plenty of those around."

"Where would I get a live trap?"

"Any good hardware. Gump's should have them. Look, don't worry about it. I'll check for you. I need a drain stopper anyway."

They agreed John would pick Mabel up in an hour, so she hurried to freshen herself up and feed her animals. As always, he arrived right on time, announced by a flurry of barking from Barnacle.

Before leaving, Mabel blocked off the space beneath her Hoosier cupboard and warned Koi to leave the mouse alone. She hoped and prayed the little critter had escaped into the basement by now, with plans to stay there. That door was securely closed.

Chapter Six

WHEN MABEL AND JOHN ARRIVED AT the tree lot, a police SUV
was parked behind the building, along with several other vehicles.
Mabel presumed some belonged to customers, since she saw people browsing the pre-cut stock. Yellow tape still warned the public
away from the hillside tree nursery though.

"I see people poking around up there." Mabel pointed a mittened hand at the edge of the woods on the hilltop.

"The forensic guys from the CHU anthro department, I imagine. I'm sure they're still combing for more bones."

"Did you talk to anybody at the station about the investigation?"

"Tried to. My friend Mac isn't working on it himself, but he
said it could take three or four months—maybe more—to get any
ID on the remains. If that's even possible."

Mabel walked toward the nearest row of blue spruces. "How
would they do that? DNA?"

John nodded. "DNA, any unique trauma to the bones, dental
records—that sort of thing."

She stopped. "Can they do that? Get DNA from a skull that's
been sitting out in the elements for who knows how many years?"

John shrugged. "They won't know till they try."

Success seemed unlikely to Mabel, but maybe something
would turn up through other avenues. Still, she pondered the mi-
raculous solving of cold cases through DNA, which true-crime
addict Lisa had told her about. She'd have to ask if Lisa knew of
any cases where DNA was recovered from skeletal remains that
were decades old.

After tramping around for half an hour, Mabel pointed. "I

can't look anymore. This one seems okay." She shook the trunk and was relieved not to see a shower of dead needles.

John stood back and tilted his head. Then he walked behind the tree and squinted. "It's kind of patchy in back."

"I don't care. At this point they all look alike. Those branches will be out of sight in the corner anyhow."

He shrugged. "Your decision."

Mabel started toward the counter, then turned back. "Aren't you getting a tree?"

"Nope. Never do. I always spend Christmas at my folks'. Plus, Billie Jean would have it ripped down the same day I put it up."

Knowing John's cat, Mabel didn't doubt what he was telling her.

Barry was swiping a credit card for the woman ahead of them when they walked up. "I'll be with you guys in just a minute, after I get this lady's tree loaded on her car."

While they waited, Mabel strolled back to peer around the corner toward the hilltop. Someone up there was taking pictures, and a few other people seemed to be scanning the ground. She wondered if they'd left the skull where Barnacle had dropped it. "Hey, John."

He motioned. "Come on back. I don't want to lose our spot."

A man with kids, and a young couple, now stood behind John. Mabel sidled up to him. "Glad Barry still seems to be doing a brisk business."

"Me too. What did you want?"

Keeping her voice low, Mabel asked, "Is our skull at the lab now?"

"I don't know. They typically photograph everything in place first and mark where each piece of evidence is located. With the iffy weather, they might have removed it after they took photos and marked where we found it."

"Or where Barnacle dragged it," Mabel said drearily.

"Guessing it came from the woods. Washed down the slope a bit in those hard rains we had. Skulls roll, you know, so they can end up farther away from the rest of the body than the other bones."

Mabel made a face at the macabre visual. "I've been thinking. Those bones might be super old, don't you think? Like maybe from one of the Native Americans who used to encamp around here."

"Hey," said a male voice from behind them. The young dad gestured toward the hill. "Do you know what's going on up there? We wanted to cut our own tree, but the guy said the nursery's off-limits today."

Mabel glanced at the wide-eyed kids next to the man. She wasn't great with kids, but even she knew rolling skulls probably weren't appropriate fodder for the three youngsters' imaginations. "Um, it's a police matter."

The dad looked frustrated. "That's what the tree guy said, but…" He glanced down at three sets of bright eyes.

Dad leaned closer and whispered, "Is it a, you know? B-o-d-y?"

"Y-e-s," Mabel spelled. "An s-k-u-l-l."

John grinned. "And a c-l-a-v-i-c-l-e."

The dad's mouth moved as he seemed to be trying to decipher what John had spelled.

"What's a 'clav-cicle,' Daddy?" The oldest boy, maybe eight, was obviously already a pretty good speller.

"Uh, we'll talk later." The man stepped back, pulling his children with him.

Barry came bustling up a few minutes later. "Sorry for the wait, folks. Help you?"

It seemed he didn't recognize them right away—or had sensibly decided to repress all memories of the previous evening.

"Hi, again." John stuck out his hand. "We met yesterday?"

Barry's face fell briefly before he collected himself and shook John's hand. His glance flickered to Mabel and back again. "Oh, yeah. Hi."

John tipped his head at Mabel. "The lady would like a tree."

"Oh, yeah, sure." Barry's relief was obvious. "Which one?"

"This way." Mabel headed back into the lot.

"Looks like you're keeping busy," John commented. "Despite the police."

"Yeah, not too bad. Considering. Man, losing the cut-your-own traffic this close to Christmas is killing me."

"I'll bet." Mabel gave him a sympathetic look over her shoulder. "I hope they get you back open soon."

"I wish—but I doubt it."

"This one." Mabel touched the tree she wanted, and Barry replaced the tag with one that said, "SOLD."

"We'll get you checked out, and then I'll help you guys load it."

"Have the police found any more bones?" she asked.

At first, Mabel thought Barry wasn't going to answer, but then he paused in his charge toward the sales counter. "Yeah. Couple bigger ones. A few fragments. It's gonna take till sometime next summer if they plan on looking for fragments."

It seemed the young farmer was done chatting. He rang up Mabel's purchase, apologized again to the waiting family, and then helped John secure the tree on his car roof.

Barry sighed. "Merry Christmas."

Though Mabel and John returned his tidings, she couldn't help wondering whether that cheerful sentiment had ever been delivered with more gloom.

Chapter Seven

BEFORE LEAVING, JOHN OFFERED TO HELP Mabel set her tree up in her living room. He'd trimmed a few ragged branches first and cut a couple of inches off the trunk so it could drink and stay fresh. With the house's high Victorian ceilings, they had no worries the room wouldn't accommodate the tree.

Mabel shut her excited animals in the storeroom, once the house's parlor, so they couldn't dart outside or trip John on his way in. While he was prepping the tree, she dug out Grandma's old tree stand and set it on a rather warped square of plywood, which she'd covered with a layer of newspapers topped by an old white sheet.

In the storeroom, she'd found a stash of boxes labeled "Christmas 1," "Christmas 2," and so on, through one numbered "5." A quick peek had revealed old-fashioned painted glass ornaments, mouse-eaten red stockings, and a plastic nativity set. Mabel remembered the manger scene from her childhood and smiled when she saw the little donkey's cross-eyed face peering out of the tissue at her.

As soon as John had gotten the tree stabilized, he left to shower and change, promising to be back in an hour. At Lisa's urging, Mabel had agreed to a little tree-trimming party including Lisa, Tim, and Nita. She felt uneasy having people over, since Grandma's clutter had taken over so much of the house. However, Lisa assured her that friends understood and said nobody should have to trim a tree all alone.

When Mabel opened the storeroom door again, her animals came to investigate the new attraction in the living room. While they sniffed around the tree, she began dragging out boxes.

"Shoo." Mabel set her box down and waved her arms at Barnacle, who was slurping tree water. When she managed to get him out of the way, she discovered Koi underneath the branches, working her claws on the trunk. "Scoot. Bad kitty."

Maybe glass ornaments weren't a good idea.

Mabel raced through the house, stashing clutter under furniture and behind doors. She hoped she didn't lose anything important in her mad scramble to make the old house company ready. Since her friends were bringing food, all Mabel had to do in the kitchen was clear counter and table space. Then, of course, freshen herself up.

All... She snorted. The clock was not on her side.

Still, by the time John returned, carrying a case of assorted soft drinks, a sealed bowl of homemade dip, and two boxes of fancy crackers, Mabel had managed to tidy the kitchen, change clothes, and feed her animals. Barnacle leapt up to sniff the food with the focus of a trained explosives dog.

Koi greeted John with a soft meow and rubbed against his pantleg, but the moment she heard someone else approach the door, she vaulted to the top of the Hoosier cupboard to observe the other arrivals from a point of safety. While John set out his contribution to the party, Mabel opened the kitchen door for Lisa, Tim, and Nita.

Once more, Barnacle's nose sprang into action, abandoning John's artichoke dip for Nita's crab puffs and Lisa's veggie pizza squares. Tim, carrying a huge bowl of tossed salad, walked past the dog unscathed.

With everyone chattering and laughing at once, and Barnacle barking his two cents, Mabel felt a flush of success. Nobody seemed to be paying any attention to the pawprints on the floor or her lack of decorating sense.

Lisa set up her phone and speaker on the living room mantel and cued up a Christmas playlist while the others loaded plates and poured drinks. Soon, everyone was gathered around the fresh-smelling spruce.

"Love your old ornaments." Nita gestured with a pizza square. "But you better put 'em up toward the top of the tree."

Mabel, already nervous, had decided after Koi's earlier attack on the trunk, to only put out a few of the fragile vintage decorations. She'd see how that went before daring to add more.

"I'm glad you decided to use your grandma's ornaments," Lisa said. "They aren't doing anybody any good if they never leave the box."

Mabel shot a look toward the kitchen, where as far as she knew—and hoped and prayed—Koi was still plumped atop the Hoosier cupboard. The precious ornaments wouldn't do anyone any good smashed on the floor either.

"I love the old card on your mantel too," Lisa said. "Was it one of your grandma's?"

Mabel paused in surreptitiously licking artichoke dip from her fingers and grabbed her napkin. "Yeah, actually, that's a kind of weird story."

Nita got up to study the card. "Nice. Did you find any more?"

"No. I didn't 'find it,' per se. More like it found me."

"So, tell us your story. Hang on." Lisa turned the music down and slid back into her seat. "Okay, go ahead."

Mabel had just picked up a pizza square. With a pang of regret, she set it back down. "I guess I haven't told any of you yet. It only happened this morning."

Four pairs of expectant eyes focused on Mabel…and one pair of hopeful brown eyes, belonging to Barnacle, focused on Mabel's uneaten pizza. She sighed. "All right."

With several interruptions for questions or exclamations over the strange mail delivery from the past, Mabel told her story. Though the rest of her audience continued to eat, Nita set her plate on the coffee table and leaned in, seeming to hang on Mabel's words with flattering intensity.

When Mabel had finished recounting her visit to the post office, and was about to bemoan being taken for an octogenarian, Nita broke in. "She said there was more mail in an old bag? I want to see that letter. Did you save the envelope?"

"Yeah, it's still here. It has a four-cent stamp on it, which is what—"

Nita's eyes glittered with something more than interest. "Where are they?"

"Um…" Nita's sudden intensity had muddled Mabel's brain, but she snapped out of her daze when she noticed Barnacle's nose hovering mere inches from Nita's plate. "Leave it, Barnacle."

She refocused on Nita as she handed back her plate. "Oh, uh, let me get the letter and envelope."

To Mabel's surprise, Nita followed her to the kitchen, carrying her plate. "Here." Mabel shoved the soft drinks aside. "Set that on the table for a minute, and you sit down."

She rummaged through her bag and came up with the envelope, which Nita claimed with eager but gentle hands. She smoothed over the wrinkled surface and looked up at Mabel. "The letter isn't in here."

"No, I put it here on the windowsill to keep it safe." Mabel raised her eyebrows as she handed over the old letter, but Nita didn't volunteer any explanation for her rabid interest.

"Oh…" Nita's breath caught as she scanned the page.

Mabel couldn't take it anymore. "Nita, what? Talk to me."

Nita's hands trembled. She shook her head.

One by one, the rest of the group drifted out of the living room and squeezed into the kitchen. John towed a reluctant Barnacle. The dog was carrying a slobbery pizza square—likely Mabel's—in his mouth.

"Bad boy." Mabel grabbed for the pizza, but Barnacle took

a quick gulp, and it disappeared.

Lisa frowned. "Everything all right out here?"

Nita closed her eyes and took a deep breath. "Sorry." When her eyes opened, tears sparkled on her lashes. "It's a lot to explain."

Mabel, for one, was dying for an explanation, but she managed to say, "That's okay. You don't have to tell us anything if you don't want to."

Lisa opened her mouth as if to disagree but shut it again.

Nita shook her head. "No, I want to tell you. It's just…a lot to wrap my own head around."

"Why don't we go back in the living room?" Lisa gestured. "You take your time, and we'll keep our mouths shut and listen."

"But your tree." Nita gave Mabel an apologetic look. "That was the whole point of the evening. You want to do that first?"

What Mabel wanted was Nita's story.

"We can do that afterward," Lisa blurted, seeming to forget or ignore she had school early the next morning.

"Or I'll do it tomorrow or whenever," Mabel said. "The point of the evening was for us to get together, and we're doing that."

"If you're sure. I didn't come here planning to hijack your party."

"Shanita Bedford, you're killing us." Lisa tugged Nita's arm. "We're all dying to find out what's going on."

Well, at least Lisa and I are. Mabel shot a wary glance at John and Tim, but even they looked curious. "Do you know where all this long-lost mail came from? Or who wrote that letter to my Grandma Mabel?"

Nita had gotten up but hesitated before answering. "Maybe. I might have an idea who wrote the letter, at any rate."

"Then, get a move on, girl." As Lisa nudged Nita toward the

front hall, Koi darted between their feet, on her way to join the party.

Once settled around the tree with a fresh supply of food and drinks, everyone waited expectantly. Nita fiddled with a cracker until it broke into pieces, then dropped them onto her plate and wiped the crumbs off her fingers with a napkin.

Mabel studied Nita with a trace of concern. She seemed "off" this evening…ever since seeing that vintage card, in any event. Nita was always buoyant and energetic, brimming with self-confidence. Was there something she didn't want to share? Or was she just trying to figure out the right way to explain whatever it was?

Nita looked up, but her eyes were focused on something beyond that room.

"This goes back before any of us were born. Back to the early sixties or so."

Chapter Eight

"I DON'T BELIEVE IN COINCIDENCES." NITA looked around at Mabel and her friends. "In two days' time, that card right there and a bunch of others came back from fifty or sixty years in the who-knows-where."

This time, she focused on Mabel. "And in that same day or two, you find a skull, and where does it come from? Maybe from where *it's* spent the last fifty or sixty years. That all happened for a reason, my friends."

Mabel found herself agreeing. Two bizarre events in one small town, within two days of each other, were more likely related than not.

"Now, I'm gonna tell you a story about another coincidence. This happened a long, long time ago, and I think it has to be connected to Mabel's Christmas card–and those remains you all found yesterday. It's too uncanny to be unrelated."

Nita nudged the carton next to her chair with one foot. "Would you mind if I started untangling this box of lights while I talk?'

"Go for it." The last thing Mabel wanted was to try untangling strings of lights that had been jumbled together for years in Grandma's storage. If working with her hands helped Nita think—or talk—more power to her.

Mabel watched Nita's deft brown fingers gently pull one light cord through a knot in another. "So, you know I grew up here. My family grew up here. I spent a good piece of my childhood on that same farm outside town where I live now. My great-grandparents bought that place back in the twenties.

"Anyhow, it all came down to me a few years ago, after my

parents retired and moved to Florida. My older brothers and I didn't want to farm, and they'd both moved away for school and settled elsewhere. Marcus lives in Pittsburgh, and Boots married a girl from St. Louis. The property's still in my folks' names, but since I'm the only one here and always loved that old place, I moved back in."

It didn't sound like any of what Nita was describing had happened back in the days of four-cent stamps, but Mabel kept her mouth zipped, as promised. She'd been known to circle around a story for a while, herself, before getting down to the meat of it.

"Growing up, my dad had two uncles—Charles and Lester. Lester was older, and my brother Boots was named after him. Boots didn't like being called Little Lester, so he gave himself the nickname when he was only about four and enamored of his cowboy boots. I never knew my great-uncle Lester, but Daddy often talked about him. Lester disappeared ten years or so before I was born, when Daddy was fifteen."

"Oh, Nita. How awful for your family." Lisa covered her mouth.

Nita nodded. "My dad's never forgotten Lester, and all the pain it caused their family when he vanished. There's never any sense of resolution when you don't even know what happened. It wasn't only their grief and the frustration of not knowing what happened. It was worse—a lot worse."

Mabel couldn't imagine anything much worse than losing a family member this way. She wanted to say or do something comforting but didn't know what would soothe such an enormous loss. "I'm so sorry," she finally said.

Nita smiled. "It all happened before my time, but my dad and his entire family have gone through something no one ever should."

"Here." Mabel got up. "I'll test the strings as you get them untangled. I doubt any of them will light anymore."

Nita handed her a strand. "There you go."

Mabel plugged the lights in, but of course, they stayed dark. John opened a fresh box of old-fashioned bulbs Grandma must have been storing for at least a decade and began the tedious job of replacing the lights one by one. She should have bought new lights that stayed cool, on strands that stayed lit even when one burned out. Served her right for trying to recreate an old-time Christmas at Grandma's house.

John cleared his throat but continued working. "I can't believe I never heard any of this. We grew up together."

Nita's mouth twisted. "We did. But it was a family matter—none of us wanted to talk about it. Like I said, everything went down long before we all were born, and Medicine Spring had been changing. It wasn't the same place, and I guess we wanted to keep old hurts in the past."

"I guess I can understand that," John said. "Are you sure you want to talk about it now?"

She grinned. "Yeah. I do. You're my friends, and we're not our parents and grandparents."

What did that mean? Was Nita saying their grandparents did something wrong? That Grandma Mabel had done something wrong? Mabel shifted her bottom in her seat, not sure she wanted to hear what Nita was about to say.

"Back around the late fifties-early sixties, my dad's Uncle Lester got hired by the post office in Medicine Spring. At first, he worked on the loading dock. It was a good civil-service job, but he was smart, and he wanted to advance. There was some competition, and it was a small post office, but finally he got a position as a carrier."

Mabel's heart lurched. "Wait, are you saying…?"

Nita nodded. "He hadn't been on that job more than a few months when he went missing. Vanished right off his route."

An audible intake of breath followed Nita's statement. Mabel was sure she hadn't been the only one gasping.

"They never found him?" Lisa clutched Tim's hand as they waited for Nita's reply.

Nita shook her head. "Right before Christmas, he disappeared along with his mailbag, and the family never got over it. He was only thirty years old."

"They searched, right?" Mabel imagined posters going up on utility poles, candlelight vigils, police dragnets.

"Oh, they searched all right. The family never wanted to give up, but they knew if he was still alive, he must have amnesia or something. They knew he wouldn't take off. My great-grandparents died never knowing what happened."

"That can be worse than mourning a death." John set aside the unresponsive strand of lights. "It's heartbreaking."

"Yep." Nita passed another light string to John. "But there was still worse." Her jaw tightened.

Worse?

Mabel couldn't imagine worse and wasn't sure she wanted to hear anything more, but she knew Nita had to get it all out. If Nita and her family had lived it, the least she could do was listen.

Nita's eyes blazed. "Before long, when no trace of him turned up, the theory was he ran off with whatever was in that sack. Christmastime—lots of people mailing presents or cards with money in them. The family knew he would've died protecting that mail though."

She held up a hand as Lisa started to say something. "Plus, a woman was killed that day, right on his route. Police were able to trace how far he'd gotten by going house to house and seeing the last place he picked up or delivered something. He disappeared right around the murder house."

Mabel gulped.

Though Nita had never known her great-uncle, tears glittered in her lashes. "He made an easy suspect. Black man, new on the job, missing mail, stuff stolen from the house, plus a whole lot of coincidences. The police got to clear a missing person case and a homicide with one fell swoop."

Mabel bristled. "That's so unfair."

Nita laughed without humor. "Fair didn't enter into it."

John frowned. "Did his car turn up?"

"Nope. He was saving for a car, so till he could get his own, one family member or another would lend him their wheels. The day he disappeared, his younger brother Charles drove him to the start of his route—it was walkable, unless he had any big packages. Charles had to run an errand of his own while Lester walked the first few blocks, but they were supposed to meet farther on. Lester never showed."

Tim drew a deep breath and blew it out. "I don't even have to know the guy. There's no way he ditched his brother and ran off. It's stupid to think he's gonna take off and disappear in the middle of winter with a mail sack and no car."

"Absolutely." Nita smacked her hand on the arm of her chair, waking Koi, who'd been sleeping behind her neck. The cat yawned, stretched, and resettled herself, purring.

Nita reached back to pet Koi. "Sorry, baby. I appreciate your support." Koi scrunched her eyes in apparent pleasure.

Mabel's thoughts whirled. "So, you're thinking my Christmas card came from Lester's mailbag? That the sack that just appeared down at the post office with all that old mail—it was his?"

Nita dipped her head. "One and the same."

"Whoa." Mabel contemplated the mailbag's bizarre reappearance. "Wonder where it's been all these years. Plus, who brought it back now—and why?"

"You got me there—but now you know why I'm so worked up over this. Do you think it's a coincidence this mail turns up right now and so do these bones?"

Chapter Nine

For a long moment, nobody spoke. Nita's words reverberated in Mabel's head. "You think it's a coincidence this mail turns up right now and so do these bones?"

They'd found a skull. Or, to be fair, Barnacle had. Next to her, the dog stretched and flopped sideways onto Mabel's right slipper.

To be honest, she'd been little more than curious about the skull, as it appeared so old. Sure, she'd felt bad for the person who'd died, but not in any personal sort of way. She'd even been more than a little bit irritated at having to deal with the police.

Now, shame washed over her, along with a sense of horror at Nita's family tragedy. She swallowed. "No. I don't see how all this can be unconnected either. Why it's surfacing now is a mystery to me though."

"It is to me too," Nita said. "But I'm sure as shootin' going to get to the bottom of it."

Lisa sat up straight. "We'll help, won't we, Mabel?"

Mabel wanted to say, "What can you and I do?" She couldn't have Nita bare her soul and share her family's grief like this, without stepping up to do *something*. She prayed this "something" would occur to her.

"Of course, we will," Mabel heard herself saying.

Nita gripped their hands. "You two are incredible. Thank you."

Mabel felt guilty. She wasn't incredible--although she'd have done anything to help Nita and her family, she was a reluctant recruit, at best. Neither Lester's disappearance nor the murder had been solvable sixty years ago. How on earth were they supposed to find any answers at this point?

As if Nita could read her thoughts, she said, "We've got one advantage today the cops didn't have way back when. We know Uncle Lester was a victim. They never got anywhere because they stopped looking."

John set another string of lights aside. "We're not getting anywhere with these. Even if we get them to light, I'm not sure they're safe. I think you ought to just go buy some more, and we'll tackle the tree tomorrow, okay?"

Mabel startled at his abrupt change of subject, but it seemed he was just clearing the deck, so to speak.

"I'm guessing none of us are in a festive mood for tree-trimming at the moment, right?"

At their head-shakes and murmurs, John pushed the boxes of decorations out of the way behind the couch. "Now, why don't you tell us what you're thinking, Nita? I take it you think the remains belong to your great-uncle?"

She nodded. "I think it's a darn strong possibility."

John rubbed his chin. "We don't have any evidence to go on, at this point."

When Nita bristled, he touched her hand. "What we've got is more of a hunch. But I have the same hunch, and it's worth pursuing."

"Does your family have any information that might help identify the remains?" Lisa asked. "Like dental records?"

Nita slowly shook her head. "I'm not sure, but I think they all went to Dr. Payne, in town. The only reason I know is they used to joke about a dentist named Payne. That office has been gone since I was in elementary school."

"Maybe somebody bought the practice and still has the old records." Mabel didn't have a lot of hope, considering neither she nor her friends had been in elementary school in almost forty years.

"We could sure check." Nita got up and retrieved her purse from the kitchen. After nudging Koi off her warm chair, she plopped back down and pulled out a pen and notepad. "Okay. Got the first item on our investigation list."

"That's good." John smiled. "Now, if they can extract DNA that hasn't been degraded over the years, that's all we need. Considering the condition of that skull, we can't count on that though."

"Hey." When Tim—who tended to be more listener than talker—spoke up, Mabel looked at him with surprise. "Lisa, you remember that show you had us watch? The one where the body had an old scar on the forehead from getting hit by a swing when the guy was a kid. Maybe there's something like that."

"Could be." John turned to Nita. "Of course, we aren't lucky enough to be able to look for scars, but Tim's right. Do you know if Lester might've had a previous broken bone?"

"I'll call my dad. He might not even know himself, but he can call my great-uncle Charles and ask him too. And I'm gonna get swabbed for DNA. If they can get DNA off the remains, I think they can compare it to mine and see whether we're related."

"Hey, Nita." Mabel held out the old letter. "You said you might know who wrote this."

"Oh, right. I got so involved with my story and IDing the remains, I lost track of where I started. I have a strong hunch it came from Lester himself."

"It had a stamp on it," Mabel said. "Wouldn't he have just handed it to Grandma, if he knew her?"

"Not necessarily. You can see he was on the shy side. He might not have wanted to put your grandma on the spot. Plus, from everything my dad says, he was real straight arrow. He would've paid for the stamp like anybody else—not just stuck it in the mailbox."

Mabel studied the letter. "So, this would be…?"

Nita traced the signature with her finger. "I think it says, 'L-e-s.' Can you find out whether your grandma knew him?"

Mabel sat back and thought. "If he grew up around here, he probably went to the same school as Grandma. I think she had a yearbook around here somewhere." She darted a hopeless glance toward the storeroom, which had become a bottomless catchall during Grandma's years of dementia. Maybe she should try looking in the attic—Grandma might have stashed memorabilia up there long before her dementia and arthritis took over.

"What about your grandma's friends? Miss Birdie and Ms. Katherine Ann?" Lisa asked.

"I guess that couldn't hurt. They both have memories like steel traps, when it comes to the old days. I guarantee they'd remember Lester's disappearance."

"I'm writing it down." Nita added to her list.

Mabel looked at the letter. "Any idea who your uncle's love interest was? The names were the hardest for me to decipher."

Nita shook her head. "If he had a crush on someone, nobody ever said. From what I've heard of him, I'm guessing he kept it to himself. He was supposed to be super shy, so he must've really trusted your grandma to share his feelings with her. I'll ask Daddy to check with his Uncle Charles though."

"I'll talk to Miss Birdie and Ms. Katherine Ann too," Mabel promised. "I'm amazed Grandma Mabel was that close to your uncle, and I never heard anything about him. She'd have been married to my grandpa by this time too."

Nita closed her notebook. "Once we get done here, maybe we can divvy up the jobs?"

"Sure, absolutely." John stretched. "We should also tell the police about our suspicions. They're going to be looking for missing persons who are potential matches for this set of remains."

Nita's lips tightened.

A pang went through Mabel. "You don't trust the police, do you?"

"I don't flat-out *distrust* them. You've got to understand our experience with them back when Uncle Lester disappeared would sour anybody."

"I understand." Mabel hesitated. She didn't want Nita to think she was defending the PD's actions sixty years ago. "However, I can promise you one thing. Lieutenant Sizemore—she's the detective now—is a straight arrow like Lester. If she sniffs a homicide, she's going to be like a dog on a bone."

Mabel looked at Barnacle and smacked her head. Too late, she realized what she'd just said.

The others groaned, and John rolled his eyes at her. "Pun, we hope, unintended."

Mabel knew she was blushing. "Of course, unintended. I only meant she won't rest if there's been a murder. She'll go strictly by the evidence in front of her. She's honest and smart— she won't make any false assumptions about your uncle."

"I don't know her, so I'll withhold judgment," Nita said. "Your opinion carries weight with me. Sounds like you're a fan of hers."

"Good grief, no!"

John burst out laughing. "They're still in their 'getting to know you' stage, but at the rate Mabel blunders into bodies, the relationship's been developing fast."

Mabel folded her arms and scowled. "Well, I didn't 'blunder into' this one, as you put it. Barnacle did—and we were all there. Except for you, Nita."

Nita laughed too. "Well…Barnacle *is* your dog, if I'm not mistaken. John's kidding, and so am I. I'm glad you and Barnacle found that skull. Call it a blunder, if you want, but you just managed to give our family our first ray of hope in a whole lot of years."

Chapter Ten

With a groan, Mabel flipped her pillow to the cool side and punched it down. Long after her friends had left for home following her tree-trimming party that wasn't, she'd still been cleaning up. There were leftovers to put away, and Barnacle had knocked over the kitchen garbage. Now that she was in bed with the lights out, her mind kept racing.

Their anonymous bones now had a possible name and people who loved him. If Nita was right, that body on the hill at the tree farm had also had somebody *he'd* loved—someone maybe forever destined not to know that. Not only that, if Nita was right, he'd died with his name falsely tarnished.

Was Nita right? Mabel had to agree it was odd, having those old remains turn up right at the same time as all that lost Christmas mail. Plus, that signature sure did look like "Les," now that Nita had pointed it out.

Coincidences did happen, she reminded herself.

Mabel hoisted herself onto an elbow and checked the time. She groaned. Almost two a.m.

She should've been sleeping hours ago. Not enough time left for a good night's sleep. However, still way too much time till she could check for old dental records or try to talk to Miss Birdie and Ms. Katherine Ann.

With a growl of frustration, Mabel flung off her covers and swung her feet over the edge of the bed to feel around for her slippers. She only found one, so she reluctantly turned on her reading light. Koi, stretched across the other side of the bed, yawned and blinked her eyes.

"Sorry," Mabel muttered.

Barnacle was already at the bedroom door, obviously figuring it was morning potty time.

"Okay, whatever." Mabel found her missing slipper under the nightstand and wiggled her foot inside. "Let's go."

Koi opened one eye a slit and scrunched it shut again.

"Lucky." Mabel turned off the lamp and felt her way to the bedroom door. A nightlight cast its dim glow over the hall runner as she made her way to the staircase, where she flipped on the downstairs entry light. For the first time since moving here, Mabel appreciated Grandma's frugal low-wattage bulb. She didn't want to wake herself up any more than necessary at this hour.

The pungent scent of spruce rose to meet Mabel as she plodded down the staircase. She paused in the doorway, looking at her undecorated tree and breathing in the fragrance of old Christmas memories. She understood John's not getting a tree if he was going to celebrate with his family elsewhere, but she wouldn't have wanted to miss having this heady aroma in her house for the next couple of weeks.

After letting Barnacle out on his run, Mabel foraged in the fridge for the block of longhorn Colby cheese she'd bought a few days ago. This had been Grandma Mabel's favorite cheese, and though Mabel wasn't any fonder of that variety than any other, she always kept some around out of a sense of loyalty.

By the time she let her dog back in, Mabel had fixed herself a plate of cheese and crackers and a microwaved cup of tea. She sat down at the kitchen table with her food and the small notebook she used for grocery lists and self-reminders.

After a brief debate on whether to make separate lists for the mystery mail and the mystery bones, she wrote "To Investigate" at the top of the first blank page and began writing down all her assignments in no particular order. Barnacle's questing nose appeared over the edge of the table. As he snuffled, a thread of drool landed on the oilcloth cover, and he licked his chops.

Mabel shoved him aside, but a moment later, a white-rimmed eyeball appeared, followed by a wet nose and a big paw. "All right."

She knew she shouldn't feed him from the table, but she'd lost that battle long ago. "So, I'm weak." She passed him a sliver of cheese.

Having her snack seemed to stimulate Mabel's foggy brain. As she considered her to-do list, she realized there was one task she could at least start right now.

After putting her plate in the sink, she took her mug and headed for the cluttered storeroom, where she remembered seeing a tub of Grandma's memorabilia. Maybe her high school yearbook was in there.

The door squeaked when she opened it. She flipped the switch. The forty-watt ceiling bulb cast more shadows than light, but she wouldn't need a lot of illumination to grab the box she was looking for.

She set her cup down on a nearby plastic bin and padded over to a stack of boxes in the far corner, trailed by Barnacle and Koi. The cat had apparently heard the door to her favorite mouse-populated room of the house creak open and decided to come downstairs.

Of course, the box wasn't where Mabel remembered last seeing it. Nothing in here was labeled either.

And it was cold. Since she only used the room for storage, Mabel kept the thermostat set to fifty and the door closed.

After poking around a while, she gave up. Tomorrow, she could either turn up the heat or bundle up—or both—and the room would be brighter. "Let's get out of here, guys."

Barnacle, at her heels as usual, followed her to the hall door. Koi was nowhere to be seen.

"I'm tempted to leave you here tonight."

She waited a moment, but the cat didn't emerge.

"I mean it."

Koi slipped out from a narrow crack between the stacks of boxes. She sashayed toward the door, languid tail plume waving behind her.

"Hurry up," Mabel grumbled. "I'm freezing in here."

Koi rubbed herself luxuriously along the base of the plastic tub where Mabel had left her tea—once hot, now iced. The mug wobbled, and Mabel made a grab for it as Koi vaulted up onto the lid.

Mabel caught her cup before it could tip over. She scowled at Koi, who now sat, tail curled around her prim front feet. "Could you please, for once, cooperate?"

Koi lay down, paws folded over the edge of the lid. She squeezed her eyes shut and then opened them, looking up at Mabel.

"What?"

Mabel looked down. Through the translucent side of the tub, she now saw a jumble of old cards, scrapbooks, diaries, and other memorabilia.

Oh, for Pete's sake. This whole time, her mug had been sitting right on top of what she was looking for.

Koi yawned and licked a front paw.

"I guess I should thank you." It never failed to amaze Mabel how often Koi seemed to "just happen" to point her in the right direction. She was walking to the kitchen when, on an impulse, she made an abrupt return to the living room.

She plopped the bin atop her coffee table and turned on the floor lamp, then cued up a Christmas CD. Barnacle lay down at her feet, but Koi continued her march to the kitchen.

As The Little Drummer Boy began to play, Mabel popped the lid off the tub. She lifted out a scrapbook covered in fabric and faded ribbons and began paging through old photos and dance programs.

Absently, she picked up her tea mug and sipped, then sputtered. Cold, naturally, after sitting in that icebox of a storeroom. She considered rewarming it but given the lateness of the hour, decided to keep going with her search. She skimmed the scrapbook but found nothing relevant, though she decided to spend some quality time looking through the book in more detail later.

Koi wandered into the room, polishing her whiskers. She leapt up onto the back of the couch, settling behind Mabel's head.

The disagreeable funk of the musty box contents clashed

with the lovely scent of the tree. Mabel sneezed and wiped her nose, then lifted out a crushed corsage. A dry crumble of brown leaves and petals showered down, leaving her holding a faded ribbon, once maybe pale blue. Beneath it, she spied the corner of what looked like a yearbook.

Mabel gently set aside the corsage, wondering what long-ago dance Grandma had worn it to. Had Grandpa pinned it to her dress? Or was this from some forgotten boyfriend?

She tugged at the burgundy cover till the book came free from beneath a bulky photo album. *Eureka. Grandma's senior yearbook.*

Eagerly, Mabel flipped pages. There she was—Mabel Josephine Spangler. Mabel was stunned to see Grandma at eighteen, prettier than she'd imagined, with long hair rolled smoothly under and a formidable rolled "bumper bang" defending her forehead.

Mabel knew Miss Birdie had never married, so she was easy to locate too, by her last name, Henry. As soon as she turned to the H's, Mabel spotted her at once. She smiled at Miss Birdie's familiar, determined, narrow chin.

Miss Birdie also stood out as one of three Black students in the graduating class—Mabel didn't recognize the other girl, but there was Nita's great-uncle, Charles. He was a handsome young man. It gave Mabel a pang, realizing Lester had once been that young and filled with potential.

After thumbing through the rest of the class, Mabel closed the book. Her head had started to droop. She hadn't found Ms. Katherine Ann, but maybe she'd been absent on picture day.

Yawning, she replaced the book and the corsage and shut the lid. Tomorrow morning, she would give Grandma's friends a call.

Chapter Eleven

MABEL WOKE LATE TO BARNACLE JUMPING on and off the bed, reminding her it was past his usual morning potty time. Koi was nowhere in sight.

Still groggy from her largely sleepless night, Mabel fumbled into clothing and followed Barnacle downstairs. While the dog took care of business, she poured food into the pet bowls. Koi came out from under the Hoosier cupboard, trailing a cobweb from her whiskers.

The cat twined herself around Mabel's leg, depositing the spiderweb in the process, before settling down at her dish.

The smell of coffee brewing, mingled with the fresh evergreen scent drifting from the living room, gave Mabel hope she might survive another day. She peeled the cobweb from her pantleg, then set a clean mug on the table to await her first mug of morning coffee—what Dolly Parton's lyrics referred to as a "cup of ambition."

She looked at the clock. Already too late to catch Miss Birdie and Ms. Katherine Ann down at the Coffee Cup Diner. Given it wasn't snowing or raining, and the thermometer outside the kitchen window read forty-two degrees, she could be all but certain the two old friends were out walking or already home. The two often ate breakfast after their usual daily walk, but on these dark winter mornings, breakfast came first.

Doggone it. Mabel poured her coffee and took a deep inhale before sipping. If she hadn't overslept, she could've had a fortifying diner breakfast and caught them there.

Just as well. It made more sense to see the ladies at one of their homes, where they could pore over the yearbook without inviting grease or maple syrup stains.

A few moments later, she'd called Miss Birdie and gotten an invitation to Ms. Katherine Ann's townhouse in the Best Years assisted living community beyond the Vo-Tech. Miss Birdie explained they were enjoying a day of candy-making and accompanying Christmas movie marathon. Mabel couldn't imagine a more perfect bonus to her investigation than fresh-made Christmas candy.

An hour later, she pulled into a spot near Ms. Katherine Ann's giant red Cadillac Eldorado, now occupying one and a quarter space. Mabel smiled. Miss Birdie often complained about Ms. Katherine Ann's casual regard for sticking to her own lane. Mabel hoped she was more careful in traffic.

Yearbook under her arm, Mabel turned to check house numbers. Ms. Katherine Ann's place seemed to be the end unit, a few steps away. As Mabel approached, she heard a TV blaring.

Ms. Katherine Ann greeted her at the door. "Come on in and make yourself at home. You're in time to test the fudge we just cut."

"Is it okay if I throw my coat on this chair?"

"Sure. We have hard candy on the stove, so I need to get back in there. Sometimes," she whispered, "Birdie doesn't let it cook long enough."

The TV noise from the kitchen drowned out Ms. Katherine Ann's words, but Mabel got the gist from watching her lips. After a moment's hesitation, Mabel left the yearbook with her coat. She feared there was no safe place to set it down in the cooking area.

She took a step in that direction, then turned back and tossed her sweater on the chair too. The thermostat had to be set well above seventy-five—or maybe the heat from the stove was to blame. Mabel pulled out a tissue and wiped her sweaty forehead.

She hoped she wasn't having a hot flash, but she'd been noticing more and more unbearably warm places lately. Soon, she'd have to start wearing shorts and tank tops under her winter clothes, so she had something to strip down to.

"You need to keep an eye on the thermometer, Birdie dear." Ms. Katherine Ann pushed Miss Birdie's hands away from the bubbling pan that wafted the fragrance of cinnamon into the air.

"I would if either of us could still read the thermometer," Miss Birdie argued. "The old-fashioned way works fine. My mother made the best hardtack you ever ate, just drizzling a little bit onto a cold plate."

"Too chancy. We're going to end up with a whole pan of syrup."

Above their gentle argument, Jimmy Stewart was serenading Donna Reed with *Buffalo Gals* at full volume. Mabel glanced at the TV on the kitchen counter. She loved *It's a Wonderful Life* and hadn't seen it in years, but clearly, now wasn't the time.

"Hi. Can I read that thermometer for you?"

"Oh, Mabel, thank you." Miss Birdie beamed. "Time is of the essence."

Mabel leaned in and peered through the cloud of steam, wishing she'd grabbed her glasses first. After having made the offer, she felt a certain pressure to perform well.

"Hard crack?" As soon as she'd read the numbers, then loudly repeated them above the TV noise, both women reacted with fire drill urgency. Ms. Katherine Ann lifted the pot from the stove, and Miss Birdie pulled a cast-iron skillet from the freezer.

Mabel watched nervously, sure Ms. Katherine Ann would slosh scalding hot syrup on her hands as the two old friends converged on the table, but they moved with the efficiency of long practice. Ms. Katherine Ann carefully poured the pan contents into the skillet.

"Would you please turn off that burner, Mabel dear?" Ms. Birdie called over her shoulder. "We wouldn't want to burn the place down with our forgetfulness."

Mabel hopped to obey. She hadn't noticed any forgetfulness on their part. In fact, she was sure she was more absentminded than either of them on their worst day.

"We always make cinnamon, spearmint, and clove," Miss Birdie said. "Nobody likes anise."

Ms. Katherine Ann made a sour face. "Used to do all three flavors at once. Back when your grandma was living. She had a nice big kitchen, and we weren't so slow then. Now, we do one flavor a day."

"We always start with cinnamon because that's our favorite. It's our insurance in case we don't get to finish the others." Miss Birdie grinned.

Ms. Katherine Ann winked. "Then we fight over which one to do next. I like spearmint, and Birdie likes the clove."

Mabel watched as Ms. Katherine Ann cut the cooling candy into bite-size pieces, and Ms. Birdie tossed them with powdered sugar in an old Pyrex bowl.

Sidelong, Mabel eyed the plate heaped with fudge, which was studded with nuts and topped with crushed candy canes. Her mouth watered. "Maybe I shouldn't have come when you're trying to work."

"Nonsense." Miss Birdie patted Mabel's hand and smiled. "We're delighted to have you join us. We miss Mabel so."

Mabel missed Grandma too, even after all these months. Maybe more so during this first Christmas season since her passing.

"Do you have time to sit and talk a bit? And look at Grandma's yearbook with me?"

"Of course, baby," Miss Birdie said. "I haven't seen a copy of *Fox Tales* since a few years after we graduated."

"All this mess needs to finish cooling now." Ms. Katherine Ann opened a cabinet door and looked back at Mabel. "Would you like tea with us, or do you prefer milk with your fudge?"

"Um, milk. Thank you."

When they'd settled in the living room with the candy and drinks, Birdie trotted back to the kitchen to turn off the TV. Ms. Katherine Ann protested that she could hear conversation perfectly well with the TV on. "We just about know that movie by heart anyway. We don't need to listen. It's just comforting to hear it in the background this time of year."

Mabel relaxed when the blare ended and silently blessed Miss Birdie. In her opinion, the movie had been a whole lot more than background. "I'm sorry, Ms. Katherine Ann. I have trouble hearing conversation myself, and having the TV off should help me, at least."

"Oh, well, then." Ms. Katherine Ann helped herself to a big square of fudge before easing back in her recliner. "I suppose it's that loud rock-and-roll music you kids listen to."

Mabel hid a grin by bringing a piece of fudge up to her mouth. "No doubt."

The fudge was divine. Mabel sighed and took a piece for her other hand.

"Now, baby, what was it you wanted to talk about?" Miss Birdie perched on the edge of an overstuffed armchair.

Mabel started explaining about the skull they'd found, but Ms. Katherine Ann waved a hand. "We heard all about that business—already been all over the news. Didn't know it was you again, though." She scowled, as if annoyed with that small failure in her intelligence sources.

"Now, it wasn't 'again.' I never found a skull before."

The women glanced at each other before bestowing a pitying look on Mabel. "Those bodies, baby." Miss Birdie shook her head. "You do end up with an unfair number of bodies."

No argument there. "I don't know why. This never used to happen to me before I moved here." She heard the self-pitying whine in her voice and stopped talking.

"Well, we never had this issue either," Ms. Katherine Ann said, "until…" Her voice trailed off.

"Katherine." Miss Birdie fixed her friend with a stern look. "If you're going to say we didn't have murders here before, that's plain not right. What about those ax murders? It's not your fault, baby."

Ms. Katherine Ann gave a grudging nod. "Nobody's blaming you for all the dead people…but you sure do have a knack for finding them."

Could she be like a human cadaver dog? This possibility had never occurred to Mabel, but now she wondered.

"Medicine Spring's not all that big," Ms. Katherine Ann went on. "We can't afford to lose many more people, you know."

"Katherine." Miss Birdie gave another, fiercer head shake. "Again, not Mabel's fault."

"No, I suppose not, but…"

"Anyway," Mabel said, "the police are trying to identify the remains, but they don't have a lot to go on. My friend thinks it might be her great-uncle, who went missing back in the sixties."

Both women perked up. "Local boy?" Miss Birdie set down her tea cup.

"Yes. He was a mail carrier back then, and he disappeared right off his route."

"Are you talking about Lester Bedford?" Ms. Katherine Ann asked.

"Yes, ma'am."

"Have mercy." Miss Birdie covered her mouth. "I'll never forget. Not as long as I live."

Chapter Twelve

"THAT WAS SUCH A SAD CHRISTMAS season. So much death and loss." Ms. Katherine Ann shook her head. "First, that poor child getting herself killed in her own place. Then, come to find out old Mr. Crawford had passed the night before…of course, that wasn't much of a surprise. He'd been ailing a long time."

"Then, Lester disappearing the way he did." Ms. Birdie's dark eyes glistened as if tears wanted to well up. "His family never got over it."

"You knew him?" Mabel leaned forward, clutching the yearbook to her chest.

Ms. Katherine Ann shrugged. "Not really. Did you, Birdie?"

"I suppose I'd have to say, 'not well.' Not to talk to." Miss Birdie looked off toward the window. "Of course, we knew the family. There weren't a lot of people of color around here back then, so we all knew each other. But when you're growing up, you don't pay as much mind to anyone a few years older than you are."

Mabel felt a sure lead ebbing away. If Ms. Katherine Ann and Miss Birdie hadn't known Lester, why would Grandma have been a close enough friend to play John Alden to his Miles Standish? Oh, well. She'd come here to ask.

Mabel held out the yearbook. "I was wondering whether Grandma knew him."

Miss Birdie frowned in apparent thought. "No…I don't believe she did. Or, I suppose I should say I was never aware of it, if so."

Ms. Katherine Ann snatched the yearbook. "Oh, Birdie, look. Your senior year. I haven't seen one of these since I don't know when."

Two gray heads bent over the musty pages. "Oh, Birdie, your hair!"

Miss Birdie sniffed. "I don't see as it's any more peculiar than yours was."

Ms. Katherine Ann cocked her head to one side and studied Miss Birdie's pouf of sculptured high school curls. She looked back at her friend. "I just like it better the way you wear it now—more natural. Not so stiff it looks stuck on."

"People said I favored Dorothy Dandridge."

Ms. Katherine Ann rolled her eyes. "I'm sure they did."

Mabel stepped in, hoping to avoid another squabble. "Where's your picture, Ms. Katherine Ann?"

"Oh, it'll be way back here." She flipped pages. "I'm a good bit younger, you know."

It was Miss Birdie's turn to roll her eyes. "Three months. You just missed the cut-off."

Ms. Katherine Ann located her photo in the junior class section and quickly slid her hand over it before flipping back to the seniors. "Oh, never mind about that now. Mabel had a question about Lester."

"Um, yeah. I couldn't find Lester in the yearbook, and I wondered if Grandma knew him somehow."

"Not that I heard of." Ms. Katherine closed the yearbook, seemingly no longer interested in strolling down memory lane. "Lester graduated before this. You'll need to find an older yearbook."

Miss Birdie tugged the yearbook out of Ms. Katherine Ann's grip. "Don't worry, Betty Grable. No one's looking at your picture. I just want to point out Charlie."

"Charles Bedford? I did see him," Mabel said. "That's Lester's younger brother?"

Miss Birdie nodded, smoothing a hand over the good-looking young face. "He joined the Army out of high school and married a girl from Louisiana. Moved down there. Only ever saw him at holidays and such after that. Except when Lester went missing. Heard he lost his job over being up here so much while they were trying to find him."

"It was a disgrace." Ms. Katherine Ann already had part of a piece of fudge in one hand, but she picked up another. "That poor family was out of their mind trying to find some trace of Lester, and meanwhile people talked like he was Public Enemy Number One." She popped the first piece of fudge in her mouth and licked her fingers.

"Shameful," Miss Birdie agreed. "They finally had to declare him dead."

She passed the yearbook back to Mabel with hands that shook. "Your friend thinks that…those bones you all found belong to Lester?"

Mabel nodded. "She does."

"Who's your friend?" Miss Birdie asked.

"Nita Bedford."

"Eugene's girl? Would that be Shanita?"

"Yes, ma'am."

"Smart girl. She'll make a good supervisor. If she thinks this is Lester, she's likely right."

"I'm afraid so. Or maybe it's a good thing, finally finding him."

"I'm sure it is." Miss Birdie lifted her chin. "Always better to know the truth."

Mabel took one more piece of fudge…it was small. "If they can prove somebody killed him, that ought to help clear his name, don't you think?"

"I do hope so," Ms. Katherine Ann said. "He never should

have been suspected of those awful things to begin with."

Miss Birdie took Mabel's hand. "You helping out Shanita, baby?"

"I'm trying to."

Miss Birdie smiled. "Good as solved then. Try your grandma's attic for an older yearbook. Lester would've been maybe three-four years older than we were. I'm sorry we couldn't help you more." She got to her feet. "Sorry too that I have to go now. I'm on altar guild this month, and we need to change the vestments."

Ms. Katherine Ann got up. "Here, Mabel, let me fix you a box of candy to take home. If you come back in a few days, we'll have our other hardtack flavors made, and a few other things."

"You do that," Miss Birdie said. "Maybe we'll think of something else to help you by then."

Mabel chewed her lip. "Do either of you know a Betty? Around your age, maybe give or take a few years?"

Both women looked blank till Miss Birdie brightened. "There was a Betty in the class right ahead of ours."

"And one in mine," Ms. Katherine Ann said. "But I believe her given name was Elizabeth."

"Was Grandma close to either of them?" Mabel asked, hope stirring.

"Not to my knowledge." Miss Birdie looked toward Ms. Katherine Ann, who also shook her head. "Why you asking, baby?"

"It's kind of a long story. I think I'd better save it for next time."

As Mabel headed toward the door a few minutes later, her shoulders dropped. She had so hoped Grandma's friends would be able to link her to Lester, or at least the mysterious Betty. Oh, well. At least, she now had a box of homemade candy.

On her way home, Mabel stopped at the drugstore, where she picked up four boxes of multicolored Christmas lights. John had made casual mention of finishing the tree after she'd bought lights "tomorrow." When everybody had left the house last night, however, they hadn't made any specific plan for finishing the decorating. She doubted they'd all want to return for a second night in a row.

Once home, Mabel checked her mailbox. As she pulled out an electric bill and a grocery flyer, she realized she'd been holding her breath. No more long-lost Christmas cards.

No new cards either. She guessed she should have bought a box of cards while she was at the store, so she could send her own. That was likely the only way she was going to receive any. Or— the easiest solution occurred to her—maybe she ought to buy a nice assortment and just hang those up.

Her cell phone buzzed in her coat pocket. Lisa had texted.

Did you get lights? Tim & I can come back for a bit if you want to finish the tree.

Mabel pulled off her mitten with her teeth and texted a reply.

That would be great. I can order a big Sicilian pizza.

Barnacle jumped at the box of candy as she came inside. "Not for you."

She clipped him to his run-out and dumped her purse and the yearbook on the kitchen table. Still wearing her coat, she plopped down on the nearest chair and rested her chin in her hand.

It was hard to shake the sense of despondency that had been settling over her ever since that skull had surfaced. Either it belonged to Nita's great-uncle Lester, which was heartbreaking, or he was still missing, and some other poor person was dead. Also sad.

Then, there was that Christmas card, which had arrived like Marley's ghost, to keep her up at night. She wasn't sure what more she could do about that. She hoped maybe Nita had been able to get a better lead from her family.

Her phone rang at the same time Barnacle began to bark. John was calling.

She answered as she went to let the dog in. "Hey."

"Hey, Mabel. What's up?"

She groaned. "A sleepless night followed by a frustrating day all around." While she unclipped Barnacle and filled food bowls, she told him about her fruitless attempts to link Grandma with either Nita's great-uncle or the mysterious Betty.

"I guess you aren't up for another evening of tree decorating then."

"Well, I didn't say that. Lisa texted a moment ago, in fact. She and Tim want to come over and finish the job."

"Let's do it then. You going to call Nita?"

"Sure. Did you find anything out?"

"A little bit. It can keep till tonight."

Chapter Thirteen

WHILE SHE WAITED FOR HER TRIMMING crew, Mabel watered her tree. It appeared to have drunk half the water she'd put in the bucket yesterday. As she walked away, though, she caught Barnacle slurping at his new "drinking fountain," and realized where a lot of the water had gone.

Mabel also poked around a bit in the attic but didn't turn up any more yearbooks. There might be some in the front room, but it was so crammed with boxes the task seemed hopeless.

Nita called, saying she'd be running late. She'd needed to get her cousin to come in and close the bookstore for her, as Zac, her college-age assistant, had left early with flu-like symptoms. On the bright side, Nita reported she'd gotten more information from her family, and she'd ordered a DNA test.

Shortly after seven, Mabel's friends started arriving. This time, the homemade goodies and attempts at healthful fare seemed to have been kicked to the curb. Besides the pizza Mabel had ordered, which arrived as everyone else came in bearing goodies, Lisa and Tim had brought chips and pop, and even John was carrying half a sheet cake from Stotz's Farm Market. He redeemed a sliver of his reputation by also producing a bag of apples, which he plunked on Mabel's kitchen table next to the bowls of homemade candy she'd brought home from Ms. Katherine Ann's.

"Let's eat the pizza while it's hot," Lisa suggested. "We can set some aside for Nita. She wouldn't expect us to wait since she wasn't sure when she could get here."

"No, she said to go ahead and eat." Mabel set out paper plates and napkins—she didn't intend to wash dishes.

Lisa slid one slice of pizza onto her plate and licked sauce off her fingers. "I do think we should wait for Nita before we talk about anything we've learned since last evening, though, don't you agree?"

"Absolutely." John tried to wave Mabel ahead of him, but she motioned him through while she set out cups. Following Lisa's lead, John helped himself to a single slice…plus an apple.

Mabel frowned and waited for Tim, whom she was relieved to see took three slices and a mound of chips. Now, she'd look restrained when she took two slices and a small handful of chips. On second thought, she also grabbed an apple.

For a while, they talked about things other than skulls and decades-overdue mail. Lisa fretted about the restaurant that had lost her reservation for the wedding brunch. "They finally located it and profusely apologized, but now we're going to be squeezed into a way smaller room."

"Stuff happens." Tim shrugged. "The holidays are a crazy time of year."

Mabel looked at Lisa with concern, half-expecting to see her eyes casting lightning bolts at the clueless Tim. "*We—*" Lisa bore down on the first person plural— "scheduled our wedding for my school break, remember? And put down a big deposit to reserve that room."

Tim grinned. "It'll be fine. Don't worry."

"Sure, it will." As maid of honor, Mabel knew when to suck it up and extend some reassurance, even at the expense of bridesmaid chores she'd have paid cash money to avoid. "We can go down there and eyeball the place whenever you want and figure out how many people we have and how we'll all fit. Maybe I can get you some money back."

"Figured it would pay off some day, having an ex-lawyer as a friend." Lisa smiled at Mabel, then reached over and took Tim's hand. "Thanks for keeping me level, sweetheart."

No question she loved this guy. He'd escaped his faux pas not only intact but being thanked—with a bit of diversionary help from Mabel.

"Have you figured out your next volunteer gig yet?" John asked Mabel.

"I decided to take a break till after the holidays and the wedding. That's plenty soon enough to get myself involved in another fiasco."

John snorted. "You hang onto that positive attitude. It'll take you far."

Lisa pulled her loving gaze away from Tim's eyes. "Didn't you mention they're looking for more choir members for the Christmas Eve service? That would be a perfect, fun way to get some volunteer time in, and contribute to the beauty of the service at the same time."

Mabel grimaced. "Believe me, my singing will never be classified as fun. Let alone contribute to the beauty of anything."

Lisa stared at her. "There is nothing wrong with your voice. I've heard you singing since kindergarten."

"I sound like a foghorn."

"You do not. You have a nice, rich voice. Some incredible singers have been altos. Etta James. Judy Garland. Patsy Cline."

"Yeah, altos. Not female Barry Whites."

"Oh, quit!" Lisa threw popcorn at Mabel, which Barnacle scrambled after when it went wide.

John gave Mabel's shoulders a hug. "You should think about it. You might surprise yourself."

"And other people," Mabel said darkly. "In fact, the shock might finish them."

"Think about it." John held her gaze till she looked away.

Tim took Lisa's empty plate and stacked it with his to take to the kitchen trash. "Ready to get the tree lights on, guys?"

Mabel breathed a sigh of relief at the change of topic. The

thought of singing in public, even with a group, was terrifying. Singing alone was the ultimate terror, of course, but when singing with others, she had the added potential of bringing the entire choir down with her.

No choir. No way.

The lights went on in a snap with the men, especially lanky Tim, able to reach the upper branches. Mabel was gratified to see the soft little gleams of red, green, yellow, and blue blossoming in the spruce, each casting its tiny glow. It took her back to childhood, when she'd wished herself small enough to live in the Christmas tree world along with the diminutive angels, teddy bears, and elves.

Lisa opened boxes, and Mabel went through them with eager hands. There was the faded construction paper star she'd made for Grandma in first grade. Her heart caught at the old painted glass ornaments, the ancient bubble lights, the tiny glow-in-the-dark plastic cherubs. Memories flooded her chest to bursting.

"Here's the manger scene." Lisa passed Mabel a brown cardboard box from a fruitcake company, still bearing its shipping label. Wavering black marker read, "Nativity."

"Is there a stable? About so big?" Mabel peered over Lisa's shoulder. "Grandpa made it out of plywood. It used to have moss and straw glued to it, but most of that crumbled off."

"Not in this tub. I'll keep a lookout."

Mabel carried the fruitcake box to the table by the front window, where Grandma used to put the display. This was a dangerous spot to set up décor of any kind, let alone the precious manger, given Barnacle's, and worse—Koi's, tendency to monitor the front of the house from there. She chewed her lip and thought, then returned to the fireplace mantel, already crowded with Grandma's porcelain animals and other kitsch.

For the moment, she just shoved the clutter back against the wall. She could deal with that later. For now, she needed to get the nativity arranged. Grandma had always said, "I figure once the manger's up, that's the most important thing, even if nothing else gets done."

The set was dime-store quality plastic, but Mabel ran loving hands over the little donkey as she placed him to the right of the Holy Family, where he'd been stationed every Christmas. One of the sheep now had only three legs, and Grandma had always leaned him against the stable for support. Mabel still hoped the stable would show up, but for now, she laid him down next to his sound brother. "Just rest for now." She smiled and paraphrased. "He maketh thee to lie down in green pastures."

She startled as John leaned in. "Talking to the little guys?"

Mabel felt herself blush. John kissed her temple. "That's adorable."

She didn't answer but smiled back. She liked being adorable. It was still a novelty to feel special to someone. John seemed to appreciate even her weirdness. That alone would have been enough to make him special to her in return.

Here was Mary in her scuffed blue robe, hands raised in adoration. She would go here. Happily, Mabel browsed through tissue paper. A camel emerged. A wise man in an orange cloak she'd always liked as a child because the color made her think of her favorite jelly-candy orange slices.

Eventually, she had baby Jesus in the manger and the Holy Family reunited. Shepherds and animals to the right, wise men to the left. Mabel looked up at the ceiling. The herald angel needed to be hooked up there somehow. "John?"

"I've got you. Do you have some fishing line?"

At her raised eyebrow, he added, "Or some thread?"

"Hang on."

Mabel trotted upstairs to the spare bedroom, where Grandma kept her old treadle sewing machine. She found a spool of white quilting thread in a drawer. Hopefully, it wasn't dry-rotted from age.

A burst of voices downstairs announced Nita's arrival.

When Mabel got to the living room, she found Nita passing out boxes of Sarris chocolate-covered pretzels. She handed one to Mabel. "Merry Christmas."

Mabel took the red box and gave the thread to John. "Aw, Nita, thanks."

"No need for thanks." Nita sniffed. "It's just a little something for you all, for being my squad."

Mabel bit the cellophane and began peeling it away. "Take your coat off. Stay a while."

"We're almost done with the tree," Lisa said. "We saved you pizza, but we figured we might as well go ahead and get as much decorating done as we could, so we'd have more time to talk about the investigation."

"Good plan," Nita said. "Tree looks nice. Let me go grab some food, and I'll be right back."

Mabel took a bite of her pretzel and admired the tree. "Great job, guys. I feel like I've hardly done anything."

"You were busy communing with the nativity scene," John said, studying the distance to the ceiling. "I might need a ladder to hang this girl up. How do you want to do it? If you don't mind a hole in the ceiling, I could try to put in a hook or a tiny nail…if you have any. Otherwise, I think a bit of tape should hold her. She's pretty light."

"There's a ladder in the back of my shed. I don't mind attaching something to the ceiling. Grandma used a hook or something when she had the set in the front window. I don't have a clue where to lay my hands on a hook right now. I guess I could pick one up at Gump's."

John walked to the front window and looked up. "I can tell you right now where to find one."

"Oh, for Pete's sake." Mabel joined John at the window. "Of course."

Nita wandered back into the room with a plate of food, Barnacle trailing her and sniffing.

"Barnacle. Leave her alone. You've already had your dinner." Mabel shooed the dog away. "Never mind the angel right now, John. It's cold out there and tomorrow's another day."

Lisa and Tim shoved the boxes and tubs into the corner while John placed the little angel on the mantel, next to the three-legged sheep. "Why don't we get drinks or whatever we want, and then we can have a status meeting." Mabel was feeling ready for some cake.

Moments later, everyone had found a cozy spot and something to eat or drink. Mabel laid the yearbook on the coffee table and reported on her visit with Ms. Katherine Ann and Miss Birdie.

"So, we still don't know how—or even if—your grandma knew Uncle Lester." Nita quirked her mouth in apparent discouragement.

"Not yet," Mabel said. "But then, I'm not done yet."

"How about a friend named Betty?" Lisa asked.

Mabel shook her head. "Came up empty there too. There were two in the yearbook, but Grandma didn't seem close enough to either of them to play matchmaker."

John looked up from petting Koi, who'd settled on his lap. "Maybe we could at least check and see if either of them is still alive."

"Might be hard," Nita said. "A lot of women still change their names when they get married."

John grinned. "PI 101."

Nita grinned back and rubbed her hands together. "See, this is awesome, having a crack team on the mission."

Privately, Mabel thought Nita might be overstating their capabilities, but she had to agree, four heads were better than one.

At least, in theory.

"How about you?" Mabel looked at Nita. "How did you make out on the family front?"

Nita wiped her fingers with a napkin and took a drink before replying. "It was…emotional. This has brought up a dark time for Daddy and Uncle Charles. Lot of bad memories."

Mabel scooted over and patted Nita's hand, at a loss for what to say.

"Daddy was old enough to remember everything vividly—how hard his dad took it. His grandma wailing. Daddy went along when they were searching for Uncle Lester."

Mabel felt a chill run over her arms. "Did he tell you about that? About the search, I mean?"

"Yeah." Nita's eyes took on a faraway expression as she gazed into the lit tree. "His memories are still so vivid, I felt like I'd been there myself. The family started looking for Uncle Lester the very first day, even before anybody else even realized he was missing."

Chapter Fourteen

NITA, NESTLED IN GRANDMA'S OLD RECLINER, drew one foot up under her as she began her tale, going all the way to the start of Lester's workday. "His old car was in the shop. Uncle Charles needed his own car, but he drove Lester to the post office early that morning and then dropped him at the start of his route. He had a full sack, so it would've been heavy, but he was sure he could walk the route okay. Uncle Charles was supposed to meet him someplace near the end of the route at a certain time, but Uncle Lester never showed up.

"At first, Uncle Charles thought he'd just gotten bogged down and was running late, so he waited a while. Then, enough time went by that he started worrying, so he began retracing the route in reverse. He was sure he'd run across Uncle Lester somewhere, but after a while, a bad feeling came over him. When he got clear back to the place he'd first dropped him off, Uncle Charles started panicking."

Mabel clutched John's hand. Nita's stark recital made her feel as if this had happened yesterday, not sixty years ago.

"So, he went to the post office, where they told him they'd gotten a couple calls from folks along the route, complaining nobody had picked up their mail that day. Uncle Charles told Daddy he thought he'd black right out at that point. He hung around for a bit, but nobody had any more they could tell him.

"After a while, a supervisor came out and told him they'd be retracing the route, to find out where Lester was last seen or had made a pickup or delivery. They told Uncle Charles they'd be in touch and then shooed him out."

"Oh, Nita, how horrible for your family." Tears stood in Lisa's eyes. "To have someone you love just—disappear."

Nita looked away. "Uncle Charles went on home and told their mom and dad—my great-grandparents. Right away, they got on the phone and called up my grandpa. Grandpa was the oldest brother, you know. He set out with Daddy, starting from the post office, to look for some trace of Uncle Lester.

"Meanwhile, Uncle Charles and Great Grandad started from the other end of the route, where Charles had planned to pick him up. Of course, it happened this time of year, and was already dark almost before they got started."

"How did they search?" John leaned forward. "Did your dad say?"

"Not really. I know they didn't go door to door. At least, not then. They couldn't be sure what kind of reception they'd get, knocking on doors after dark. That evening, they drove around, got out here and there, flashed their lights into the bushes and around the yards and sidewalks. Just looking for some sign of what happened. Any sign at all, of like a struggle or anything out of the ordinary."

John raised his eyebrows.

"I think you know where I'm going with this."

John made a wry face. "Did people try to run them off?"

"Well, to be fair, I guess I might be a bit concerned if I saw someone outside my house flashing a light around," Nita said.

"But...?" Mabel frowned. Nita was describing a living nightmare. "Why assume you've got intruders when people are on a public sidewalk and looking in gutters too?"

"I'd figure they lost a ring or something," Tim said. "Or a kitten. Sometimes they might go into an inlet."

"Thank you." Nita gave thumbs up. "I would too. Some people only wanted to ask what was going on, which is a normal question to ask. But a couple hotheads threatened to shoot if they didn't keep stepping."

"Good grief!" Lisa's eyebrows shot upward.

"So, they did move on. They didn't need any more trouble. If anyone came outside wondering what was up, they went ahead and explained what had happened and asked if the residents knew anything."

"Did anybody tell them anything?" Lisa asked.

"They managed to get a rough idea of how far Lester had gotten on his route, but they would have to come back in the daylight to be able to search very well. They found out one other thing simply by being on the street and running into the cops, who stopped and questioned them."

Mabel frowned. She didn't get it. "Why? Were they searching too?"

"At first, they thought so." Nita snorted. "Daddy and Grandpa had gotten to an area the police had all taped off, and it was lit up like a block party. But searching for Lester wasn't on top of the cops' priority list."

Mabel hit her head with the heel of her hand. "They were there because of that woman who was found murdered on his route."

"And just because your dad and grandpa show up, that makes them suspects?" Lisa's outrage trembled in her voice.

Nita shrugged, palms up, her gesture conveying this was the way things worked, like it or not. "They'd chased all the neighbors away quite a while before. Daddy said you could see them peering through the windows. Some even had binoculars. Then, these two Black guys come strolling up, poking around and shining lights into people's yards. That was all the police needed to make them suspicious."

"That doesn't even make sense," Mabel said. "Why would

anybody who'd just murdered someone decide to cruise on into an active police crime scene? Not to mention call attention to themselves by waving lights around?"

"Hey, no argument here. After Grandpa told them why they were there, the cops only took their information and told them to stay clear of the scene. It seemed to Daddy they already had a theory that Lester was involved. Now, when his relatives show up, they start putting the pieces together and decide Daddy and Grandpa might be hiding Lester someplace and were just nosing around to find out what was happening with the murder investigation."

What a horrible situation. "They must've been half out of their minds with worry by that point," Mabel said.

"They were. My poor great grandma was sitting back home all this time with no word."

"Did they pick up any clues whatsoever?" John asked.

Mabel wished John had been there—wished someone trained to look for evidence had been there to help. Darting a glance at him, she felt sure he wished so too.

"Not at that point. It was dark, and he clearly wasn't there…assuming he was conscious or capable of communicating."

Lisa's quick intake of breath reflected the cold feeling in the pit of Mabel's stomach. Of course, they'd have had to consider the possibility that Lester was out there in the December cold, still alive and in danger of dying of injury or exposure.

"Did they continue searching the next day?" Tim asked.

Nita nodded. "For days and weeks. They risked their jobs while they looked for any sign at all of Lester. They hounded the police, which of course, irritated the cops. The last thing you want to do when they're already suspicious of you."

"They found nothing?" Mabel asked.

"Like I mentioned, the police had closed off the area around the murder house. That also meant part of the general area where Lester was last seen alive, or where mail had been picked up or delivered, was off limits too. Anything they might've found, either the police got it first or it got obliterated by the wet snow that started coming down before the next morning."

"Nothing at all?" Lisa seemed unwilling to give up on the sixty-plus-year-old search.

Lisa's tenacity coaxed a small grin from Nita. "A soggy receipt a block from the house where the woman got killed. Pretty much unreadable. Might or might not have been Lester's. It was from Bud's Esso station—no longer in business, of course. That's where Lester bought gas for Charles's car that morning."

Nita sighed. "In a book or TV show he'd have gotten a uniform button torn off. The police would've somehow missed it, and then Daddy would've found it. Even if that had happened, all it would've done was put Lester right at the scene of the murder."

John leaned forward again. "Did your family look elsewhere? I mean like leave the sidewalk area or question anybody other than the homeowners who came outside?"

Nita stretched. "I'm sorry." She unwound the leg she'd been sitting on. "I'm getting all kinked up—and kind of emotional. I knew some of this before, of course, but it isn't something my family likes talking about. This is the first time I'm hearing a good chunk of this myself, and it feels really raw—like it just happened."

Mabel hopped up. "Want tea or something?"

She shook her head. "Maybe in a bit. Let me finish telling what I know first. Get it all out."

Mabel sank back into her seat.

"Yeah. They did leave the route in a few spots—like there was a vacant lot with a fallen-in shed or barn toward the back of it. They couldn't get access to very many places though. Everything was private property. There wasn't any trail to follow either—the snow didn't come till later that night."

"Interviews?" John prompted.

"Lester had a guy at the post office he ate lunch with sometimes, when he still worked in the back. They managed to get hold of him, and the guy told them Lester had a kind of enemy over there."

John pulled out his phone. "Did they mention any names? Like either who they talked to or who this supposed enemy was?"

Nita shook her head. "Neither of them could remember. Daddy had a name on the tip of his tongue, but he couldn't bring it up. He said he'd let me know if he remembered."

John raised his eyebrows. "A name for which guy—his lunch buddy or the guy he said was an enemy?"

She shrugged hopelessly. "A name. For one of them. He didn't say which—if he even knew. Guys, I have to admit I'm bummed out. Everything happened so long ago, and for all we know these people are dead now, anyway. Or if they aren't, who's to say they're still in their right minds?"

"Hey, quit that." Mabel scooted over and knelt next to the recliner. She jiggled Nita's arm. "They're not necessarily dead. Look at Miss Birdie and Ms. Katherine Ann—they're not only alive, they're out there powerwalking every day. Which is more than I can say for myself. They're still sharp too."

"Oh, I know, but not everybody's like that. Not to mention we're working against Father Time here, if not the Grim Reaper."

Lisa moved in from Nita's other side and jiggled her other arm. "Now, listen, Nita. Not everyone's going to be in their age bracket. Look at your dad. He was around back then, and he's only in his seventies. The guys Lester worked with might be too—well, at least, their early eighties."

"I'm tired, okay?" Nita rolled her eyes and waved a hand.

"I got a bunch of Christmas promotions going on at the shop, and in a few weeks, I'm gonna have to learn how to be a township supervisor. So don't expect me to do that math right now. I just know we need to get cracking, and things aren't looking great to me at the moment."

"Don't worry." Mabel smiled. "We've still got a bunch of other trails to follow."

Nita gave Mabel a skeptical side-eye. "Such as?"

"Lots of them. Like finding out more about that woman's murder. Whether that letter to Grandma really came from Lester. Who is this Betty he was in love with—and is that really her name? How did Grandma know all these people?"

"Of course, Lester wrote that letter," Lisa said. "It's a three-letter man's signature, and it clearly isn't Bob or Dan. It looks like Les…or Leo, right?"

"It does." Mabel struggled to her feet again—her knees weren't what they used to be. "If we can confirm it's from Lester, that ought to be evidence in his favor. Lester was a family man— and this letter proves he was looking forward to getting married and starting a family of his own. He's not going to run off and disappear. Not when he's asking my grandma to help him get a date with the woman he loves," Mabel argued.

Nita held up her hand like a traffic cop. "The police will say he got tempted to rob that woman and ended up killing her. That he might not have planned it, but maybe she surprised him, and he had to run."

Mabel shook her head. "Woman, you just refuse to be en-couraged."

"Can I say something?" Tim had raised his hand. Mabel wondered if this was something that happened when quiet men married kindergarten teachers.

Nita smiled. "Of course, you can. Don't mind us."

"I was just wondering whether you showed that letter to your dad and uncle, so they could tell you if they recognized Lester's handwriting or the signature."

Nita's smile broadened into a grin. "No, I haven't, and that should've been one of the first things we thought of. There are too many different pieces of this puzzle."

"Which is why it's lucky we have so many good heads on this job." Lisa beamed at Tim and squeezed his arm.

Mabel picked up the letter. "Why don't you take this with you? Just let me make a copy first. Did you get a chance to ask whether they knew if Lester was sweet on someone in particular?"

She shook her head. "It took so long, talking about his disappearance and the search and all. It took so much out of them too—Uncle Charles in particular. I decided that was enough for one sit-down."

"Of course." Mabel patted Nita's hand. "All this has to be so upsetting."

Nita covered Mabel's hand with her own. "What happened to my great-uncle Lester was upsetting. It's upsetting going back and reliving it too. But the idea that maybe now we can *know*—maybe right some old wrongs, bring his remains home for a proper burial—that's *exciting*."

They had to find those answers. After all these years, Nita's family deserved some resolution and peace. And though they could never bring him back to realize his hopes and dreams, Lester still deserved justice.

Chapter Fifteen

MABEL'S FINGER HOVERED OVER THE "SEND" button. Again, she drew it back. Maybe she should read over her article one more time. Her account of volunteering at the soup kitchen had seemed like the perfect story for *The Shopper.* It was warmhearted, could be tweaked to make it a bit more seasonal—and of course, it was one of the few volunteer experiences she'd had so far that hadn't involved a homicide.

After talking to her writer friend Jackie, she'd been determined to submit something—however modest—before the end of the year. However, Mabel thought with a small sense of relief, it wasn't the end of the year yet.

Last night, John had stayed a while after everyone left. They'd sat in the glow of the tree lights, Koi on John's lap and Barnacle lying across Mabel's feet and snoring. At first, they'd talked about the mysterious skeletal remains and Lester's equally mysterious disappearance and speculated about what Nita's family might be able to contribute concerning the long-lost card and letter.

But soon, Mabel's brain began to feel fuzzy and overloaded. Her eyelids started to droop, and John gently pulled her closer so she could rest her head against his shoulder. After that, they'd just sat in each other's company and let the soft lights wash over them. At some point, Mabel had roused, realizing she'd dozed off. In fact, she'd been so sound asleep, she'd drooled a bit on John's shoulder—if she hadn't begun snoring, she'd likely still have been dreaming.

He'd left soon after that, saying he was subbing at the high school in the morning and had to get up early. Mabel hoped her drool hadn't been a contributing factor.

Now, she considered her day ahead. She still had Christmas shopping to do—a task she never enjoyed in the best of times. Her worries about making the money last, which she'd inherited from Grandma and recovered in the settlement from her old law firm after her firing, had further dampened her shopping enthusiasm.

What about John? As her boyfriend—how she loved that word—he was entitled to something nice. What to give him? He was a bigger problem than Nita.

Having made her list and written down a few ideas for family members, Mabel put a reminder on her phone to place orders tomorrow. If she didn't do this soon, she wasn't going to get guaranteed delivery before Christmas. Somehow, writing that list and setting a reminder made her feel more in control.

"Come on, Barnacle. Let's take a walk."

The air was crisp with a dusting of snow on the branches, as well as Mabel's car. Perfect for a brisk walk around the field behind her house.

The only problem was that Barnacle didn't seem inclined to be brisk about his business. She hadn't been taking him out so much lately, with the impending holidays, as well as everything else that had been going on in her life.

The dog seemed very invested in performing a detailed nasal analysis of every bush and pebble, none of which he'd had the pleasure of snuffling in the previous few days. When he resisted being tugged along, Mabel resigned herself to her fate. Let him do his thing.

They'd only reached the midpoint at the far end of the small field when two deer came bounding out of the Sauer hedges a few yards away, headed toward the woods. Barnacle shot to the end of his leash, nearly jerking Mabel off her feet.

She tightened her grip in the nick of time and held on as he yipped, barked, and lunged at the fleeing deer. "Okay." Mabel panted. "That's enough. I don't want to chase deer."

Once she'd managed to redirect him toward home at last, Mabel felt her pocket vibrate. She dug out her now-ringing phone. "Hey, John."

"Do you have time to talk?"

"Sure, but listen. I'm out with Barnacle, and he tried to take off after a couple deer. Give me a minute to get back inside, so I won't have to hang onto him at the same time."

Back in the house, Mabel pulled off her coat and gloves and distributed treats to her pets. She reheated a cup of coffee and grabbed the Christmas tin of caramel corn, which she'd bought for Miss Birdie before realizing caramel corn in all likelihood didn't mix well with dentures. Better eat it now, she reasoned, before it got stale.

Once resettled on the couch, she redialed John. "Sorry, I'm back. What's up?"

"I had lunch with Mac—my buddy at the PD. Thought I'd catch you up on what I found out."

"Ooh, good." Mabel pried open the tin. This was a perfect time for popcorn. "Tell me everything."

"Well, for one thing, the back of that skull had a noteworthy fracture."

"What?" Mabel tried to exclaim through a sticky mouthful of popcorn. "I didn't see any fracture."

"We only got a good look at the front, remember? The way it was turned, we couldn't get more than a glimpse of the back. Anyway, this guy had a significant fracture that could have been fatal."

Mabel wiped her fingers on the damp paper towel she'd wisely provided for herself. "Are they sure it wasn't an old injury?"

"They don't think so. It wasn't something that a person could typically walk away with."

"But there's a chance he did?"

"Not a big chance. At a minimum, his brain would've been scrambled. Staggered, maybe—but not walked."

"Could it have happened after death? Like if the body or skeletal remains got banged around?"

"Sure, I guess that's also possible. The examiner suspects it happened either antemortem or perimortem—at or around the time of death—but after all this time, there's no conclusive answer."

Koi jumped up, and Mabel reached out to pet her. She managed to stop in the nick of time, realizing sticky fingers didn't go with cat hair any better than caramel corn with dentures. The cat chose not to accept the rebuff and began butting her head against Mabel's wrist, her cue for petting time.

Mabel stood. "Maybe Lester fell on the ice or something and cracked his head. He might've been confused and wandered off into the woods and then died of his injury or exposure."

"Good thought. He might have made it to the woods, anyway. I always like brainstorming. Sometimes you hit on the right answer that way."

Koi stretched out a paw and hooked her claw in Mabel's pantleg with a sharp jab. "Ow." Mabel struggled to lift the claw out without injury to either herself or the cat, not to mention her pair of jeans. "I'll talk to Nita about it."

"Well, when you do, here's another question for her," John said. "The police turned up a mostly intact femur with an old, healed fracture. See if she can find out whether Lester broke his leg at some point, okay?"

"Sure. That sounds like a clear identifier for Lester. If it turns out he never broke his leg, this isn't him. Now what about teeth?"

"Surprisingly intact. Photographs and impressions were taken. If they can get dental records for any missing persons who might fit the size and assumed age and gender, they'll have something to compare for ID purposes."

Mabel eased back onto the couch. "Starting with Lester." Koi crept onto her lap. If she'd wanted to snuggle, the cat would have shunned her.

"He's at the head of the line, since he's the only name they've got right now. Hopefully, I made points with the cops by being able to give them a dentist they can start with."

"I'm sure you did." Barnacle had now gotten up from the floor, stretched, and was in the process of shoving his big head into her lap, snuffling at the popcorn tin. Koi hissed and swatted.

Mabel grabbed the tin and dumped both animals before heading for the relative safety of the kitchen table. While she was shooing away both pets and trying to walk, John said something she missed.

She plunked the tin on the table and sat. "Sorry. What did you say?"

"I asked if you submitted that article today."

Mabel grimaced. "Not yet. I thought I'd go over it one more time."

"It's what? Three hundred words? Two-fifty?" She heard skepticism in his voice.

"Yeah."

"How many times have you gone over it already?"

She squirmed. "A bunch. When you have so few words, you can't afford to waste any of them. I don't want to send it in till I get it right."

"Come on, Mabel. Don't be chicken."

When she started to sputter, he cut her off. "It'll never be perfect—nothing is. Tell you what. Send it to me right now. Or send it to your writer friend Jackie. We'll take a gander, and if it looks okay, I want you to send it right away tonight. Just do it. You have to bite the bullet sooner or later."

She wanted to bristle but knew he was right. She didn't have to like it though. This felt like she was shivering at the end of the high board, and John was trying to shove her off into the deep end of the pool.

Of course, she could swim…metaphorically speaking. Couldn't she?

"Come on, Mabel. It's *The Shopper*, not the *New Yorker*. I'm sure they don't expect Pulitzer material—just a good little article. You can do this."

Mabel hadn't expected it to be so hard, a few months back, when she'd first hatched this idea of a writing career. She was going to sit at her charming desk every day like Louisa May Alcott and write things. Before long, her books would be making people laugh and cry and maybe put her on the bestseller list.

Three months later, she didn't even have the desk. She had a kitchen table. The kitchen table which now held her laptop, stacks of paper, a partial loaf of bread, and a festive popcorn tin.

"Oh, all right." Mabel was unable to keep the sourness out of her voice. "I'm sending it to you right now."

Chapter Sixteen

MABEL SCROLLED THROUGH OLD EDITIONS OF *The Medicine Spring Statesman*, which in 1962 had still been a daily. The library was silent, apart from the clacking of somebody's keyboard or an occasional click from the heating system. On this workday afternoon, very few patrons occupied seats around the scattered tables.

She'd forced herself to send her soup kitchen article to John before leaving the house but couldn't help feeling some trepidation. After three months of hearing her hold herself out as a writer, he was about to get a glimpse of her work product, scanty as it was.

Sure, she'd written the biography of local philanthropist Margarethe Sauer for the historical society. To her regret, Mabel's name appeared as co-author, below the late Helen Thornwald, who'd written most of it before her unfortunate ax murder. As proud as Mabel was of her own contribution, it still rankled that her name was now forever linked with Helen, who in life had been Mabel's nemesis.

This little one-page ode to the soup kitchen, on the other hand, was Mabel's own brainchild. Sending it to John had left her feeling somewhat…exposed.

Too late to undo sending it. Gritting her teeth, she focused on the first article she'd turned up regarding the death that had coincided with Lester's mysterious disappearance. Although John was supposed to be trying to get a look at the police murder file, Mabel reasoned newspaper accounts might still be informative.

The headline read, "Woman's death shocks village of Medicine Spring." This was followed by a subheading, "Mystery killer still at large." A photo, likely from the victim's high school yearbook, showed a sweet-faced brunette in a white-collared blouse and black pullover with a circle pin on the left. Looking at the young graduate, who would die so tragically only a few years later, made Mabel sad.

Another, grainier, black-and-white photo, imaginatively captioned "Murder House," depicted an old mining company cottage, recognizable at once by its cookie-cutter similarity to others Mabel had seen. The tiny house, which the victim had rented, had been built by the coal company for its workers many years ago.

Several houses still survived down near the railroad tracks, in this old mine patch section of Medicine Spring known by locals as Tippytown. All identical, but for changes made by the owners over the years—an addition here, aluminum siding there. The covered porch on this one set it apart from its neighbors, as did a high privacy fence, which—even in this fuzzy shot—clearly needed painting, around the small front yard.

Mabel squinted. She couldn't see any snow on the ground that might have shown tracks.

She read.

The body of twenty-two-year-old Catherine Abramovich, who resided at 14 Douglas Street in Medicine Spring's Tippytown section, was found deceased in her home shortly before 11 am Tuesday morning, after she failed to appear for work at the Collier Construction Company in Bartles Grove, where she was employed as a clerk-typist and receptionist. Police were still at the scene at the time of this report. Though the official cause of death must await the coroner's ruling, police at this time characterize the death as "suspicious."

Mabel frowned. The headline writer had come in, guns blazing, with his "mystery killer" and "murder house," when the article made it quite clear the cause of death was still undetermined.

According to the rest of the story, a coworker sent to check on Cathy had found her body in the living room of the unlocked house.

The coworker, a file clerk named Mrs. Mildred Green, reported she'd fled the house to call police from a drugstore in town. When asked why she hadn't phoned from the "murder house," she'd told the reporter, "I watch Perry Mason. You don't ever touch the telephone. Fingerprints, of course." Later, she'd admitted she was also "scared out of her wits."

Though she'd seen no sign of forced entry, Mildred said the living room looked "quite disheveled," with cabinets and drawers standing open. She hadn't examined the body after finding no pulse, but "There was a whole lot of blood around Cathy's head."

Mabel fought down a wave of nausea. She'd once found a body in this condition and could too easily imagine the sight and metallic odor of blood. She took several deep breaths, looking off toward the fiction stacks, where an old gentleman was browsing, and then out the window. A few snowflakes drifted in the air, aimless and in no hurry to settle down anywhere.

After she'd collected herself, Mabel went back to scrolling. Later articles reported the coroner's homicide ruling, with head trauma indicated as the immediate cause of death. Still later articles covered Cathy's funeral, which drew curiosity seekers, as well as legitimate mourners such as Cathy's parents, grandparents, and sister Bonnie Ann.

According to several reports over the ensuing weeks, police were pursuing "several promising leads," about the details of which they remained close-mouthed. It hadn't taken long, however, for Lester Bedford's name to pop up.

Mabel didn't think she had the stomach for those articles yet. On an impulse, she began looking for coverage of Lester's disappearance. She didn't find much.

The disappearance wasn't mentioned at all for a couple of

days, as the focus remained on the Abramovich murder. Even Vietnam War coverage only merited a brief paragraph on an inside page.

Mention of Lester first appeared two days after the murder, largely in connection with complaints of undelivered mail, though it did say his disappearance was being investigated. No wonder Nita's family had been so angry and frustrated. Someone they loved had vanished, and people seemed more concerned with their Christmas cards and parcels.

Before long, the two threads merged, with public speculation turning to Lester as a potential suspect in Cathy's murder. Anyone who'd seen Lester the day of the murder or since was urged to come forward. While police never officially characterized Lester as a suspect, then-Police Chief Richard Barnhardt made repeated pleas for him to contact police. This had to have been maddening for the family.

In fact, this was rapidly becoming maddening to Mabel, as well. She took another calming breath, hoping to stave off a growing desire to punch somebody in the nose. "Contact the police?" she muttered. "How's he supposed to contact the police?"

She became aware of the librarian eyeing her and turned away, clamping her lips shut. Mabel logged out and slammed her notes into her bag before walking over to collect the articles she'd sent to the printer.

Two other patrons stood in line ahead of her. As the man at the front gathered his printouts, he turned his head, and Mabel studied the slight dent in his strong nose.

She looked over as he passed her on his way out, and they made eye contact. She startled when he gave her a big smile. Though he kept walking, Mabel looked after him, staring at his back. She knew him from somewhere.

A library assistant was clearing a paper jam for the woman

next in the line. While she waited, Mabel cast an idle glance toward the parking lot below. The man who'd smiled at her was popping the locks on a black Mercedes sedan. He had to be in his eighties but moved like a younger man.

In a flash, she remembered. This was the customer she'd exchanged glances with at Demitasse. As he drove away, Mabel wondered if he lived in town and was single. She entertained herself by thinking which of her older friends would make the best match for him.

A few snowflakes drifted in the air. Mabel watched them, her thoughts returning to the sad story of Lester's disappearance.

She had wanted to help Nita, simply because Nita was her friend, and she felt her and her family's sorrow. But reading those articles, just as events had unfolded nearly sixty years ago, had been enraging.

Now, it was personal.

Chapter Seventeen

MABEL ARRIVED HOME TO THE RACKET of Barnacle's barking. Her lackadaisical handyman, Acey Davis, sat in his truck, occupying her usual spot in the side driveway. Rolling her eyes, she pulled up to the curb.

"Hey, Acey, I'm home now." She waved her arm out her open car window.

Instead of starting his truck to move it out of the way, Acey got out and walked over to her. "Where you been, Mabel? I got here right about two, and there was no sign of you."

Oh, no. Instead of calling her or driving away, it seemed he'd been napping in her driveway for the last hour. An hour he'd bill her for.

"I'm sorry. I forgot you were going to try to stop by this afternoon. Would you mind moving your truck, so I don't block you when I pull in?"

He reached under his worn blue-plaid lumber jacket and scratched his belly. "All righty. I guess I still got about another hour, hour and a half, I can give ya."

"That's great. You should be able to clear a good bit of the basement in that time."

Acey had been turning toward his truck, but he stopped. "You didn't tell me I was supposed to be working down cellar. It's a right dank day to be down in there."

"I know, and I'm sorry, but the township's given me till spring to deal with the soggy area in the field, and I'm hoping I can get the state to declare it a protected wetland by then. That just leaves the house, and you know Linnea next door keeps threatening to report me to the health department over Grandma's clutter."

Acey spat. "That dang woman. She wanted me to rid her house of snakes. She must think I'm St. Patrick or something. I ain't touching any snakes."

Mabel averted her eyes. She wouldn't mention she'd recommended Linnea give him a call.

"Okey-dokey." He heaved a sigh. "I guess I can manage an hour or so. Seeing as that witchy woman's sticking her pointy nose into your business."

Mabel watched him climb back in his truck. The antagonism between Acey and Linnea had only worsened during the recent race for the township board of supervisors, when they were rabidly supporting opposing candidates. Acey, in particular, seemed determined to carry the grudge, as his candidate was his own cousin Cletus. While the feud was, of course, unfortunate, it seemed to be working to Mabel's advantage in this instance. She only hoped the hostility didn't extend to Nita, who'd ended up beating both candidates without even running for the job.

A few minutes later, Mabel was parked in her own spot, and Acey had maneuvered his truck around to the other side of the house and backed up to the basement bulkhead door. This had necessitated his driving through the back yard, but she recognized it was a reasonable request, since he'd have to drag a lot of heavy stuff up the stone steps to load onto his truck. She hoped he wouldn't get stuck and churn up her yard.

Mabel had encouraged Acey to work a tad harder than usual by promising he could keep anything he wanted from the basement. She was confident there were no treasures down there. At this point, even if he turned up a few antiques, like a coal scuttle, he was welcome to them—all she wanted was to see an empty cellar. Anything he found was bound to be in poor shape, anyway, knowing Grandma's devotion to the principle of "use it up, wear it out, make it do, or do without."

Once inside the kitchen, she dumped her stuff on the table and started rooting around in the fridge. Caramel corn hadn't made a very sustaining lunch. She grabbed a jar of blackberry jam and bread, planning to slap together a PBJ to tide her over, but became sidetracked by Koi and Barnacle.

Both animals were focused on the noises coming from the basement. Barnacle was whuffing and scratching at the door, while Koi had crouched down to insert her small pink nose into the crack beneath. Next, she hooked a paw under the door and began banging it.

"What the heck you want, Mabel?" Acey yelled from below.

"Not me, it's the cat," she yelled back. "Come on, guys." She peeled the animals away from the door and blocked it with a couple of chairs. "How about an early dinner?"

"Dinner" was a word both knew well. It might not occupy them long, but maybe she'd buy enough time to make her own sandwich.

To Mabel's amazement, Acey worked steadily till nearly five o'clock. By then, it was dark outside, and the solitary basement lightbulb would be all but useless for trying to see into the gloomy corners. She heard the bulkhead door clang down, followed by the whirring sound of Acey's tires, as he tried to get traction to pull out with a presumably heavy load of junk on the back of his truck.

Mabel cautiously opened the kitchen door to the basement and peered down, crowded by her pets. Barnacle stood at the top and barked, having been shut down there on occasion, but Koi scurried down the steps to explore.

Mabel was gratified to see a lot more clear area than the last time she'd ventured a peek into the dank, spider-infested space. She jumped at the rap on her outside door.

Acey was standing outside.

"Hey, you got a good start down there. Come on in."

He stepped inside, to be beset at once by Barnacle's busy nose. "I'll try to finish her up mebbe tomorrow."

"That's great." Mabel tried to keep the astonishment out of her voice but failed. Who knew she could light a fire under Acey, simply by letting him have whatever he removed from her house? Sadly, this wasn't an incentive she was ready to offer him anywhere but the disgusting basement.

Buoyed by actual signs of progress in getting her house decluttered, she offered him a seat while she wrote him a check. "If you want to wash your hands, I can get you a couple of Christmas cookies."

Acey eyed her warily, seeming as amazed by Mabel's show of goodwill as she was by his unusual productivity. "Well, I didn't get all that dirty. I wore my gloves and all."

At the sight of the cookie container, however, he relented and went to the sink. Mabel tried not to take too close a look at the smears of dirt all over his clothing or the festooned cobwebs dripping from his cap. She had better put his cookies on a plate, she decided, rather than let him dip into the box.

Back at the table with his cookies and glass of milk, Acey glanced down at Mabel's sheaf of photocopies from the library. "Well, lookie here. That old-time murder."

He picked up the top paper and began reading, lips moving. "Before my time, but my ol' Aunt Adelaide sure did talk about it." Acey shoved a gingerbread man into his mouth.

This afternoon was getting better by the moment. Mabel hadn't dreamed Acey, of all people, would know anything about Cathy Abramovich's murder. She plopped down in the only other chair not heaped with paper or occupied by a cat. "What did she say?"

"Oh, she took it all real personal, Aunt Addy did. She was so upset about that mailman taking off with all that mail."

Mabel gritted her teeth. "I don't think we know he did that. He might've been another victim, you know."

"I 'spect that's true enough. I guess Aunt Addy was only repeating what she heard. She was mostly worked up about that mail going missing, however it happened."

"Why was she upset about the mail? Did something of hers go astray?"

"Nah." Acey helped himself to another gingerbread man, and Mabel had to wait for him to chew and swallow. "It was this guy here."

He pointed to the part of the article that mentioned various items that had disappeared along with Lester. Mabel peered at the paragraph.

"Edmond Crawford?"

"Yeah."

Mabel was having trouble following the thread of Acey's disjointed story, punctuated as it was by gingerbread men. Edmond Crawford had been a wealthy old man whose will was supposed to have been in the mailbag. She couldn't imagine how any relation of Acey's would have had anything to do with Crawford's will. "What about him?"

"Addy was a young girl at that time, and she worked for old man Crawford. She was his housekeeper, like. She came in days, and he had whatcha call a secretary—but it was a man, the secretary was. He lived right there in the house.

"Anyways, Aunt Addy always told the story that the old man was having a real sickly spell. One evening right before time for her to head home, he sent the secretary out to pick him up some medicine and called her in. She said he had her go get his will out of his desk drawer, then turn to the last page and write down what he was saying. After that, he signed it and had her sign as a witness. On her way out, she was supposed to stick it in the mailbox, addressed to his lawyer."

Mabel frowned. "It disappeared?"

"Yup. You know, my mom used to make these." Acey took another cookie. "She was a terrible cook."

Mabel's frown deepened. She wasn't sure whether that had been a commentary on her own baking, but he sure seemed to be inhaling plenty of them, either way. "Then what happened?" she prompted.

"Oh, well, old Crawford passed overnight. He left Aunt Addy five hundred dollars in his will. That was a lot of money in those days."

"She didn't get her money? Because the will was gone?"

"Nah. She got it, all right. It was the same under his old will, and his lawyer had another copy of that in his office."

Mabel pushed Barnacle's inquiring nose away from the edge of the table. "But Adelaide was still upset."

"Yeah." Acey reached for his pocket. "You got a ashtray?"

"No, I don't. You know I don't like cigarette smoke in the house. Why was she upset?"

"Well, she felt bad, 'cause she liked the old goat. He told her right where he wanted his money to go, and that was different from the old will."

"Do you remember how the estate was supposed to be distributed? How did it end up?"

"You mean where the money and all went? Some to the church, some to Aunt Addy, and his nephew got the rest, as it turned out."

"Where did the testator—Mr. Crawford—intend the money to go?" Mabel asked.

"She said he had it going to his secretary, but that young fella hadn't been around more than a year by then. Nobody believed Crawford would've let himself get suckered that way. He was a sharp old so-and-so."

Mabel was beginning to get the picture. "So, people didn't believe Adelaide's story about a new codicil?"

"A what?"

"I mean they didn't believe her when she said he'd changed his will to favor the secretary over his nephew."

"Right, little lady. They acted like Aunt Addy made the whole thing up. Or was too dumb to know what she signed to." Disgust dripped from Acey's words.

"I can understand that would have been very upsetting. So, the nephew inherited? Did Crawford's secretary file some sort of contest over it?"

"No ma'am. I guess he didn't have anything written to stand on. Pretty much everybody knew Aunt Addy had a crush on him too. The secretary, I mean. So, they were all saying she made the whole thing up."

"Are either of these guys still around, do you know? Or your aunt?"

"Aunt Addy's still kickin'. I don't know about the secretary guy." He scrunched up his face in apparent concentration. "What was his name now? She'd remember."

"How about the nephew?" Mabel asked.

"Heck, Mabel, everybody knows Ricky Putnam."

"Ohh…the big house." The lightbulb went on in Mabel's head. "With all that land. Isn't that out past Tippytown?"

He nodded. "The very one. Ol' Ricky took it over just as soon as the will got…whatchacallit."

"Probated?"

"That's right. Took over the house, the grounds, and got himself a wife. All in no time after that."

Mabel thought for a moment. "I'm sure you believe your

Aunt Adelaide, and I don't want to cast any doubt on what she says took place. Did she happen to say why Mr. Crawford would disinherit his own nephew in favor of an employee he'd only known for—what? A year, I think you said."

"Sure did. She always said Ricky was a punk kid who didn't give a darn about Crawford. The old man liked Ben—hey, that was his name. Just now popped into my head. He got to know him over that time, livin' in the same house. According to Aunt Addy, the feeling was mutual."

Acey's account seemed plausible enough, assuming Aunt Adelaide was a credible witness. She could see how a grumpy old man could get sick and tired of a relative who didn't show him any respect or affection. On the other hand, it was also possible this secretary of his was no more than a schemer, trying to take advantage of a frail, elderly person with a lot of money. From what Acey had told her, Adelaide might well be an unreliable narrator since she was supposed to have had a crush on Ben.

Did Ben's failure to file a contest suggest the story of the missing second will wasn't true? Or did it mean Ben actually was the decent person Crawford and Adelaide thought him to be—a person more interested in his boss's welfare than his money?

How did any of this connect to Uncle Lester's disappearance?

Chapter Eighteen

MAYBE IT HAD BEEN A MISTAKE to let herself get swept up in relief over the basement, complicated by a sense of Christmas cheer. Mabel had found it easier getting Acey installed at her kitchen table, eating her cookies, than it was to get rid of him.

But worth it, she decided. He'd been a fount of information about at least one valuable piece of mail gone missing along with Lester and his mail pouch. This tended to confirm an idea Mabel had been ruminating on, that somebody had been so desperate to intercept something in that bag they'd been willing to kill for it.

Adelaide's story had already served up one likely suspect—Ricky Putnam, the heir to the Crawford estate. She was already familiar with the Crawford estate, a landmark in the greater Medicine Spring area. As with most local landmarks, the preferred name hadn't changed along with changes in ownership.

After Acey's eventual departure with a rattling truckload of Grandma's clutter, Mabel booted up her computer. Online information was limited, but a half-hour later she'd learned Edmond Crawford had made his small fortune in the pop-bottling business. Sure enough, he'd died in 1962 and according to his obituary, left no widow or children. Richard Putnam was listed as his sole survivor.

Try though she might, Mabel found little background on Putnam. As far as she could determine, he still lived on the Crawford estate with a wife named Bonnie. Though she couldn't dig up any direct evidence of his working at anything, it didn't seem he'd run the bottling business into the ground. In fact, he'd sold it to a bigger bottler several years after Crawford's passing, at a much-appreciated value. Maybe he'd retained capable managers.

There weren't many photos. One was of Putnam signing a document when the business changed hands. He still appeared quite youthful—maybe thirty at that point. Another appeared with his wedding announcement, next to a dark-haired bride in long, sleek, white satin, short veil attached to a white pillbox hat. Mabel's gaze lingered on the beautiful bride. There was something familiar about her—perhaps the unmistakable, and no doubt deliberately accented, resemblance to Jackie Kennedy.

Soon, Mabel found herself scrolling through photos of "other" Richard Putnams, a few of an actor from the Golden Age of Hollywood named Richard Widmark, and inexplicably, a few seemingly unrelated subjects, including rocker Mick Jagger and cartoon hero SpongeBob SquarePants. What possessed search engines to do this?

She'd abandoned the image search and gone back to look for a wedding announcement when John's ringtone came from her purse.

"Hi—I was wondering whether you might like to come over for dinner."

"Sure. What time?"

"You can come whenever. I'll put you to work, and we can talk while we cook."

"Sounds great. Give me forty-five minutes or so to clean up and get over there."

John's house sat in a well-kept older neighborhood on the outskirts of Medicine Spring. When she pulled up outside his bungalow, his cat Billie Jean was watching from a front window. The cat had loathed Mabel from Day One but had of late shown signs of softening her feelings to more of a low-grade dislike. Still, Mabel took a beat to prepare herself to face whatever the cat had in mind.

Mabel hurried up the sidewalk as a cold wind swooshed across her path. The cat jumped down from her perch in the window as Mabel came up the front steps.

John met her at the door with a quick kiss and took her coat. Billie Jean, now sitting on the armchair nearest the door, turned her back in a pointed manner and began grooming. Mabel called that a win.

She sniffed the air. "Smells good. What are we having?"

"Pot roast. It's been simmering for a while."

"Oh, yum—I haven't had pot roast in forever. I thought I was helping you cook."

"You're helping with dessert. That okay?"

"Sure." As Mabel trailed him, she wondered what they were making.

John pulled a set of ramekins from the shelf overhead and handed them to Mabel. "If you'll give them a quick wipe down and a squirt of cooking spray, I'll get the other fixin's."

He brought a ball of dough out of the fridge and plopped it on a cutting board dusted with flour. Then, he disappeared head first into his pantry cupboard and backed out carrying a big Mason jar of fruit. "I'll take care of the pastry, and you can do the filling."

Mabel raised her eyebrows. "What do you have there?"

"My mom's spiced peaches."

Something about spiced peaches on a cold December night sounded glorious to Mabel. She watched John roll out the pastry, cut six circles of dough, and press one in each depression in the tin.

"Okay." He popped the jar lid. "Let 'er rip."

Mabel divided the peaches among the pastry cups and sprinkled them with flour, while John produced a bowl of crumb topping. As soon as they'd covered the mini pies, John slid the tin into the preheated oven and set the timer.

Mabel stared. "You're so efficient."

John shrugged. "No more than average."

She quirked the corner of her mouth. If John's kitchen performance just now was merely "average," Mabel was in a heap of trouble. She was a modern woman—maybe it shouldn't bother her that John was way more skilled in the domestic arts than she was—but it did.

Not for the first time, Mabel wondered what John saw in her.

She shook herself to clear the negative thoughts.

John laughed. "What was that?"

"I don't know. Just shaking off a funny feeling, I guess."

"Come on." John took her hand. "Let's go sit on the couch till dinner's done."

Mabel couldn't help noticing John had done little to decorate for Christmas, as he'd told her. A greenery garland lay across the mantel, with white-flocked doves perched here and there. A Holy Family—carved of olive wood, she presumed—sat in the center, unsupported by shepherds, wise men, or even a donkey or sheep. A few bright cards lay in a shallow bowl on the coffee table.

John snapped his fingers. "I'm sorry. I forgot to offer you a drink. What would you like?"

"That's okay. If we're going to eat soon, I can wait."

He looked at his phone. "About twenty minutes. Can you manage?"

"No problem. So where should we begin?"

"If you mean the investigation, let me say something else first." John touched her hand. "I liked your story about the soup kitchen. You shared your experience, and even gave a little glimpse of how it changed your attitude. Send it in—do it tonight, okay?"

She must've made a face because John gave her a stern look. "Tonight. They only publish once a week, and we're getting close to Christmas."

Mabel squirmed, pleased he'd liked her work, but nervous about letting someone who didn't love her see it next.

"Tonight," he repeated. "And why not give contact information for a few places readers can call to get involved? The editors should love that."

She chewed her lip. "All right. I guess all they can do is reject me."

John shook his head. "Not *you*. They may need to reject your story, but it's not personal. Maybe they already have enough articles to fill the paper for the holiday season. Just do it."

She caught herself nodding and made herself stop. "Hey, not to change the subject, but did you get another chance to talk to anybody down at the police department?"

"I did. Nothing more on the ID, unfortunately. They're hopeful they'll have some luck with Dr. Payne's records. The big news is Mac got me a look at the Cathy Abramovich casefile."

"Really?" Mabel's head popped up. "Can I read your notes? Did you take any pictures?"

John grinned. "Slow down, girl sleuth. You know it's a major miracle I got to look at that file at all, right? I only had about twenty minutes to skim the whole thing before Chief Dunlap got back from lunch. Taking notes wasn't on the table—let alone photographing files like 007."

"Oh, well." Mabel couldn't help feeling a bit let down. "If I know you, you managed to zoom in on the highlights and glean a lot of good info in whatever time you had. Right?"

John waggled one hand. "I'd've loved to have time to read,

but I did the best I could. Most everything back then was hand-written, you know—and some of those cops' writing was bad enough they could've been doctors."

Despite her disappointment, Mabel laughed. "So, what were you able to find out…and remember?"

To her surprise, he reached behind him and pulled a few papers off his desk. "I couldn't take notes at the station, but I did a brain dump as soon as I got back to my car."

He cleared his throat. "Here are the main things. First, there were no fingerprints in the living room, where she was discovered, or on the doors—aside from the coworker's who found her."

"Hmm. At least the victim's prints should have been there," Mabel said.

"Right. So somebody took time to wipe everything down. They did find prints elsewhere in the house, but nothing that wasn't traceable to people with a legit reason to be there, like her family members."

"Footprints?"

He shook his head. "Not inside or out. That was a bit surprising, since it was winter, but it didn't appear anybody had walked around inside the house with wet feet. Apart from Mildred the coworker, again. With no snow on the ground, they wouldn't expect good footprints outside."

"Was anything taken?"

"Yeah, a few things. Some costume jewelry, a camera, and her purse. The purse, empty—and also wiped clean—was recovered later in a dumpster in Bartles Grove."

Mabel thought. "Not a lot, considering somebody got killed for it."

"No, but that's not necessarily unusual. Murder isn't sensible."

"I guess not." They chatted awhile about motives for murder. Mabel startled when the kitchen timer went off.

John stood and gestured for her to lead the way to the kitchen. "To be continued over dinner."

The food, as always, was delicious. While they ate, they returned to John's perusal of the Abramovich casefile.

"Did you get any idea of their suspect list?" Mabel hoped there had been more people on the list than Lester.

John laid down his fork. "Like Nita told us, they focused on Lester early on. As my buddy pointed out, what happened that day is something beyond coincidence. A woman's murdered, and very close to the same time, a postman walks right off his route along with the mail and disappears within a block of her house."

Mabel buttered another slice of bread. "It does seem like there has to be some connection. I think it seems more likely Lester was the second victim that day, not the killer, though."

"I tend to agree, but you also have to recognize we might be more than a little prejudiced in Lester's favor." "Fair enough," Mabel said. "But doesn't it seem to you that the cops were pretty darn quick to zero in on him to the exclusion of anybody else?"

"Whoa—I never said they didn't look at anyone else."

Mabel's ears perked up. "They had other suspects?"

"Other people were questioned."

That phrasing still made it sound like Lester was the primary suspect. "Who did they talk to—did the file say?"

"Yeah. They did a house-to-house. Questioned everybody along the route."

Once again, it sounded more like the police were looking for information, not interrogating suspects. "Did they talk to Richard Putnam?"

John's eyebrows shot up. "They did. What makes you ask about him in particular?"

Mabel capsulized her earlier chat with Acey. "Assuming his Aunt Adelaide is a reliable narrator, Ricky Putnam had a strong motive to snatch that mailbag."

A grin twitched at the corner of John's mouth. "Um, that's assuming a good bit for that particular family. Besides which, a motive to pilfer something from the mail, while a federal crime in and of itself, doesn't prove murder of either the mailman or a nearby resident."

Mabel waved an airy hand. "Maybe not, but it would put him on the scene, if only as a witness." She thought a moment while chewing on her bread. "If he knocked Lester down, say, while grabbing the mail pouch, and Lester sustained a fatal head injury, it might make it felony murder. I'd need to do some research on that. I think that would depend on what was in the pouch."

"Murder, maybe—but not of Cathy Abramovich."

"Oh, phooey. So, there are a few holes to fill in." Mabel scooped up another delicious forkful of pot roast but paused before putting it in her mouth. "I think Aunt Adelaide is as likely to be giving an accurate account as not. Being related to Acey doesn't mean she makes up stories—or doesn't know what happened to her."

"Is she still living?"

"Acey says she's still kicking. Now, since you point out Ricky had no motive to kill Cathy —that we know of—maybe you saw some other potential suspects in that file? I hope."

"There was an ex-boyfriend as well as a current boyfriend."

"Well, there you go. Wouldn't they typically be the first people police would look at?"

He nodded. "I believe they alibied out."

"Sometimes alibis can be broken. Did you get names?"

"I did." He made a shushing gesture as Mabel started to ask if he knew their present whereabouts. "Let's finish our nice dinner before we dig any deeper into ancient homicides, okay?"

Chapter Nineteen

MABEL HAD COUNTED ON MISS BIRDIE and Ms. Katherine Ann's predictable routine, and she was pleased to see they hadn't let her down. As she closed the door of the Coffee Cup diner with a jingle behind her, she saw the two old ladies at their usual breakfast booth.

Ms. Katherine Ann glanced up with a smile, and Miss Birdie turned to look. She scootched over and patted the seat next to her. "Come join us, baby. We're just getting started."

Mabel slid into the booth with a shiver. "The temperature's dropping out there again."

"They say there's another front blowing in—it's awful. I wish they'd make up their mind." Ms. Katherine Ann scowled at her chocolate sprinkle doughnut.

Miss Birdie smiled. "Now, I don't believe WXAT has the power to control the weather."

Ms. Katherine Ann spared a gloomy look out the steam-clouded window. "I realize that, Birdie. My goodness, though, you'd think that new meteorologist fella they hired would get it right once in a while. Say what you will, Tom Greenway was accurate occasionally."

The waitress appeared at Mabel's elbow. As she offered a menu, Mabel shook her head. She had established a regular order since deciding she was going to eat a bit healthier. "Everyday Breakfast, please. Scrambled with whole wheat. Peppermint mocha latte, uh, small. Thanks."

The waitress smiled. "Got it."

Mabel cast a glance at Ms. Katherine Ann's plate. "Oh, and a chocolate doughnut with sprinkles, please."

As she watched the waitress walk away, Mabel reproached herself. She shouldn't have ordered both the latte and the dough-nut. At least, the latte had been a small.

Miss Birdie savored a grapefruit section and set her spoon down, pacing herself as always. "How are your investigations go-ing, baby? What have you learned about Shanita's case so far?

"Not enough, at this point." Mabel had been about to dis-claim investigating anything but had to admit that wouldn't have been true. She was in it up to her eyeballs.

She reached into her purse. "I was hoping maybe you ladies could help. You know I was asking about Grandma's friend Betty, but I never got to tell you why."

Mabel explained how the long-lost mail had begun to turn up, including the Christmas card and letter addressed to Grandma. "Nita believes Lester wrote it."

"Oh, my land." Ms. Katherine Ann's eyes widened. "Can you imagine?"

Miss Birdie patted Mabel's hand. "That must have given you quite a turn."

"It did, but what the letter said was even more disturbing."

"Oh, dear." Miss Birdie exchanged a startled look with her friend. "Are you wanting us to look at it? Does it mention this Betty you were asking us about before?"

"Yes, on both counts. Maybe you'd like to sit next to each other to read? I can switch seats with Ms. Katherine Ann, since the light's a little better on this side."

Ms. Katherine Ann didn't hesitate to get up. "I can't believe it. Of all things. I'd have said your grandma never knew the man."

Miss Birdie wiped the table in front of her, removing a few tiny spatters of grapefruit juice. When Ms. Katherine Ann had set-tled beside her, Mabel handed over the letter, and Miss Birdie spread it out in front of them.

Mabel was surprised to find her heart chugging as the two

old ladies squinted at the scrawling handwriting. In a moment, she might learn something earthshaking.

Or nothing at all.

One of the ladies gasped. Mabel couldn't be sure which, but Miss Birdie had covered her mouth. Ms. Katherine Ann's mouth hung open.

When neither spoke, Mabel blurted, "What is it?"

Miss Birdie, always calm and sensible, seemed overcome. She shook her head, hand still to her mouth. Were those tears glimmering in her eyes?

Ms. Katherine Ann finally found words. "Land's sake. That letter isn't talking about Betty. It's Bertha."

Mabel didn't get it. She gave her head a little shake and raised her shoulders.

"Ber-tha." Ms. Katherine Ann enunciated the name slowly and clearly, pointing at Miss Birdie. "Ber-tha."

"Bertha," Mabel repeated, feeling as if she were Jane trying to communicate with Tarzan for the first time.

"Honestly, Mabel." Ms. Katherine Ann pointed again. "He's talking about Birdie."

This time, Mabel clamped a hand over her own mouth. When she'd gotten a grip on herself, she lowered her hand and managed to say, "But…"

"You didn't know Birdie was Bertha?" Ms. Katherine Ann managed to make it sound as if Mabel hadn't understood a basic scientific fact, like the earth revolving around the sun.

"No, I didn't." Mabel reminded herself Ms. Katherine was elderly. She probably hadn't intended to suggest Mabel was a dolt.

"You saw her in the yearbook, didn't you?"

"Well, I did, but I recognized her picture. I didn't have to read the caption."

"Katherine…" Miss Birdie seemed to have recovered some-what from her initial shock. "Of course, Mabel doesn't know our ancient history. That's why she's asking us questions."

Mabel studied Miss Birdie with some concern. Although she sounded calm enough, it was clear she'd received a massive shock. The kind of shock that might give someone her age a heart attack. "I'm so sorry," she whispered. "I had no idea, or I'd never have sprung that letter on you this way."

"I know you didn't, child. There's no way you could have known. I never imagined…" Miss Birdie stopped and took a deep, shuddering breath.

Mabel pushed a water glass across the table to her, still half-expecting her to collapse. "I'm sorry," she repeated.

"Mabel." Miss Birdie took her hand. "You did nothing wrong. Whenever or however I found this out, it was always go-ing to be the shock of my lifetime."

Ms. Katherine Ann put an arm around her friend. "Are you all right, Birdie?"

Miss Birdie gave her head a brisk shake, as if to clear her thoughts. "Of course, I am. I just…"

Mabel had never experienced a time when Miss Birdie was at a loss for words or what to do. This reaction made her feel cu-riously unsettled too. She didn't like seeing Grandma's oldest friend so vulnerable and fragile looking.

Pulling herself together by apparent force of will, Miss Birdie cleared her throat and looked down, running a thumb along the crease in her napkin. "I never knew. I wish…"

Mabel covered Miss Birdie's cool little hand, all bones like a tiny sparrow, with her own. "Men," Mabel said, at a loss for what else to say.

Miss Birdie looked up then and laughed. Ms. Katherine Ann cackled. "You're right about that."

Miss Birdie sobered. "I scarcely knew him, except to see.

He was big and handsome like his brother Charles, but I never even thought he looked my way. The idea he could have been my… And he met such an awful end. I'm sorry I'm rambling."

"It's okay." Mabel patted her hand again. "We understand. You've had a shock."

"How do you feel, honey?" Ms. Katherine Ann asked.

Miss Birdie looked up, frowning a bit, as if taking a reading on her own feelings. "I feel as if I lost something…precious. Before I even knew I had it. Maybe it would never have worked out anyway, but we lost the chance to find out. I'm angry, Katherine. I'm so angry at whoever took that away from us."

Mabel nodded her understanding, but Miss Birdie wasn't done yet. Her dark eyes blazed with unshed tears.

"I'm angry at Les Bedford too. Pussyfooting around behind my back instead of speaking up all those years ago. Thinking I wouldn't give him the time of day unless he had money." She smoothed her hands over the wrinkled letter with the same tenderness she might show somebody she loved. "Darn fool."

Chapter Twenty

MABEL LEFT THE COFFEE CUP WITH most of her breakfast in a bag. She could have it for lunch later. Her chat with Miss Birdie and Ms. Katherine Ann had rattled her to the pit of her stomach.

Snowflakes were dancing in the air again but showed no signs of settling anywhere. All the shop windows were dressed for the holidays with snowmen and poinsettias, tumbling elves and silver bells. The lights and big red bows Acey had helped string along Main Street had created a magical transformation in the village.

She wanted to be happy and festive, full of Christmas cheer, but all she felt was worry. Money would soon be tight if she didn't start doing a better job of watching her pennies. Lisa's bridal shower was coming up, which Mabel was supposed to be coordinating. Dear Miss Birdie, wise and kind and never flustered, had been dealt a cruel blow she hadn't deserved. Plus, Nita's family was in turmoil over their old loss. Mabel felt helpless to bring her friends any peace, except through prayer, and she could use some of that herself.

Better to face things head on. She stowed her leftovers in her car and started for Reader's Retreat Book Shop at a brisk walk. At least, she could let Nita know the mystery of the old letter had been solved.

"Mabel!" Before she could turn the corner, the familiar voice stopped her.

"I'm so glad I bumped into you." Mabel's seventy-something friend from the historical society came puffing up to her from behind, so to be technical, she hadn't exactly bumped into her. It had been more like a low-speed pursuit.

Nanette was angular, dressed as usual in sensible, tailored clothes—a navy wool coat and sturdy oxfords. A blue-and-white striped beret sat atop her salt-and-pepper bob. "I was supposed to give you a call this afternoon, and here I run right into you. It was meant to be."

Anytime Mabel heard somebody say they were "supposed to," rather than "wanted to," call her, her inner radar went off. "I'm glad to see you, Nanette, but if Cora wants me to do something for the historical society, I'm afraid I can't take anything on right now."

Nanette smiled. "No, bless your heart. This isn't for the society. It's for the Lord."

Checkmate.

"Um, I really am wrapped up in something right now," Mabel mumbled with a sense of hopelessness.

Nanette squeezed Mabel's hands. "This won't take too much of your time, and I do know how busy you are, especially this time of the year. It will just be the next few Tuesday evenings, and only for an hour and a half. The choir is critically short of altos, especially since Alma moved to Florida, and now Cora has come down with bronchitis."

This was a nightmare. Mabel made a frantic mental inventory of excuses, starting with the most accurate one, "I can't sing."

"The music isn't difficult, and you still have two other ladies to support you."

"Oh, Nanette."

"Two anthems for the Christmas Eve service, and of course, we lead the congregation in the carols."

"I can't," Mabel croaked. Maybe she was losing her voice. Was it wrong to pray for laryngitis?

"Please, Mabel. Your grandmother was such a faithful member of the choir."

Mabel began backing away. "Let me pray about it, okay?"

"Oh, that would be wonderful. Choir practice is at seven, but come a bit early, and I'll help you find a robe."

"But I—"

Nanette squeezed Mabel's hands again. "Side entrance. The other doors will be locked. You know where the choir room is, don't you?"

A moment later, Mabel found herself alone on the street. Nanette's phone had rung, and Mabel could hear Cora's voice, still booming despite the bronchitis. After giving Mabel yet another squeeze, Nanette trotted off to find Cora some throat lozenges and pick up her prescriptions for decongestant and an antibiotic.

Deep in gloom, Mabel continued around the corner on her way to the bookstore. Visions of her third-grade spring concert rose in her mind. No matter how she tried, she couldn't blot them out. She'd towered above everyone in her row, including the boys, in the fussy white Jessica McClintock prairie dress with lace bib her mother had insisted she wear.

Mabel had almost survived till the end. However, for the next-to-final number she'd somehow been selected to sing the round, *By the Waters of Babylon*, as part of a small group. The practices had been torture, but by the time of the dress rehearsal, she'd managed at last to sing her part without messing up. Then, standing in the spotlight, glowing in her white dress, Mabel's fatal inability to sing her part while everybody around her was singing something else had come back with a vengeance. Decades later, the awful moment still haunted her.

Of course, she'd promised Nanette to pray about it, but all she could manage was, "Not me, Lord. Never again."

The bell above the bookshop door jingled as Mabel shoved it open, starting the shop dog, a small, grouchy terrier named Tabasco, to barking. Nita's face brightened as she came from behind the counter, fashionably seasonal in a wine-and-hunter checked pullover over a gray midi skirt and black boots. "What brings you here?"

"I'm coming from breakfast with Miss Birdie and Ms. Katherine Ann, and thought I'd stop in." Mabel unwound her scarf and unzipped her coat. "I found out something huge I thought you ought to know right away. Plus, I probably should pick up a few Christmas gifts while I'm here."

"Better and better. Zac should be done with his break any minute. We can go in the back to talk, okay?"

"That would be best." Mabel shoved at Tabasco with the side of her foot as he continued sniffing at her ankles. The last thing she wanted was to step on the little guard dog.

Nita stuck her head in the breakroom. "Can you please keep an ear out for customers? Mabel and I have some business to attend to in the back."

Nita's office was an island of order and serenity, with its heavy old furniture, gleaming with polish, and healthy green plants creating an atmosphere of natural beauty. Her gray cat, Gaiters, stretched his long white legs and yawned as he rose from his spot in the guest armchair to meow at Mabel.

Nita sank into her desk chair with a groan. "Been on my feet all morning. Did you notice the window display when you came in?"

"It's really nice." Mabel threw her coat over the chair back, picked up Gaiters, and sat, settling him on her lap. Despite her guilty realization that she hadn't even noticed the display in her deep funk, she was confident anything Nita did was bound to be beautiful.

"Thanks." Nita leaned forward. "Okay, what did you find out?"

"I'd tell you to sit down, but you already are. I showed the letter to the old ladies, and they were sure it's from Lester. Now, here's the real news—Lester's love interest wasn't named Betty. It was Bertha."

When Nita failed to react, Mabel drew a deep breath and let it out. "Bertha is Miss Birdie."

Shock flattened Nita's strong features. "You've got to be kidding. Uncle Lester had a crush on Miss Birdie?"

Mabel felt a surge of protectiveness for her elderly friend. "Well, she was young and pretty back then."

Nita waved an impatient hand. "No, of course, she was. I just can't believe Miss Birdie might've been my great-aunt, and I never knew it. I love Miss Birdie."

"Everybody does. Miss Birdie never knew either."

"How did she take it? Was she shocked?"

"Reeling. Anybody would be."

"Aww." Nita sank back in her chair. "She never even married. Sixty years later, she finds this out." She gave Mabel a studying look. "Do you think she would've had him?"

"I couldn't say for sure, but I wouldn't be surprised if she would have. She and Ms. Katherine Ann both said how handsome he was, and Miss Birdie took the news hard."

"It makes me so darn mad," Nita said. "They had their whole lives ahead of them, and somebody cut all that off."

"Even worse, we don't know why." Mabel quirked her mouth. "Almost sixty years gone by now, which doesn't help."

"Well, I can't accept that." Nita slammed her fist down on the arm of her chair. "I don't care how many years have gone by. We can't bring Uncle Lester back, but I want answers. He deserves that. Miss Birdie deserves that."

"I agree. Who knows? Maybe some things will be easier now than they were. If there are still any witnesses who didn't come forward back then, maybe they'll speak up now. Maybe they won't want to die with this on their conscience."

"We've got DNA now too," Nita added.

"Plus, we already have all this new evidence." Mabel

stopped petting Gaiters and started ticking things off on her fingers. "We've got a body. The missing mailbag has turned up. We found that letter from Lester, and we know he wanted to marry Miss Birdie."

She paused. "It's too bad neither she nor Ms. Katherine Ann really knew him at all. That's sad, of course, but it also means I doubt they'll have a lot more to contribute to solving this."

"That's all right." Nita took a swig from a takeout cup that had been sitting on her desk and made a face. "Cold."

"Did you learn any more from your family?" Mabel asked.

"Oh, yeah. Not as dramatic as what you just told me, but for one thing, my dad's sure that the signature's Uncle Lester's. He didn't know who he was interested in, but of course, Daddy's much younger. We likely need my great-uncle Charles for better intel. Miss Birdie and Uncle Charles wouldn't have been in Lester's class in school, though. So, they wouldn't have been at a lot of functions together for Charles to observe him making cow eyes at Miss Birdie."

"I wonder how he and Grandma Mabel knew each other." Mabel frowned. "Miss Birdie and Ms. Katherine Ann had no idea they were even acquainted."

"It must have been something outside of school." Nita appeared to ponder, looking up at the ceiling. "Did your grandma work outside the home at all?"

The idea took Mabel by surprise. She'd only ever known Grandma as a housewife, as was typical of her era. "I don't think so…but I guess to be accurate, I'd have to say I don't know for sure."

"From the sound of the letter, Uncle Lester didn't have any real good jobs previously. I can ask my dad. If he doesn't know, he ought to be able to find out."

Mabel nodded. "I'll check with Ms. Katherine Ann about Grandma. I don't want to bother Miss Birdie right now."

Nita made a sour face. "I can't imagine losing a potential fiancé you never knew you had, let alone this way. The 'what ifs' could drive you crazy."

The office door opened. Zac stuck his head inside. "Hey, Nita. I've got a customer out here wants to talk to you."

"Be right there." Nita sat up.

"Real quick before you go," Mabel said. "Did your dad happen to remember the name of the coworker Lester had a problem with?"

Nita got to her feet. "Yeah. It was Jerry Kalchik. I got a bit more on that, but it'll have to wait. We'll talk later."

"Excuse me." Mabel shifted Gaiters off her lap. "One other quick question while we're walking. Do you think it's possible Lester just fell and got a head injury that day? Maybe he was trying to get home and became confused and wandered off into the woods. He could have died from the injury or exposure."

Nita tilted her head. Her side-eye spoke volumes. "That makes no sense to me. From everything I've ever heard that man wouldn't have abandoned his route if it was four in the morning, and he was dying. Besides, why would he head home through the woods, when he could have knocked on a door somewhere nearby?"

"I don't know." Mabel chewed on her lower lip. "Confused, maybe."

Nita opened her door. "Not likely. Even if someone's got head trauma, I can't see them leaving the nice, level sidewalk and heading through people's yards and up a hill into the woods."

The wheels continued to turn in Mabel's head. "But if he *was* attacked, he could have headed into the woods, trying to escape."

Chapter Twenty-One

Mabel returned home past her usual lunchtime. Of course, she was carrying her breakfast leftovers, so that would take care of that.

Ignoring Barnacle's barking and Koi, sitting in the front window watching her, Mabel checked the mailbox before going in. A couple of bills and some advertising. She let out a breath she hadn't realized she was holding. Ever since the arrival of the 1962 Christmas card, she hadn't been able to open the box without trepidation.

Mabel shoved the mail into her bulging bag of Christmas books from Reader's Retreat. It made her feel almost holly jolly, knowing she'd not only taken care of most people on her Christmas list, but also had given Nita some sales to smile about.

Inside, she turned off her security system and clipped her anxious dog to his outside run. Koi jumped up onto the kitchen table to sniff Mabel's parcels. Unsurprisingly, most of her interest seemed directed toward the Coffee Cup takeout bag.

After shooing away her nosy cat and bringing the dog inside, Mabel reheated her leftovers and booted up her laptop to check email while she ate. Reheating hadn't improved her breakfast, particularly the bacon, but it was still edible.

As she scrolled, Mabel deleted the usual influx of advertising from companies she must once have bought something from, since the spam filter hadn't weeded them out for her. Suddenly, her hand froze an inch above the delete button. She had never gotten an email from *The Shopper* before.

It occurred to her that this might be the newspaper notifying her that her article had been rejected. Mabel pressed her fist against the queasy lump in her stomach before clicking to open the email.

"We are delighted to let you know your article about your experience serving in the soup kitchen will be appearing in our Good Neighbors section on the 12th of this month. Thank you for your contribution."

Stunned, Mabel re-read the email. There seemed to be no mistake about it. Her article had been accepted. She was being published.

She jumped up and spun around before sitting back down to read the message again. No, the words hadn't changed. "I'm a success," she whispered, following the whisper with a little shriek of excitement.

Who could she tell? Everybody would be at work now, except her parents. Mabel grabbed her phone and began texting everyone she could think of—John, of course, and Lisa. Nita. Her sister Jen and niece Betsy. Jackie from the writers' group Mabel had yet to attend.

After spraying most of the people she knew with her good news, Mabel debated calling her mother. Mom would be happy for her, but she also had an uncanny knack for bringing Mabel back down to earth with a thud.

Finally, she dialed.

"Mabel. Is it you?"

"Who else would it be, Mom?"

Her mother sniffed. "I don't know. It's been so long since you used that phone to call home, I thought maybe it was stolen."

"Haha, Mom. It hasn't been that long, and you know it. I've just been so busy with my writing and the house and Christmas stuff."

"And that skull you got yourself mixed up with, I'm sure. I wish you'd stop getting involved with every dead body that comes down the road. Ever since you decided to be a writer, you've been acting like you think you're Jennifer Fletcher."

"It's Jessica."

"What?"

Mabel drew a calming breath and exhaled. "It's Jessica Fletcher. On *Murder She Wrote*. She was twenty years older than I am. Besides which, I do not involve myself with dead bodies. They keep involving themselves with me."

"Well, I don't understand how a dead body can involve itself with anybody. Be that as it may, I worry about you. Sooner or later, you aren't going to squeak out of one of these homicides as easily as you get involved in them."

Mabel heard the love behind the words and controlled her irritation. "I know, Mom. I appreciate your concerns. I do try to be careful."

"It wouldn't be so bad if you were married. I don't like your living all alone there." Her mother tsked. "I never realized Medicine Spring was such a dangerous place. It always seemed so quiet when Grandma lived there."

It was on the tip of Mabel's tongue to mention the infamous 1939 double homicide right down the street, but she realized just in time that bringing up the old ax murders was unlikely to calm her mother's fears.

"Listen, Mom. I have some good news."

"You're coming home for Christmas, aren't you? We're having people over Christmas Eve. Maybe you can invite your young man so we can finally meet him."

"Um, of course, I plan to come home. I don't know about John. He may have plans."

"Better ask him now," Mom said. "If he hasn't made plans yet, I'm sure he soon will."

"Okay, but, Mom, I wanted to tell you about my writing." Mabel's words came out in a rush as she tried to steer the conversation away from her mother's two favorite topics—Mabel's so-called "murder hobby" and her marriage prospects. "I sold a story—I'm going to be published."

"Oh, my goodness. Mabel, that's wonderful. Where will it be appearing?"

"It's going to be in *The Shopper* on the twelfth."

Though her mother seemed to have muffled the receiver, Mabel could still hear her calling in the background. "Dad—Mabel's having a story published." Pause. "A story."

There was another pause, presumably while Dad responded.

Mom again. "I said a story. She wrote a story, and they're putting it in the paper."

Pause.

"No, it's just *The Shopper.*"

Mabel felt herself deflate a bit.

Her dad came on the line. "Hey, Muffin. Congratulations. Your mom and I are so proud of you. We'll have to pick up a copy. I don't think they deliver over here."

"Thanks, Dad."

Mom said something in the background, but Mabel couldn't make it out. It seemed Dad had covered the receiver, and Mabel heard some muffled back and forth, followed by Dad saying more clearly, "I'm not asking her that."

Mom came back on the line. "How much are they paying you, dear? Don't let them rip you off."

"I'm sorry, Mom. Someone else is trying to reach me. Love you both."

Mabel collapsed in her chair. Her phone had been pinging with text messages, and she was more than ready for the interruption.

As she scrolled through the texts and tapped out replies, Koi jumped up on the table, apparently to read over her shoulder. Everybody was excited for her, and thankfully, no one else asked how much she was getting for the story because the answer was nothing.

It took Mabel a while to settle down after the thrilling email about her story. She dug out last week's edition and turned to Jackie's UFO story. That was how Mabel's story would look. Finally, she'd have a clipping to put in her empty "Clippings" folder. Between this success and her biographical booklet about Medicine Spring's late local philanthropist, Margarethe Sauer, her writing career was taking off at last.

She knew she should sit down and do some writing right now but decided to savor her success for a while. She hadn't heard from John yet, but expected he'd call when he was done teaching or had a break. His schedule was unpredictable, at least to her. Though he taught a couple courses at community college, with random faculty meetings and office hours thrown in here and there, he'd said he was done for the semester. He also worked as a substitute teacher, though, and she had no idea what his day looked like.

While she waited to hear from him, she could call Ms. Katherine Ann and find out whether Grandma Mabel might have worked somewhere with Lester before he became a postman, and she became a housewife. She didn't have Ms. Katherine Ann's phone number, so she looked that up first.

Barnacle laid a paw on her knee.

"What? You want your walk? It isn't even lunchtime yet."

The dog lifted mournful eyes to her face.

"Let me make this one quick call, and we'll take a nice little walk. All right?"

Barnacle's ears came forward at the "W" word.

"Wait one little minute, okay?"

The dog sighed and lay down. He knew that other "W" word too.

Mabel dialed and was gratified when Ms. Katherine Ann answered right away. "Mabel Browne, what on earth?"

"Hi. I wanted to ask you something real quick, but before I do, how's Miss Birdie? I feel awful about giving her that shock earlier. I had no idea."

"She's doing fine," Ms. Katherine Ann shouted. "She's right here—we're making candy. You want to talk to her?"

"Oh, no, that's all right but maybe you could put your phone on speaker. That way, we could all talk together."

"How do you do that?"

"Your phone ought to have a button, maybe marked "speaker," or with a little picture of a horn under it…?"

"Where would that be?"

"I'm not sure, Ms. Katherine Ann. Never mind. I'll just ask you, and if you aren't sure, maybe you could ask Miss Birdie."

Mabel explained Nita's idea that Grandma might have once worked with Lester.

"You know, you might have something there. Birdie, what was the name of that place that Mabel worked when she first got out of school? I can still see it plain as day, but I can't remember the name. It got tore down, and the Ford dealership's over there now."

Mabel heard no response from Miss Birdie, but knew she was much more soft-spoken than Ms. Katherine Ann.

"Swan's," Ms. Katherine Ann said. "Swan's Drug. She worked there on weekends, her last year of school, and then went fulltime till she took a secretary type job in Bartles Grove. That other one lasted right up till she got married and was expecting your daddy."

Quite apart from her investigation, Mabel was fascinated by this glimpse into Grandma's "secret life." Of course, she guessed it wasn't all that secret, but Mabel had never heard anything about it before.

"I suppose Lester might've worked at the drugstore a while. Maybe doing deliveries or sweeping up. What, Birdie?"

Ms. Katherine Ann came back on the line. "Birdie thinks he did. She went in once and bought a soda when Mabel was working the fountain. She says Lester came out of the back with a brown paper package, so he might've been making a delivery. Birdie says he smiled at her."

Mabel was about to reply when Ms. Katherine Ann exclaimed. "Oh, my land, Mabel. I've got to go. The candy's boiling over."

Mabel sat looking at her phone. Ms. Katherine Ann hadn't hung up, because Mabel could still hear clanking pans and excited voices in the background. After waiting a bit, Mabel clicked off. It was clear the conversation had ended.

"Okay, Barnacle, your turn." Mabel shrugged back into her coat and collected the leash and a potty bag. "Let's go."

Barnacle cavorted like a child leaving school on the last day before Christmas break. How Mabel wished she had his ability to enjoy life's simple pleasures without getting bogged down with worry. He had no concept of money, and nobody would ever ask him to sing in the church choir…though if they did, he'd undoubtedly be happy to give it a try.

Chapter Twenty-Two

MABEL APPROACHED THE CHOIR ROOM ON reluctant feet. The sound of voices and laughter didn't encourage her. She dreaded the moment everyone would turn and look at her, and it would be too late to run.

It wasn't too late yet. She could still turn around and take the back stairs to the parking lot, hop in her car, and go home. She could put on her pajamas, make some popcorn or hot chocolate, and turn on a Christmas movie. For a moment, she stopped and considered it, almost able to visualize the angel on one shoulder and the little devil with his pitchfork on the other.

"Mabel!" The ladies' room door swung shut behind Nanette as she stepped into the hallway. "I'm so glad you decided to come."

She grabbed Mabel's arm and towed her along behind her through the choir room door. Mabel could now appreciate Barnacle's emotions when being dragged into the vet's office.

The assembled choir was incredibly small. This wasn't a good sign for someone hoping to lose herself in the crowd and lip-sync as needed.

The choir director laid a sheaf of music down on the piano. "Who do we have here?"

Nanette shoved Mabel forward despite her resistance. With a flourish, she introduced her with an eagerness worthy of a talent scout who'd discovered the next Taylor Swift.

Mabel recognized the choir director, Amanda Bonney, but it seemed the recognition wasn't mutual. Amanda was a petite and brisk redhead, likely somewhere in her thirties. Red-framed glasses sat on her freckled nose.

"Hi, Mabel." Amanda smiled with apparent delight. "We're thrilled to have you join us. Nanette, would you mind matching Mabel up with a robe while I grab her some music?"

"Mabel!" The screech had come from Rosalyn Andrianakis, a historical society member on a perpetual quest to find her son a bride.

Mabel gave Rosalyn a feeble wave as Nanette led the way to the choir robe closet. "Where are the altos?" Mabel whispered, looking back over her shoulder.

Nanette laughed and patted her chest. "Right here. Rosalyn and I are the entire alto section at this point."

Well, this is dire. Mabel hadn't spoken the words aloud, but as John had once said, her face tended to broadcast her thoughts as effectively as a Times Square billboard, rolling across her forehead.

"You'll be fine." Nanette held a robe up to Mabel's neck. "This should do." She picked a twist-tie up from the floor. "Here, we'll fasten your hanger to mine, so you can find it."

As they headed back past the piano, Amanda handed Mabel her music. "Nothing too difficult in there. With as few singers as we have, and seniors for the most part, I try to keep it simple. We never know who'll be able to be there Sunday morning."

Before sinking into her chair, Mabel cast an envious glance at the five sopranos. She'd have stood a chance over there, singing melody with numbers in her favor…if only she'd been able to sing above a D, on her best day.

In fact, the bass section, another five strong, looked more promising than the altos. Regrettably, even her range didn't go that low.

Rosalyn reached over and gave her a hug. "I'm so excited I can finally introduce you to Tommy." Taking Mabel's shoulders, she pointed her at the basses. Tommy, Mabel figured, must be the one guy under seventy. He was turned, listening to the fellow next to him with an intensity that might have been calculated to avoid making eye contact with his mother and her latest marriage prospect.

Bespectacled, with a mop of salt-and-pepper hair, and wearing a navy V-neck over a plaid shirt, he looked a bit professorial and not unattractive, for a man whose mother seemed to think couldn't get a date without her intervention. But he wasn't John.

"I guess there aren't any tenors?" Mabel whispered to Nanette as soon as Rosalyn reluctantly released her.

"Only Clive." Nanette pointed to a distinguished-looking man with a shock of silver hair, ramrod straight in charcoal dress slacks and white Oxford shirt, who'd just entered the room. "He's ex-military, originally from the UK. Of course, everything we sing is SAB—because with just the one tenor, Amanda doesn't want to take any chances. He has a beautiful voice, though, especially given his age. She's hoping he'll sing *O, Holy Night* for Christmas Eve."

Amanda cleared her throat, and the chatter stopped. "Let's warm up on some scales." She played a note on the piano, and everyone, including Mabel, obediently began to sing. "Do, re, mi, fa, so, la, ti, do."

She'd done this ever since kindergarten, so she felt herself relax a bit. At least, until they'd moved up an octave. Soon, Mabel was lip-syncing. With luck, they'd ask her to leave.

The rest of the rehearsal was a blur. She tried to follow Nanette and Rosalyn, but neither was a very strong singer—nothing to compete with the mighty phalanx of sopranos singing melody to mostly familiar songs. She struggled to hear her part and, despite trying to stick with the altos, kept slipping into the soprano line and cutting out when it got too high. Once, when the men had the melody, Mabel even found herself singing with them. When she sang with the altos, she had the distinct feeling she was hitting a lot of wrong notes—considering the way she felt Nanette cringing next to her.

When the rehearsal came to a blessed end, Mabel scrambled to gather her things. Unfortunately, several people came around to welcome her, and Rosalyn dragged her over to meet Tommy—*Tom*, he emphasized. He was pleasant, but clearly embarrassed by his mother's blatant efforts to marry him off. Mabel hurried to excuse herself when Nanette came to extricate her.

"Thanks for joining us this evening, Mabel. You did fine for your first rehearsal—I hope we didn't overwhelm you. We've been going over this music for more than a month now, don't forget, so it's natural to need a little time to get up to speed. It's not difficult music."

Mabel mumbled something noncommittal—or at least unintelligible. She considered leaving her music on her chair and pretending she'd forgotten it, but somebody would be sure to chase her down with it. Resignedly, she tucked the sheets under her arm and made a beeline for the door.

"Mabel," called a melodic voice from behind her.

Darn it. She'd already gotten one foot outside the choir room door.

The director was beckoning her. Amanda had to have heard her struggling earlier. Mabel wrestled with conflicting emotions. On one hand, her fear of humiliation if she was about to be kicked out of the choir before she could ruin the Christmas Eve service…on the other, a cowardly hope that maybe she would be asked to leave and wouldn't have to flounder through another practice.

Amanda smiled, perhaps to soften the blow.

"I so appreciate your joining us." Amanda stepped from behind the piano. "You can see we're struggling to attract new members—particularly younger singers. As it is, we're one cataract surgery, a hip replacement, and a new winter home in Florida, away from not having a choir at all some Sunday."

Mabel smiled vaguely, not knowing what to say to that.

"But…"

Here it came. Amanda was about to say she was desperate for new choir members—but not desperate enough to take on Mabel.

"I'm sorry," Mabel mumbled. "It's okay. I'm really too busy anyway, and…" She trailed off, belatedly realizing Amanda had finished what she'd been saying, and Mabel had missed it. "Huh?"

Amanda laid her palm over Mabel's hand. "I couldn't help noticing—"

Mabel cringed.

"What I'm trying to say," Amanda said, starting over and enunciating each syllable as if Mabel were a new student of the English language, "is that I have in mind a different project where your talents might be better utilized than in singing with the choir."

Ouch. She was being excused at the very first choir practice. Mabel foresaw an assignment in the nature of choir robe management or sheet music librarian. It would be okay, she told herself…someday. Though she wished she hadn't first disgraced herself by trying to sing.

As the last of the other choir members slipped out the door, Amanda pulled Mabel over to a chair in the first row and sat down next to her. Now, she took both Mabel's hands in her own and looked into her eyes. "I couldn't help noticing you have an unusual lower range—and your intonation is quite good."

"What?"

Puzzlement creased Amanda's brow. Fingers in her ears, she shook her head as if to clear them. "Here's the thing. Clive—the tenor—did you meet him?"

"Nanette pointed him out."

"Yes, good. Clive was supposed to sing *O, Holy Night* as a prelude Christmas Eve. Now it seems he's gotten a call from his sister back in the UK. She's been scheduled for an unexpected operation next week, and he's needed there. Since he doesn't know how long he'll be away, we need to replace him."

Mabel nodded but couldn't see where she came into the picture. She wasn't a man, so Amanda wouldn't be asking her to take over Clive's solo. She couldn't sing the soprano arrangement, either, as Amanda must have noticed.

Amanda released Mabel's hands and got up. She trotted back behind the piano and returned with a piece of music, which she handed to Mabel.

Mabel looked down. She was holding a copy of *O, Holy Night* with Clive's name penciled at the top. "I don't…"

"Mabel, you're a godsend. Until you walked through the door this evening, I didn't know what I was going to do to fill that spot." She tapped the music drooping from Mabel's limp hand onto her knee. "This should be well within your range, and the tune should be mostly familiar."

Fear tightened Mabel's chest. "I can't." She tried to shove the music back at Amanda.

"You can." Amanda's voice rang with conviction. "I'll work with you and Janet. You know our organist, don't you? By Christmas Eve, you'll be able to sing this in your sleep."

Mabel wished she *could* sing it in her sleep. Or, better yet, not at all.

She could say no. In fact, she'd been seeing a lot of articles encouraging that very thing. "Oh, I don't think—"

"I realize this comes as a surprise but give yourself a chance. You have a lovely voice—believe that, okay? God gave it to you for a reason." Amanda gave Mabel a sympathetic smile. "Just try, Mabel. Don't say no until you've at least tried it."

Trying it meant making a fool of herself by singing all alone in front of Amanda and the organist. She couldn't do it. If she refused now, she could simply walk away.

Could she come and sit in a back pew on Christmas Eve after that though?

"Remember, Mabel—'I can do all things through him who strengthens me.'"

I don't want to.

For a fleeting moment, Mabel thought she'd said the words aloud. But there sat Amanda with a hopeful look on her face, still waiting for Mabel's answer.

Mabel opened her mouth to say, no, I can't. To make up some excuse. Sadly, her brain wasn't coming up with anything that didn't make her look selfish and lazy.

Was she selfish and lazy? Of course not. At least, not more than a little bit. What she was, was scared.

"Why don't you take the music home and try it there?" Amanda asked gently. "Is your email in the directory? I'll try to send you a link to a few tenor *O, Holy Nights.* If I can find one singing this arrangement, you can use that to help you get a handle on it."

That is how Mabel ended up walking back to the parking lot with solo music in her hand and a cold weight in the pit of her stomach.

Chapter Twenty-Three

MABEL'S CAR WINDOWS HAD FOGGED DURING choir practice. While she ran the engine, waiting for the defroster to do its work, she turned her phone back on to check for messages. There was a text from John, telling her how proud he was of her for submitting her story and getting it accepted.

A missed call from Nita also sat at the top of her notifications. Mabel dialed her back. "Nita, sorry—I had my phone off during choir. What's up?"

"Hey, wanted to let you know Great-Uncle Charles came home this evening. We've been talking on the phone, but he decided he needed to be here with us right now. I wondered if you might want to come over tomorrow sometime and talk to him."

"I'd love to." Mabel hesitated. "How about the others?"

"He and Daddy are anxious to talk to you. I'm thinking we might do better with just you and me. Don't want to overwhelm Uncle Charles with a bunch of people, you know?"

"Yeah, you're probably right. When do you want me?"

"How about you come on over for supper? Here to the farm—I got Uncle Charles staying here with me, and I already invited my folks to join us."

They set a time, and Mabel entered it on her phone calendar. "How's your driveway?" Mabel remembered the long farm driveway as soupy in rain or snow.

"Not bad right now. It's been cold enough to keep it in good shape."

"Good shape" for Nita's SUV might not be considered good shape for Mabel's aging Kia hatchback. Hopefully, she'd make it from the road to the house and back.

Mabel spent a restless night, stewing over her new career as a tenor soloist. Next morning, she stood in the shower a bit longer than usual, trying to wake herself up.

The steady beat of the water on top of her head seemed to stimulate thought, at least. By the time she was drying her thick mass of chestnut hair, she'd decided to return to the post office to see if she could learn anything more about the mysterious reappearance of the old mail sack. It had occurred to her that a security camera might show the stealthy figure dropping off the bag of Christmas mail like a postal Santa.

An hour later, she'd eaten a less-than-satisfying breakfast of cold cereal, fed Barnacle and Koi, and gotten dressed for her expedition. "Be good," she told her animals without much hope. Barnacle tended to find things to scatter or chew, and Koi had a habit of leaving half-eaten mouse corpses in unexpected places.

She wasn't going to talk to that counter clerk again. For one thing, she didn't think she could pull off impersonating a septuagenarian much longer. At least, she hoped not, though the lack of sleep last night hadn't fostered a youthful bloom.

For another thing, the clerk had struck Mabel as much too tight mouthed for her purposes. What she needed was either to see a camera with her own eyes, or find some chatterbox working the loading dock, who was eager to spill his guts.

Hers was the first car in the post office lot, not counting mail trucks, delivery vehicles, and what she presumed were postal employees' personal rides, all parked on the other side of a chainlink fence. Luckily, the gate was open.

Mabel parked in the public lot, then walked back toward the loading dock on the other side of the fence, jingling her keys as she went. No postal workers were in sight.

She stopped a few yards back from the dock and looked around. There was no sign of a camera anywhere that she could see.

As she stood, contemplating, and watching her breath cloud the cold air in front of her, a stocky man in dark-blue coveralls emerged onto the platform from somewhere inside the building. "Can I help you, lady?" He came to the edge of the dock. "You're not really supposed to be back here."

"Oh, I'm sorry." Mabel didn't have to pretend to be flustered. "I was just looking to see if you had a security camera back here."

The man's unruly, sandy-colored eyebrows shot up.

"I mean," Mabel clarified, "I got one of those old pieces of mail that turned up recently and was told somebody dumped the old mail pouch back here one night. It made me wonder whether you might have a camera that captured video of the person who dropped off the bag."

He shook his head. "The gate's locked at night. Whoever dumped that sack just heaved it over the fence."

"I see." Mabel shifted her feet but wasn't ready to retreat. "Um, do you guys have any theories about where it came from?"

The man shook his head again. "It got stolen—what? Sixty years ago? Maybe whoever took it finally got an attack of conscience. Or maybe somebody stumbled on it, wherever it's been stashed all these years. No clue."

"Anybody's guess, huh?" Mabel decided to try one more question before she got herself thrown out. "You think it could have been that mailman who went missing back then?"

He shrugged. "I suppose some people think so. Myself, I figure the guy must be dead by now, and I say let him rest. From what I hear, he wasn't on that particular job too long at the time, but he worked here in back quite a while before that, and he was a good employee, or he wouldn't've been promoted."

Mabel would be sure to share this guy's opinion with Nita's family. They could no doubt do with an endorsement of Lester's conscientiousness right now.

She took a step back. "You figure somebody jumped him?"

"I wasn't here sixty years ago, lady. Not a clue."

"Me neither. Thanks for your help. I guess that's all then."

As she trudged back to her car, Mabel reflected on what the mail handler had told her. If the sack had been tossed from this side of the fence, maybe a camera across the street had caught the moment it happened.

A chilly wind tossed her hair, interrupting her study of the row of businesses opposite the post office. Mabel got back in her car and squinted at the shops. She doubted Trout's Secondhand had a security camera—or Sally's Hair Hut, though you never knew. Gump's Hardware looked promising, though. At least, something was protruding from under the eaves.

She got back out and locked her doors before trotting across the street. Unless she was mistaken, the dark cylinder she'd noticed was, in fact, a camera.

The bell rang as she opened the door, and the cashier—a woman with faded brown hair threaded with gray—looked up with a smile. The Santa on the cashier's green sweatshirt was smiling too. Her comfortable figure stretched Santa's smile to extra welcoming proportions.

"Hi." Mabel smiled back at them both. "I have kind of a weird question." She gestured behind her. "I noticed you have a security camera out there, and I was wondering whether you have a view of the post office parking lot."

Though Santa continued to smile broadly, the clerk's smile began to fade.

"Here's the thing," Mabel said. "I recently got an old card in the mail that had been lost somewhere for many years. Over there—" She gestured behind her again. "They told me somebody had tossed an entire bag of old mail across the fence. Their camera range doesn't cover where the person must've been standing, and I'm curious whether yours does."

The cashier's growing frown lightened a bit. "Oh, honey, no, ours wouldn't reach that far. It's trained on the front of our building. Might reach a little of Trout's there to our left, but that's about it. Nothing across the street."

Well, Mabel guessed that was that.

"You got one of them real old cards, you say?" The clerk leaned back in her seat. "Was an article in the *Statesman* about that. I heard a couple other people here lately, saying they'd gotten stuff from way back in the sixties."

"Yup."

"Where you think it's been all this time?" the woman asked with a musing expression.

"That's what I'd like to know too. Well, thanks for the info."

Back on the street, Mabel checked the time. Too early for lunch, but her bowl of cold cereal was a distant memory at this point. Her stomach gurgled sadly.

This would be the perfect time to stop by the Coffee Cup for a maple-walnut honey bun and something warm to drink along with it. The diner was only a few steps down, so Mabel hustled in that direction.

When she stepped inside, a warm cloud of coffee-scented steam enveloped her. She took a deep breath and blew it out. Looking around, she was surprised to spot Ms. Katherine Ann, walking from the restrooms to a back booth. This was much later than the two old friends' routine breakfast stop.

"Miss Birdie? Ms. Katherine Ann? What brings you out here this time of day?"

As Ms. Katherine Ann slid into the booth, Miss Birdie looked up. "Hello there, baby. Why don't you have a seat? Katherine and I were doing a bit of Christmas shopping, and we decided we could use a little pick-me-up."

Miss Birdie's pick-me-up, Mabel saw, was what appeared to be a cup of chicken noodle soup with a side of saltines. Squelching a twinge of guilt, Mabel gave the waitress an order for her pastry, grilled with butter on the side, and a large peppermint mocha latte.

"How are you ladies doing?" Mabel eyed Miss Birdie, sitting next to her, as the waitress walked away. It might be her imagination, but the usually chipper old lady didn't seem quite as bright-eyed as normal.

"Well, my feet are killing me," Ms. Katherine Ann pronounced. "My podiatrist gave me these orthopedics and I think they've made them worse. We walked all over the mall this morning, and I never had this kind of trouble before."

"I'm sorry to hear that. Maybe you should talk to your doctor. He can probably change your orthotics to something that fits you better."

Ms. Katherine Ann swallowed a bite of cinnamon toast and dabbed at her lips with her napkin. "I don't know if I want to go back to that quack. Maybe I'll try that lady doctor over in Bartles Grove. Thelma Neuhaus swears by her."

Miss Birdie looked up. "I never knew you to take Thelma's advice for anything, Katherine. I don't think the problem is those orthotics—it's trying to cram your feet into size seven-and-a-half shoes. Didn't Dr. Carver warn you about that?"

Ms. Katherine Ann grunted. "I told you. The man's a quack. My shoes are only tight when my feet swell—he should have allowed for that."

Miss Birdie rubbed her forehead and kept her further opinions to herself.

Mabel laid her palm over Miss Birdie's delicate, childlike hand. "Are you feeling all right, Miss Birdie?"

Ms. Katherine Ann shook her head. "She's been blue ever since she heard about Lester. It hit her hard."

"I suppose it's everything about it." Miss Birdie looked off toward the shelf of stacked coffee mugs. "The way Lester was slandered back then. How hard it was on his family when he disappeared like that…the talk around it, the never knowing. It's all coming back now."

She looked down at her bowl of soup but didn't pick up her spoon. "And now, thinking of him dead all these years. Still not knowing what happened to him."

"And what might have been." Ms. Katherine Ann's look was shrewd. "If the man had just spoken up while he had the chance."

Miss Birdie tightened her lips, sealing in whatever she might have said. What Mabel wanted to say was that it might have been even harder on Miss Birdie if Lester had declared himself back then…if she had lost the man she loved and planned to marry. Look how hard it was even now, the way things had ended up.

At the far end of the room, the diner door opened.

"My land, isn't that Charlie Bedford?" Ms. Katherine Ann exclaimed.

Mabel and Miss Birdie turned to see two men enter. Mabel recognized Nita's father, even now, with silver overtaking his black hair, and the full, natural style she'd remembered now replaced by a closer crop. She didn't know the older man with him but could see the family resemblance. If this was Uncle Charles, he was still a fine-looking man with an erect bearing, well-dressed in charcoal pants and a dark red V-neck woolen sweater over a white dress shirt.

"Oh, my," Miss Birdie whispered as she peered over the booth back. "I think you're right. That's Eugene with him."

On impulse, Mabel waved a hand. Miss Birdie sank lower in her seat.

Mabel got up and trotted over to the pair of men, a little bit sorry now that she'd attracted their attention, as it seemed to upset Miss Birdie. "Hi," she greeted Mr. Bedford. "I'm Nita's friend Mabel from back when we were kids, and I used to visit my grandmother in the summer."

"Little Mabel Browne." He smiled and put a hand on her shoulder. "Nita said you were back in town—and we're going to have the pleasure of your company at supper this evening, right? We were all so sorry about your grandma. She was a good lady."

"Thank you. I miss her terribly."

"Nita says you've taken over the house?"

Mabel nodded. "It's a work in progress." *To say the least.*

"I'm sorry." Mr. Bedford rested a hand on the older man's back. "I should have introduced my Uncle Charles. Charles, this is Mabel Browne, as I'm sure you've already figured out."

It seemed Charles had been focused on the booth where Miss Birdie and Ms. Katherine Ann were sitting. He shifted his gaze to Mabel and took her hand with a smile. "Imagine, another Mabel Browne. I'd have guessed they broke the mold with your grandmother."

"They did," Mabel agreed. "I might be her namesake, but she was one of a kind."

Charles gestured at the booth behind Mabel. "Don't I know these ladies? My goodness, it's a lot of years, but I believe I do."

Here goes, Mabel thought, realizing Miss Birdie might not be ready to talk to Lester's family right now.

As Miss Birdie straightened her back and looked up, Mabel saw she'd underestimated Miss Birdie's inner reserves. "Why, hello, Eugene."

"And Charlie," Ms. Katherine Ann interjected. She patted her chest. "Katherine Ann Landis—McArthur now. You might not remember me—I was a year behind you and Birdie." She gestured at her friend.

Charles smiled at Ms. Katherine Ann, then took Miss Birdie's hand and looked into her eyes. Mabel wondered if Nita had told him yet about Lester's letter.

"I'd know you anywhere, Bertha. You're looking well."

"You are too, Charles. Louisiana has agreed with you, I see."

"I liked it there, but I miss the seasons up here." Charles smiled, still holding Miss Birdie's hand. "And the people."

"Have you moved?" Ms. Katherine Ann asked. "You did say 'liked.'"

Charles turned his attention to her, slowly releasing Miss Birdie's hand. "I'm thinking about coming back up here. One of my boys is still down there, but the other one's in Chicago now."

"Understood you married a Louisiana girl," Ms. Katherine Ann said. "Won't she miss home?"

"Belinda passed several years ago."

"I'm so sorry." Miss Birdie took Charles' hand again and squeezed it.

"Thank you. It was a long time ago, but we all miss her very much."

"Excuse me, ladies." Mr. Bedford tapped Charles' shoulder. "I believe our pickup's ready, Uncle Charles. We'll look forward to seeing you this evening, Mabel."

Mabel watched Charles bid the old ladies goodbye, then follow Mr. Bedford back to the register. When she looked back at her seatmates, Ms. Katherine Ann was jiggling Miss Birdie's wrist. "Well, he's still looking fine, isn't he?" she hissed.

Miss Birdie shifted in her seat. "Hush, Katherine. He'll hear you."

Mabel grinned. Nothing like a good-looking man to brighten up the gloomies. She felt as if she were sitting and listening in at the eighth-grade lunch table.

As her grilled maple-nut honey bun arrived, Mabel felt her own spirits lift. Tragedy had taken a lot from her friends, but it was Christmas again, and miracles still happened.

Chapter Twenty-Four

On her way to Nita's, Mabel came in view of the nearby Crawford estate. She paused at the end of the sweeping drive and admired the big, handsome old house of white brick. It wasn't ostentatious, like the mansions she'd seen in a couple of recent upscale developments, some of which looked more like private sanitoriums than one-family suburban residences.

Still, the curved sweep of paved driveway drew her eye up the hill, to where the house sat amid mature trees and winter-dormant gardens complete with fountains. Lawns sprawled away towards woods and fields. A drystone wall, the likes of which Mabel wasn't used to seeing outside New England or the UK, set the property off from the roadway. Candles glowed at each window, and swags of evergreen gathered by massive red bows graced the pillars at the ungated entrance arch and the front of the house.

The effect was monied but unpretentious, almost to the point of appearing welcoming. Almost—except for the prominent security signs.

Mabel moved on past what might once have been an old wagon road, now overgrown with encroaching trees and brush, then another long driveway leading to a modest farmhouse and barn. This must be the Mennonite neighbors.

It had been at least thirty-five years since Mabel had been to Nita's own family farm. She was relieved to see they'd heavily graveled the long driveway, prone to mud and deep ruts back in Mabel's childhood.

She couldn't help smiling at the sight of the red-roofed barn and big Victorian farmhouse nestled in spruces and hemlocks. Trucks and cars crowded the farmyard—Nita's entire extended family must be here.

Mabel's cell rang as she pulled up to the house—John's ringtone. She'd texted him earlier, to let him know she was eating dinner with the Bedfords.

She parked under a spruce that had lost most of its lower branches and answered her phone.

"Just wanted to give you a heads-up," John said. "Police have made a presumptive ID based on medical and dental records, plus postal uniform fragments. The remains appear to be Lester's."

Mabel drew in a sharp breath. "Do the Bedfords know?"

"They should've heard by now. They were supposed to be notified this afternoon. Still awaiting DNA confirmation—assuming there's enough that isn't too degraded to process."

Mabel cast an uneasy eye at the yellow-lit farmhouse windows. "Those poor people—and Miss Birdie. I saw her earlier today, and I've never seen her so troubled."

"It's a tragedy." John sighed. "An old tragedy, but I'm sure the wound's still raw for Nita's dad and uncle—anybody who lived through the disappearance and the days of searching and wondering."

"I won't say anything unless they do," Mabel decided. "I'm not sure if I should let on that I already know or not."

"Play it by ear. I doubt it matters as long as they were informed first."

"I guess I'd better go in. Call you later, okay?"

"Okay, but, hey—I wanted to tell you again how proud I am of you for being brave and submitting your article. I can't wait to see it in print with your name on it."

Mabel couldn't help the flush she felt wash over her cheeks, or the little smile twitching at the corner of her mouth. "Thanks. I know it's nothing—it's just *The Shopper*, and I'm not getting paid, but—"

"Now, stop that. You wrote something the editors felt deserved publication. People are going to read your article the same as anything else in print. You took a big chance and put yourself out there. Now, take some pride in that. Let yourself enjoy it."

"Thanks. I'll try."

"Well, *I'm* proud. As a matter of fact, I'm going to pick up extra copies when it comes out."

"Stop it."

"Nope. I'm going to keep telling the world how great you are. Consider me your publicist."

Talking to John had boosted Mabel's spirits. She now recognized how nervous she'd been about coming here tonight, knowing how much turmoil the family had been thrown into in recent days. She was an outsider, especially after all these years. Still, for some reason, they'd wanted her here.

After a moment's hesitation, Mabel walked around to the back door leading to the utility room off the kitchen. This had always been the "friends and family" entrance and the one she'd used throughout her childhood.

She raised her hand to knock, but she'd never done that as a child. "The door's always open to you," Nita's mom had told her. Since Mabel could hear all the voices inside, she wasn't sure anybody would notice her knocking back here, anyway.

She pushed the door open. "Yoohoo."

A flurry of tiny growls and sharp yips came her way from one of the front rooms. Scruffy little Tabasco burst into the back entry. One scraggly lower tooth had caught on his upper lip, creating a sneer.

Nita barreled into the utility room behind him. "Settle down." She scooped her watchdog up in her arms. "Sorry. He's guarding the compound."

"Just doing his job." Mabel peeled off her coat and added it to the heap of outerwear atop the clothes dryer.

"Thanks for coming. Let's get in there, and I'll introduce you."

"Who all's here? I ran into your dad and Uncle Charles down at the Coffee Cup earlier."

"Oh, yeah, Daddy told me. It's them, my mom, my brothers—do you remember them?"

Mabel grinned. "Yeah. Marcus and Boots."

"Right. Plus, wives and kids, Uncle Charles' son Raymond, my son Omar, his wife Belle, and my grandbaby Brooke."

"You know I'll never keep everybody straight, right?"

"I wouldn't expect you to. Mama calls everybody by the wrong name herself, and I definitely misspeak half the time. Anyway, we're just gonna have a nice dinner first—and I'm saying it's nice because I didn't cook. I was working so Mama, and my sisters-in-law and daughter-in-law all did potluck."

The delicious smells wafting from the kitchen were already making Mabel lightheaded.

"Then, after dinner, it'll just be you and me, Uncle Charles, Raymond, Daddy, and my brothers."

Mabel added in her head. "That's seven people."

"Still kind of a lot, I know, but they'll sort themselves out. I expect it'll be Uncle Charles and Daddy doing most of the talking."

As they started toward the lights and chatter beyond the back entry, Nita stopped and caught Mabel's arm. "They IDed the body today, at least as far as they could. It's Uncle Lester."

"John told me a moment ago. I'm so sorry, Nita."

"After all these years, it's better to know. Daddy and Uncle Charles are relieved. They're already planning a memorial service."

"It's still an awful way to go."

Nita nodded briefly. "All right. Time to eat."

As anticipated, Mabel was overwhelmed by Nita's large

family. A leaf had been added to the big farm table, and card tables and TV trays set up through the living room and front hall. Kids were laughing and racing up and down the staircase and around the downstairs. As Nita's mom called for grace, every head bowed before the chaos resumed.

"Hey, Mabel." Nita's brother Boots shook her hand. "Long time, no see. Glad to hear you're in Medicine Spring to stay."

"I'm glad too. It's been good getting back together with Nita."

Boots grinned. "The terror twins."

He waved Mabel ahead of him in line and handed her a plate. A fabulous array of food had been jammed into every available inch of counter space, on top of the stove, and along the old Hoosier cupboard's pull-out shelf. A church-basement-sized coffee urn sat on a metal serving cart next to stacks of coffee cups.

Nita line-jumped between Boots and Mabel, drawing a joking objection. "I saved us seats at the big table," she said. "Desserts are all on a table out in the garage, so save some room."

"I'll do my best." Mabel felt more than a bit dazzled by the spread in front of her. She'd known Nita's mom was a great cook but had never experienced the glory of a Bedford family potluck before. This was going to take some strategizing.

As she inched forward, Mabel forced herself to take tiny portions of whatever would fit the plate. The last thing she wanted was to slight one of the cooks.

"You want more mac-and-cheese than that," Nita hissed in her ear. "My sister-in-law uses a secret ingredient she learned from her mother, and it's out of this world."

"No problem." Mabel was partial to mac-and-cheese. Obligingly, she heaped a bigger mound onto the edge of her plate, then shoved the overflow to safety with her handful of tableware.

"Save space for the pulled pork over there." Nita nodded toward an old-fashioned electric roaster on a wobbly-looking side table. "Tender as a grandmother's kiss."

It was helpful, having a buffet-line coach. Nita steered Mabel's hand away from some delicious-appearing baked beans. "I wouldn't eat anything that came out of her kitchen." She pointed. "Have some of those. You could eat off her floor."

Corn pudding joined the party, along with bread-and-butter pickles, scalloped potatoes, broccoli casserole, green beans swimming in a bacon-laced broth, and cornbread. The first layer of food was almost hidden by later additions by the time Mabel headed for the table.

"Settle yourself, and I'll bring us a couple coffees, okay?"

"Thanks." As Mabel spread her napkin over her lap, she looked around at the others who'd scored seats at the "big table." Nita's parents sat opposite, along with Uncle Charles, with son Raymond next to him. Mabel and Nita were flanked by Nita's brothers, with Boots to Mabel's left. The wives sat beyond Raymond, Boots, and Marcus. Mabel presumed she wouldn't have to interact with them, since they were seated too far away for conversation.

It occurred to Mabel that the seating arrangement suggested circling the wagons.

Mr. Bedford cleared his throat. "Once again, I was sorry to hear about your Grandma Mabel. I guess Nita's told you we don't live in Medicine Spring anymore, but we remember her fondly."

"Thank you." Mabel lowered her forkful of mac-and-cheese onto the plate. "I'm so sorry for your loss too. I had no idea about any of this until…"

"Nita told us you found Lester's remains." Mr. Bedford's voice, though steady, had gone soft—even hard to hear above all the chatter around them. Considering the background laughter and conversation, Mabel guessed that for many in the younger generations, the shock and sense of loss were somewhat muted.

"Um, yes." She'd have credited Barnacle with the discovery, but no doubt Lester's family wouldn't appreciate that detail. "We did."

He dipped his head in a grave nod. "We're grateful you did. The years of waiting and wondering have been hard."

Mabel looked down at her cooling mac-and-cheese, wondering whether they'd mention the recent identification.

"I wish Mother and Dad could be here," Uncle Charles said. "Lester's disappearance killed them. They were never the same."

Mrs. Bedford rested a hand on his wrist. "Now, Uncle Charles, look at it this way. They've all three been together in heaven for decades. We're the only ones who didn't know."

Uncle Charles smiled and covered her hand with his own. "You're right as usual, Edie. No more dark thoughts. Now, we'll be able to give Lester a proper burial. Soon, we hope we can put an end to all the ugly speculation we've lived with for so long too."

Nita appeared at Mabel's left shoulder and set a mug down in front of her. "That's the next job." Nita squeezed into her seat. "Figuring out what did happen to Uncle Lester that day."

"And to that poor young woman." Uncle Charles's forehead creased. "I don't think Lester can ever rest with an untainted memory till that murder's resolved as well."

"Mark my words." Nita gestured with her table knife. "Solve one death, and we're gonna solve the other. Mabel here has already brought a whole slew of murderers to justice. She'll get to the bottom of this in no time."

"Oh, hey, now." The weight of this family's expectations was something Mabel did *not* want to take on. "I'm not some crime-solving Bat Girl. I got lucky a couple times, but I don't know the first thing about investigating a murder."

Nita scoffed. "We're all looking into it right now—Mabel, me, Lisa, and the guys. John actually *is* a private eye."

Mr. Bedford brightened. "Is that right? Maybe you really can get to the bottom of what happened, even after all this time. Stranger things have happened, you know."

From the far end, next to where his daughter Brooke sat at one of the kids' tables, Nita's son Omar snorted. "Come on, Mom. You've gotta be kidding."

"We always suspected Ricky Putnam." Mr. Bedford leaned forward, meeting Mabel's eyes with great intensity.

Again, she reluctantly set her fork down.

"Have you heard how he got his money?"

Mabel shoveled a big spoonful of corn pudding into her mouth and nodded. Hurriedly, she chewed and swallowed, chasing the food with a sip of coffee. "He inherited it from his uncle—but the housekeeper always said the uncle had intended to disinherit him."

Mr. Bedford nodded and slammed a fist onto the table, making the cutlery jump. "He did more than intend to disinherit him. He wrote him out of the will the very night he died, but the will—which went out with the mail the next morning—disappeared."

"Let the girls eat, Eugene." Mrs. Bedford gave him a placid look. "It's not good for anybody's digestion to get worked up like this at the table. You can talk all this over after the meal."

Mabel patted her lips with her napkin. "Right—but I agree the whole thing about the will is very suspicious."

Mr. Bedford sat back with a look of satisfaction. "I think maybe he killed the girl too. You know she lived right around where Lester disappeared."

"After supper, Daddy," Boots said. He and Nita's other brother exchanged a look and shook their heads.

Chapter Twenty-Five

DINNER WAS OVER. MABEL HAD CLEANED her plate, as well as slivers of hummingbird cake, sweet potato pie, zucchini bread—one of the many zucchini-centric items Nita said her mother served year-round, thanks to a freezer full of shredded squash from her garden—plus a smidge of cobbler from a sister-in-law's home-canned blackberries. She was overstuffed but found it hard to be regretful—except for the basket of buttermilk biscuits she'd been forced to leave untouched. She'd cut back tomorrow.

Mabel had made a halfhearted offer to help with the dishes, but Nita had herded her past the door of the overcrowded kitchen full of chattering women. "Keep moving—you're needed in the front room. Anyway, we're not wanted in there. Number one, you're a guest. Plus, I know it's the twenty-first century, but only married women allowed. I not only birthed a baby, but I'm a grandmother, for Pete's sake—and *I'm* not welcome either."

Mabel looked over her shoulder as Nita towed her along. "But why—?"

"Hey, I didn't make the rules. I just benefit from them. I'm divorced, so I'm not a member of the club anymore. I'm guessing because this is their time to talk about the husbands."

"Why am I wanted in the front room then?"

"We're going to talk about Lester. Daddy and Uncle Charles have it in their heads that you're going to bring him justice."

Mabel spun around to look into Nita's eyes. "What? Where did they get that idea? We *all* said we'd help, but…"

Nita shrugged one shoulder but wouldn't meet Mabel's gaze. "They've seen you in the newspaper, solving that Sauer ax murder that went back even further than what we have right here.

And they know you're on our side."

Mabel opened her mouth, then shut it. She knew from Nita's reluctance to look at her that Nita had likely been the one touting Mabel's detective prowess.

Mabel *was* on their side, and she did want to help. However, she most decidedly did not want to be in the position of "lead detective." Every murder investigation she'd been involved in—and there had been more than she'd like to acknowledge—had been resolved as much around her as through her direct efforts. Mabel couldn't bear to have these dear people counting on her for results, couldn't bear to be the latest person to fail them.

Still, here they were in the doorway to the front room, once the farmhouse parlor, and Nita was shoving her inside.

To Mabel's relief, there were only three people in the room. Uncle Charles sat in the overstuffed armchair to the left of the unlit fireplace, one foot resting on the fringed burgundy hassock, and Mr. Bedford occupied the matching chair to the right. Raymond stood in the shadowy corner by the bookcases, looking out toward the long driveway. All three men turned their eyes on Mabel, and the old men got to their feet.

"You girls have a seat," Mr. Bedford said. "Is the loveseat all right? Maybe you'd like the chair." He motioned toward the armchair he'd just vacated.

Embarrassed by all the attention, not to mention their courtliness, Mabel waved a hand. "The loveseat's fine." She gave an awkward laugh. "I *should* be standing. Give that big dinner a chance to digest."

Nevertheless, she and Nita sank onto the loveseat. Their generous derrieres took up all the available space, which made Nita giggle.

Mabel grinned. "Your old cat used to be able to sit between us. What was his name?"

"Cedric." Nita snickered.

Mr. Bedford joined the laughter. "Old Lord Cedric. Nita was in her Sherlock Holmes phase when she named him. It was British everything."

"He was a noble cat," Nita insisted, despite her grin. "A mouser without peer."

"No room for him now." Mabel watched as Tabasco leapt onto Nita's knees and curled his wee lip at Mabel.

She tried to edge away, but that was an impossibility. Hopefully, Tabasco would get used to sharing Nita and the loveseat with her.

Uncle Charles settled himself in the armchair once again, with his son helping get his foot positioned on the hassock. "Doggone ankle's swelling. Don't know why."

"They both are, Daddy." Raymond shook his head. "You ought to have them both elevated. You need to call your doctor tomorrow morning."

Uncle Charles shook his head. "Eh, she'll just say too much salt. I'm not supposed to have it, but everything tastes like cardboard without it."

Mabel studied the feisty old man. He might have some swelling in his ankles, but otherwise he looked in great shape for his age—not to mention remarkably clear-headed.

"So, what are you girls thinking about the case?" Uncle Charles asked.

The case?

Nita looked at Mabel, as if expecting her to take the lead.

Mabel cleared her throat and shifted. "To be truthful, I believe Lester was a victim here. I suspect Nita's right—if we find out who killed Cathy Abramovich, we'll find out who killed Lester, and vice versa."

Uncle Charles leaned forward eagerly. "How do you plan to do that?"

This was the problem with making pronouncements. People

expected you to have a plan.

"Old-fashioned legwork." Mabel echoed something she'd once heard John say. "Not going to guarantee we'll find answers so late in the game, but we'll give it our best."

Seeing a flicker of disappointment in Uncle Charles's face as he sank back in his chair, she added, "I was at the post office earlier. A guy who worked back on the loading dock told me no one there thinks Lester ran off with the mail. He said Lester had worked in the back for a long time at that point, and been a good employee, or he wouldn't have been promoted."

Mr. Bedford gave a satisfied nod. "What we've said for years. The post office muckety-mucks weren't so supportive back then."

"Which is why it's a good thing it's a new day, right?" Mabel tapped her lower lip. "Speaking of the post office, I meant to ask about Jerry Kalchik."

Uncle Charles reared forward again. "That's where you should start looking. Eugene insists Putnam was behind every-thing, but my money's on Kalchik. He hadn't been working at the post office as long as Lester, but he was convinced he should've gotten that promotion to carrier."

"But why?" Mabel frowned.

"Felt entitled," Uncle Charles said. "There hadn't been a Black mail carrier in Medicine Spring before that, and I guess he didn't stop and think how Civil Service worked."

"So, he was…disappointed when he lost the promotion to Lester." Mabel stated the obvious.

"Disappointed isn't strong enough. He spread lies about Lester. Threatened him. Said he and his buddies knew how to wipe the smile off Lester's face, and that Lester had better watch his back when he left the post office."

A sick feeling roiled Mabel's stomach. She'd never imag-ined anything like this in Medicine Spring. "Did he follow through on any of his threats that you know of?"

"Other than killing him, you mean?" Uncle Charles's face was grim. "Little things at first. Air let out of his tires in the post office parking lot. Threatening notes under his windshield wipers."

Mabel and Nita spoke at the same time. "Everything focused on his car?" Mabel asked.

"Do you still have any of those notes?" Nita clutched Mabel's hand. "Maybe there are prints, or we could check the handwriting."

"The police took the last one," Mr. Bedford told Nita. "As far as I know, it'd still be in evidence. Lester tossed the others."

"Yep." Uncle Charles looked at Mabel. "Everything I heard had to do with the car. Usually, it happened in town or the post office lot."

"The same car something went wrong with on the day Lester disappeared." Mabel's brain clicked through the implications. "So unless he could borrow a car, Lester would likely be on foot and burdened with a heavy mailbag."

Uncle Charles slapped his hand on the arm of the chair. "Dang, you're good, Mabel. Nita was right. This all could've been planned."

Mabel grimaced. "Coulda, shoulda, woulda. It's just a thought. It doesn't account for Cathy Abramovich getting killed in almost the same place Lester disappeared, either."

Uncle Charles sat back again. "Maybe not, but I think you're on the right track. Maybe she was a witness to what happened to Lester."

"Do you know if Kalchik's still alive?" Nita asked.

The old men looked at each other. "I don't know." Uncle Charles shrugged. "Lost track of him a long time ago."

"Same here." Mr. Bedford scratched his chin. "But I still think ol' Ricky Putnam's the villain in this piece."

"Tell me what you know." Mabel wished she had her notebook with her, but it was still on her kitchen table, where she'd been making out a grocery list.

Nita pried herself out of their too-snug seating arrangement. "Hang on a sec. Need my notebook."

Moments later, she returned, flipping to a blank page, pen clenched in her teeth. She wedged herself back beside Mabel. "Okay, Daddy. Shoot."

"Ricky Putnam was a spoiled brat. Everyone around here knew that. He was old man Crawford's solitary living heir—at least, by blood. He broke Crawford's heart, since Ricky was his late sister's only child. So, he gave the kid a lot of second chances, but after a while, Crawford reached his limit."

Mabel pondered. "How do you know that? I'm not doubting you, but we need witnesses, if we can still find any."

"Like I say, anybody who was around back then could tell you that. He went through cars like other people go through jugs of milk. Crawford sent him to school a couple different places, and Ricky got himself kicked out of both of them. Never kept a job. He'd work a while and quit—or get fired."

"Blood's thicker than water though, right? What makes you think Mr. Crawford gave up on Ricky? Is there any evidence that Crawford didn't keep right on giving him second chances?"

"You said it yourself, Mabel. There's a witness. Adelaide Pettigrew was there. She literally watched Crawford sign the new will. The next morning, it disappeared from the mail. I don't believe in coincidences."

Mabel slowly shook her head. "Adelaide's still around, according to Acey. The sooner we talk to her, the better. Remember though—the gossip also says she hated Ricky and had a big crush on the secretary, Ben Whatever. She wasn't the most disinterested witness."

Mr. Bedford waved a dismissive hand. "No matter who she

liked or didn't, nobody considered her a liar by nature. She wouldn't have gained anything by lying anyway."

"We'll look into it." Nita made a note. She glanced at Mabel. "Maybe you could follow that one up?"

"Um, sure."

"I figured I'd see if I can find out if Kalchik's still living," Nita said. "Or maybe Lisa could do that." Nita looked back at her dad and uncle. "Did he ever get that promotion, after Uncle Lester disappeared?"

Uncle Charles growled. "He did. He was next in line. Stayed at it till he retired."

"Even after all those threats? That's awful." Mabel couldn't begin to imagine how grating that must have been for the family, having to see Lester's enemy and possible killer on that route, day after day, for years. She could begin to understand Uncle Charles's vehemence.

"No proof." Mr. Bedford lifted a shoulder.

Yet, sixty years later she and Nita were supposed to come up with enough evidence to convict him?

"So, we're thinking either Putnam or Kalchik killed Lester?" Nita tapped her pen on her lower lip. "And Cathy Abramovich was collateral damage?"

The old men exchanged another look. "Well…to be honest," Mr. Bedford said, "one of her boyfriends is probably likelier. You know what they always say."

"Crime of passion, right." Nita scribbled something. "Domestic partners, romantic partners. Cops always start there. Do we have names?"

"You'd have to look back. I don't know whether they ever published names at the time." Uncle Charles shifted his bottom in the deep chair. "Raymond, give me a hand, would you? Eugene, this chair is too soft. A person sinks right down into it so's you can't get up again."

Once Raymond had towed his dad out of the depths of the cushions and propped him farther forward with a couple of throw pillows, Charles sighed with relief. "There was a lot of talk at the time that the two men were jealous of each other, and each of them thought Cathy was two-timing him with the other guy."

Inwardly, Mabel groaned. Nothing but gossip. It might all be very true, of course, but they had nothing concrete to work with. "Hey, Nita, make me a note to look for those names, okay?"

Mabel snapped her fingers. "You know what? I'll bet John could find them in the police file if his buddy can get him back in. There might even be interview notes."

"This investigation's really shaping up." Uncle Charles rubbed his hands together. "Anything else you need from us, girls?"

Mabel opened her phone. She ought to get home and check on her animals. "One last thing, I guess. You've seen that letter I got—addressed to Grandma? It looks to us like Lester was asking Grandma's help getting a date with Miss Birdie. Is that what you think?"

Both men nodded. "It's Lester's handwriting and signature," Mr. Bedford said. "No question."

"Does this make sense to you?" Nita asked. "Did you have any idea Uncle Lester was crushing on Miss Birdie?"

"Or why he'd be asking my grandma to put in a good word for him?" Mabel added. "None of us, including Miss Birdie and Ms. Katherine Ann, had any idea he and my grandma were friends."

Uncle Charles smiled. "I never knew for a fact, but I'm not surprised. Les always kept his feelings pretty much to himself, especially if he thought he'd end up embarrassed or let down. Birdie was always a beauty." If Mabel didn't know better, she'd think Charles looked dreamy-eyed, himself. Maybe Miss Birdie had more than one male admirer.

She nudged Nita, who looked up, confused. "Huh?'

"Never mind. I'll tell you later."

"I wasn't aware your grandma knew Lester any more than to say hi to," Mr. Bedford said. "Were you, Uncle Charles?"

"Not unless they worked somewhere together. I'm sure your grandma wasn't a member of our church. Les had a few other jobs before he took the Civil Service exam…he made deliveries for Dave's Appliance, did janitorial work for the school. I think he made deliveries for the drugstore for a while too."

"Guessing that was it, then. I only found out lately that Grandma Mabel worked at the drugstore before she got married."

"I imagine he saw the girls together at school or around town and realized they were close. Yes, assuming he and Mabel got along well at work, I can see Les asking her to serve as a go-between," Uncle Charles said.

"Well, I know for a fact that Miss Birdie was at the soda fountain on at least one occasion when Grandma was working, and Lester came out from the back and smiled at Miss Birdie. She and Ms. Katherine Ann told me about it."

Uncle Charles wore a musing expression. "That must have been quite a smile. Imagine remembering it all these years. Did she…have a crush on Lester?"

Chapter Twenty-Six

A LIGHT WINTRY MIX WAS FALLING by the time Mabel left the Bedford farmhouse, and it sparkled in the outside lights. Some of the family had already left, so she had no trouble backing and turning. The driveway was clear of accumulation, but Mabel knew road conditions tended to be most slippery when the first light precipitation contacted previous oil leaks.

She couldn't say she enjoyed driving in snow or rain, but she'd grown used to it since moving to Medicine Spring. "Slow, but steady" had become her motto. She knew better than to creep along, which could cause as many problems as speeding.

Looking through spatters of what she thought of as thick rain hitting the windshield, she drove up to the road and looked back before turning right, amazed again that Nita chose to live out here alone. Of course, Nita had grown up here, so she more than likely didn't share Mabel's sense of scary isolation.

Before long, she passed another long farm lane cutting off through the fields and trees just beyond Nita's place.

This must be where Nita's Mennonite neighbors lived—Grace, the barista from Demitasse, and her family. Mabel couldn't see any lights, other than a faint gleam that might have been a lantern inside the farmhouse, coming through the trees. She wondered if they were part of a conservative Mennonite branch or just early-to-bed farmers. She imagined it was the latter, based on what she knew of other local Mennonites, who drove cars and had telephones.

Mabel was glad Nita had such close neighbors, and it seemed they had a friendly relationship. It made her consider the relative isolation of her own house down at the dead end of Carteret Street, with the trees of Willow Creek Park on two sides and fields on the others. Even with other houses less than a long block away, she didn't know the inhabitants well. In the few months since she'd moved into Grandma's house, she hadn't made getting acquainted a priority—and neither had they.

She certainly knew Linnea, who lived through the patch of woods beyond Mabel's small field at the back of her house. Linnea was not a plus.

She would add this to her list of New Year's resolutions, Mabel decided—getting to know her neighbors. She was glad she didn't have to do it now.

As soon as she got home and had let Barnacle out on his run, she kicked off her shoes and called John.

"How did it go? Did you get enough to eat?"

"Haha. I had to waddle out of Nita's house, and I brought home a big box of leftover food, which I'm now trying to find room for in my fridge. If you want to come over for dinner tomorrow, I'll share the wealth."

"You won't need to ask me twice. So, tell me. The plan was to talk to Lester's brother Charles, right? How did that go?"

"Good, I guess." Mabel laughed. "Nita said something about not wanting to overwhelm him, but he and Mr. Bedford had their own agenda. They're convinced that you and I and the others can do what the entire Medicine Spring police force couldn't accomplish in 1962."

"Close two homicide cold cases?"

"Bingo. Hey, who knows? They might be right—looks like we already closed a missing person case."

"We did promise Nita we'd do what we could," John admitted.

"Glad you're taking that attitude. I picked up an assignment for you."

"Like what?" John's voice was leery.

"Cathy Abramovich had two boyfriends, one current and one former. I guess the cops gave them both a close look at the time."

"That's true."

"You already knew." Mabel was unsurprised. "Do you have names? Or any further information on them?"

"James 'Bud' Bender was the former boyfriend, and Mark Enlow was the current one. Both were jealous types, Bud in particular, and there were public altercations—not to mention a neighbor's report of a man screaming at Cathy one night not long before her death. The police could never pin it on one or the other of them."

"Do you know if either's still alive?"

"Haven't had time to look further."

"Did they find any physical evidence to tie one of them to the scene?"

"Nope." Mabel heard John blow out a forceful breath that might've been from discouragement. "Nothing usable. Of course, their prints turned up in the house, along with Cathy's parents' and sister's, all of which were latent and could've been left at any time. No fingerprint or shoe print in her blood, or anything like that."

"Latent?"

"Not visible like a fingerprint in the victim's blood, for instance."

"I see." Lisa would have known that. Mabel chewed at her lower lip. "Are you able to look into whether either or both of these men are still alive?"

"Sure. I'm proctoring an English exam tomorrow morning, so it'll be afternoon before I get to it."

Koi leapt up and rubbed her head along Mabel's jaw. Mabel rubbed the cat's warm, round, little head. "No rush, obviously.

I've got my own assignments."

For the rest of their conversation, Mabel filled John in on what she'd heard from Nita's family. After they'd hung up, she looked at the time. It was almost 9:30, the tail end of Lisa's pre-bedtime availability. She decided to text, figuring Lisa could decide for herself whether she wanted to chat or just go to bed.

You up? Had dinner at Nita's and learned a bunch of stuff. I think Uncle Charles might be sweet on Miss Birdie.

Her phone rang in her hand.

"Tell me everything—but I need to get to bed so I can get up for the early student drop-offs, so don't take the scenic route."

Mabel snorted. "You're the one who always takes the scenic route. I'm nothing, if not succinct."

"Whatever. Meter's running, so get to it."

For the second time since she'd gotten home, Mabel ran through her sit-down with the Bedford elders. "You want to look into whether Jerry Kalchik still walks the earth?"

"On it." Mabel heard what sounded like a yawn on Lisa's end, but a beat later, Lisa continued. "What, pray tell, are you in charge of?"

"I'm going to follow up with Adelaide Pettigrew—or whatever her last name is these days. Acey never mentioned whether she ever got married."

"Well," Lisa said, "we might never get the answers we're looking for, but at least we're getting organized."

Being organized was something Mabel had never been accused of in her life. In fact, it felt as if she were getting herself deeper and deeper into the hole as time went on and her to-do list spiraled out of control.

"I've got to get to bed." Lisa gave another audible yawn. "One last thing though. You didn't tell me the best part yet."

Mabel frowned. "Huh?"

"Miss Birdie," Lisa hissed.

"Omigosh…duh. How could I forget? Yeah, Uncle Charles mentioned what a beauty Miss Birdie was, and I'm telling you the truth, his eyes kind of glazed over like a man in love."

Lisa chuckled. "I don't know. You might be reading a lot into a case of indigestion or something, given the size of that meal you described. Anyway, he hasn't even seen her in…what? Seventy years? You think she might have changed a tad since he last saw her?"

"Since this afternoon? He just saw her today at the Coffee Cup. He held onto her hand a whole lot longer than he needed to. Plus, the last thing he asked me seemed aimed at finding out whether Birdie might still be pining for Lester."

"I didn't know she was ever pining for Lester to begin with," Lisa said.

"She wasn't. Of course, she and Ms. Katherine Ann thought he was cute, but that was as far as it went. I do think Miss Birdie is really sad about his death and thinking about what might have been, but I didn't tell Uncle Charles that because it wasn't what he asked. I didn't want to discourage him."

Lisa's yawn sounded bigger than the previous two. "Well, I hope you're right, and they can make a love connection, but sounds to me like you're getting ahead of yourself. Now, I have *got* to get to bed."

"Me too. I mean I hope so too. It would make me feel much better if something happy came out of all this sadness. Good night, Lis."

Chapter Twenty-Seven

THE NEXT MORNING, MABEL DECIDED TO face her demons and try singing *O, Holy Night*. As a tenor. At least, she could ease into it by looking at the music first. If, as she expected, it was too awful when she started singing, she'd simply call Amanda and let her know it wasn't going to work out.

Mabel had never been a delicate flower, but being asked to sing a man's part was a new low. If she couldn't sing with a whole group around her, how could she sing a solo? The idea was plain crazy.

She hadn't gotten that video link the choir director had said she'd try to send yet, but Mabel presumed she could find something. She opened her laptop and searched for tenor performances of the familiar Christmas solo she'd only ever heard sung by high-soaring sopranos. She was startled when the search results spilled out video after video.

Unsure which, if any, resembled Clive's arrangement, she decided to listen to one at random, just to hear how the piece sounded in a tenor voice. Where to start? Pavarotti? Mabel shook her head. She didn't want to set the bar at that level right off the bat.

There were a few church videos, but she doubted the acoustics would be as good as a professional recording. Jonathan Antoine looked like a good place to start. Professional, but he also looked friendly. Not quite so terrifying as Pavarotti in his tuxedo.

Mabel clicked play, and Antoine's voice filled her kitchen. For a moment, she forgot why she was listening.

So beautiful.

As she listened, Mabel felt the impact of the long-ago angelic message as if she were one of the shepherds on that chilly hillside surrounded by grazing sheep and looking up at a star-scattered night sky. Mabel pressed her fingers against her stinging eyelids.

She wasn't sure if she wanted to cry because of the beauty of the message or her own desperate sense of inadequacy.

Hmphh.

Confused, Mabel looked up. Of course, nobody else was there but her animals. Maybe Barnacle had snuffled.

Just sing.

Mabel frowned.

You're the only thing stopping you.

Oh, good grief, Grandma was in her head again. As long as she'd been living here, she'd had a tendency to hear Grandma's commentary. Usually, it consisted of her grandmother's well-worn sayings, but this message seemed a bit more pointed. Mabel couldn't recall Grandma's ever telling her to sing before.

Then, she remembered. After the third-grade disaster, hadn't Grandma said something like this? Mabel had refused to listen back then, resorting to lip-syncing for the rest of the year—but maybe forty-plus years was long enough to live with being afraid.

They can catch you, but they can't eat you.

"All right, Grandma. I get it—but when you hear me, you'll be sorry you didn't leave well enough alone."

Mabel looked at her animals. Barnacle lay on the floor next to her. He'd seemed to enjoy the music up to this point. Koi was occupying her favorite perch atop the Hoosier cupboard. It was hard to make out the cat's expression, but it seemed to Mabel that Koi usually agreed with Grandma.

"I won't be hurt if you guys decide to leave." Mabel closed her music, which wasn't quite the same version as Antoine's, and took a sip of water. Right now, she just wanted to test-drive her range. She cleared her throat and sipped again. Realizing her palms were sweating, she rubbed them over the knees of her jeans.

"Okay." She restarted the video.

As Antoine began singing, Mabel joined him, though she kept her voice soft so as not to offend Koi and Barnacle. The beginning part had some low notes, which had worried her, but she found she could pretty much reach them. They wouldn't be as full and rich as Antoine's, but they were there.

After a while, she felt herself relaxing and simply singing. By the time they reached "Fall on your knees," she nearly drowned out the recording and even flung one arm out in a melodramatic gesture.

When the song ended, Mabel closed her laptop. She looked around. The angels had returned to the heavens and her animals were still here with her. She hadn't driven them away with her singing voice.

For the first time, she felt an inkling that she might be able to do this. As long as she stayed here in her kitchen, and Jonathan Antoine sang with her, that is.

After practicing her solo, Mabel tried to write for a while. She didn't have much to say yet about volunteering to sing with the choir—not much good, at any rate–but she did manage to make a few notes and create a rough outline for an article. Since she intended to write for seniors, she wanted to include something Amanda had mentioned to her—that because people were so busy these days, it was hard to recruit younger adult choir members or youth. Church choirs were shrinking or even disappearing for this reason, but retirees were well-suited to step in and fill the need.

Mabel didn't want to be a retiree. Not yet. However, that had been taken out of her hands when she got fired and hadn't been able to find another good job. Her writing wasn't bringing in any money yet, either. She promised herself she'd look for something part time after the New Year.

Mabel looked at Grandma's atomic sunburst wall clock. Time for a lunch break.

Her laptop chimed as she removed the flash drive. Hearing the familiar signal, Barnacle laid his chin on her knee.

"I agree, buddy. Break time."

Mabel opened her refrigerator, now all but bulging with leftovers from dinner at Nita's. She was tempted to start pulling some things out for an impromptu feast but thought better of it. She wanted John to have a chance to appreciate the riches she'd brought home before they started getting depleted. Besides, she wouldn't even know where to begin.

At last, she dug a TV dinner out of the freezer and stuck it in the microwave. While it heated, she dialed Acey's number.

"What can I do for you, little lady? Hope it's no emergency or nothing. I was countin' on an afternoon off to do a little Christmas decorating around my place here."

"No emergency. Hey, Acey, I was wondering if you might be able to put me in touch with your Aunt Adelaide."

"Actually, she's my great-aunt, but I never did call her that."

"Great-aunt, yes. Could you put me in touch with her? I had something I wanted to ask her about."

"I guess so. Whatcha want to talk about? Is this about old man Crawford's will?"

Mabel hadn't intended to explain everything to Acey. She didn't want what she was doing spread all over town, but she couldn't see any way around it. Less said the better, though.

"I guess what you told me the other night got me curious. I'd like to hear her story firsthand, you know."

Acey was quiet for several seconds, such an unusual state

for him that Mabel was afraid he might be planning to refuse to help her. At last, he said, "This must be something for your writing, huh?"

Mabel couldn't in good conscience bring herself to outright lie. It did seem though that her weird writing habit might be an acceptable excuse in Acey's eyes for all sorts of aberrant behavior. At some point, this might prove useful.

"Just curious."

"Well, I suppose it'd be okay. Aunt Addy lives in one of them retirement apartments over at whatchacall Best Years?"

"I know the place." Mabel had just visited Ms. Katherine Ann there, in fact.

"You want I should call her first and let her know?"

"That would be terrific, since she doesn't know me. Thanks. You say she's still clear in her mind?"

"Oh, Aunt Addy's sharp as they come. She'll talk your ear off and then start in on the other one."

Mabel wasn't sure whether that was good or not, but she was glad to know Adelaide still had her mental faculties and Acey would run interference for her. When they'd hung up, he'd promised to give Adelaide a call—and if Mabel heard nothing further by tomorrow morning, she should consider it okay to approach her herself.

Chapter Twenty-Eight

LATE THE NEXT MORNING, MABEL WAS once more walking up to the doors of the Best Years apartments, this time bearing a box of what Acey had told her were Adelaide's favorite chocolates. On the phone, the old woman had been quite pleasant and amazingly clearheaded, considering she was one of Acey's relatives. She was not, however, concise—and her hearing seemed more than a tad spotty.

Oh, well. Given Mabel was investigating sixty-year-old events, it had been a great turn of luck to find a key witness not only available and willing, but with apparent good recall of the critical facts. Beggars couldn't be choosers.

Mabel found the second-floor apartment door decked for Christmas from top to bottom. A huge wreath of faux pine entwined with red-and-silver ribbon and studded with pinecones and red and blue balls occupied the upper center. Christmas cards, decorative cutouts of teddy bears, tin soldiers, and snowmen covered every remaining inch of the door. A candy-striped crocheted stocking hung from the doorknob, with "Addy" embroidered diagonally, top to bottom.

For a moment, Mabel searched for the doorbell. She finally found it under a sprig of plastic holly and pressed the button.

The buzzer, obviously set to rouse the entire building, reverberated inside the apartment. Moments later, Mabel heard the telltale thump of a walker, which abruptly stopped.

After a delay that began to make Mabel wonder what was going on inside, the door opened. Apparently, the break had been due to Adelaide's leaving the hard surface of the kitchen tile to cross the carpeted living room. Christmas carols blared from an old-fashioned tape player on an end table. It was a wonder the woman had heard even her extraordinarily loud doorbell over the sounds of good cheer.

Mabel beheld a person as physically dissimilar to Acey as humanly possible. Where the handyman was scrawny, Adelaide was as round as Mrs. Santa. Instead of his dark mop, she wore her iron-gray hair in a teased and shellacked Marlo Thomas flip. Even at her age, she had a few inches on Acey in height. Her floor-length quilted housecoat featured a seasonal print of tumbling elves waving drums and candy canes.

Adelaide beamed a welcome. "You must be Acey's good friend Mabel."

"Uh…" Mabel wasn't quite ready to acknowledge any truth in Acey's exaggerated version of their relationship, but she did want Adelaide to feel comfortable enough to talk with her. "Yes?" She *was* Mabel, after all.

"Come right in. I see you looking at my housecoat. Isn't it a beaut? It was an early Christmas gift from the kids. I guess I shouldn't call them kids—my oldest turned fifty this fall. Look at my feet."

When Mabel's gaze had completed the trip down to the floor, she was startled to see red-and-green slippers with curled-up toes, completing the elf look, peeking out from beneath Adelaide's hem. "Amazing," Mabel managed to say.

"Part of my gift. I love Christmas, don't you? I thought you might, so I turned on the carols for you."

Mabel hoped they wouldn't have to scream at each other to be heard the whole time. She had to save her voice if she was going to be a tenor soloist in a matter of days, so she merely smiled and handed Adelaide the box of candy.

"Oh, how lovely—thank you! Do you like sweets? I just love them. Come, sit in my kitchen and let's have some goodies while we talk. I've started my Christmas baking, so we have

Santa's thumbprints, date pinwheels, fantasy fudge, church windows—you know the ones you make with the little colored marshmallows? Would you rather have hot chocolate or coffee? Or I could make you some tea."

Mabel had a sweet tooth she'd have thought ranked near the top of anyone in Medicine Spring—or perhaps all of Bartle County. But in the sweet-loving department, Adelaide left Mabel in the dust.

"Coffee, please," Mabel requested—quickly, before Adelaide could serve her a hot cocoa heaped with marshmallows and whipped cream along with her cookies and fantasy fudge. "With a bit of milk." For once, Mabel left her usual three sugars off her order.

Blessedly, the carols became somewhat muted when she stepped into Adelaide's kitchen. The room reflected her sweet, holly-jolly disposition. "I've never seen a pink kitchen before." Mabel gazed, agog at a very pink refrigerator, pink countertops, pink gingham curtains and tablecloth, and strawberry-covered wallpaper.

"I'm *so* glad you like it." Adelaide clasped her hands to her heart. "My boy found me the refrigerator. Isn't it the most precious thing? He said, 'Mom,' he said, 'you won't believe what we just took out of this house,' and I *didn't*. He works in the construction field, and sometimes when they get called in on a remodel, they end up being told to just rip out perfectly nice fixtures and junk them. Isn't that a crime?"

While she was talking, Adelaide had been shoving cookies and fudge at Mabel. Despite a sugar high from the fudge fumes alone, Mabel heard the word "crime," and attempted to redirect the conversation. "Funny you should mention—"

"Now, there's your coffee. Yes, I know it's a lot of pink, but what little girl doesn't dream of growing up and living in Barbie's Dream House?" Adelaide chortled.

Mabel resisted the urge to raise her hand and say, "Me."

"Anyway, I did manage to Christmas things up in here with the holly garland and such. Did you want sugar?"

"No, the milk is fine, thanks. I wanted to ask—"

"How is young Acey doing these days? I don't get to see much of the family since I moved in here. My kids and grandkids visit, people from the church, but that's about it."

Mabel started at the phrase "young Acey," which sounded as if he were the proverbial boy in knee pants. For a few seconds, she struggled to control her twitching lips. "Um, he seems to be doing fine. I—"

"I know he took the election real bad. I never saw that boy work so hard. It was a blow when Cousin Cletus lost his supervisor position."

In the several months Mabel had employed Acey as a handyman, she felt qualified to say she'd never seen him work that hard, either. She zipped her lip, however, when it came to shedding a tear for Cletus Pettigrew, since she'd personally written in Nita Bedford for the job and was grateful she'd scraped a win.

"Yes, I know he was upset, but he does seem to have moved on a bit since then. What I wondered was—"

Adelaide dunked a cookie in her hot chocolate. "Do you like the pinwheels? So many people seem to dislike dates these days. I don't know why. My late employer, Edmond Crawford, God rest his soul, always loved them. He always said, 'Adelaide—'"

Desperate now, Mabel leapt at the name. Her words ran together as she spit out her question along with a few cookie crumbs. "Yes, I was curious about Edmond Crawford's will. Acey told me you—"

"Oh, yes, I witnessed it all right. A travesty that was. A total miscarriage of justice. Mr. Crawford, God rest his soul, must still be spinning in his grave like that ice skater, whatshername. Oh, who was that now?"

Realizing they'd get nowhere till Adelaide recalled the particular skater, Mabel called out names. "Kristi Yamaguchi? Oksana Baiul? Um…Peggy Fleming? Sonja Henie?" Darn it, she couldn't remember any more names now that the pressure was on.

Adelaide shook her head. "No…" She tapped her lips in apparent thought. "The one with the hair."

Mabel creased her brow. She didn't think Adelaide was going dotty, but as far as Mabel could recall, all of them had hair, except maybe Scott Hamilton.

"You know, she was so doggone cute with the hair. Everybody cut their hair like that for a while. Dorothy, wasn't it?"

"Hamill?"

"What?"

Mabel began to realize Adelaide's machine-gun chatter might be due as much to her hearing issues as to her excitement at having a captive audience. Whenever Adelaide was looking at her, she seemed to hear at least some of what Mabel said, but when she was otherwise occupied or looking away, she talked right over Mabel.

Mabel made sure to catch Adelaide's eye. "Dorothy Hamill?"

Adelaide clapped her hands together. "Dorothy Hamill—of course! I could have sat here all day and never came up with that. Now, what was it we were talking about?"

"Mr. Crawford's will?"

"That's right. I will never forget that day as long as I live. Poor Mr. Crawford. He was struggling for every breath that evening. He sent Ben—that was his secretary, Ben was—to pick up medicine for him." Adelaide shook her head mournfully. "Then he called me in, and he said, 'Do you know where my will is?' and I said, 'I believe so, sir,' and he said…"

Things continued in this vein for some time, until at last, Adelaide came to the crux of the matter. Mabel leaned forward.

"I wrote down word for word what Mr. Crawford told me, and—I can't remember just how he put it, but he changed his will, so his nephew Ricky didn't get anything, but I got five hundred dollars. His church got something too. I guess the only change, from what I heard later, was he took Ricky right off and put in Ben Holt instead."

Here, a small sigh escaped Adelaide's lips. Mabel remembered her reputed crush on the old man's secretary-companion. There seemed to have been a lot of love in the air back then. Cupid must have been shooting his arrows right and left, but so far, none of the budding romances Mabel had heard about had come to anything in the end.

"It was so unfair. I heard what Mr. Crawford wanted to do with his money, right from the horse's mouth, and I wrote it all down just like he said, and he signed it. I signed it too and put it in the mailbox, just like he said. Later that night, well… Do you want some more cookies?"

To Mabel's horror, she realized while she'd been listening to Adelaide, she had eaten every single cookie and square of fudge on her plate. "Uh, no, thanks. Go ahead with your story."

Adelaide dunked another cookie in her hot chocolate. A moment later, no doubt having found the hot chocolate not so hot, she got to her feet to hobble to the microwave.

Mabel hopped up. "I'll do that. You go on with what you were saying."

"Well, now, this is the sad part, and I hate to tell it. Later that night, Mr. Crawford passed into glory, God rest his soul. I felt so bad he was all alone at the end." Adelaide's eyes welled with tears, and Mabel could never doubt Crawford had had a loyal and caring housekeeper in her. "Ben had come down to work right then, and he always checked on Mr. Crawford first thing, which I did too. So, we walked in together, and I said, "Time to rise and shine," like I always did, as I opened his bedroom draperies.

"Mr. Crawford, he always used to grumble at that, but I knew he secretly liked our little routine. That morning, though, he didn't say a word, being dead as he was, though I didn't know it quite yet. I was too upset to do a thing, but Ben went right over and checked his pulse and then he shook his head and said, 'He's gone, Addy.'"

At that, Adelaide sobbed and put a hand over her mouth, clearly reliving the emotions of that moment. Mabel rested her hand over Adelaide's till the sobs subsided.

Adelaide pulled a tissue from the deep pocket of her quilted robe, held it to her nose, and blew a vigorous blast. When she was composed enough to go on, she said, "Ben held me and patted my back." She gave Mabel a somewhat watery smile at that. "And then, he called the police, and a minute after that, I called to let Ricky know."

"How did he take it?"

Mabel wasn't sure Adelaide had heard her, but her question was answered anyway.

"I told him Mr. Crawford was gone, and I was sorry for his loss, and do you know what he said to me? All he said was 'thanks,' and then hung up."

"Wow." Mabel understood people had different reactions to grief, but Ricky's response seemed uncommonly cold.

"He never did show up at the house that day at all. In fact, I called him the night before too, and told him, 'Ricky, your uncle is doing real poorly. I think he might be near the end this time, in case you want to come see him once more.

"Of course, he never did come then either, when he might have given Mr. Crawford that bit of comfort, having his solitary living relative with him. The first we saw him there at the house afterward was a few days after Mr. Crawford passed, looking over his inheritance." Adelaide's disgust was written in the downturn of her cheerful mouth.

Mabel had so many questions, if only she could make Adelaide hear them. She cleared her throat. "Do you have any idea why Mr. Crawford would disinherit his own flesh and blood and leave everything to his secretary?"

Adelaide's eyes widened. "Haven't I been telling you? Ricky didn't give a fig for his uncle. He only ever called or came by when he wanted money. It was shameful, and it hurt Mr. Crawford—I know it did."

Mabel wondered if she could get a straight answer about Ben Holt—one uncolored by Adelaide's girlish crush on the man. All she could do was try.

"I take it Mr. Holt treated Mr. Crawford better than that?"

"Oh, my goodness, yes. He lived right there, of course, so he saw Mr. Crawford all the time. He was so considerate of him." Adelaide patted her heart.

"Do you believe Mr. Holt was honest?"

'Oh, yes. I never doubted that, and neither did Mr. Crawford."

In Mabel's experience, a little bit of doubt was often a good thing.

"He wasn't after Mr. Crawford's money, if that's what you mean. When the new will disappeared from the mail the next day, and Ricky was set to inherit the money, I told everybody who'd listen that there was a new will in Ben's favor. Ben was shocked to hear about it—Mr. Crawford never said a word to him—but he refused to fight. I'd have testified for him in court, but he said no."

"Does Ben Holt still live around here, do you know?"

"What?" Adelaide shook her head and cupped a hand to her ear. "Would you like more coffee?"

"No, thank you." Mabel repeated her question.

Adelaide sighed. "No. He moved on not long after the funeral. Never did hear what became of him."

"What about Ricky? He's still around, isn't he?"

"Who?"

"Ricky."

"The lord of the manor." Adelaide sniffed. "Still living it up in Mr. Crawford's house. Got himself married soon after his uncle passed away, God rest his soul. It was a real fairytale romance, some say.

"Married that Abramovich girl that lost her sister. People said it was such a blessing amidst all that grief, but he was no prize. They never did have any kids, but they're still up there. He never had to work a day in his life afterward, not that he worked all that much before, anyway."

Ricky was married to Cathy's sister—Mabel's mind churned to digest this new bit of information, linking Ricky to the dead woman. "You don't like him." Mabel stated the obvious.

"I pray every day for his benighted, heathen soul," Adelaide said comfortably. "But no, I never did."

Mabel wrestled with how to phrase her other questions delicately. Well, anyone who credited Ricky Putnam with a benighted, heathen soul was likely to be entertaining suspicions of her own, and Mabel wanted to hear what they were.

She patted Adelaide's plump, soft hand. "Please don't take this wrong, ma'am, but why do you say that? Is it because he neglected his uncle, or do you… You don't think he…?"

For all her cheeriness and chatter, Adelaide fixed her with a shrewd look. "Do I think he bumped Mr. Crawford off?"

Mabel gasped. That thought had never occurred to her. From the other room the Andrews Sisters sang *Santa Claus Is Coming to Town*…a fitting soundtrack to this discussion of what Ricky had been up to, right before Christmas, 1962.

"No," the old woman said with seeming reluctance. "I never saw Ricky as a murderer. He didn't have the gumption."

Mabel pulled herself together. "I didn't mean to suggest he

did anything of the kind." As the words left her mouth, she real-ized she sort of *had* meant to suggest something of the kind—albeit with a different victim…or two.

"What I meant to ask was whether you believed Ricky might somehow have gotten hold of the second will and maybe disposed of it. Is there some way he could've found out that he'd been dis-inherited?"

Adelaide didn't say anything right away. She'd been looking right at Mabel while she was speaking though, so hopefully, she'd heard and understood the question.

Finally, Adelaide nodded. "My fool brother Harry ran into him down at Doc's bar the same evening the will was signed. He told Ricky right to his face."

Chapter Twenty-Nine

MABEL COULDN'T SETTLE DOWN TO HER writing. For starters, all the cookies and candy had given her a bellyache, as her mother had always warned her. She also struggled with what she'd learned about Ricky Putnam and his uncle's will. If he had heard about his disinheritance the same day the will was executed, wouldn't he have stolen it out of the mailbox that very night?

If that's the way things happened, Ricky would have had no reason to go anywhere near the mail route the next day or to attack Lester. Maybe he didn't know the will was already outside? Maybe he'd only decided to go check the next day, after it had already been picked up. She should've asked Adelaide if Harry was still living—or if she knew whether he'd blabbed to Ricky about the will already having been stuck in the mailbox outside the Crawford mansion.

She picked up her phone. Almost four. She hadn't heard from John since last night and wondered if he was still on the trail of Cathy Abramovich's two boyfriends. He was supposed to be here for dinner at six, so she guessed she'd have to be patient.

Lisa might be free by now, but she'd been working and wouldn't have had time to locate the disgruntled coworker Jerry Kalchik yet. Once again, Mabel reminded herself to be patient, though she didn't feel like waiting.

Nita. Mabel could get hold of Nita at Readers' Retreat and let her know what Aunt Adelaide had told her.

She settled herself in Grandma's rocker and dialed. Koi leapt into her lap the instant her bottom hit the hand-sewn chair pad. Stroking the cat with one hand, she heard the phone ring at the other end.

Nita picked up. "Mabel?" Her voice was muffled. "You'll never guess who's in the store right now."

"You're right." Mabel frowned. "Who is it?"

"Bonnie Putnam. She's shopping for Christmas presents."

"What?"

"Ricky Putnam's wife, Bonnie," Nita hissed. "She never comes in here. She's been asking advice on what to buy. If you come right now, you can get a peek at both of them—Ricky dropped her off, so he'll be coming to pick her up."

Mabel wasn't sure what a peek would do for her, but curiosity won out. "I'll be there."

Koi held onto Mabel's sweater when she tried to ease her onto the floor. One by one, Mabel pried the cat's hooks from the cable knit. Snags occurred.

"Come on, sweetie, let go. I've got to get to the bookstore before our suspect arrives."

As if sensing an opportunity to be of assistance, Barnacle jumped up, planting his big paws halfway on Mabel's knees and halfway on the cat. Koi screeched and spat. She yanked her paw out of the sweater knit, leaving a small hole and a huge snag as she pulled free and shot across the kitchen with Barnacle in pursuit.

Koi leapt onto the Hoosier cupboard shelf and then vaulted to the top, where she perched with her fur blown out to epic proportions. Barnacle stood on his hind legs, front paws resting on the Hoosier shelf. As he danced around, Mabel's stacks of paper and miscellaneous small items from pens to vitamin containers fell to the floor. The dog barked with the ferocity of a hound treeing a coon, but his happy grin said it was all a good-natured game.

"Barnacle!" Mabel shrieked. "Get down."

The dog dropped to all fours and turned to smile at her, dripping drool, his fluffy tail gently wagging. From her vantage point, Koi hissed her lack of appreciation for the game.

"Good boy," Mabel said with mixed emotions. He *had* obeyed when she told him to stop. "It's not a game if the other guy isn't having a good time, though, all right?"

After reassuring her unhappy cat, Mabel studied her damaged sweater with a rueful eye—she hoped she could pull that snag through to the back side and close up the hole, so it didn't show so much. Oh, well, at the moment, she needed to hustle. She tugged her coat over the damage, grabbed her purse, and headed for the door.

When Mabel pulled into a space a couple of blocks from the bookshop, she couldn't help noticing the brand-new Land Rover parked right in front of the store. She raised an eyebrow at the RICKYP vanity plate. "Looks like Bonnie's ride is here," she muttered.

Mabel stepped inside the store. The bell above the door woke Tabasco, who'd been sleeping in the window. He growled with his eyes half open before flopping onto his side with a groan and closing them again.

"Hi, Mabel." Zac smiled at her from his spot atop a rolling ladder as he was shelving an armload of books. "You shopping or visiting? If you want Nita, she's in back with a pair of customers." He rolled his eyes for Mabel's benefit.

Mabel hesitated. "Maybe I should stay up here and browse a bit till she's free."

He beckoned her closer. "I put out some new cozy mysteries on the end cap back there. You might want to peruse them while you're waiting."

"Um, sure." Mabel loved cozies, as Zac must have known, but from his winking, and shooing gestures with the book he was holding, she guessed his main goal was to get her into a good spot to observe the Putnams.

As she wandered casually toward the back, she could hear a woman talking. Mabel positioned herself in front of the "New Paperback Releases" at the end of the mystery shelves. She picked up the latest in a favorite series of hers and flipped it over as if to study the back cover copy—not that she needed to. She knew she'd be buying this one.

From her vantage point a few yards from the register, she had a clear view of a well-heeled couple...their backs, at least.

The well-preserved older woman wore a long, fuzzy, green plaid coat with tall brown leather boots. This had to be Bonnie Putnam. Her silver-streaked brown hair was cut in an expensive-looking bob that just crested her coat collar. Mabel didn't like most showy, high-end bags, and the big purse resting on Nita's counter was no exception, but she could tell even from here that the price tag on that one had been a doozy.

As Bonnie went on talking, the man next to her shifted his feet, and his shoulders lifted in a sigh.

As well put together as his wife, he wore a camel woolen dress coat with a plush fur collar over velvety, dark-brown, wide-wale corduroy pants and polished loafers. His steel gray hair was still full and obviously styled.

Mabel was in the process of studying the man's impatient body language when he turned and looked straight at her. Instantly, she dropped her eyes to the book in her hand.

She'd seen Ricky Putnam before, behind her at the post office counter when she'd been investigating the origin of the mysterious Christmas card. He'd been annoyed then too—at her, for taking too long.

From the deep lines etched in Putnam's face, Mabel reflected that if he'd killed to inherit his fortune, it hadn't made him a happy man. She ventured another peek through her lashes.

He had turned back to the counter and was taking out his wallet. While he paid the bill, his wife stepped away, as if watching the transaction was in poor taste.

Bonnie walked past Mabel and paused to run her fingers over one of the silklike scarves displayed on a rack. All had literary themes. This one was imprinted with books and teapots.

Mrs. Putnam had scarcely touched the scarf before dropping

it with an expression of distaste.

Must be polyester.

"Zac," Nita called.

When he appeared, she gestured at two bulging cloth Reader's Retreat shopping totes. "Would you please carry these to the car for Mr. and Mrs. Putnam?"

"Sure thing."

Zac trailed after the couple, giving Mabel a smirk as he went by.

Mabel scooted to the counter. Nita sat on the stool, eyes closed and fanning herself with an advertising circular.

"Are you okay?" It was only now occurring to Mabel that Nita had just been forced to conduct a polite business transaction with the man who might well have killed her great-uncle.

Nita nodded and opened one eye. "I worked for it, but that was more than a $700 sale. They aren't either of them book people, but they wanted tasteful gifts for the folks on their list, and they wanted it all 'one and done.' We walked around here for over an hour, and I had to ask questions about everybody from their relatives to the housekeeper and Ricky's accountant, so I could suggest books they might enjoy."

"Wow. That's quite a job. I couldn't have begun to do that."

Nita shrugged. "I'm an independent bookseller. I know books, and I'm used to hand selling." She winked. "Plus, how could I mind getting gifted the perfect opportunity to ask a lot of nosy questions?"

"Ooh…" Mabel tipped an imaginary hat. "Well done."

Nita grinned. "Sometimes you get lucky."

"I was afraid it was painful for you having to be all nice and polite to the guy who maybe murdered somebody in your family and then made himself rich off of it."

Nita pushed herself onto her feet. "Didn't let myself think about it. Felt a bit queasy at first, but then I just thought of it as part of our investigation." She winked. "And about the money, naturally."

"Naturally."

The bell over the door rang, and a moment later, Zac appeared, bringing a breath of cold air with him from outside. He stretched out a twenty-dollar bill so they could see and beamed. "Nice tip."

"I should've carried their dang books myself," Nita grumbled with a grin. "Hey, my girl and I are gonna go back to the office for a bit. That woman walked my feet off."

As Zac headed back to shelving, Nita opened the door behind the counter. Gaiters the office cat looked down from atop the office bookshelves and yawned.

"Want a coffee or tea? My mom and dad gave me one of those pod coffeemakers for the office as an early Christmas present. It's my new toy."

Mabel eyed it with suspicion. "Is it hard to use?"

"Easy peasy. Look through that basket and pick what you want. I'll show you how it's done."

Mabel dug through dark roasts, light roasts, green tea, chai tea, cider…her brain was starting to feel overwhelmed.

"There's flavors on the bottom. I don't like them, but knowing you, I imagine there's something down there to tickle your fancy."

Plunging her fingers all the way down, Mabel came up with a pumpkin spice. She knew the fall season was over, but not for her. "Here we go."

When Nita had delivered a perfect coffee and gestured for Mabel to take the cushy armchair, she made herself a boring black coffee and took it to her desk. "So, do you want to hear what I learned from the Putnams or fill me in on Ms. Adelaide's story?"

Gaiters leapt from the bookcase and landed with delicate feet on the end table next to Mabel, narrowly missing her cup of coffee. Mabel picked her drink up just as the cat stuck his little pink nose over the rim.

"I guess I can go first. Adelaide told me a couple things. She confirmed everything Acey said earlier. Plus, she was sure Ricky knew he'd been disinherited the night before Lester and the will disappeared. Her brother Harry ran into him at the bar and told him so."

Nita paused with her mug a couple of inches from her lips and fixed Mabel with a thoughtful look. "Which was also the night old Mr. Crawford died."

Mabel stared. "Are you thinking…?"

Nita set her drink down. "Well, you have to wonder, don't you? Bump the old guy off, steal the will, and bam, you're rich."

"I can't believe you and Adelaide both went there. It never even occurred to me that Ricky might have murdered his uncle. I must be unusually dull-witted." Mabel shook her head. "Though Adelaide said she didn't think Ricky had the gumption to have killed Crawford, anyhow."

Nita picked up her cup again. "Doesn't mean he didn't."

"No, I guess not but there didn't seem to be any suspicion of that at the time. The death went down as natural. What I don't understand…" Mabel paused. "Well, two things. First, if Ricky knew the night before, wouldn't he have snagged the will out of the mailbox right away? Then, he never would've had to grab the mailbag from Lester at all, right?"

Nita stroked her chin. "True. Adelaide for sure put it in there?"

"She says she did."

"I'm not sure what to think about that." Nita leaned back in her desk chair and turned to look out the high window behind her desk. She spun back. "Maybe he was too drunk to go get it."

Mabel shrugged. That explanation seemed flimsy to her.

"Well, let's put that aside for the moment." Nita sipped her coffee. "What else don't you understand?"

"The other murder. Cathy Abramovich. Everybody thinks your great-uncle Lester must've killed her and that's why he ran off, right? I keep coming back to her, because even if Ricky had a motive to kill Lester, why would he kill her?"

"Maybe…" Nita paused as if in thought. "We need to do some digging there. See if we can find a link between him and Cathy. She was very pretty—you saw the newspaper pictures. For all we know, he could've been involved with her too. Might've been a love triangle."

"Good thought. Adelaide gave me another unbelievable link I'll share in just a minute—not sure it provides a motive though." Mabel straightened. "Or considering where the house is, she could've witnessed Lester's murder, and he had to eliminate her."

"Ooh, I like that."

Mabel sagged again. "That sure complicates things. Because now Ricky's got the mailbag and two dead bodies. One's out on the street on full display if somebody comes by, and…"

"Yeah, her body was inside the house. How'd that come about? Did he chase her inside? And you're right. How's he gonna dispose of both bodies plus the mailbag before someone comes along? Where would he take 'em?"

"Well, the murders could've been unrelated, I guess." Mabel pulled out her tiny notebook and scribbled a reminder to ask John about Cathy Abramovich's time of death.

She tapped her pen on her chin. "Here's the other thing Adelaide told me. Bonnie Putnam was Cathy Abramovich's sister."

"No way."

Mabel nodded. "Quite a coincidence, huh? What if Ricky married her to quiet any suspicions of his involvement with Cathy or her death?"

Nita slammed her hand on her desk, sloshing coffee. "Hey, maybe she discovered something questionable." She mopped the puddle with a wad of tissues. "Aren't spouses prevented from testifying against their partners?"

Mabel waggled a hand. "I doubt she'd have married him if she knew."

"Maybe she didn't know what she knew."

Mabel processed that sentence and decided to move on. "Maybe. Now, what did you find out about the Putnams?"

"Not a whole lot," Nita admitted. "But it was amazing how rich they are and how alone in the world. You know who they were buying for? Of course, you don't—I'll tell you. His accountant, the housekeeper, a gardener, their financial advisor…who else, now?"

Nita took a swallow of coffee and grimaced. "Excuse me." She walked over to the coffeemaker and made herself a fresh cup.

"Okay, now. This ought to lubricate my brain. I guess that might be all the people who work for them that I can recall right now, not that it matters. Then, they also bought for her handful of friends from the club and his golf buddies. That's it. One cousin, but no other family at all."

Mabel quirked the corner of her mouth. "I guess that makes sense for him, at least, if he was Mr. Crawford's only surviving heir. Plus, they might have bought something else already, you know. Not everybody buys for extended family."

"I guess you're right, but she said they were doing their whole list all at once. I hear what you're saying about extended family, and I hope for their sake they've got someone. When you get older, you ought to have at least a few relatives to fall back on. Like you say though, Ricky looks like the last of his line. She talked like she was too."

"What did she say?"

"I made a point to ask about family." Nita winked. "Like, did she need anything for family—and she said, nope, everyone was gone. Her parents and sister were all she'd had, and now they were gone too."

"Sad." Mabel tried but found it hard to dredge up any warm feelings for the snooty pair. "At least, they have each other."

Nita snorted. "That's the other thing. They don't strike me as a couple of lovebirds, either. He just dropped her off to do their Christmas shopping, and when she called for him to come pay for the books and pick her up, I could hear them squawking at each other. She wanted him to pick out his own books for his golf buddies, and he wanted no part of that. Said he'd as soon buy them a bottle of something. And when it came time to pay—whoo-ee!"

Mabel shrugged. "Sounds like a lot of couples, from my experience. Not to mention this is the Ho-Ho-holiday shopping season. Tempers fray."

"You got that right. I deal with the public, and it isn't pretty."

"It goes to show you," Mabel said. "Money won't buy happiness. If Ricky killed your great uncle, and maybe Cathy too, what did it get him? Nice clothes, a fancy house and car—so what?"

Nita tilted her head and looked at Mabel. "Am I a bad person for hoping he's miserable?"

Mabel hesitated. She knew what Grandma might say, but she also had more than an inkling of how Nita felt. "I think that's natural. Sometimes it's hard to feel the way we think we should. Feelings don't always behave."

"They sure don't." Nita blew out a big puff of air. "Dr. King said, 'The arc of the moral universe is long, but it bends toward justice.' Well, I believe there's justice in heaven, but for once I'd like to feel there's some kind of justice down here somewhere."

"Me too." With a sigh, Mabel dislodged Gaiters and set him on the floor before getting up. "Which means I guess we need to keep plugging."

Chapter Thirty

JOHN ARRIVED EARLY FOR DINNER, CARRYING a bouquet of white carnations and sturdy spruce and holly. He caught Mabel in the middle of cleaning the tiny half-bath under the stairs. At the knock on the door, she jumped up from wiping down the floor with sanitizer and whacked her head on the low, sloping ceiling.

"Ow! Darn it." She pulled off a rubber glove and rubbed her head on the way to her kitchen door. She'd hoped to change clothes and freshen up before John arrived.

Barnacle jumped at the door, barking, slobbering, and leaving snout marks on the glass. The moment she opened the door, the dog threw himself on John, about bowling him over.

John thrust the flowers at Mabel with a laugh. "Hi, you two!" He grabbed Barnacle by the ruff and gave him an affectionate little shake while the grinning dog whined and tried to lick John's face.

Mabel rolled her eyes. She guessed she ought to be offended that her boyfriend greeted her dog before her, but it was kind of sweet. Their happy interlude also gave her a moment to peel off her other rubber glove and run a hand through her tangled hair.

Once Barnacle had settled down, John pulled Mabel in for a kiss. "I'm a bit early—sorry."

She wondered if he mentioned that because she smelled of cleanser. "I'm glad you're early. I did want to change clothes though—can you give me a minute? I've been cleaning."

"Go right ahead. I hope you weren't cleaning just for me."

"Well, I do clean for myself from time to time, you know."

"I'm sure you do." He grinned. "I didn't mean to suggest otherwise. Does Barnacle need to go out?"

"Would you mind? That would be great if you'd put him out on his run. Or his leash is hanging over there, if you'd rather walk him up the block. He'd love that."

"I would too. If it were daylight, I'd take him into the park." Barnacle perked up.

"Shh. He knows more than the 'W' word—if you say, 'P-A-R-K,' he's ready to charge."

While John wrangled the squirming dog onto his leash, Mabel hurried upstairs to wash and change. If she was quick enough, she might have time to straighten up a bit downstairs before man and dog returned. Contrary to what she'd suggested, she *had* been cleaning just for John, and she wasn't done yet.

By the time they got back, Barnacle bursting through the door with enough force to make it thump against the wall, Mabel had managed to dash and stash the kitchen and living room into some approximation of order. "Hey, guys, chow time."

Koi oozed out from under the Hoosier cupboard and went to inspect John's feet and pantlegs. He reached down to let her sniff his hand before rubbing her chin.

Now, why couldn't John's jealous cat Billie Jean be that hospitable to Mabel?

After John had hung his coat on a peg by the door, he came up behind Mabel while she was dishing up pet food and wrapped his arms around her. This gave her a little shiver that distracted her completely from what she was doing.

He planted a kiss on the back of her neck before stepping back and holding out a hand. "Once you get those filled, hand them to me, and I'll feed the livestock."

Minutes later, the animals were eating, and Mabel was passing John containers of leftovers from dinner with the Bedfords. This was less efficient than it might have been because John kept prying off the lids and peeking at the contents.

"Oh, my gosh, this food." He sniffed. "These smoky greens.

They must have bacon in them."

"I'm sure your arteries will survive one night of red meat and carbs."

"No, of course. All of this looks and smells fantastic. Are these…" Another sniff. "Shrimp étouffée?"

"Yep. You wouldn't believe the variety—and amount—of food in that kitchen."

"I'm not a fanatic," John said. "I enjoy an occasional splurge—like when somebody's put the time and TLC into a beautiful meal like this."

"I'm glad. Otherwise, it's all on me. Barnacle, get down." Mabel shoved at the dog with her hip. "I'd better give them a bit more to occupy their attention."

John grinned. "He's simply offering to help take care of the surplus. Why not let me bribe them while you get the rest of the food out? Tell me what to do."

It was pleasant, working together. While John picked up the bowls and added a smidge more pet food, she finished setting the beautiful array of leftovers out on the table and Hoosier shelf, the way they were, figuring John could pick and choose whatever he wanted and microwave them on one plate.

Sadly, Mabel soon realized she had very few serving spoons. This was puzzling, since she remembered a great army of spoons, ladles, and serving forks from holiday meals here in her youth. Since moving here several months ago, she hadn't needed more than one at a time. Pulling out a few soup spoons to fill the gap in inventory, she filed the small problem of the missing spoons away in the back of her brain as a mystery for another day.

By the time she'd brought out plates, bowls, napkins, and cutlery, Barnacle was plowing through his second helping, sending kibble flying around him. Koi sat plumped next to her bowl, nibbling one bite at a time, fluffy tail curled around her body.

When Mabel and John settled to eat, John asked her to fill

him in on what she and Nita had discovered before he told her what he'd learned about the Abramovich police file. It was impossible to eat much and tell John what they'd learned at the same time. As a result, her food was already getting cold when John excused himself to refill his plate.

Mabel stared. "I've never seen you do that."

"What?"

"Go for seconds."

"These aren't seconds. I wanted to try a taste of everything, so I just took a tiny spoonful of what would fit on my plate to start."

"Ahh… Well, I guess I've finished what Nita and I had to report, so I'm going to gobble this down and then grab some dessert. That makes it your turn to report, okay?"

The microwave timer dinged, and John removed his plate. "Why don't we finish eating first? All right?"

"Sure. We can be civilized."

John laughed. "I suppose I wasn't, since I made you talk while I snarfed my food."

"Help with the dishes and we'll call it square."

"Sounds like a good deal to me." John threw a look over his shoulder at the food containers. "Since we don't have any prep dishes or utensils—and we didn't even empty the containers we started with."

After dinner, Mabel returned the leftovers to the fridge while John stood at the sink and washed. She couldn't help imagining how nice it would be to have him here all the time…not as domestic help, but as her husband. Her heart did a little dance.

As if he'd heard her heart doing the buck-and-wing behind him, John looked back and smiled. "Almost done."

"Me too."

They'd decided to wait and eat dessert later, when their meal had had a chance to settle. "I'll make tea," Mabel said, "to be followed by your debriefing." While she was boiling water, John took a moment to drag the hassock over in front of the fireplace and hang the angel above the nativity.

As soon as John sat on the couch a few minutes later, Koi leapt onto his lap as usual. Mabel hesitated, then plopped down in Grandma's recliner. If she sat next to John, things might get too distracting for her to pay adequate attention to his report.

Barnacle looked from one to the other, yawned, then dropped his bulk onto Mabel's foot. At least her faithful Velcro dog hadn't abandoned her for another.

"So, tell all. Did you manage to find either of Cathy Abramovich's boyfriends?"

He grinned. "I did, in fact."

"Yeah?" Mabel sat up straight, a bit of a feat since she had to leverage herself out of the depths of the saggy recliner.

John nodded. "Neither's decrepit either. Bud, who used to be in and out of trouble for his temper, got drafted. The service seems to have settled him down. He went to school on the GI Bill, is twice divorced, playing the field of local widows at the moment, and a grandfather of five."

Mabel thought. "I'm glad he cleaned up his act, but that doesn't necessarily have a lot to do with who he was in 1962."

John acknowledged her point with a thumbs-up.

"You said 'local.' Where's Bender now?"

"You must not attend local theater productions. He's the director of the Medicine Spring Playhouse—has been ever since he retired as a high school English teacher ten or fifteen years ago. He acted in their productions before that."

"I've never been to a single show. I guess I was busy moving in and trying to get a job. I think they knocked off for the season right about the time I started getting involved with all the volunteering and writing."

"And murders." John lifted a corner of his mouth and both eyebrows at Mabel.

"I wouldn't say I get involved with them. They just happen, and there I am." She hated when people suggested she had some sort of sick hobby involving homicide. John was clearly only joking, but even he was doing it.

"To be fair, I've tended to be on the scene too," John admitted. "Though that only started since you moved here."

"Stop it." Mabel covered her ears.

John came over and gave her a hug. "I'm kidding—but you can still see a Bud Bender production before the ball drops on New Year's Eve. The Playhouse is reopened for a limited run of *A Christmas Carol*. They do it every year to benefit Children's Hospital."

"That might be fun."

"It is—if we can get seats. It's very popular. They do a meet-and-greet reception with the director and cast in the lobby afterward."

Was John asking her to go to the show with him? "Do you want to go?" Mabel asked.

"Sure. We can combine business with pleasure."

"The only commitment I have right now is choir practice Tuesday night." Mabel's heart took a little dip, along with her stomach. "But something else might crop up. It's a busy time of year."

"Right. Let's see if I can get tickets, and we can nail down a date before I leave. Hang on."

John pulled out his phone. Several minutes later, he'd managed to get them seats for an upcoming performance. "Whew. I was beginning to think we were out of luck."

Mabel entered the date and time on her online calendar. "Wait a sec." She ran into the kitchen and wrote the same info down on her wall calendar.

"Belt and suspenders, huh?"

Mabel shrugged. "It's complicated, okay?"

"Whatever works for you." John raised both hands in surrender. "Now, the second boyfriend—who was the most recent man in Cathy's life at the time of the murder—"

"Mark Enlow," Mabel interrupted.

"Your memory serves." He winked. "Enlow seemed a bit more serious relationship. The police interviews with family and friends, for the most part, said they'd met and liked him, unlike Bud, whom she'd kept more on the down low. She'd brought Enlow to a couple parties and it seems like he'd met her parents."

Mabel paused in scribbling notes. Though John had met her sister, she still hadn't introduced him to her parents. She'd never met his, either. Would one of them take that step over Christmas?

"Mabel? You zoned out again."

"Oh, sorry. You said, 'seemed like' he'd met her parents?"

"Yeah, guessing he did, but then the chief returned from lunch, so I never did get to finish reading that part of the file. In fact, I'd barely gotten to the boyfriends when my friend snatched away the folder."

"What makes you think he'd met the family?"

"One of the parents—mom, I think—was quoted as saying she'd thought they might make a good couple, and Cathy had seemed happy with him. She just hoped…something I didn't get to read."

"John! You missed the most important part."

"Maybe so. That's why I need to go back."

Mabel finished writing what "mom" said, and looked up, pen poised. "Where can we find Enlow?"

"*You* aren't going to find him. I'll pursue the boyfriend angle myself." From the firm set of John's chin, Mabel realized she'd have to do an end run to get the information she wanted.

John cleared his throat. "What are you looking at now?"

"I messaged Lisa earlier about Bonnie Putnam being Cathy's sister." Mabel exited her phone screen. "I'm wondering why I haven't heard anything back. I thought she'd call or text about Lester's coworker by now. She was going to follow up on him."

"She worked today, right? Plus, she's probably caught up with some wedding nonsense or—" John froze. "I didn't mean 'nonsense.'"

Mabel stared. Was this what he thought?

"That came out wrong. I meant 'wedding stuff.' All the traditional event-related mysteries men are not privy to."

John looked so sheepish and repentant Mabel couldn't bring herself to call him on it. Being on the practical side herself—and more than a little introverted—she even had to admit she'd be more than willing to skip a lot of the hoopla, given the choice.

His Freudian slip, though—if that's what it was—did make her wonder if his negative opinions about weddings ran deeper. What did that mean for their relationship long term?

The awkward moment passed, and John nicely made up for it. They enjoyed an assortment of desserts over more tea, and John ceded the larger sliver of hummingbird cake to Mabel. As he was leaving, he gathered her into a big hug and pressed a kiss on her forehead.

"Thanks for sharing the bounty. I'll call you tomorrow, okay?"

Mabel nodded but felt somewhat blue. They'd learned a few things, but it still didn't seem like they'd gotten very far toward finding Lester's killer, let alone Cathy's. Theories—even strong theories—were all well and good, but they weren't admissible in court.

Chapter Thirty-One

Mabel had been watching for Lisa's car and ran out as soon as it pulled into Mabel's driveway. The moment she'd hopped in and buckled, Lisa began backing out.

"Where are we going?" Mabel stared at her friend's profile. "You're being awful mysterious."

Lisa smiled. "I am, and I'm enjoying it, so just relax and wait for the big reveal."

"I'd been starting to wonder where you were. I told John last night I was expecting to hear back from you."

"I'm sorry. I was on the phone with Tim, and it got late. By the time we got off, I knew you'd still be up, but I needed to get to bed. We're rehearsing for the kindergarten program on top of all our regular reading and math work, and it's been like directing a show at the zoo…heavy on monkeys."

"Do kids that young get winter break fever?"

"You're kidding, right? Every passing day is another step deeper into kiddie madness."

"Be sure to tell me when your program is, and I'll put it on my calendar." Mabel's queasy stomach rolled over. Her December and January calendar pages were already too full, with Christmas and New Year's activities, the wedding frenzy…and *O, Holy Night.*

She swallowed. "Did I tell you what I got roped into at church?"

"Yeah." Lisa darted a sidelong glance at her. "You joined the choir. How's that going?"

"Like the last few yards on my way to the gallows."

Lisa snorted. "Come on now, Mary, Queen of Scots. I know

you have issues about singing, but that's rather, shall we say, extreme? You're part of a group—lots of cover. It's not like you have to stand up there and sing a solo, is it?"

Mabel shot Lisa a brooding look through lowered brows. "In fact, it's exactly like that. I'm supposed to sing *O, Holy Night* with no back-up but the organ. I'm Gladys Knight without the Pips. No, even worse—I'm Elvis Presley without the Jordanaires."

Lisa's jaw dropped. Her glance telegraphed alarm. "Oh, honey, I'm sorry. How'd that happen? What do you mean…Elvis?"

Mabel explained about the vacant tenor section, and Clive's fleeing the country. "So I guess not having a girl's voice means now I've got to sing a man's solo."

"Listen, Mabel. A quote-unquote girl's voice is whatever the good Lord gave you. You obviously have a girl's voice, and you can totally do this. Women sing tenor all the time…or at least it's not uncommon. It's an honor being asked to sing a solo—you'd agree if it was someone else being asked, wouldn't you?"

"I wish they were, but they're not." Mabel grabbed her hair with both hands. "I'm dreading this. As soon as I start feeling like maybe I can do it, my nerves take over again."

Lisa hesitated, as if reflecting on what to say. "You're a good singer, Mabel Browne. You've always been a good singer. You're not an eight-year-old kid anymore. We both know kids can be cruel. Believe me—I spend six hours a day with them, and my kids are still young enough to be on the sweeter side."

Mabel knew she was still acting like she was in third grade, but the fact remained—she had messed up. That little girl still lived inside her. She didn't want to debate Lisa over it. "Hey, you never told me what you learned about Kalchik. Are we going to see him?"

"I'm, uh, still checking. I have a different surprise for you at the moment. "

Mabel narrowed her eyes. "Where *are* you taking me?"

"To see Santa."

Mabel rolled her eyes. When Lisa got like this, there was no use trying to pry anything out of her. On the other hand… She looked out the window. Lisa did seem to be driving in the direction of the mall.

Sure enough, Lisa turned on her left blinker at the intersection for the Countryside Outlet Shops. Mabel began to suspect she'd been shanghaied for another craft supply excursion for wedding reception favors.

"Do you mind if we stop at a couple places so I can look for gifts for my mom and dad?" Mabel asked. "They're both so hard to buy for—my dad in particular."

Again, Lisa gave her an enigmatic smile. "Of course. No problem."

Mabel's friend seemed extra perky, even for her. "That smile's starting to creep me out, *Mona* Lisa."

Mabel's snark only earned her another of those secretive smiles.

The vast outlet parking lot made Mabel want to hum the theme from *Oklahoma*. A fierce wind always came sweeping down the plain here, especially in the winter. Lisa had to park in the overflow lot. Mabel pulled her hood close to her cheeks and put her head down for the long hike to the nearest stores.

Carols floated on the frosty air from giant speakers, doing nothing to infect Mabel with Christmas cheer. When they reached the huge sports store, she veered in that direction. In part, because it was closest and presumably warm, and also because she was sure she could find socks or something for Dad.

Lisa grabbed her arm and tugged.

"But I wanted to look for something."

"Later, little elf."

Mabel dug in her pocket and found a tissue. The stinging

wind had made her eyes tear up and her nose run.

When she looked up again, they were standing in front of the department store outlet. A fake tree stood by the doors, draped with tinsel garland and hung with oversize plastic trumpets, drums, and gingerbread men. Mabel hustled past it into the embracing warmth of the building and the blare of *Here Comes Santa Claus*, competing with the forceful cheer of *Jingle Bells,* which still pursued them from the outside speakers as the doors were closing.

"Come on." Lisa gave Mabel's sleeve another tug.

They threaded their way, starting and stopping with many an "excuse me," through a crowd of bag-laden shoppers. Mabel scanned displays as they went, thinking her mother could always use another nice scarf or maybe some high-end face cream.

Lisa flung out an arm to stop Mabel. "There."

Mabel's gaze followed the direction of Lisa's head tip.

Fake snow covered a raised platform in a back corner near the toy section. Enormous candy canes stood in a curving row, holding up a rope line, which led to a couple of steps up onto the platform, where Santa sat enthroned. Young kids swarmed around the base, accompanied by harried-looking parents or grandparents. Many of the kids, dressed in their holiday best, were resistant or even crying.

Quite a few of the adults, Mabel couldn't help noticing, seemed near tears themselves as they coaxed, cajoled, tugged, or threatened their little angels. She shuddered, having found store Santas terrifying when she was a child. The resulting photos were never worth it.

"I guess you weren't kidding."

"I wasn't. There's your Santa—Mark Enlow."

Mabel squinted, trying to relate the jolly old elf before her with the grainy news photo she'd seen of a handsome young man. Of course, Santa costumes made a pretty impenetrable disguise.

Even if she'd known the guy before, all she could see of him at this point were eyes and a nose.

"You know," she said, "you hear about these suspects from back in the day, when they were young and fighting over a twenty-something girlfriend. It's hard to imagine them as eighty-year-old men. Let alone Santa Claus."

"Are you in line?" asked a strained female voice behind them.

"No," Mabel said at the same time Lisa said, "Yes."

Mabel stared at her friend.

"Which is it?" the voice asked.

"Um…" Mabel turned to see a woman with smudged eye makeup—were those tear stains?—surrounded by three squabbling boys between about ages two and six. The middle boy shoved the smallest one, sending him backward onto his bottom. The toddler wailed as the mom pulled him to his feet while delivering a scolding to the perpetrator.

"It's all right," Lisa said. "You can go ahead of us. Looks like you've got your hands full."

The woman cast a grateful look Lisa's way, as Lisa ushered them ahead and reached into her purse to pull out a plastic baggie. "Are they allowed a sticker?"

"I don't think some of them deserve it." The mom gave the shover a dirty look.

Lisa seemed to consider before holding out the bag to the aggressor. Mabel was sure this moment of pondering was an act, but it was pretty convincing. "How about we let this guy pick out two stickers? One for him and one for his little brother? Then, maybe we can let the youngest pick out stickers for both of them."

A smile started to relax the harried lines of the woman's face. "You must be a mom."

Lisa smiled and shook her head. "Teacher." She held out the bag to the naughty boy. "Which do you think your little brother would like?"

"What about me?" The oldest wormed his way close to Lisa.

"You look like a good boy. Is he a good boy, Mom?"

Mabel let Lisa do her thing, relieved to see the brothers settle down. While they went through the sticker bag, she studied the Santa. He seemed a natural for the role, patient and gentle with the kids—not bellowing that awful, hearty ho-ho-ho she'd hated as a child.

The line moved painfully slowly. When at last they'd gotten within a few spots from their goal, Lisa turned her attention back to Mabel.

"What's your plan here?" Mabel waved a hand toward the jolly man in the red suit.

"Oh, I figured you could casually say something like, 'Hey, aren't you Mark Enlow?'"

"Whoa. First of all, why am I the one asking him anything? And how are we supposed to explain our presence here to begin with? Maybe you haven't noticed, but we're the only fifty-year-old people in this line unaccompanied by children."

Lisa snapped her fingers. "Easy. You introduce yourself and ask if you can talk to him when he gets off, which should be…" She double-checked the sign. "In about half an hour. Tell him you're a writer doing research for a true-crime book and would like his recollections of Cathy Abramovich."

"But I'm not—" Mabel stopped mid-sputter. She wasn't writing a true-crime book about the Abramovich murder—but she could be.

"There." Lisa beamed. "You see. Two problems solved."

"I only see one problem solved." Mabel grumbled. "Yours. You cook up this scheme and then get me to carry it out."

"Well, I can hardly introduce myself as a kindergarten teacher and explain why *I'd* need to talk to him, can I?"

Lisa had her there. "What's the second problem solved?"

"Your next writing project, of course."

As if Mabel needed another writing project. Her volunteer book was barely creaking along, going nowhere fast. Besides which, she already had a true crime project—a complicated, multigenerational ax murder saga that she still hadn't figured out how to take hold of.

However, she had to admit it would be nice to have another project to work on, when she wanted to avoid working on the other two. Was that an unworthy thought?

"Hey, how did you find Enlow, anyway?"

"Elementary, dear Mabel. I called John to ask a question about Kalchik, and he'd located Enlow's home address. So, I decided to contact Enlow. His daughter told me where to find him."

"Does John know we're doing this?" Mabel asked uneasily, remembering his declaration that *he* would follow up with the boyfriends.

"Not yet. Shh…we're here." Lisa bounced up the steps with a happy smile for Santa.

The old man looked confused, scanning behind them for a tiny tot with his eyes all aglow. "Did you want to…see Santa?"

"We did," Lisa chirped.

"I can only see one of you at a time. And…" Santa's glance flitted over Mabel. "No sitting on Santa's lap."

He beckoned Lisa closer and lowered his voice, likely to avoid traumatizing the waiting children. "I don't ordinarily see adults. Is this for the photo? I suppose we could pose both of you with Santa, if you want. Were you good girls this year?"

"Of course, we were, but that isn't why we're here," Lisa said.

Santa's eyes widened and he beckoned for a helper elf. "If you're a process server or something like that, please leave. You'll upset the kids."

"Oh, good grief." Mabel stepped in front of Lisa. "I'm sorry to bother you at work, sir, but we—or, that is, I—was hoping you might be willing to chat with me—just for a moment—when you're done here."

"I don't understand."

"My name's Mabel Browne, and I'm a writer. I'm interested in doing a true-crime book about a young lady named Cathy Abramovich. I understand you knew her. Would you be willing to give me some insight into who she was? So I can flesh her out as a person, and not simply a crime victim."

Santa rested his head in a white-gloved hand. For a moment, Mabel was afraid he wouldn't say anything. Or that she'd given the old man a heart attack.

He looked up and waved the elf back before turning his attention to Mabel. "I loved her," he whispered. "I never would have hurt her. Do you understand? I couldn't tell you, even today, who might have killed her."

"I'm Ms. Browne's research assistant. Please," Lisa begged. "We're not here to accuse you of anything. We just want as much background as you can give us."

Mabel gave the old man an anxious look. "We understand this is painful."

"You have no idea." He heaved a sigh, already waving the next child in line forward. "Why not let her rest in peace?"

Mabel met his eyes, which at this point looked teary, above the Santa beard. "I want to honor her memory," she told him. "And get her story out there again in hopes of finally getting some answers about what happened to her."

She felt Lisa stiffen next to her, but as the old man gestured for them to move on and make room for the remaining children, he said, "Food Court in about half an hour. I'm running late." He gave them a look that spoke volumes as to why. "I'll be in blue plaid flannel and a gray jacket by the baked potato place."

Chapter Thirty-Two

"I DIDN'T REALIZE THIS PLACE HAD a food court." Mabel studied the posted menu while she and Lisa waited for Mark Enlow. "Some of these baked potatoes look delicious. I want to try the pizza supreme one. Doesn't it look good?"

"He ought to be here by now," Lisa fretted. "We should've kept an eye on him."

Mabel shrugged. "He must know we'd keep coming back. If we don't catch him today, we can still get a potato."

"Could you forget the potatoes for a minute? What did you think about Enlow?"

Mabel thought. "He seemed sincere to me. You know what's funny though, is I'm having the darnedest time not thinking of him as Santa, aren't you?"

"No, I'm not. We can't let ourselves start confusing a man who may be a cold-blooded killer with our cozy childhood impressions of Kris Kringle."

"Hey." Mabel pointed. "Isn't that him? Look. He's still wearing his beard. Maybe it's real."

Lisa gave Mabel the side-eye. "Maybe. Just don't say, 'Maybe he *is* Santa,' or I'll have to slap you to bring you back to your senses."

Enlow was remarkably agile and energetic for his age. As he approached, Mabel came close to making a joke about how Santa never aged, but she kept her mouth shut. She was pretty sure Lisa was kidding about that slap, but she didn't want to risk it.

Instead, she said, "Isn't it amazing how the senior citizens of Medicine Spring manage to stay so healthy and spry? Look at Miss Birdie and Ms. Katherine Ann. Almost makes you think those Medicine Spring waters are as healing as Native Americans claim."

"It kind of does," Lisa admitted. "Makes me glad I live here."

"Me too. Maybe only a legend, but why not keep that hope alive?"

As Enlow came within hailing distance, Lisa called, "Are you Santa?"

A smile split the old man's face. "No, he's very busy up at the North Pole right now, getting ready for Christmas Eve. I'm just one of his helpers."

"Well played." Lisa stuck out her hand and reintroduced herself.

Mabel also shook and repeated her name. "Can we buy you a potato?"

"No need. I'm not sure yet what I want, but I'll buy my own."

Enlow seemed to know the place well. He placed his order without glancing at the menu, then took a seat at a nearby table to wait.

"Do you eat here a lot?" Lisa asked.

Enlow nodded. "I'm here almost every day this time of year, and I know all the food court menus." He turned an eye on Mabel. "You're writing about Cathy?"

She hesitated. "Thinking about it." That much, at least, was true.

He sat and looked at her till it began to feel uncomfortable. "Why?"

Mabel darted a glance at Lisa. She hadn't expected to be the one being questioned.

Lisa took her cue. "It's unsolved after all these years. Plus, the unexplained disappearance of that mailman makes it all the more puzzling."

Enlow shook his head. "It was the worst day of my life."

"I'm sorry to bring up sad memories," Mabel said.

"I remember anyway." His gaze drifted far away from the busy food court. "Cathy was a nice girl—a good girl. She couldn't help attracting attention. She and I were never that serious—in fact, she told me she'd recently met somebody she thought might be 'the one.'"

"Who was that?" Lisa asked.

Enlow shook his head. "I never knew. It was very recent. I wish she'd gotten to live out her happiness."

"You weren't upset?" Mabel prodded.

"I was happy for her—like I said, we weren't serious, but she was still very special to me." Enlow gave her a quivering smile. "Sixty years later, I've got the most wonderful wife in the world, five kids that grew up to be a credit to us, eight grandkids, eleven greats…a satisfying career and a happy retirement. Despite all that, I still can't forget that awful day."

Mabel squelched an impulse to apologize and leave Enlow to his memories. "Do you mind telling us a bit about Cathy?"

He sighed and shook his head. "No."

"Your potato's ready," the counter attendant called.

"I'll get it," Lisa told him as he started to rise. "Can I pick anything else up for you?"

"Thanks. A packet of chives, salt, and pepper, and they should give you the plasticware and my cup of water."

"I'll be right back."

Enlow didn't wait to begin his story. "She was smart. That's the first thing you ought to know. Everybody talks about how beautiful she was, and that was true enough, but I loved how quick she was. She had a brain for physics like you wouldn't believe. It was wasted as a file clerk, but like a lot of girls back then, they didn't encourage them to use their potential. She had a great sense of humor… Oh, thank you, dear."

Lisa sat back down. "You're welcome." She seemed to accept Enlow's endearment as an inoffensive reflection of his vintage, as did Mabel.

"Mr. Enlow was just saying how bright Cathy was."

"A good student?"

He paused in trying to rip open the packet of plasticware, which seemed wrapped for doomsday storage. "Book smart, sure, but also just very quick-witted. Whoever—" He fixed them with an unreadable look. "Whoever killed her must've taken her by surprise."

After holding their gaze for a moment, he resumed work on the sealed packet.

Mabel exchanged a glance with Lisa. Was he trying to convince them of his own innocence? If so, it was an odd gambit, considering her boyfriend might be expected to be well-trusted enough to stage a surprise attack.

"Here, let me." He was driving Mabel crazy with that blasted packet. She snipped a little slit in the top with her nail clippers and handed it back.

The other thing driving her crazy was the aroma of baked potato. Her tummy gurgled. She might have to get one to go.

"Who do you think did it?" Mabel asked. "If you have a theory."

"I've always suspected Bud Bender. He was the insanely jealous type, and what you might call macho. Not sure that's the right word, but he always wanted to prove how tough he was, always wanted to be in control. He didn't like her breaking up with him."

"I saw a report that some man was heard screaming at Cathy not long before the murder."

"There you go. Excuse me. I've got to eat fast, so I can get back to the North Pole." He began shoveling food into his mouth.

Mabel stared. Was he crazy or just joking?

He caught the look and laughed. "That's what they call the Santa display."

Lisa leaned in. "How about the mailman? It seems a lot of people back then suspected him."

Enlow shrugged. "I never bought that. It's a definite possibility, but there wasn't all *that* much taken from the house…unless robbery wasn't the motive. I think she would've fought more if a strange man came inside the house. Even if he made up some story, she would've been on guard more. At least, I think so.

"But I'll tell you who's most likely, in my opinion, to have killed that postman."

Mabel already had her own suspicions, but she asked anyway. "Who?"

"Ricky Putnam. I'm not saying old Mr. Crawford wasn't a hundred percent right in disinheriting Ricky, but I think he yanked Ricky's chain once too many times."

Mabel wrote a note. It felt like marking answers on an opinion poll. "What about that guy from the post office who wanted Lester Bedford's job—Kalchik?"

Enlow looked blank. "Never heard that story." He shrugged. "Guess he could still be in the running, but I don't know."

"I'm guessing police questioned you too?" Lisa asked. "Were you ever cleared?"

He frowned and swallowed a big bite. "I had a perfect alibi. I was an orderly at that time and was at work at the hospital. Bud's story was a whole lot shakier. In fact, he changed his story at least once. First, he claimed to be at work stocking shelves at the grocery store, but it turned out he left soon after he got in that day, claiming he was sick. Later, he said he got the days mixed up. Considering how soon after Cathy's death we were being questioned, I don't think so."

When Mabel and Lisa left the food court en route to Mabel's Christmas shopping goals, it became clear the piped-in carols had ceased in favor of the mellow sounds of a live, young people's orchestra. Lisa paused.

"They must've bused in people from senior living for the concert." She squinted. "Is that Miss Birdie?"

"Sure is, but she doesn't live over there—she must've come with Ms. Katherine Ann." Mabel spotted another familiar figure and squeaked with surprise. "Look. Do you see the man on the other side of Ms. Katherine Ann?"

"Does she have a boyfriend now too?"

"Not that I know of. It's Nita's Uncle Charles." Mabel frowned. "As far as I know, he hasn't moved to Best Years either—and I have no idea what he's doing here with Ms. Katherine Ann."

"Didn't you say you thought he was interested in Miss Birdie?" Lisa giggled. "Maybe Ms. Katherine Ann's chaperoning."

Mabel saw Uncle Charles steal a peek at Miss Birdie. "I'll bet he and Miss Birdie are just shy."

"Well, that's something Ms. Katherine Ann will never be accused of," Lisa said.

"Oh, hey—that's Acey's Aunt Adelaide on this end of the back row." Mabel nodded at the round figure in festive attire.

Lisa squinted. "What's she doing?"

Adelaide was craning her neck to stare at a cluster of people on the sidelines. Whatever she was up to certainly had nothing to do with the concert in progress.

Mabel had just turned her attention to the standees as the orchestra's rendition of *Greensleeves* came to an end and applause erupted. Adelaide shrieked.

Mabel started so violently she dropped her bag and whirled to look back at the seniors. As Adelaide half rose from her chair, the woman seated next to her grabbed Adelaide's arm.

Mabel and Lisa bumped heads as they both bent to retrieve Mabel's bag from the floor. "Ow." Lisa rubbed her head.

"Sorry." Mabel looked back at the disruption.

Adelaide waved her arm in the air, making the bells on her sweater jingle. "Ben!" she screeched.

Stunned, Mabel whirled around. The handsome older man she'd run into at Demitasse and again at the library emerged from the group of standees. Dressed as before in worn jeans and boots, he'd added a dark blazer with a red woolen scarf at the neck. His smile spread from ear to ear, and it was for Adelaide alone.

Adelaide shook off her neighbor's hand and got to her feet. An aide scrambled toward the back row. She made a shushing gesture, which Adelaide ignored, chattering at full volume. As she reached both arms out to Ben, Adelaide tripped.

"Oops." She caught the back of the chair in front of her, almost tipping the frail old man from his seat. Adelaide's seatmate shoved her tripod cane at her.

After a startled silence, the orchestra burst into a lively rendition of *Sleigh Ride*, which covered at least part of the ruckus. Mabel inched closer as Ben Holt caught Adelaide's shoulders and planted a kiss on her cheek.

Mabel couldn't hear the exchange between Ben and the aide, but a moment later, the aide moved Adelaide's chair over to the railing some distance away from the audience, so she could sit while renewing her old acquaintance. Smiling, the aide pulled an empty chair into Adelaide's vacated spot and sat, keeping one eye on the two old friends.

"Do you suppose that's the famous Ben Holt?" Lisa asked.

"Who else could it be? It looks like he's already charmed the attendant too." Mabel shook her head. She couldn't help noticing how many of the old women kept turning in their seats to eye him up, several with an envious glance at Adelaide.

"Anyone that charming could have ingratiated himself with old man Crawford, right along with Adelaide and the rest of the female population," Lisa mused.

Mabel was reluctant to admit she hated to think ill of Ben, who seemed to be every bit the paragon Adelaide had described. He leaned over Adelaide's chair, still holding her hand. While Mabel doubted the handsome man shared Adelaide's infatuation, he was showing her kind and respectful attention, and his fondness seemed genuine.

Lisa cut into Mabel's ponderings. "Wonder what brings *him* back to town after all these years."

"I do too," Mabel admitted. Possible ulterior motives thrust themselves into her mind. What if he'd come to avenge himself on Ricky for stealing his inheritance? Or for killing Cathy… *if* he even knew her? On the other hand, while Mabel doubted he'd been pining for Adelaide, maybe he had felt nostalgic for the holidays in Medicine Spring.

All these people who'd played a role in the events of December 1962 seemed to be resurfacing. It almost felt as if there were some otherworldly convergence at work—brought about by Lester Bedford's return from his shallow grave like a brooding ghost of Christmas past.

Chapter Thirty-Three

MABEL THREW HER PURCHASES BEHIND LISA'S passenger seat. Two more gifts taken care of. On the way back to the outlet mall parking lot, she'd picked up appropriate, if not exciting, presents for her parents. Mabel had never placed those orders she'd planned to get around to, and now it was too late. She'd decided Jen and her family were getting gift cards this year, so that took care of five more people on her shopping list.

As they drove out, Lisa put on her right-turn blinker and braked for the signal at the main mall entrance. "What did you think of Enlow's theory of the case? Or should I say, 'theories?' And/or 'cases?'" Lisa frowned and shook her head. "I guess we have to consider Cathy's murder and Lester's disappearance separately, as well as also potentially connected."

"I think we do. Well, I'm not too sure about his rationale for Bud Bender. He's basing an awful lot on Cathy's caution about strangers. If Bender was bad-tempered and giving her problems, wouldn't she have been cautious around him too?"

Lisa nodded. "You'd think so, but she also might have thought he was more hot air than anything. Or that she could manage him okay. She did know him—and dated him."

"True. Also, we're taking Enlow's word as fact. He was Bender's rival, after all. We don't know whether there were signs of a struggle in that house or not. Or whether she cracked the door to talk to whoever was there and he—or she, I guess—shoved right in and grabbed her before she could fight back."

Lisa grinned as she made her turn out of the mall. "You doubting Santa's word?"

"Let's just say I know better than to take *anyone's* statement at face value. That's a slippery slope, which you know as well as I do. If not better."

"Agreed. You can check with John whether it looked like there'd been a struggle. What do you think of Enlow's alibi?"

Mabel shrugged. "There might have been some way he could've slipped out mid-shift, but I'd think the cops checked that out. Seems like his alibi would've been easy to verify. Or debunk."

"Yeah, I think so too." For a moment, Lisa drove in silence. Then she glanced Mabel's way. "I couldn't help liking him."

"Me too," Mabel admitted. "Of course, it's hard to think ill of Santa. Even allowing for that, he showed what looked like real emotion about Cathy and her death. Everything he said seemed reasonable and sincere."

"Not that we scratch him off our list yet," Lisa said.

"No, ma'am."

At the next red light, Lisa looked over at Mabel. "You and I both have an unfortunate tendency to focus on people we don't like. You wouldn't believe how many murders I've seen committed by guys whose neighbors all say he was the nicest man you'd ever meet and wouldn't hurt a fly."

To Mabel's knowledge, Lisa had never seen a murder committed. She was referring, as always, to the true-crime podcasts and TV shows she followed.

"I'm sure that's true, but there are still red flags. At some point, we have to consider the evidence and decide whether or not to trust somebody." Even as she said it, Mabel couldn't help remembering how long she'd harbored suspicions about John and his motives…probably too long.

"Of course. In most cases, I'm not talking about people we spend a lot of time with and get to know well. More often, it's neighbors, classmates, coworkers—people like that. We only get a limited view of someone in that one setting. A slick criminal can deceive anyone, though, including their wives who never suspected they had a secret life."

"But—" Mabel didn't want to be forever wary, and she didn't think Lisa did either.

Lisa rambled on. "Look at Ann Rule, the queen of true-crime authors, not to mention a former cop. She sat alone at night next to Ted Bundy, of all people, on a suicide hotline, during the time he was actively out killing people. She knew him for years and considered him a friend. He totally bamboozled her."

"You trust Tim."

Lisa stared as if Mabel had gone daft. "Naturally."

"Okay. Just checking." Mabel smiled. "We all make judgments about who to trust, and I have to believe if we're cautious and take our time, we're right *most* of the time." As she said it, she stifled the unpleasant memory of somebody she'd liked and trusted, only to have her judgment turn up flawed, almost fatally.

"Granted," Lisa said. "For what it's worth, I trust John too. If that's your subtext here."

"No, I just…never mind."

Lisa grinned.

Mabel rolled her eyes. "Leaving aside Santa—and our boyfriends—for the moment, catch me up on where you are with tracking down Jerry Kalchik."

"Okay. That's a quick answer. I located a death certificate for him—I think—down in Florida, but there wasn't enough information for me to be sure it was him. John's trying to confirm."

Mabel eyed her friend. "Are you going to confess to John where we went?"

Lisa winked. "I figured that could be your department."

"You're a pal."

When Mabel arrived home, Barnacle jumped all over her,

sniffing and pawing, and danced between her and the back door. Koi was nowhere in sight, but as soon as Mabel had gotten Barnacle out on his run, the little cat emerged, sat down just out of reach, and squawked.

"I'm sorry, okay?" Mabel took a step toward her, hoping to make amends, but the cat trotted away to sit in a corner.

Food was the universal language, so she picked up the pet dishes and began filling them. As soon as Koi relented and started eating, John called. Mabel put it on speaker and went to bring the dog in.

"Hey, have you seen *The Shopper*?"

Mabel caught her breath. "Is it out? Is my article in it?" She headed back to the door.

"Yes, to both, and it looks beautiful."

"I'm checking right now."

Mabel hustled to the mailbox, picking her way through the slush. She'd gotten the usual mix of holiday advertising and yes, there was *The Shopper*. "I've got it. Hang on, I'm going back inside now."

As soon as she reached the kitchen table, she opened the paper with shaky hands and began flipping pages. "It's here," she breathed.

John chuckled. "I know. What do you think?"

"It looks so…real."

"It is real—the first of many more to come."

"They even got a photographer out there—and put in a sidebar with all the local food pantries and other places that need volunteers to help feed people." Mabel felt a stinging sensation behind her eyes. Was this how a new mother felt, holding her child for the first time?

"I'm so proud of you, *ma belle*."

"Thanks." She couldn't even complain about the teasing

play on her name. "I can't believe they published it. With the picture and all this other fancy stuff too."

"Well, I can believe it."

Koi leapt onto the table, coming down smack onto Mabel's pride and joy. "Hey, careful there." The cat was sniffing the paper, but looked for all the world as if she were reading Mabel's literary efforts.

With very slow and gentle hands, lest she startle Koi into digging in her claws, Mabel lifted the cat down, then folded the paper and stuck it in her purse for safekeeping. She pulled off her coat and went into the living room to plop down for a chat.

Shaking off the excitement over her publication as best she could, Mabel changed the subject. "Did you learn anything new on the Abramovich front today?"

"A little. Death was likely caused by her hitting her head on the corner of the coffee table within six hours, give or take, of the time her coworker discovered the body around eleven am."

Mabel chewed on that information for a moment. "So, that means her death could've been caused by an accidental fall, right? Rather than homicide?"

"Yeah, based on the lack of any obvious weapon such as a blunt instrument, but the coroner took into account the extensive perimortem bruising on her arms—some of which looks like possible handprints—as well as evidence somebody had pulled her hair."

"How big were those handprints?"

"You've got to understand they were just *possible* handprints. If so, they could've been from a small to medium male or medium to large female."

Mabel thought hard. She wished she'd had John's update earlier, when she and Lisa were talking to Enlow. Just how big *were* his hands? He hadn't been a huge man, but he might well have shrunk with age. How he looked now was no predictor of hand size at that time.

"Hey." John's voice cut into her thoughts. "You drifted again."

She startled guiltily. Now, she guessed, was the time to confess what she and Lisa had done.

"Sorry, I was thinking about hand sizes and…oh, promise you won't get mad?"

"I'm not making any promises when you lead into something that way." Suspicion laced his usual calm voice.

It occurred to Mabel to be grateful they weren't in the same room, for her to watch the thunderclouds form. "Well, in my defense, I didn't plan any of this—it was Lisa. I didn't even know where we were going." She heard her whiny tone and grimaced.

"Tattletale." The good-natured grin had returned to his voice, despite the wariness.

Mabel took a deep breath and jumped in. The entire account of their interview with Enlow spilled out, along with her impressions of the man.

"Santa?" John snorted. "You girl sleuths interrogated Santa? At least, you did it in a public area. Just because someone puts on the red suit doesn't place him above suspicion."

Mabel bristled. "We know that. We were very objective." Then, she couldn't help adding, "But the beard was real."

"How very *Miracle on 34th Street,*" John said dryly.

"I know, but it was hard to overlook the resemblance."

John chuckled. "Since you can't see me right now, imagine the eye roll."

"I already was." Mabel relaxed. He wasn't mad. Their conversation moved on to other topics, including their date for the local dinner theater. She was excited about that—both seeing the show with John and getting a chance to size up Bud Bender.

Chapter Thirty-Four

MABEL TOOK MORE TIME THAN USUAL getting ready for the show at the Medicine Spring Playhouse. Granted, it wasn't a Broadway opening, but she felt like dinner theater called for more glamor than a movie, with supper at the Coffee Cup. She couldn't bear the thought of putting on a dress, but she did pull out the cranberry velvet blazer Jen had found for her at the thrift store, and paired it with her new, slinky black pants, lacy black camisole, and chunky necklace of garnets and big silver beads.

As she turned and studied her backside in the old full-length mirror, she wished she could wear devastating black stilettos. The very thought made her snort. It would be a toss-up as to where she ended up first—the podiatrist or the ER.

When John knocked, she took one last look and hustled downstairs. Despite nearly tripping over Koi, lying in the shadows on the staircase, Mabel made it to the kitchen intact. Barnacle was jumping at the door and wagging frantically.

John stood back and whistled when she opened the door. Then he pulled her into a hug. "You look like dynamite."

Mabel felt herself blush. She still wasn't used to feeling attractive, but thanks to John's obvious approval, she'd started to wear better-fitting clothes like these new pants. Being around Nita had also been an eye-opener. Nita was far from wispy, but she never tried to camouflage her figure, the way Mabel always had, and Nita never failed to look stunning.

As Barnacle continued his affectionate onslaught, John leaned over and rumpled the dog's ears, but looked up at Mabel. "You ready?"

"Sure. Let me grab my coat and my purse."

It was the mildest night they'd had in the last couple weeks. Though a dusting of snow still lay in the shadowy areas around the house and bushes, the air was calm under a sky blanketed with clouds. Barnacle stood at a front window, silhouetted against the light, and barked.

Mabel settled into the passenger seat. "This weather's not very Christmasy, is it?"

"Fairly typical nowadays." John looked over his shoulder to back out of the driveway. "We seldom get much snow till after Christmas. All the accumulation we had the last couple weeks has been unusual."

"The almanac says it'll be a white Christmas. A very white Christmas."

"We'll see," John said, seemingly not putting much stock in the almanac's predictions. "The forecast did say a major blizzard is headed this way, but it's expected to go south. I hope so—this car isn't much good in the snow."

"Neither is mine." Mabel hated driving in snow, shoveling snow, scraping snow…but she did love a white Christmas.

Playhouse parking was overflowing by the time Mabel and John arrived, so they ended up in a spot halfway off the edge of the pavement, where the lot faded away into weedy, winter-brown pasture. A few other patrons trudged ahead of them, talking and laughing, as they made their way to the theater building, a big, old barn with peeling white paint and a new-looking red roof. A few smaller outbuildings clustered around the main structure, sheltered by tall, bare trees.

Mabel not only had never attended a performance here, but she'd never even been down this narrow country road either. "This is exciting."

John smiled and squeezed her hand. "Even if we don't get to meet Bud Bender, we should at least have a nice dinner and enjoy the show. It's gotten good reviews."

They stood in line for the coat check, then made their way into the cozy auditorium, where dining tables were set with white tablecloths and wait staff were pouring ice water and taking drink orders. As Mabel and John had preordered their meal, their salads and dinner rolls were already waiting when they found their table number.

Most other tables were occupied already, and the efficient servers buzzed around the room, delivering plated main courses. "They have this down to a science," Mabel murmured.

"They do. The goal is to have everyone done eating, the main course cleared, and dessert and coffee served before the curtain goes up."

While they ate their salads, Mabel and John chatted about getting his paperwork filed in hopes of having his PI license reinstated in the New Year. He told stories about his students at the community college, and she bemoaned getting Grandma's house decluttered, despite Acey's recent burst of productivity.

John laughed. "I'm sorry. I know you're worried about the house, but I can't help cracking up at the way you incentivized Acey. Unfortunately, I doubt you want to use the same tactic for the rest of the house."

"Good grief, no. He'd clean the place out in two days, and I wouldn't have a stick of furniture left."

When their main courses arrived, conversation lagged somewhat over roast turkey with stuffing and all the traditional trimmings. By the time the eggnog crème brûlée and coffee followed, Mabel had to remind herself why they were here.

"I'm enjoying myself so much, it's hard to get my mind back on the investigation."

John cleared his throat and tilted his head toward a table off to Mabel's right. "Speaking of the investigation, another member of our dramatis personae is here for the show."

"Huh?" She swung her head around to see what he was talking about.

"Shh…not so obvious. I mean another character connected to our investigation is in the audience tonight."

Mabel squinted. "Is that Ricky Putnam?"

"The same. And his wife, Bonnie."

"They clean up good." Mabel eyed Bonnie's sparkling indigo cocktail dress and chunky silver statement necklace. Ricky was also resplendent in a dark suit with snowy dress shirt and a pocket handkerchief and tie that picked up Bonnie's color scheme. "In fact, they make the rest of us look like hillbillies at a jug band festival."

John snickered. "From what I gather, he has the money, she has the taste."

The house lights flickered, and a few patrons who'd headed for the restrooms after the main course scurried toward their tables. Idly, Mabel watched the race for seats before glancing back at the Putnams. He hunched over his phone, scrolling and frowning. Bonnie leaned back in her seat, watching him over the rim of her wine glass with a scowl that more than matched his.

Mabel looked back at John, who caught her eye and smiled. She smiled back, grateful to be here with somebody who'd rather look at her than his phone, even if they *weren't* the most polished couple in the room.

The lights went down, and the curtain came up. Mabel settled back, ready to be whisked back to Victorian London and the old tale of an impoverished family rich in love and the miserable rich man who needed ghostly intervention to learn where to find true wealth. She'd seen so many versions, she could have recited the key dialog along with the actors, but soon she was lost in its spell. By the time the play ended, she was frantically trying to wipe her eyes and swallow the lump in her throat before the house lights came back on.

"I'm impressed." John blew his nose and stood. "For a bunch of local amateurs, they did an amazing job."

"They had good material to work with." Mabel stood, along with most of the audience, to applaud Bud Bender, as the director came on stage to join hands with his cast. "Bender deserves a lot of credit though too. He really got the most out of his actors."

She studied the man, trying to fit her image of him sixty years ago with the way he appeared today. Though now rather stoop shouldered, he must have been tall once. Lean and rugged featured, with a prominent Roman nose and a lot of dark, but receding hair, he'd aged well, appearance-wise, though Mabel suspected his mane of dark hair had to be dyed. Black-framed glasses gave him a serious, almost intellectual appearance.

"Come on." John took her hand. "If we slip out now, we'll be able to pick our spot for the reception before everybody else crowds into the lobby."

As Mabel grabbed her purse, she glanced toward the Putnams' table, which was now empty. "Looks like they had the same idea."

"Nope. They left right as the third ghost appeared."

"Huh. I totally missed that."

John leaned close to whisper into her ear, and Mabel had to strain to hear him over the noisy ovation. "You were in the zone, but I was facing them when they left. During the first act, he was just sitting slouched in his seat. They were hissing at each other all through the beginning of the second act. Finally, he shot to his feet and marched out, with her chasing after him."

"I'd pay money to know what they were talking about." Mabel rebuked herself for getting caught up in the play and failing to keep an eye on their suspect.

"Might be nothing, but we'll never know." John scanned the growing crowd in the lobby. "Maybe the people who were next to them do though."

Mabel cast an eye over the festive, chattering mass of people before focusing on a young man and woman, who looked to be in their twenties. "Could that be them?"

John sighted along her surreptitious pointer finger. "I think so. Let's find out."

He wended his way toward the couple, Mabel following in his wake. She paused to snag several cheese puffs, a scoop of candied pecans, and a couple of light-green meringue Christmas trees decked with tiny, multicolored, ball-shaped sprinkles. She knew she wouldn't be able to eat and hold a drink, so she'd have to stop for punch later.

"Excuse me." John tapped the bearded young man—underdressed in jeans and a gray ragg pullover—as if asking to pass. Mabel was impressed with John's own acting ability as he feigned a doubletake. "Hey, I think we were sitting near you in there. Sorry you were stuck next to that chatty pair. I could even hear them from where we were."

The young woman, a smooth-cheeked blonde in tight jeans, short boots, and an asymmetrical cardigan splashed with bright geometrics, rolled her eyes. She leaned in. "Guess what they say is true—'Money talks.'"

Mabel laughed at the surprising witticism. "Money?"

"Oh, yeah," the guy said. "That was the Putnams. You know."

"I do." John shook his head. "Surprised they'd be that rude. I heard they donate quite a lot to the Playhouse every year."

The young man sniffed. "Doesn't mean they care about theater."

"Did you miss much of the dialog?" Mabel asked before popping a cheese puff into her mouth.

"Some." The young woman looked around the packed lobby. "Of course, we all know the story anyway, but our friend was playing the Ghost of Christmas Yet to Come, so I was glad they cut out right after he came on stage."

"Looked like they were arguing over something?" John dropped the leading question before helping himself to one of Mabel's cheese puffs.

"I could only make out a few words. Whatever it was, it got pretty heated." The young man joined the young woman in scanning the room.

"I think something he said started it, and she lit into him," the woman said. "All I could hear was her swearing."

The man pointed and waved. "There's Erik." He tugged at his date's arm. "Excuse us."

Mabel watched them greet their friend before turning back to John. "Interesting, but I wish they'd heard more of what was going on."

John shrugged. "Could be nothing. Here comes Bender now."

The director took his time strolling into the room, beaming, and shaking hands right and left. Though he had many admirers congratulating him on the performance, Mabel was glad she and John weren't trying to get an audience with Ebenezer Scrooge or Tiny Tim, who seemed to be the real focus of attention as they sat on stools next to each other, sipping punch and posing for pictures.

"He's putting a lot of weight on that cane," Mabel observed.

"At his age, he's allowed to have a limp." John threaded his way through the Scrooge and Tiny Tim roadblock. "Just because a few seniors you know are supernaturally spry, like Miss Birdie and Ms. Katherine Ann, you can't expect everyone else will be."

"No, of course not. Grandma had her hip replaced years before she died. I guess I'm still having trouble envisioning this elderly guy as a homicidal twenty-something hothead."

"Shh…" John put a finger to his lips. "He approacheth."

A moment later, they found themselves directly in Bender's

path. "Bravo, sir." John planted himself and stuck out his hand. "That was an excellent treatment of *A Christmas Carol.* I enjoyed the subtle comedy you introduced. Like that aside and exchange of glances between the gentlemen soliciting charitable donations for the poor."

"Thank you, young man." The director smiled and bobbed his head in acknowledgement. "The material's so familiar one has to freshen it up in some way. Wouldn't want to overdo the levity though."

"No. It was the perfect amount."

"We were sorry to hear this will be your final season at the Playhouse." Mabel ignored the guilty twinge she felt, as this was the first show she'd managed to attend.

"One must retire sooner or later. I already left teaching several years ago, you know. Directing made a nice retirement activity, but I simply don't have the energy anymore."

A middle-aged man shifted restlessly behind John, waiting his turn with Bender. Mabel realized they'd soon lose their opportunity to extract any information from the director. "I hope you don't mind my asking you an unrelated question."

Bender smiled politely but raised an inquisitive eyebrow.

"I'm a local writer." Mabel reproached herself for still not having printed any business cards. It was so hard to make a professional impression without a card to offer.

Bender chuckled. "If you have a script, I'm afraid I can't help. If I were you, I'd hold onto it till my replacement's on board in the next few weeks, once the holidays are over."

"Oh, no—I didn't mean that." Though she was flustered, it occurred to Mabel that she might want to add "playwright" to her business cards when she got around to having some printed. She cleared her throat, keeping one eye on the impatient man behind John. "I'm researching a potential true crime book about the unsolved murder of Cathy Abramovich."

Given the dim lighting, Mabel couldn't tell whether Bender blanched. There was no doubt his right hand on the cane seemed firm. He frowned. "About Cathy?"

"I understand you knew her, and I'm wondering if you might be willing to give me an interview, help me get a better understanding of who she was."

"I don't know. It's very…painful for me."

Mabel touched his sleeve. "I understand, sir, but we want to honor her memory. Too often, true crime gives more attention to the criminal than the innocent victim."

"I quite agree. I'm just not sure about discussing it. You may contact me through the Playhouse for the next two weeks. At some point after that, I may be relocating to Arizona."

"Thank you. Before we go, could you tell me your reaction to the discovery of the skeletal remains of the mailman who disappeared off his route the day Cathy was murdered?"

Bender shook his head. "I'm not sure what you're talking about. I need to go now, but if we speak later, you can explain then." He peered around John. "Hello, there. Sorry to have kept you waiting."

John tugged her arm, towing her toward the exit. "True crime book?"

"I might write one. If the ax murder book turns out okay. Anyway, it's a perfect excuse for asking nosy questions about the Abramovich murder. Bender didn't seem rattled, did he? He looked blank when I mentioned Lester."

"Yes." John held the door for Mabel as she stepped back out into the cold. "But don't forget—Bender was an actor long before he was ever a director."

Chapter Thirty-Five

BY THE TIME MABEL AND JOHN left the playhouse, a few large, wet snowflakes had begun drifting down. The pole lights in the parking lot caught them as they followed the currents, making each flake glitter as it danced. John only needed to use the brush on his back window, but enough snow had already accumulated on the windshield for him to turn on the wipers. The blades on his old classic car had two settings—on and off—so after two swipes, he turned them off again.

The roads hadn't gotten too bad yet, though the snowfall increased as they went. Even with John's taking it easy on the curves, he'd delivered Mabel to her door with a lingering kiss in what felt to her like no time at all. She knew in this weather it would be selfish to ask him in for a cup of tea before he left. So, she just rested her head against his neck for a moment, then sighed. "Let me know when you make it home, okay?"

The snow continued to fall through the night. When Mabel got up to use the bathroom sometime well after midnight, she looked out at a world of white, gleaming despite the darkness, as more heavy flakes pelted down, obscuring everything beyond her yard. Her shed and all the trees and bushes had turned into shrouded mounds.

By morning, the snow was still coming down, but it had diminished to a slushy spatter of wintry mix as temperatures crept upward. Mabel stretched luxuriously, reveling for once in her state of unemployment. She would wear her sweats and cozy slippers and stay in all day.

Koi rolled over on the pillow next to Mabel, stretching too while she yawned enormously, showing pink tongue and pointy white teeth. Mabel reached out to pet her and was rewarded by getting her wrist grabbed between the cat's front paws and her hand gently bitten.

"Ow!" Mabel had learned not to move till Koi released her unharmed.

Mabel inspected her undamaged flesh and scratched at an itchy claw depression. Even if Koi didn't actually injure her, Mabel was still sensitive enough to cat allergen to end up with a maddening itch the rest of the day. "Why do you do that?" she demanded.

Koi blinked, yawned again, and rolled in the other direction.

Mabel swung her legs over the edge of the bed and felt around for her slippers as she picked up and unmuted her phone. Barnacle pawed at her knee, then romped between her and the door. "Hang on."

Mabel shivered. She'd been keeping the thermostat low to save on her utility bill, but soon she'd have to inch it up. She knew it would be worse if John and Tim hadn't weatherproofed her windows in November.

As she shuffled toward the staircase, her phone pinged. Only 7:13 am, and she'd already missed calls from Lisa, John, and Nita.

Lisa's was first, since she got up before six to make it to school on time for her early drop-offs. Mabel played the voice message while clipping Barnacle to his run.

"Have you heard anything about that fatal accident out by Nita's last night? That's all I got. Please text if you know more."

Mabel's heart began to pound. *Nita.* Her fingers fumbled as she moved to the next voicemail.

"Mabel? This is Nita. Did you hear someone got killed in the road out my way last night? Don't know if their car broke down or what, but it sounds like they were walking in that blizzard. I can't believe it."

Mabel set out the pets' dishes and began filling them while

Koi stropped herself on Mabel's ankles. The last voice message came up.

John's call had come in a few minutes before Mabel got out of bed.

"Call me when you get a chance, okay?"

She couldn't help a little lopsided smile. That was John. No content—just "call me." Maybe he'd invite her to breakfast at the Coffee Cup.

She set the bowls down and let Barnacle back in, then dialed.

"Mabel, hi. Thanks for calling back. Are you up for a quick breakfast at the usual? I need to get to the high school to cover an exam, but there's still a bit of time if you don't mind keeping it short."

Though road crews had been plowing and salting for hours, the Coffee Cup was emptier than usual. Even Miss Birdie and Ms. Kathryn Ann weren't here, Mabel was relieved to see. Ms. Kathryn Ann shouldn't be driving on iffy roads and Mabel prayed she realized that.

John waved from their usual booth in the back. She started to slide in across the table from him, but he moved over and patted the seat next to him.

Mabel smiled. "What brings this on?"

He helped her off with her coat and threw it on the other bench seat. "I wish I could say I just wanted to snuggle, which of course, I do. But I also want to keep our conversation private."

Mabel frowned. "I already heard from Lisa and Nita there was a road fatality last night. Is that what this is about?"

He nodded, but didn't speak, as the waitress appeared with her pad open.

"Good morning, Genevieve. Two coffees, right?" John raised an inquiring eyebrow at Mabel, who nodded, realizing this was a healthier choice, but disappointed at passing up a seasonal latte. Darn it.

They placed their orders—John's usual and Mabel's dreary Everyday Breakfast, though she added a maple walnut scone for later. Once their coffees had arrived and Mabel was picking through the new assortment of flavored creamers, John began filling her in.

"So, I put out some feelers. Ricky Putnam was the fatality."

Mabel gasped, hand to mouth. "Omigosh. I heard he was on foot. What on earth?"

John shrugged. "No one knows. He was less than a quarter mile from home, possibly walking home from Doc's Lounge. You know it?"

"Vaguely."

"Kind of divey, but a neighborhood place on the main road near Nita's. Been there for many years. I'm sure police have been talking to his wife, but I haven't heard anything back from that yet."

Mabel stirred her salted caramel creamers into the black coffee. "Do you know how he died?"

John shrugged. "Looks like he was halfway onto the road and half on the shoulder when the plow clipped him, but already down when that happened. That's where they found him, anyway. For all I know, he was dead even before that. We'll have to wait for more."

"I can't believe it. We just saw him a few hours ago."

"I know. It's crazy. I hate to see anybody die like this, let alone right before Christmas."

The wheels in Mabel's head were turning. If Ricky Putnam had killed Lester Bedford—and maybe Cathy Abramovich, as well— now they might never know.

After John had headed to work, Mabel sat in her car outside the

Coffee Cup while her windshield defrosted. She sent Lisa a quick text, promising to talk when Lisa was off work. Then, she dialed Nita's cell.

Nita picked up on the first ring. "You got my message?"

"I did. I was just now talking to John about it."

"It was Ricky Putnam." Tension vibrated in Nita's voice.

"John told me."

"Listen, Mabel. Are you doing anything right now?"

"Sitting in my car outside the Coffee Cup. Why?"

"Can you pick me up?"

"Of course." Mabel put her car in gear. "Your house, right? Wouldn't your car start this morning?"

"No, I'm at Suds. I'll explain when you get here."

Mabel frowned. "Suds the beer distributor or Suds the carwash?"

"Mabel," Nita snapped. "Sorry. I'm a little bit stressed. The carwash, of course. Not to mention the beer place is Foamy's."

"I'll be there in two shakes."

The carwash lot crawled with salt-spattered vehicles creeping their way toward the mouth of the wash tunnel, like June bugs crawling into an insect trap. When Mabel pulled up at the curb, she saw no sign of Nita's SUV, which she guessed had failed to restart when she'd come to the exit.

She found a spot along the side of the lot and parked, then dialed Nita. "Where are you?"

"I'll be right out. Where are you?"

Mabel told her, then watched till Nita emerged from the building and trudged toward her. Everything about her drooped, including the red swing coat Mabel so admired.

Nita got in, shut the door, and immediately dropped her head in her hands.

Mabel caught her shoulder. "Hey, what's wrong?" She felt a jolt of alarm. She'd seen Nita stressed before, angry, or sad but never like this. "Nita?"

Nita looked up at her. Tears glittered in her lashes, but Mabel wasn't sure whether they were from sadness or fury. Maybe both. "That…" She seemed to swallow what she'd been about to say. "That lousy Ricky Putnam. As if I wasn't already having the worst morning." Nita looked off through the side window.

"What happened?"

Nita whirled back. "They towed my dang car." She gave a forceful huff. "Can you believe it? I wanted to go in early today to work on my displays and holiday promotions, so I'm cranky to begin with. I always check online weather and local news before work, so I saw the first report about the accident when I got up this morning—with no ID for the victim, of course."

Mabel frowned in confusion. "But why…?"

Nita held up an impatient hand. "So, I'm heading out my driveway toward town, and the other direction's chaos because he got hit just up from my place, and it's a crime scene. Flashing lights, official type people, backed-up cars getting redirected.

"I drive away, planning on running through the carwash here before I pick up some breakfast to take to the store with me. My car's less than two years old, and it was covered in salt, not to mention I slid coming home in all that mess last night and hit a tree. Put a dent in my front bumper and cracked my headlight, so now I have to deal with replacing the light—at least—so there goes my deductible."

"Oh, Nita, that's—"

"Not all." Nita put up her hand again. "I'm tired. I'm cranky. My baby's got a dent in her. I haven't had my coffee. So, I pull in here, and there's Johnny Law in my rearview."

"Johnny…?"

"The cops. What my granddad used to call 'em. Stay with me, Mabel."

"Okaay…"

"They wave me over to the side and tell me it's Ricky dang Putnam who got killed in the road back there."

"But why…?" Mabel felt like her side of the conversation was pretty limited, but none of what Nita was saying made any sense to her.

"Hold up. First, they ask if I saw or heard anything last night. I say I'm way back off the road in my house, fast asleep, and with the snow and all, I never even heard the plow go through."

As Mabel opened her mouth, Nita held her hand up again. "Let me get it all out. So, they say they wanted to come talk to me, but someone saw me leave, so they sent a patrol car after me. When they see me pull in at the carwash, and with a dent in my front end, they want permission to do a forensic examination."

"Wait. You gave them permission?" Mabel's eyes widened. "You didn't demand a warrant?"

"I was not at my best." Nita shook her head. "Plus, I was raised to never argue with the police. They said it was either that or wait while they got an emergency warrant. Anyway, I'd rather they give it a good look, because I know they sure as heck won't find any of Ricky Putnam's DNA on my car. With any luck, they'll find tree bark."

"I'd still have asked for a warrant, but okay. For goodness' sake, don't talk to them anymore without counsel." Mabel chewed her lip. "Just in case, I can line up a lawyer for you. You know I can't represent you, okay?"

Nita rolled her eyes. "In case what?" She waved her hand. "Never mind. I know. Don't worry—I wasn't going to ask you."

"Hmphh."

"Mabel, I know you don't want to do law stuff anymore. Besides, I know you were never a criminal lawyer. So don't get your feelings hurt." Nita patted Mabel's hand. "I appreciate your help."

"No worries." Mabel put her car in gear. "So, two questions. First, where to? And where's Tabasco?"

"To the shop. By way of a drive-through, so I can grab us some breakfast. Tabasco's home today. He loses his mind in the carwash."

"There's no drive-through on our way. Is the Quick Shop all right? No need to buy me anything. I just ate."

"I guess so, thanks. The way the fast-food places get backed up in the morning, it's as easy to run in and order off the screen."

Fifteen minutes later, they pulled into a spot in front of Reader's Retreat. "Come on in for a bit and eat your doughnut," Nita said.

"Sure." Mabel gathered her purse, along with a bag containing two apple cider doughnuts delivered that morning to the Quick Shop from Stotz's Farm Market. With a twinge of guilt, she stowed her maple-walnut scone in the console for an afternoon snack.

She hadn't intended to get any more food, but fresh apple cider doughnuts were rare as wild roses in December. Besides, she'd need the extra energy to deal with this latest crisis.

The shop wouldn't open for business for another hour. Nita took out a big brass keyring and unlocked the door, which opened with a jingle from the overhead bell, then relocked. "Woof, it's cold in here." Nita set her stuff on the back counter and turned up the heat.

"Come on back." As they entered Nita's office, Gaiters, curled in the armchair, yawned and stretched, then rolled onto his back to study them upside down.

"He'll move," Nita predicted. She hung up her coat on the

walnut-and-brass coat tree in the corner and popped the lid on the cat food bin.

Gaiters leapt lightly onto the floor, and Mabel stole the vacated armchair, which had been nicely warmed by its previous occupant. As Nita scooped food into the cat's dish, she looked over at Mabel. "Buy you a coffee? What do you want?"

"Oh, thanks. Another pumpkin spice, if you've got it. Or maybe a hazelnut."

Seconds later, Nita delivered a perfect hazelnut coffee. "Cream? I've got regular or hazelnut. Maybe a salted caramel."

"Hazelnut would be great, thanks."

Once they were both settled and eating, Mabel wiped cinnamon-sugar off her fingers and took a sip of coffee. "Now, back to this morning, did the cops tell you why they were so hot on your trail? Not to mention, towing your car."

Nita wiped her fingers. "Since Uncle Lester's remains turned up, they'd been going back over their old files. Putnam was looked at for the disappearance, I was happy to hear. The downside is they think finding Uncle Lester's remains might've reinflamed our suspicions—which they consider a motive to go after Putnam."

"Oh, come on." Mabel sputtered. "That's ridiculous."

Nita frowned and shrugged. "I kind of get how it must've looked, my driving off, straight to the carwash, and with a brand-new dent in the front. Like I say, unless somebody plants it, they won't find any evidence, because I didn't do anything to him."

She gave a short laugh. "I'm sure not going to kill off a customer who just dropped that much money in my shop."

"It sounds like they're looking at it as murder?"

Nita snorted. "Other than pointing out my own motive, they weren't sharing their theories with me."

Mabel thought. "John once told me police always go in considering a death as possible homicide. That doesn't necessarily mean they believe it's murder—they just need to eliminate it first. What about tire tracks? Wouldn't they be able to use those? To clear you, at least."

Nita quirked her mouth. "Doubtful. Most of the snow fell between when I got home at 10:30 and sometime toward morning. My tracks were covered up long ago, along with anybody's that might've hit Putnam before the plow came through. In fact, it seems the snow pretty much covered Putnam too, which is why the plow operator didn't see him."

Mabel blew a random curl back from her forehead and popped the last delicious morsel of cider doughnut into her mouth. "Did the cops say how long they expect to have your car?"

"At least a day or two." Nita groaned.

"Do you need a ride home?"

Nita shook her head. "I can ask to snag a ride from Zac. If not, I've got a bunch of family to call."

"It'll be okay," Mabel told her, with more conviction than she felt, as she collected her things. "Try not to think about all this too much—you've got work to do. Let me get out of here and see what I can find out. We'll be in touch."

Chapter Thirty-Six

Back in her car outside Reader's Retreat, Mabel texted Lisa a quick update. Then, she called John. As expected, he didn't pick up, but she left him a message about Nita. She knew he'd get back to her as soon as he was free.

She jumped as a reminder popped up on her phone. Oh, no. In the confusion of the morning, she'd forgotten she was supposed to meet Janet the organist, to practice her solo. Now, here she was in town without her music, at the ten-minute reminder. She texted Janet she was running five minutes late, then dashed home.

Seventeen minutes later, Mabel scooted into the choir loft, shedding her coat and dumping it onto a chair along with her purse. "Sorry. It's been a morning."

Janet smiled and motioned for Mabel to sit. "Relax for a few minutes. No need to rush. Get your breath back."

Mabel dropped into the first choir pew and tried to slow her breathing. It hadn't been just the rushing around and the news about Ricky Putnam—and Nita. The moment she'd stepped out of her car in the church parking lot, her nerves had grabbed her by the throat.

"Are you ready for Christmas?" Janet asked the standard question people raised all December long. Though she realized the organist likely intended to offer a less stressful topic to think about, Mabel found her lack of Christmas prep almost as anxiety-provoking as her solo.

"Not really."

Janet laughed. "Me neither. As my mom used to say though, Christmas will come anyway, and whatever we didn't get done won't matter. I'm so happy you're singing. You're putting what matters first."

Mabel attempted to swallow, but her mouth and throat were so dry, the gulp turned into a choke and cough.

"Oh, goodness. You need a drink. Hang on." Janet rummaged in her bag and brought out an unopened eight-ounce water bottle.

Grateful, Mabel cracked the lid and drank. "Thanks. That's a lifesaver."

Janet stretched, extending her arms in front of her, laced fingers outward. She must have been seventy or older, but her smooth Asian features and black hair threaded with a bit of gray made her appear closer to Mabel's age.

"Are you always this calm?" Mabel blurted.

"No." Janet snort laughed. "I'm a work in progress, but I'd rather be progressing than a perpetual basket case, wouldn't you?"

I'd love to, Mabel thought, *but progress is awfully slow.*

"Are you ready to play with this for a bit? We won't try to polish it right away. Let's just sing it through for fun a time or two first, shall we?"

An hour later, Mabel stepped back out into sharp December sunshine that threw the landscape into sharp relief against dark shadows and crisp blue sky. She felt a surge of energy and took a little skip that made the scattered salt crunch underfoot. Mostly, she was flooded with relief that practice was done. Only a couple more run-throughs before Christmas.

Mabel also felt a glimmer of hope for her Christmas Eve performance.

Janet had surprised her by singing along with her—an octave higher, of course—the first time through. Apparently, she'd been literal when she said, "Let's just sing through it." Having a second voice join Mabel seemed to make singing easier.

The second time, Mabel had soloed, and most of the song was, at any rate, not a disaster. Not to say, there weren't some issues. The biggest thing Janet kept saying was to sing out and not be so timid. "I'd rather you hit a wrong note with some confidence than waffle over it."

Before Mabel left, Janet had secretly recorded her last attempt and played it back for her. Mabel had felt a lump in her throat. She could almost forget it was her own voice. Even if she sang no better than this on Christmas Eve, Mabel would count it a victory. She hadn't frozen and she hadn't thrown up.

The song itself was beautiful. Hopefully, listeners would respond to that and not her fumbles.

Both Lisa and John had replied to her messages. Nita had also left a voicemail, wailing that getting DNA back from the bumper of her SUV could now take weeks, given the holiday season. Mabel sighed. No surprise there. Poor Nita. Her message had ended with, "Getting mixed up in this mess is *not* a good look for somebody who just barely got herself elected supervisor."

Lisa's message had been simple. "Call you at lunchtime." That should be any moment now.

John's text read, "Done here at three. Will stop by police station and see if I can ferret out any tidbits. Pizza later?"

Mabel replied, "When/where?"

"I'll swing by. Around five-thirty? Let's go out. I've been wanting to try Three Bad Cats."

Mabel replied with a smiley face. Then, not wanting to sit and chat with Lisa in the church lot, she headed home. She hadn't quite made it when her phone rang.

"Hi, Lisa. Hold on. Let me get parked and in the house. Do you have a minute?"

"Yeah. The kids have grandparent's day, and I'm not on lunch duty. So, tell me everything."

Tucking the phone under her chin, Mabel reported everything she'd learned from John and Nita, while letting Barnacle out and getting sandwich fixings out of the fridge for herself. Lisa punctuated her debriefing with repeated gasps.

"Ricky Putnam? What on earth would he be doing out there in the road—and in a snowstorm?" She moaned. "He was such a good suspect too."

"I guess nobody knows, unless the police have figured it out by now."

Lisa blew out a breath. "How horrible for Nita and her family. After everything that happened with her great-uncle, and just now recovering his remains, it feels like they're getting beaten up by the system again."

"I know, but at least so far, Nita's waiting to see how things play out. She admitted she might've looked kind of suspicious this morning. She had no idea what was going on when she left her house."

"Is Lt. Sizemore investigating?"

"I haven't heard. Hoping John knows something. I never thought I'd be saying this, but I hope she does take over the case. She's smart and honest."

"I'm sure she will, if they think it's murder," Lisa said. "I guess it may be accidental, right? I mean he was hit by a snowplow, for goodness' sake."

"Well, he was, but John told me he was already down and snow covered when the plow struck him. The impact might not be the actual cause of death—he might already have been dead at that point."

"Huh. Maybe he collapsed from a heart attack or something. Or fell and died of exposure."

"I'm hoping John will know more by this evening." Mabel thought for a moment. "Let's assume Putnam *was* murdered. Who had a motive—other than the Bedfords, that is?"

The silence on the other end of the line, Mabel presumed, was due to Lisa's thinking. Finally, Lisa spoke up. "I suppose it could be any of our other suspects. Enlow said Cathy had a new love interest. Either of the boyfriends could have gone after Ricky, if he was involved in a love triangle with her…or quadrangle…or whatever. Of course, we have no evidence of that, but then again, we haven't looked yet."

"Even Ben Holt, if he was part of a love pentagon," Mabel mused. "He's back in town, which seems odd, after all these years."

"Aaghh," Lisa wailed. "Too much geometry and not enough facts."

Silently, Mabel agreed. "Looks like Kalchik's out of the picture now. Even if he had a motive to kill Ricky, which I can't see. I guess Ben Holt could also be seeking revenge over the inheritance, but sixty years later?"

"Well, that's kind of the problem with all of them. Why now?"

Mabel's head had begun to hurt. "Maybe Bonnie got sick of him." She dug through a drawer for ibuprofen, but all that was left in the bottle was the desiccant pack.

"Look," Lisa said, "I've got to go now, but keep me posted, okay?"

"All right. We'll be in touch. I'll let you know if John gives me anything important."

Three Bad Cats Pizza occupied an old brick house on the outskirts of Bartles Grove. Even on a weeknight, the bar and dining room were both crowded. Mabel could have swooned like a southern belle at the aroma of marinara and sausage.

"I can't believe I've never been to this place." She looked around the dimly lit bar and then toward the dining room. "We won't be able to hear ourselves think, let alone talk, in the bar."

"Agreed." John took her elbow and aimed for the hostess station. "Let's see if there's a booth open in the dining room."

As it turned out, only tables in the middle of the room were available, but they could wait for a back booth. The dining room was many decibels quieter than the bar. While they waited, Mabel studied a menu and drooled over passing trays of pizza.

"Oh, this says deep-dish is their specialty."

"Yep." John nodded. "The three guys who own the place are lifelong friends. They grew up in two competing Chicago pizzeria families. There was an article in the *Statesman* when this place opened last year."

"What on earth brought them to Bartles Grove?"

"One guy married his college girlfriend, who came from here. His brother and their friend had always wanted to open a pizzeria, and they decided this would be a great place to give it a whirl. The cost of living is way lower, and they have no deep-dish competition whatsoever. Plus, they wanted to get away from their harsh winters."

Mabel raised her eyebrows.

John laughed. "Yeah, I know. But if you've ever experienced Chicago lake-effect wind and snow, you'd be scampering back here too."

A young server with straightened shoulder-length black hair

and creamy tan complexion approached with table menus and rolled silverware. She smiled. "If you'll follow me, your booth is cleared."

Mabel noticed a couple emerging from another back room. "Is that another dining area?"

The server turned. "Yes, that was once a little viewing room, when people lived here many years ago. Despite a bit of kitchen noise, it's a little quieter. Would you rather sit there?"

Mabel looked at John, who smiled. "Sure."

"Hang on a sec while I take a peek." The server peered around the corner. "One being cleared now. Please wait here a moment, okay?"

When they'd settled at their table, Mabel looked around the back room. It was as broad as the dining room, but much shallower. Only three well-spaced tables occupied the space, with theirs against the outside wall. "What were they viewing? I expected there to be paintings or a lot of windows or something."

John grinned. "Read the back of your menu."

"Oh, dear. How appetizing."

The house history revealed that in the early 1800s, the main dining room had been the front parlor, where deceased family members had been laid out for visitation. That room still had a "death's door," designated for removing the body, with no outside steps for the living to come in. This shallow back room had later been partitioned off and was used for viewing the body, and the front room became a "living room." After commercial funeral homes had come into vogue, the little parlor became an all-purpose room.

After Mabel and John had placed their order, with sausage in Mabel's half and vegan sausage in John's portion, they settled in to discuss Ricky Putnam's unexpected demise. "Did you learn anything new? Like what happened to him—or why he was out in the snow instead of sleeping in his mansion?"

"I did. Remember what I said about Doc's Lounge? Well, it seems Ricky and Bonnie went straight there from the Playhouse. They each had a couple drinks, but reportedly continued squabbling till Bonnie got up and left with the Land Rover. People who saw her said she didn't seem all that tipsy. Ricky didn't close the place down, but he nursed another drink for a while after she left, then started for home on foot."

"At his age, and in all that snow? That's crazy."

John shrugged. "He was offered a ride, but he refused it—a bit belligerently, I might add. Apparently, Doc's was his bar of choice since he turned twenty-one, and he'd been walking home like that for many years. He was in good shape for his age—as I'm sure you noticed—and all he had to do was cross the road, walk up about forty feet, and he'd be in his own driveway."

"A very long, snow-covered driveway."

"Which his Mennonite neighbors had already plowed for him earlier that evening. More snow had come down, of course, but it should still have been passable at that point, since he didn't stay all that long. For a change."

Mabel frowned. She couldn't imagine letting a man his age walk home in that snow.

John seemed to read her expression. "I know. The barkeep did say they called to let Bonnie know he was on his way but had to leave a message on her voicemail. By that point, I expect she'd turned off her phone and gone to bed."

Mabel shook her head. "Was he drunk?"

"Of course, the bartender would deny he was visibly drunk when he left there. He wouldn't want to run afoul of the Dram Shop Act, but the other patrons agreed he seemed okay. They were all regulars, like he was, and they'd been observing him for years. The most they'd say was he'd reached the argumentative stage, which wasn't all that unusual for him—and he staggered…a bit…when he stood up."

"So, at this point they're waiting on a tox screen, I suppose?"

John started ticking off a list on his fingers. "All the stuff from the medical examiner—I'd think tox screen for blood alcohol and the most common barbiturates. Physical exam to determine whether his injuries all came from the snowplow or maybe a separate impact from another vehicle or even a blow from a blunt instrument."

Mabel opened her mouth to comment, but John held up his hand. "And of course, whether he might have died from natural causes, like heart attack, stroke, or falling and either hitting his head or not being able to get up before dying of exposure."

She moaned. "For all we know, he could've been shot, stabbed, or strangled."

"As far as I know, all possibilities are on the table right now," John said. After a pause, he added, "At least in theory."

Mabel looked up sharply. "You know something, don't you? There must be at least some suspicion another vehicle was involved. Just ask Nita."

"Oh, they have some kind of evidence, but police aren't sharing."

Mabel rubbed her forehead. "Have they talked to Bonnie yet? Did she ever get the message from the bar?"

"I don't know. When police arrived to notify her Ricky was dead, she went into hysterics and has been heavily sedated ever since."

"What do you think?" Mabel studied John's expression. "*Was* it murder?"

"Even though they're being careful to eliminate other possibilities, the cops seem to think so. So does my gut—because it's such a huge coincidence. Yeah, an old guy walking home from the bar getting hit on the road looks like an accident. But I can't get past his connections to Lester's death, resurfacing all of a sudden after all these years."

"That's where the cops seem to be looking too." Mabel chewed on her lower lip. "They think Nita and her family have a motive to avenge Lester's death, and I hate to say, I don't see anybody with a stronger motive than that, sixty years after the fact."

"Ben Holt had one, but yeah," John said. "Why wouldn't he go after Ricky back then?"

"If Putnam was murdered, it had to be something unrelated to the old murders—or else somebody discovered new information lately, tying him to one or both of them."

They continued to chew on possibilities till their pizza arrived, and it was every bit as luscious as promised. For the moment, Mabel managed to shake off the visions of murder that danced like poisonous sugarplums in her head.

Chapter Thirty-Seven

Mabel tossed in bed, her heavy dinner and heavy thoughts keeping her awake long past midnight. Finally, she got up in search of an antacid. She stared out the window on her way back to bed, thinking about each suspect and what he or she might have discovered that would've stirred homicidal feelings toward Ricky. For that matter, how could they have made such a discovery when Mabel and her team of crack investigators had so far come up with nothing?

Koi emerged from the bedroom, yawned, and stretched. She padded over to Mabel and meowed.

"I agree. Snack time."

Mabel shivered. She didn't want to turn up the kitchen thermostat but grabbed a hoodie from the back of a chair. Koi sat next to her food dish and meowed soundlessly.

Mabel was pouring a few kibbles into the bowl when Barnacle clattered downstairs to join them. She rolled her eyes and grabbed the dog food.

After feeding her animals, Mabel opened a cabinet and considered her options, then firmly shut the door again. She was already having trouble sleeping. A mug of orange-spice green tea would probably sit better.

While the tea brewed, she mentally reviewed her suspect list. This felt so wrong. Christmas ought to be a time of joy and peace. As if holiday bills and to-do lists weren't already stressful enough, here she was trying to figure out which of these suspects was naughty or nice.

Mabel's mind balked at considering any of the Bedfords serious suspects in Ricky's death. She was sure police were way more anxious to solve that homicide than the others, already decades old—especially with Bonnie Putnam there to pressure for an arrest.

Poor Bonnie, losing both a sister and husband to homicide…and both during the Christmas season. Now, she seemed to have no one.

Mabel gave herself a shake. She might feel sorry for Bonnie, but Nita and her family came first. The best thing she could do for any of them was try to figure out who killed Ricky.

She couldn't expect the police to share her conviction that the Bedfords were above suspicion. Mabel rubbed her forehead. Maybe the medical examiner would rule Ricky's death accidental, but she couldn't count on it.

Who might have wanted to kill Ricky? The sooner they figured that out, the sooner Mabel could get back to worrying about *O, Holy Night*—and stop thinking about the unholy night that had left Ricky dead and Nita a police target.

Mabel opened her notebook to the suspect page. Kalchik, whether dead or alive, had no motive Mabel could see.

Bud Bender remained a suspect for Cathy's death, at least in Mabel's mind. Maybe even for Lester, if the mailman had surprised him in the act of murder. However, if Bender *had* killed Cathy, there went the one slim motive she could think of for his killing Ricky—revenge for Ricky's murder of the woman Bender had loved.

Hold on—might Ricky have been wrestling the mailbag away from Lester at the moment Bender tried to flee Cathy's murder scene? Mabel paused, her finger on Bender's name on her list. She kind of liked this scenario.

The water was boiling. Mabel turned off the burner and started her tea steeping.

Why now? She kept coming back to that question. Maybe Bender thought at the time that he'd escaped Ricky's notice, but

Ricky might've recently given some indication he knew what Bud had done.

Why would Ricky open his mouth now though?

There were practical problems too—maybe not insurmountable, but they did make Bender a less probable suspect. For one thing, he'd just been at the reception after his big show, surrounded by enthusiastic audience members. Would he have scampered right out, stalked Ricky Putnam till he emerged from Doc's Lounge, and then committed murder?

For another, Bender seemed frailer than several other Medicine Spring seniors. Still, how much strength or agility would it take to drive a car into someone?

Mabel shook her head. She'd seen his vanity plate on a Mini Cooper in the Playhouse lot. Bender would've been lucky to get his tiny, lightweight car home in that blizzard, let alone make a homicidal detour.

Mabel shuddered. What would it take to steer into a human being? Besides being horrifying, it might take a bit of skill. You'd want to make sure the victim was dead, lest he identify you later. And in the process, you'd have to maintain control of your vehicle, or you'd end up in the ditch yourself with your wheels in the air.

What about Ben Holt? Quite a coincidence, his returning just as all this murder business was filling the air. He, at least, had an obvious and longstanding motive to kill Ricky, assuming he'd been stewing in dreams of vengeance for the past sixty years. He still appeared quite vital, and given his worn boots and jeans, she could easily imagine his driving the sort of four-wheel-drive vehicle cowboys now used to ride the range.

Mabel was about to focus on Mark Enlow when her messenger app pinged, making her jump and Barnacle bark. *Nita.*

Apparently, Mabel wasn't alone in being unable to sleep tonight. She read the message: *You up?* Nita wanted to video chat at—what was it?—1:16 am. "Hey," Mabel said when Nita appeared on her screen, wearing a ratty beige robe over what looked like Halloween pajamas with big orange jack-o'-lanterns on them.

"Thank the Lord you're up. I feel like I'm going to crawl right out of my skin tonight."

"I couldn't sleep either. I was going through our suspect list. I don't think we can deal with what happened to your Uncle Lester till we get to the bottom of this Ricky Putnam thing."

Nita sighed. "Agreed. But, hey, I have something crazy I want to run by you. Think Lisa's awake?"

It was Saturday night, but… "Nooo...but she'll be madder about missing something than being wakened at this hour."

A moment later, Lisa's drowsy face appeared on screen. "What is this? A middle-aged slumber party?"

"We couldn't sleep," Mabel said. "We've been talking about Ricky Putnam's death. Nita has an idea."

Lisa perked up. "I'm gonna make tea, but I have my volume up. Keep talking."

"I saw Bonnie in town today," Nita said. "She was driving her Mercedes sedan."

"So?" Mabel frowned.

"I know the roads are a little better now, but why wouldn't she be driving the Land Rover, as usual?"

Lisa popped onscreen. "Yeah, considering that long lane of theirs."

Mabel shook her head. "I heard the neighbors plowed the lane. Plus, that was Ricky's car—I not only saw him driving it, but it had his vanity plate on the back."

"They did plow it," Nita said, "and mine too. It's still not like driving on pavement though, and the mansion has that big hill you'd have to climb back up. They aren't confident drivers. I've never seen either of them out in snowy weather without the four-wheel-drive."

Mabel shrugged. "Interesting, but…"

"Bonnie drove Ricky's car all the time in bad weather. He didn't go out a lot, so I guess he didn't mind."

Wheels began turning in Mabel's head. "Wait. Are you saying there's something wrong with the Rover?"

"Like a dent from hitting a human being in the road?" Lisa asked.

Nita nodded. "Guessing. Wouldn't that be something—if Bonnie was the culprit?"

Lisa yawned and tottered offscreen. She came back carrying her tea mug. "Motive?"

Nita and Mabel spoke at once. "I haven't gotten that far," Nita said.

"What about this?" Mabel realized this theory had been incubating in the back of her brain for a while now, simply waiting for the right conditions for it to mature. "Ricky killed Bonnie's sister. Not sure why. Maybe he had a thing for her and she spurned him. Or maybe she surprised him when he was killing Lester, and he had to eliminate her as a witness."

"All right." Lisa nodded, and so did Nita, who added, "Assuming for purposes of argument, right?"

"Right. Ricky had no known connection with Cathy, so Bonnie had no idea he was guilty. They had a whirlwind courtship, which is pretty weird in itself, don't you think?" Mabel asked.

"Surprising for somebody like Ricky, who was very young and suddenly very rich." Lisa rubbed her chin. "Perfect set-up for someone in his demographic–not to mention someone known for his immaturity—to go out and party and enjoy a wide variety of beautiful female companionship. *Not* get married and tie himself down right away."

Nita jumped up and began pacing, going in and out of screen. "Ooh, this is good."

"Motive for marriage?" Lisa tented her fingers and rested

them against her lips.

"For her?" Mabel looked aside, collecting her thoughts, then back. "Hey, something good in her life at a bad time. A good-looking guy with a ton of money wants to marry her. Wouldn't be surprised if she wasn't thinking real clearly under the circumstances."

"Easy enough. But what about him?"

Nita stuck her face close to her camera. "He'd want to get Bonnie on his side. Quiet her suspicions. Or to give her something else to distract her from pushing for answers. Maybe there was evidence he thought would mean something to Bonnie if she focused in on it."

"Then suddenly, after all this time, something makes Bonnie realize her husband's the monster who killed her sister—and had also betrayed Bonnie. Took advantage of her, made a fool of her, used her." Mabel realized she'd raised her voice in her excitement and put a hand over her mouth.

Nita slapped her table and both Mabel and Lisa jumped. "Who'd know Ricky's routine better than his wife? Who'd be in a better position to snoop around in his things? Who'd be able to find out stuff an outsider wouldn't?"

"Omigosh," Lisa breathed. "Did we just break the case?"

"Maybe one of them." Mabel sank back in her chair, and Koi leapt onto her lap and rubbed her chin against Mabel's. Mabel petted absently. "We do have three bodies and only a potential solution for one of them." She emphasized "potential."

"How do we get the police to go find the Land Rover and check it over?" Nita frowned. "Guessing she's already scrubbed away any blood or hair evidence. Might even have it at a body shop somewhere out of town by now."

Lisa rubbed her chin. "Scrubbed it, maybe, but with modern equipment and chemicals, you'd be surprised what police can still find."

Mabel sat back up. "I don't know if she's had time to get the Rover to a body shop. Ricky's accident—or murder—just happened. The police were on the scene practically in front of Bonnie's driveway all night and a good chunk of the next day. It would take nerves of steel to drive the murder vehicle out onto the street so soon. Let alone with a Ricky-shaped dent in the front."

Nita smiled. "Good point. Back to my question. How are we gonna get the police to go take a look at the widow's own car?"

Lisa straightened, no longer looking sleepy, with a grin the size of Kansas. Her expression was one Mabel had learned to dread.

"Oh, no," Mabel said. "No, no, no."

Chapter Thirty-Eight

"NITA." LISA HAD A GLEAM IN her eye. "How close are you to the Putnam's?"

Nita scoffed. "No more than to nod to."

Lisa snorted. "I don't care whether Bonnie invites you to her Tupperware parties. I'm talking geography. How far is their place from yours?"

"Short walk. They're the other side of the Stoltzfus farm."

"Couple miles?"

It was Nita's turn to snort. "This isn't Wyoming. Twenty to forty acres or so, and deeper than they are wide. Half a mile, maybe three quarters."

Alarms clanged in Mabel's head. "Lisa, no."

Lisa waved a dismissive hand, still looking at Nita. "Dogs? Alarm systems?"

Now, Nita had a troubling gleam in her eye, as well. "Stoltzfuses have a collie mix. They've been keeping her inside since the weather got bad. Far as I know, the Putnams aren't animal lovers." She frowned. "An alarm…I'd have to bet they do."

Lisa took a sip of tea, then warmed her hands around the mug, resting the rim against her chin. "What do you think—on the perimeter or just the house?"

Nita shook her head. "I wouldn't know. Best guess…alarm on the house, security lights and cameras outside."

"Well, shoot, then."

Mabel gave Lisa her sternest look. "I know what you're thinking, and somebody *might* shoot. Too risky."

Lisa pointedly ignored her. "Safest route?"

"Through the woods." Nita groaned. "Not the driveway. We

wouldn't want to climb that hill in full view of the windows—and cameras, if any, which I bet there are."

"Through the woods? You've got to be kidding." Mabel couldn't believe a respectable middle-aged kindergarten teacher and business owner were having this conversation. "There's snow out there. We'll get caught. I mean *you'll* get caught."

"There's an old wagon road, at least through the back of my property and Stoltzfuses."

"And once you get to Putnams' property line? Still a road—do you even know? Is there a fence? Will that car be parked outside where we can see it, even if we get that far?" Mabel wanted to shake some sense into them.

"Well, we don't know till we reconnoiter." Lisa shrugged. "Where's your sense of adventure, Mabes? We always planned to be investigators, didn't we? Investigators have got to take a few risks."

"*You* planned to be an investigator. I was going to be Perry Mason. And we were twelve years old—at our age, the 'risks' include breaking a hip out there." Mabel inserted air quotes, breathing hard.

"Hey, you don't have to come." Nita's voice was soothing. "You've already done way more than your share for my family and me. Just stick close to your phone, okay?"

Mabel shook her head. "Oh, no. I'm not letting you two go it alone. If anyone's staying back, it's you. If the police are already suspicious of you, the last thing you need is getting caught creeping around Bonnie's property in the dead of night."

Lisa set her mug down. "So we're agreed we're going?"

Nita got to her feet. "All of us or none of us. I'm gonna go get dressed."

"Me too. I'll pick you up in ten or fifteen, Mabes. Watch for us, Nita, and everybody make sure you have your cell phone and a flashlight with good batteries."

"Wait." Mabel's feeble objection was drowned out by scraping chairs, and her friends disappeared from the screen.

The full moon was still a week away. It was surprisingly bright, nonetheless. Mabel had mixed emotions about that. When the foolish, overage Nancy Drew, Bess, and George crept into the open area behind the Putnam mansion, this moon might still be bright enough to reveal what they were up to. Yet the additional light was helpful as the trio made their way through the snowy woods.

The wagon road was in better shape than Mabel had feared, and most of the heavy, wet snowfall had melted away. Once their eyes had adjusted, the moonlight showed the clear outline of the road edges. Sadly, the ruts, rocks, and fallen branches weren't as easy to see, as she noticed every time she tripped or skidded.

It was cold under a cloudless sky. Mabel shivered, and her teeth were beginning to chatter. She wished she'd had the time and foresight to put on long underwear. She caught the back of Nita's parka. "Where are we?"

"The Stoltzfus barn ought to be straight down that way, but there's a field between us and it."

"Ought to be? Don't we know?"

"Give me a break—we're in the woods. I've walked this road since I was two or three, but I haven't been up here in over a year. Plus, it's dark, and everything looks different in the winter."

"I was just asking." Mabel felt in her pocket, in case she had a candy bar or something to take her mind off what they were doing, but all she found were old, crumpled tissues. If John knew where they were, he'd blow his top.

That reminded her. "Hey, did either of you leave word about

where we were headed?"

Of course not.

Nita shook her head, and Lisa told her to stop worrying.

Mabel clamped her lips shut and returned to worrying.

Soon, the wagon road made an abrupt left and began descending the slope. Mabel's boots slipped in the slush, and she grabbed at bushes to keep her balance. "Where is this taking us?"

"It heads down to the road. Or did. I don't know…if it goes all the way through…anymore." Nita was puffing now, and her words came in short bursts.

Lisa looked back. "We're not on your property at this point?"

"Right. We're on the line between Stoltzfus and Putnam."

Mabel frowned in thought. "I think it does. I remember seeing some kind of opening in the brush at the side of the road along there, but it was pretty overgrown."

"No one's used it in years," Nita said, "but it doesn't matter. We can't stay on the wagon road anyhow. If we don't want to call attention to ourselves, we need to come in at the back of the property. Through the woods."

So far, they hadn't needed their flashlights, but if they were going to leave the relative openness of the wagon road and scramble over rocks and fallen trees, they'd have to turn on some light. Mabel checked the time. "It's almost 3:30."

"Thanks for the update," Lisa said dryly. "Let's keep moving. We need to get in and out while things are still quiet. It won't be daylight for a few hours, but for all we know Bonnie might be an early riser, particularly if she decides to sneak the Land Rover off the property before people start stirring."

The woods were snarled with thickets of brush and crisscrossed with downed trees. Mabel stumbled and caught herself on a twig that snapped in her hand. She landed on one knee in the slush and struggled to get up till Nita reached back and gave her a tug.

"How much farther?" Mabel knew she sounded grouchy, but she couldn't help it. This whole escapade was nuts, and she devoutly wished she'd gone back to bed.

"We should be getting a glimpse of the gardens behind the Putnam house in the next five or ten minutes." Nita steadied Mabel till she had both feet firmly planted. "We ought to be able to stay in the shadow of the woods while we look around outside for the Land Rover."

"And if we don't see it?"

Lisa stopped, bent over, resting her hands on her knees as she caught her breath. She was many pounds lighter than Mabel, but it didn't appear she was in much better shape. "Whew." Her flashlight beam danced crazily as she straightened. "There's a garage, I presume?"

"Yeah." Nita rubbed her chin. "I haven't been back here since I was a kid, but at that time, there was a big garage, a shed, what looked like an old stable, a barn—and the pool house, of course."

"Of course." Mabel narrowed her eyes. "Are you guys seriously thinking of breaking into buildings?"

Nita and Lisa exchanged a glance. "Well…" Lisa looked away. "No breaking and entering, of course." She looked back at Mabel. "Maybe try to sneak a peek inside. Somehow."

Mabel's stomach lurched. "Once we step into the yard, there are bound to be security lights and cameras. If we lay so much as a finger on one of the buildings—"

"We run the risk of alarms," Lisa concluded.

"You understand you're risking your job if we get arrested."

"I'm willing to bet the alarms are only attached to the house," Nita said. "With lights and cameras on the grounds. We'll pull up our hoods and sneak a quick peek. If the Rover's here, we'll take a few quick pics and get out."

Mabel pulled out her phone and began searching penalties for trespass. She had a weak connection, but it was too slow. Her friends were already moving, so she moaned and stowed the phone in her pocket.

The Putnam mansion lay in darkness below them as they emerged at the edge of the woods. Of course, a light might be on in front, but it was a big house, and Mabel doubted anyone on that side would see or hear them.

"I don't see a car," she whispered.

"Me, neither."

Mabel glanced at Nita and was startled to see her scanning the grounds through a pair of binoculars. "What do we do now?"

"I think we should do a quick reconnaissance of the perimeter," Lisa said. "Everyone set your phones to vibrate. I'll go clockwise. Nita, you want to go counterclockwise?"

Nita gave a quick nod and began moving.

"What about me?" Mabel hissed.

"You've got the birds' eye view up here. You want to be lookout for now? Call us if you see anyone, okay?"

"Um, sure. You guys stay back in the shadows, all right? Stay off the lawn."

"Roger that." Lisa giggled, as if this were fun.

Minutes ticked by as Mabel scanned the house and gardens. She soon lost sight of Lisa and Nita as they melted into the woods edge. No lights flashed on inside the house or outbuildings, and the gardens and pool area remained dark. Shadowy mounds here and there remained motionless, and Mabel concluded they must be bushes or statuary.

Mabel's pocket vibrated, and she jumped. Fumbling, she

brought out her phone. Lisa had texted, *Mercedes parked in front. No sign of Rover. Headed back.*

Nita replied, *Nothing this side. On my way.*

This property had clearly once been farmed, and despite later gentrification, it still retained the outbuildings Nita had described from her childhood memories. While she waited for her friends, Mabel studied the buildings. The garage was right next to the house. The shed was too small, and the pool house didn't have big enough doors. She chewed her lip. The one-level stable had four stalls across, each with its own Dutch door.

Mabel squinted. It was hard to be sure without binoculars, but she didn't think the doors were padlocked. They'd be too narrow for the Rover, though.

She turned her attention to the barn, set way back by the trees. One narrow door on this end that she could see—big enough for a person or a horse or cow to pass through. She knew, however, that most barns had a wide entrance in back, built to accommodate hulking farm equipment and towering loads of hay. If she were Bonnie and wanted to hide the Land Rover for a while, her instinct would be to stash it in back, on the upper level.

"Hey." Nita's voice sounded so close to her ear that Mabel startled and dropped her phone.

"Sorry." Nita shone her light on the phone, now sticking up out of a clump of snowy leaf litter. She stomped her feet, likely because they were turning into frozen stumps, like Mabel's.

As Mabel stood back up, phone in hand, Lisa approached from the other direction. Nita motioned for her to hurry over and pointed. "I passed right behind that barn. There's a road curving up around to the upper level, where the hay and equipment would be stored. I saw car tracks leading up there."

Mabel's heart lurched. "What now?" From what she knew of barns, there wouldn't be many windows up there.

"We'll have to look." Lisa's words were decisive, but Mabel

heard the quiver. It was one thing to imagine oneself a detective, but quite another to sneak around in the dead of night, searching for clues on someone else's property.

Nita must have heard that quiver too. "I'll go. It's my problem, not yours."

"Nita, no." Mabel and Lisa spoke at once. "The cops are already suspicious," Lisa said. "You can't afford to get caught."

Mabel blew out a gusty breath. "Well, neither can you." She gave Lisa a stern look. "You can't risk your job, which is what you'd be doing."

Mabel gulped, choked when spit went down her airway, and coughed till she could breathe again. "I'll go."

Chapter Thirty-Nine

"THAT'S NOT FAIR." LISA GRABBED MABEL'S wrist. "None of this was your idea to begin with."

Nita put out her arms and blocked Mabel's path. "Hey, the last thing I want is for you guys to get in trouble for helping me."

Mabel swallowed hard and lifted her chin. "I'll be careful. The worst they can do if I get caught is charge me with trespass and make me pay a fine."

"Then we should all go," Nita said.

Mabel shook her head. "I've already been over this. If I get caught, they'll send me home. If Lisa gets caught, she might lose her job—something I, of course, don't have to lose. If they catch you—" Mabel gave Nita a severe look. "The cops already have your car. If they catch you prowling around here, they'll be sure you had something to do with Ricky's death."

Mabel pried Lisa's hand off her arm. "We can't all risk getting caught. If things go bad, I need you well out of range. Use your heads…and your phones."

"Who should we call?"

As much as Mabel hated the idea, there was one obvious answer. "John. You've got his number, right? At the very least, he can give us a ride home. I think I have hypothermia at this point, not to mention frostbitten toes."

Mabel surveyed the building below them. There was no way she was going to walk across that wide open area, with all those windows facing her. She chewed her lip. Nita had gotten close to the back barn door without any security lights coming on, so maybe she ought to retrace Nita's route. As much as she hated the thought of scrambling through more woods, that's what she'd have to do.

She gave her squad one last thumbs-up and started making

her way through trees and brush. It wasn't all that far to the barn by this route, and the woods sloped way down to the level of the dirt ramp leading to the back door. Short minutes later, she stood facing the barn door from a few yards away.

Mabel hesitated before leaving the tree cover. This was it. Would she be flooded by a blaze of lights the moment she stepped out? See the flash of a security camera?

What should she do if that happened?

Complete the mission. There was no other choice. Once her picture was taken, there'd be no need for a line-up. Just about everyone in the Medicine Spring PD would recognize her right away.

Mabel grimaced. They not only knew her, they'd all interrogated her at one time or another. Nobody on the force needed directions to her house anymore. Did that make things better or worse?

Visions of Detective Lieutenant Sizemore's face swam before her eyes. *Okay, definitely worse.*

But she was committed. Taking a deep breath, Mabel pulled her hood around her face, bent forward, and darted for the door.

No security lights. No camera flashes.

Mabel threw herself against the rough boards of the barn siding and panted with relief. She'd made it. It was darker between the trees and the shadow of the building. She turned on her flashlight app and focused the point of light at the door.

Mabel couldn't believe her luck. The closure was an old-fashioned iron latch bar that slid into a metal bracket. *No lock!* She texted.

Did this mean Bonnie wasn't a husband killer, hiding the car she'd used to do him in? Or just extremely cocky?

Mabel shoved to open the rusty latch, but it stuck. She jiggled the latch with cold-stiffened fingers and shoved again.

Nothing.

Again. Finally, the latch gave way. She grunted and heaved the big sliding door aside as her boots slipped in the slush.

Horrified at the door's loud squawking and rattling, Mabel

stopped pushing as soon as she'd made an opening big enough to squeeze through. She stood inside for a moment, listening. All she heard was her own heartbeat in her ears. Smells of old hay or straw, mixed with the funk of motor oil, made her sneeze.

Mabel blew her nose, then shone her light around the open space. The haymow above looked empty, though bits of hay from long-ago harvests still littered the floor.

In the near left corner under the loft was a small, built-out room like a shipping crate with a locked door, and next to it, what looked like a grain chute for stalls below. Mabel's eyes were drawn at once to the vehicles parked to her right—a full-size John Deere tractor, a gleaming garden tractor that looked for all the world like the bigger tractor's younger brother, and most notably, the missing Land Rover.

The car had been pulled straight in, so its front end lay hidden in shadows. Her light caught the "Ricky P" plate. Now, for the moment of truth. Would she find front-end damage? Even blood?

Heart slamming, Mabel opened her camera app and crept forward. She held up her light for a better look at the left front bumper and quarter panel. *Pristine.* The sole visible blemish was dried salt spray.

Mabel's stomach lurched. What if they were wrong? Bonnie had seemed like such a good suspect.

Well, she hadn't seen the right side yet. The vehicle sat with its nose jammed up against a stack of moldy-smelling haybales, so Mabel had to turn around.

She rounded the back of the Land Rover. When she shone her light toward the right front panel, Mabel drew in her breath with a gasp. Almost at once, she heard rustling behind her, accompanied by a squawk from the door.

"What do you think you're doing?"

Chapter Forty

At the sharp female voice behind her, Mabel spun around. Lisa and Nita stood in the doorway, Bonnie Putnam between and a half-step behind them, holding a gun. Society matron though she was—and old enough to be Mabel's mother—Bonnie might've been a Bigfoot hunter in heavy black parka, ski pants, and boots, eyes obscured by night vision goggles.

"Toss me your phone."

Mabel stepped forward but held onto her phone. She'd gotten her cheap case online and suspected it hadn't been built for bouncing off the floor.

"Stop right there." The gun came up a bit higher. "I said, 'Toss the phone.'" Except that Bonnie used a bad word to modify "phone."

"Here's the thing," Mabel said.

"Toss. The. Phone." Bonnie grabbed Lisa's coat collar and turned the gun on her.

Mabel gasped. "Hey, wait. I just don't want to break my phone."

"Mabel," Lisa snapped.

"Don't shoot. But…could you hold out your hands to catch it? I don't throw too well."

"I don't shoot too well either, but if you don't throw that thing right now, I'm going to try shooting it out of your hand. It might be fun to see what I hit." The gun swung toward Mabel.

"Throw it, Mabel." Lisa was gritting her teeth now.

Nita caught Mabel's eye and tossed her head up, as if trying to convey some message Mabel wasn't sure she could read.

"I *am* throwing it." Mabel took a couple little practice swings, then hurled her phone directly at Bonnie's face.

The instant the phone left Mabel's hand, Nita lurched sideways, shoving Bonnie off balance. Predictably, the phone went wide and smacked Lisa in the head, knocking her over as Lisa tried too late to duck. The gun went off as Bonnie toppled, firing a shot into the barn ceiling.

Mabel drew a deep breath and piled on top of the three struggling women. Nita slammed Bonnie's wrist against the floorboards. Bonnie screamed but wouldn't let go of her gun.

Lisa, squashed beneath Nita and Bonnie, wheezed, "Mabel, get the gun."

Pushing with her hands and feet, Mabel tried to roll aside, in an attempt to gracefully exit the four-woman pileup. The bodies beneath her lurched and bucked, throwing Mabel back and forth, and finally pitched her off. She landed on her right shoulder with a jolt of pain before crashing onto her backside.

By rocking on her bottom and paddling with arms and legs, Mabel scrambled, staggering, to her feet. Where was the gun?

"Stomp on her hand," Nita ordered.

Mabel looked around in the dim, dusty light shed by her cell phone, which had landed facedown a few feet away. At last, she spotted the firearm. Nita was still forcing the muzzle away from the group of people, but Bonnie would not let go.

Mabel put out a hand to balance herself against Nita's shoulder, but Nita kept moving as Bonnie struggled. "Can you hold still a sec?"

"Sorry," Nita muttered. "No can do. Just stomp."

Mabel planted a tentative booted foot on Bonnie's gun hand.

"Ow! You're going to get charged with that." Bonnie gasped but still held onto her weapon.

Mabel gritted her teeth. She suspected Nita, like she herself, felt a weird and unhelpful reluctance to hurt the older woman. Belatedly, she also remembered Pennsylvania law imposed enhanced sentencing for serious assaults on victims over sixty.

"Are you okay, ma'am?" Mabel picked up her foot and tried to peer at Bonnie in the bands of moonlight breaking through gaps in the barn siding.

To her surprise, Bonnie spit at her, though Mabel was blessedly far enough away to miss the projectile.

"Come on, Mrs. Putnam—be nice. We don't mean any harm."

"Yeah," Lisa wheezed as she struggled out from beneath Nita and Bonnie. "We might've just gotten lost in the woods and been seeking shelter, you know."

"Is that your story?" Bonnie snorted.

"Well…"

"I didn't think so." Bonnie's fingers moved slightly, as if relieving stiffness in her gun hand.

Mabel swallowed. If she picked her moment, she might be able to snatch the firearm right out of Bonnie's grip. "Why don't we all wait for the police to sort this out?"

Again, the rude snort from Bonnie. "What police? You three broke into my property and attacked an elderly woman. Nobody would blame me if I shot to defend myself."

Mabel looked at Nita and Lisa, but there wasn't enough light to make eye contact. Had this batty old lady just said she planned to shoot and kill them if they let her up?

"If that's how you want it." Nita gave a complacent yawn. "You keep the gun, and we'll take our chances with the police. As long as I'm sitting here, you're not going anywhere. You tell your story, and we'll tell ours."

"Good luck with that," Bonnie sputtered. "You broke into my building in the middle of the night. Try explaining that."

"I did not break in," Mabel insisted. "We were walking

through the woods, and the door was unlocked. There's no harm in being curious, is there?"

"It killed the cat."

Lisa stretched the kinks out of her back. "Have it your way. Like my friend said, we can tell our story to the police, and you tell yours."

"Yeah." Mabel fixed Bonnie with a hard glare, though she didn't imagine Bonnie could see it in the dim light, and with her cheek pressed to the floor. "I'd love to hear you explain where that huge dent in the front end of the Land Rover came from."

Bonnie's hand twitched, and Mabel swooped to grab the gun. Bonnie's hand tightened, but a beat too late. Mabel kicked the weapon well aside, afraid to touch it.

Bonnie swore. "So, I hit a deer. Everybody does, sooner or later."

"Then explain why the blood and hair contain your husband's DNA."

"What blood and hair?" As Nita helped her to a seat on the haybales, Bonnie gave Mabel a sly smile.

"Maybe you washed it, but the police will still find it," Lisa said. "There's bound to be a trace in a crack somewhere."

Bonnie tapped her upper lip in apparent thought. "I'm willing to work with you. Let's trade. I don't report you three for breaking and entering, assault and battery, attempted theft…and whatever. You pretend you were never here and keep your mouths shut—deal? I'll even sweeten the pot. How does ten thousand apiece sound?"

"Like you're trying to bribe witnesses." Mabel shook her head in disgust.

"Just resolving an awkward situation." Bonnie waved a dismissive hand. "I'm a grieving widow. Have any of you been married almost sixty years? Do you know what it's like to be devoted to someone that long, and all at once they're gone? How terrifying it is to wake up in the middle of the night and see security images of people creeping around your property? I don't even have employees here overnight. Anyone would panic."

Mabel swallowed. Was she bluffing? There hadn't been a single flash. Then it struck her, and she almost groaned aloud. Infrared cameras. Of course.

"The police seem to think you might be responsible for Rick's death, Miss Bedford. I disagree, as you've always been a quiet neighbor who minded your own business. We both have a tiny bit of body damage on our cars. Very common around here in the winter months, but awkward. Since we're both innocent of anything worse than an ordinary fender bender, it's in our mutual interest to keep our mouths shut. Agreed?"

When Nita just stared at her, Bonnie went on. "All you need do is leave me to my grief, and I let you return to your warm, comfy beds. No harm, no foul."

Lisa gaped at her. "What are we supposed to tell the police?"

"Don't worry." Bonnie smiled. "I didn't call the police—and I've already handled the security company inquiry."

Now it was Nita and Mabel's turn to gape. For a self-described grieving and frightened widow—who must be pushing eighty—her choosing to avoid police intervention was almost as good as a confession. Plus, they'd all heard her dummy up a reason to shoot and kill them all, after hunting them down in her ninja assault get-up.

Mabel sidled close to Lisa and whispered. "Did she take your phones?"

Lisa nodded. "They're somewhere out there in the woods. She made us toss them, but we'd already heard her coming and I texted John first."

"Not 9-1-1?"

"Perfect," Bonnie interjected. "So, no problem with the police."

Lisa ignored her. "I figured we were busted, and that she'd already called the cops on us. But then I realized if she *had* killed Ricky, things might go very bad."

"We didn't know *who* was out there," Nita said. "I was about to bite the bullet and dial 9-1-1, when she yelled to toss the phones and put our hands up."

Mabel shivered. They might in fact have bitten the bullet. She shuffled past Bonnie to look for her phone, which no longer seemed to be giving any light.

Lisa and Nita continued questioning Bonnie, while Mabel crawled around the floor. Finally, she felt her phone under her hand.

"My screen's cracked!" She pushed buttons. "My battery must be dead. It was still lit up earlier, after I threw it. I—"

Abrupt, thunderous pounding rattled the door, and blinding lights blazed through the cracks in the siding. Mabel jumped and screamed, along with everyone else in the barn.

"Police—open up!"

Chapter Forty-One

Bonnie stumbled to the door.

The moment it opened, two officers shoved inside, guns drawn. Detective Lieutenant Sizemore followed, wearing old jeans and a heavy wool blanket coat in olive buffalo plaid. Looked like she'd gotten out of bed for this.

Sizemore stared at Mabel and shook her head.

Mabel tried a smile. "Hi."

"Is this the whole cast of characters?"

Mabel nodded, and Bonnie said, "Yes."

Sizemore tossed her head toward the open door. "Jerry, tell the guys we'll be escorting these ladies down to the house for questioning."

Nita raised her hand. "Could somebody check the Land Rover for damage? It's—"

Sizemore waved her hand for silence. "We don't have a warrant, and as far as I've heard, the Constitution still applies to barns."

"But you're already here, and there's—"

"Doesn't matter." Sizemore held up her hand like a traffic cop. "We're *not* going to violate Ms. Putnam's rights. After we get your stories, we'll see what we have. Never fear, Ms. Bedford—if there's probable cause, we'll deal with it then."

One of the officers took Bonnie's elbow and headed her toward the door. Bonnie sniffled and held her arm. "These women are criminals. They broke in and attacked me when I came to investigate."

"Yes, ma'am."

Two other officers stepped over the doorsill and came inside.

One gestured for Nita to come with him, and the other took Lisa's arm.

Mabel swallowed hard. This was the worst mess she'd ever been in.

Sizemore looked at Mabel and shook her head again. "This is a bridge too far, Ms. Browne."

Mabel looked away and blinked back the tears that had forced their way up from her aching chest. She pointed. "Uh, there's a gun over there somewhere."

Sizemore's eyes widened.

"It belongs to Bonnie, um, Putnam."

Sizemore spoke into her mic, asking Jerry to come back to the barn. Then, she turned to Mabel with a wry look. "I hope no one's expecting you home for breakfast, Ms. Browne."

By the time John treated Mabel, Nita, and Lisa to all-day breakfast at the truck stop by the interstate ramp, the "most important meal of the day" was hours late. Tim had been invited, but was due at the woodworking company, which had a big custom order to get out the door. Nita had texted her long-suffering assistant Zac to cover for her. For the next two hours, Mabel and her friends had talked about their overnight mission and tried to explain to John why it had seemed like a good idea at the time.

When Mabel stumbled through her own door at last, the sun was riding high. She felt both exhausted and overstimulated. She suspected if she lay down to sleep, she'd toss and chase her thoughts for hours.

At least, it looked like Bonnie wouldn't be preferring charges against them for their well-intentioned but ill-advised trespass. As John had pointed out, she was in a world of far more serious trouble of her own.

According to a text John received as they'd pulled into the

truck stop lot, Bonnie had confessed to killing Ricky. If Bonnie's confession was to murder—and not a tragic accident on bad roads—Mabel assumed she might well receive a life sentence, though even an early release, or a reduced sentence of twenty years or so, would still keep her in prison till she was approaching 100. Pennsylvania hadn't executed anyone in decades, but murder was still a capital crime.

Barnacle whined and jumped till he knocked her off balance and sent her crashing into the kitchen table. Mabel steadied herself and pushed him down. "I'm sorry, buddy. Let's get you outside and then feed you."

By some miracle, the dog had waited to potty. While she appreciated the gesture, she also felt a wave of guilt for making him wait. She didn't deserve him.

There came those tears again. Mabel scrunched her eyes shut till the moment passed. Her emotions were extra fragile after the night she'd had.

As she got out the pet food, she spied Koi sitting atop the Hoosier cupboard, tail tip twitching with disapproval. "I'm sorry," she repeated. "Come down and get your breakfast, okay?"

Though Barnacle inhaled his food the moment she set it down, Koi was still eating when Mabel gathered her strength to climb upstairs to bed. She had just pulled on a pair of leggings and a big sweatshirt and started to get into bed when her phone rang.

She'd planned to silence her phone but hadn't had a chance to do it yet. Because it was John, she picked up. "Hey."

"Are you trying to sleep?"

"Not yet. What's up?"

"I got more info on the Putnam case just now. Should I fill you in, or do you want to take a nap first?"

"I wouldn't be able to sleep now anyway. Go ahead and tell me."

"Mac says they were about to apply for an emergency search

warrant to prevent Bonnie from destroying evidence, when she confessed. I guess she realized the jig was up, with three witnesses against her and the police about to go over that huge dent in her car for Ricky's DNA."

"What did she say? Was it an accident?"

"I don't know yet. All I know is she confessed to hitting him. I suppose she could make out a case that she'd gone back to pick him up but slid in the snow and panicked when she hit him."

"What happens now?" Mabel asked.

"Last I heard, she was conferring with her attorney. That's been going on for a while now. I'll let you know if I hear more."

After John hung up, Mabel tried to fall asleep. Despite her exhaustion, sleep wouldn't come. It was hard to sleep with daylight seeping into the room, and intrusive thoughts of the night before pushing their way into her head, along with burning curiosity about what Bonnie would ultimately confess to.

Maybe now, they could get back to resolving Lester's death, not to mention Christmas and *O, Holy Night*. Thinking of her solo was so agitating, Mabel gave up and got out of bed.

Her feet dragged on her way downstairs again. Koi, who'd ordinarily have come upstairs to bed with Mabel, seemed to be expecting her. The cat was stretched across the back of the living room couch, staring at the unlit tree. When Mabel approached, Koi turned her head and meowed silently.

"Okay." Mabel plugged in the lights and felt her spirits lift as the colors bloomed to life. For a moment, she stood and stared, along with the cat. "Good idea," Mabel told her before plodding into the kitchen.

While the coffee brewed, Mabel inhaled the rich aroma and tried without success to push all thoughts of murder out of her mind. Christmas Eve was almost here. She'd wanted all this homicidal business cleared away by now, in time for a happy Hollywood ending.

She regretted not solving Lester's murder—or Cathy's for that matter. That's what she'd promised Nita and her family to begin with. That she was going to figure out who'd killed Lester—and clear his good name. With the help of her friends, of course.

Then Ricky Putnam had gone and complicated everything by deciding to get himself killed too. Of course, his death had to take precedence over decades-old events, but she knew Lester's fate still hung over the Bedfords' Christmas.

At least, Mabel told herself, now maybe Nita could have her car back.

In the front room, Barnacle was barking.

When Mabel peered out the window, the mail carrier was turning around in her driveway. "Settle down," she told the dog. "It's just Nancy."

Mabel hunched into her parka and made her way to the mailbox. As usual, it was crammed with colorful holiday advertising. Also, an electric bill, she noticed with a grimace. Plus, two—no, three cards.

Of course, Mabel had never gotten around to sending any Christmas cards herself. So, she wasn't surprised she'd received a mere handful in the mail. In fact, one of these was addressed to Barnacle and Koi. She flipped it over and saw her vet's return address stamped on the flap.

Back inside the kitchen, Mabel kicked off her shoes. "You guys got mail."

Barnacle jumped up on her, an old habit Mabel had been unable to break. She doubted he was interested in his Christmas card. He just about always greeted her this way—whether she'd been gone overnight or only out to the mailbox. Unsurprisingly, Koi didn't bother to rouse herself from her perch on the couch.

Mabel poured her coffee and sat at the kitchen table to go through her other mail. Two cards were addressed to her, one in her niece Betsy's handwriting. She didn't recognize the other, addressed to Miss Mabel Browne, complete with title, which had become unusual these days.

Out of curiosity, she opened it first. An old-fashioned card showed a couple in a one-horse sleigh, winding their way through a snow-covered landscape to a church in the valley.

Mabel shook off an unsettling sense of déjà vu. Nonetheless, she picked up the envelope again and was relieved to see substantial postage in the form of a current stamp with a Madonna and child.

All the same, a folded sheet of stationery fell out as she opened the card. History seemed determined to repeat itself.

Mabel took a fortifying drink of coffee before opening the letter. She spilled a few drops as she set her mug back down.

For pity's sake, there's no need to be nervous.

All the same, her heart jolted as she began to read.

Dear Mabel Browne,

I hope you are well. My family and I appreciate your help in finding justice for Lester.

Please forgive my imposing on your holiday season. I hope you won't mind this small intrusion too much, especially considering how much you already have to deal with. I'm writing to you because I believe you're in a unique position to do a great kindness not only to me, but also for someone I know is a dear, lifelong friend of yours.

If I'm asking too much, please forgive and think no more about it. Or if you believe I'm wrong to pursue this, I'll be grateful if you'd let me know. I suppose it's best for me simply to say it.

Since returning to Medicine Spring, I find I'm developing feelings for Miss Birdie. You may think this is foolish at my age, but love has no season, as an old song says. As you grow older, God willing, you'll learn how true this is. My two questions are:

1. Do you think it would be appropriate for me to approach

Birdie and ask for a date?

2. If so, I'm wondering whether you might be willing to put out a feeler for me first.

I wouldn't want to appear insensitive by approaching Birdie right now, with Lester not even in the grave yet—especially if she cared for him and is grieving. I would never want to trespass on whatever feelings they had for each other. But I'm an old man, and what time I have left here on earth is looking mighty precious. I hope you understand.

Birdie is such a good woman. I want whatever is best for her—whether that includes me or not. (I considered asking Katherine to talk to Birdie for me, but I believe you know Katherine well enough to understand why I'm asking you instead, as much as I like and respect her.)

Thank you, Mabel. You are a good woman too.
Sincerely,
Charles Bedford

For a moment, Mabel sat in stunned silence, rereading the letter to be sure she understood, but it still came out the same. The Bedford brothers were both interested in the same woman—and Mabel didn't blame them. Nearly sixty years after the older brother had asked Grandma to intercede for him, here came the younger brother, asking the same thing of Mabel.

"Why me?" she moaned. Koi stared at her with an expression that suggested she might be questioning Mabel's mental stability.

Yes, Mabel had known Miss Birdie her entire life, and yes, she did love her and want the best for her. Did Mabel have the right to decide whether Miss Birdie ought to know someone cared for her though—perhaps enough to propose marriage?

Mabel groaned. Of course, she didn't. Miss Birdie had already lost one chance at love. Not to put too fine a point on it, but Miss Birdie was a big girl. If she couldn't make her own decisions by now about whom she should go out with, then neither could Mabel.

Might Uncle Charles's approach be inconsiderate or hurtful? Mabel didn't think so. Miss Birdie had barely known Lester. As shocked as she'd been to learn he'd been interested in her long ago, there had never been any kind of relationship between them. Now, here was a man who seemed ready to offer her one. From everything Mabel had seen of Uncle Charles, she couldn't imagine his ever being anything other than considerate and gentlemanly.

Not to mention, Mabel had plenty on her own plate to deal with.

God bless them.

She smiled and texted Nita: *Please tell your Uncle Charles Mabel says, Go for it.*

Chapter Forty-Two

THE DAY BEFORE CHRISTMAS EVE, MABEL sat at her kitchen table, wrapping presents and inserting gift certificates into cards. The radio station was already playing Christmas music almost non-stop, but for news and commercial breaks. Tomorrow through Christmas Day, little short of a Martian invasion would justify interrupting the sounds of cheer and goodwill.

Mabel checked off gifts as she went, feeling satisfied that there seemed to be nothing left to buy. John had been her biggest problem. Their relationship was only a few months old, so she didn't feel she could give him anything too personal. On the other hand, a boyfriend deserved something a bit more thoughtful than a gift card.

Then she'd remembered John's interest in true crime. She'd talked to Nita, who'd recommended a police detective's memoir about his career solving cold cases. She hoped he'd like it.

Almost at the end of her list, she froze. *Acey.*

Should she give him something? He still hadn't returned to finish the basement—probably because nothing was left down there that he wanted. Mabel sighed. Knowing him, he'd expect something. Maybe she could just stick a bit of money in a Christmas card. That would probably please him more than anything else.

As Mabel pondered this final hole in her gift-giving, the music stopped.

"We now interrupt our programming to bring you this breaking news, just in from our WXAT-AM newsroom. Medicine Spring Police now announcing an arrest has been made in the

1962 death of local resident Catherine Abramovich and disappearance of local resident and federal employee Lester Bedford, also presumed dead pending positive identification through DNA analysis.

"Police now informing us local resident Bonnie Abramovich Putnam, currently in custody and charged with homicide in the recent death of her husband Richard Putnam, has been additionally charged in connection with both 1962 deaths. A news conference is expected, and we will as always keep you informed."

Mabel gaped, trying to process what she'd just heard. It was hard to imagine Bonnie's killing her own sister. She wondered what evidence the arrest was based on.

She grabbed her phone. Who to call first?

John, of course. He was likeliest to have an inkling of what was going on. Though if he knew, wouldn't he have called her already?

Of course, he didn't pick up, so she was forced to leave a voicemail. After that, she texted Lisa and Nita. Then, Mabel puttered around the house for a while, checking her phone periodically for a missed call or mysterious battery failure.

Finally, she grabbed her coat and bag. Nita and her family needed to hear this news right now, if they hadn't already. John was AWOL, and Lisa was having high tea at some fancy place with Tim's mother and grandmothers that afternoon, so she doubted either would pick up the phone. However, Nita, being her own boss, could usually shake loose for a few minutes.

Barnacle trailed her to the back door, pushing his body in front of her knee. "I'll be back soon, guys."

All the same, she had to force her way through the door while shoving at her dog. Koi watched from her command post atop the Hoosier cupboard, and then turned pointedly away.

Reader's Retreat was doing a lively business when Mabel arrived. She slipped through the crowd, thinking maybe this had been a bad idea.

Nita was handing a bulky hardback to a middle-aged woman. "I know he'll enjoy this. Please let me know."

The woman headed to the register, where Zac was checking out another customer. "Come over here a second." Nita pulled Mabel into a back corner lined with shelves of home repair and how-to books.

Two padded chairs faced each other. Nita took one and motioned Mabel to sit in the other. "People like to sit and use the 'library.'" Nita air-quoted. "I wish they'd either buy or learn to use the internet. Still, I always give them a chance to browse, since they might be deciding whether they want one of them. Don't want to get a reputation for being crabby with the customers."

Mabel winked. "That's Tabasco's job."

"Right." Nita laughed, then leaned in. "Now, what was that weird text about Uncle Charles?"

Mabel grinned. "Before I answer that, did you tell him?"

"I did. He got a grin bigger than the one on your face right now and he's been humming tunes and cackling to himself ever since."

"I hope I didn't make a mistake. I've never given advice to someone old enough to be my father or grandfather before." Mabel explained the note she'd gotten in the mail.

"Oh, that's so sweet. You did the only thing you could. They're old enough to run their own romances. I hope it works out for them—I'd love if she became my Aunt Birdie."

"And I'd be jealous." Mabel glanced around. "Look, I don't want to hold you up too long, but I'm here for a reason. I wanted to make sure you and your family knew. Did you hear Bonnie Putnam's been arrested for both Lester and Cathy's deaths?"

Nita leapt to her feet and did a happy dance, hands over her mouth to muffle her shrieks. After a moment, she caught Mabel's hands and they both jumped up and down till Mabel got winded and had to pull away.

"Tell me everything," Nita said between pants.

"That's all the news bulletin said. There's supposed to be a news conference at some point. Don't know when. Don't you think they'll call you guys because you're Lester's family?"

Nita was already dialing her phone.

When Mabel got home, she'd barely slipped her coat off before John called. "Hey. You got my message."

"On my way over. I found out a ton of stuff. Doubt it's anything they won't make public—I just got it a little early. But you have to promise to keep it to yourself till after the news conference."

"What about Lisa? She just now came up on call-waiting."

"Tell her you'll call back. She and Nita deserve the inside scoop, but we have to be careful not to steal Chief Dunlap's thunder, or we'll never get another one."

"All right, but I hope they announce something soon."

Mabel tidied up her gift-wrapping mess—and the mess underneath that—barely in time to start a pan of cider with a couple of cinnamon sticks heating on the stove before John's car pulled up. Barnacle set off a frenzied barrage of barks and jumped up to put his paws on the kitchen door so he could look out. When he recognized John, he added tail wagging to his display.

Koi, unperturbed, strolled over to the kitchen table and leapt up to arrange herself for John's maximum appreciation. "Off," Mabel ordered.

Koi scrunched her eyes and purred.

Mabel threw up her hands and went to open the door.

John came in and wrapped her in an embrace, which Barnacle struggled to turn into a group hug. John's shoulder was cold and damp from the freezing drizzle, and when he kissed her, his lips were cool on hers. In his arms, Mabel felt warm all over. She melted against him for a moment, but business was business.

"Tell me everything." She towed him in the direction of the table.

John laughed. "May I take my jacket off first?"

"Of course. I'm sorry." She took his coat. "Would you like some warm cider?"

"Love some. Your kitchen smells inviting."

Mabel smiled—that had been her goal. "Do you want to talk here or the living room?"

"Might as well go in there and make ourselves at home."

When they'd made themselves comfy on the couch, cider mugs steaming on the coffee table in front of them, John rubbed his chin. "We've got a lot to talk about, but let me catch you up on the murders first."

"Please." Mabel shifted in her seat. "I mean…Bonnie? Her own sister?"

"I know. It's crazy. A lot of our theories were correct, but obviously not all the players."

John was silent for a moment, sipping his cider, till Mabel started tapping her fingers on the arm of the couch. "Sorry. I'm trying to figure out the best way to tell it. Should I start with her deciding to confess? Or the story she gave Lt. Sizemore?"

"Why *did* she confess? She might've been able to pass off Ricky's death as an accident, in all that snow. Why even confess to his murder—let alone the other two?"

"Only she can say. Maybe Christmas is a good time to

cleanse the soul of old sins. I don't think she's had a happy moment in the past sixty years."

John tilted his head. "Besides, I think she realized trying to fight charges on Ricky was pointless—between the vehicle damage and her highly suspicious failure to call the cops or her security company about your intrusion. Plus, she had three witnesses telling fairly consistent stories about the deal she offered you. I guess she felt she might as well unburden herself as to the other two at this point."

Mabel attempted to curl one foot under her, but right away her leg cramped. She massaged the muscle. "What was her story—why would she kill her sister?"

"Basically, she told police she was always in Cathy's shadow, and Bonnie felt like she herself never got anything."

"Like what?"

"Guys seemed to be the big thing. Cathy was older and more popular, and according to Bonnie, boys threw themselves at Cathy all the time. Bonnie resented her sister getting all this attention. She felt like all anybody needed was one good boyfriend and blamed Cathy for hoarding."

"That sounds a bit…unbalanced." Mabel had never attracted boys the way Cathy did either, but it was hardly fair to blame the girl for what guys did.

John set his drink down. "She finally snapped when she learned Cathy had not only started dating the man Bonnie was obsessed with, but for the first time, told Bonnie she thought she was in love."

"Oh, dear."

"Bonnie exploded, because she felt he 'belonged' to her." John shook his head. "In fact, it almost seems as if she still believes that."

Mabel leaned forward. "Mark Enlow? No, wait—he told us there was someone else at the end."

John leaned back and grinned. "Ben Holt."

"No!" Mabel thought about his smile and incredible charm, even today. Yes, she could see how both sisters fell for him. "So Bonnie attacked Cathy?"

"She says it was an accident. It started as a typical catfight, with some shoving and hair pulling, but Cathy got knocked down and hit her head. Bonnie was devastated, or so she says, and she panicked. She grabbed a few things to make it look like a robbery gone bad, then did a quick clean-up and tried to flee the scene."

"Then there was Lester." Mabel could see the scene almost as clearly as if she'd been an eyewitness.

"There he was."

"How could she kill him?" Mabel waved a hand. "I mean—not morally, but a full-grown man?"

"At first, she darted back behind the fence and bushes, trying to decide what to do. When she stuck her head back out, she was just in time to see Ricky grab the mailbag from behind and knock Lester down."

"So, Ricky killed him. Why did Bonnie confess?"

John laughed. "Slow down. You're getting ahead of me. Ricky ran for the woods, but Lester didn't get up. Bonnie crept back out and saw Lester had hit his head on the sidewalk. Then, his eyelids fluttered."

"So, she had a live witness who could place her at the house right about Cathy's time of death."

"Yeah. I guess she could've claimed she'd merely discovered the body, but she was a wreck. She didn't think she could hold it together. In that moment, she decided it would be easiest just to kill Lester and let someone else discover the bodies. As Cathy's sister, and far from the scene, she'd be a lot less likely to attract police attention."

Mabel swallowed. Poor Lester—in love, and with his whole life ahead of him.

"She banged his head against the sidewalk a few more times, till she was sure he was dead."

"How could she? And this time I do mean morally."

"I don't know. I've heard killing gets easier after the first time."

Mabel shuddered.

She reflected in silence for a moment, then straightened. "You know, all this started with Ben Holt, didn't it? With Crawford writing Ricky out of his will so he could leave his fortune to Holt—and two women in love with him, one to the point of violence."

"You're right—I hadn't thought about it." John gave her a small salute.

"Do we know why he chose to come back now, after being away all those years?"

John nodded. "Police had already talked to him earlier. By the time Cathy was killed he'd developed serious feelings for her. Her terrible death on top of Crawford's, and the mess with the inheritance he'd never known about, were too much. Everything in his life seemed to have fallen apart. So, he simply left town and stayed away."

"Why—?"

John held up his hand. "Lately, all the news reports started bringing back those days—between the reappearance of the old mail, and the recovery of Lester's remains. Holt said he decided it was time to 'lay a Christmas ghost to rest.'"

Her phone was ringing. "It's Nita."

"Go ahead." John picked up his cider.

Mabel muted the call. "She wants us to come to her house."

"Oh, good grief." John groaned. "I'm *not* reciting this story for the entire family. Listen, I give up. Tell her to come on over here, but *all* this is confidential until after Chief Dunlap has her moment."

"Wait, hang on." Mabel read an incoming text. "Now, Lisa's inviting us over too. Why don't we go there, since she's kind of midway, and we won't have the entire Bedford family to deal with."

An hour later, they were all sprawled around Lisa's apartment living room, except for Tim, who was still at work. Lisa's one-eyed tomcat Ulysses curled purring on John's lap as John repeated his account of Bonnie's confession.

Nita, who'd earlier been dancing so ecstatically at the news of Bonnie's confession, sat somber. Mabel perched on the arm of the chair, her hand on Nita's back. "I know," Mabel whispered. "It was awful. Completely senseless."

"To make a very long story shorter," John said, "Bonnie was still kneeling beside the body when Ricky came back to check on Lester. He wasn't a hundred percent sure he hadn't been seen, and was rattled, of course. All he'd wanted was the will. Bonnie looked up and said she'd seen everything, but they could 'fix it.'"

Nita's hand clenched.

"They just needed to dispose of the body." John gave Nita an apologetic look. "Bonnie let him think he'd killed Lester and told him they were in this together now. She explained about Cathy, saying it had also been an accident, but they couldn't count on anyone believing that. With any luck, if Lester disappeared, people would start thinking he'd killed Cathy and gone on the run."

Lisa growled, making Ulysses jump. "That's obscene. Bonnie Putnam must be colder than dry ice."

Mabel put her arms around Nita, who'd begun to tremble.

"They're gonna go lenient on her—I know they will," Nita said. "Because she's old. She murdered Uncle Lester, and now she's lived her whole worthless life. Long enough to get a soft landing because she's an old woman."

There was nothing to say to that. Privately, Mabel was afraid Nita was right.

"So," John continued, "Ricky and Bonnie made their unholy pact. Bonnie insisted on two things—silence and marriage. I'm guessing it was a miserable marriage, but Bonnie got what she wanted out of it anyway. Ricky stayed quiet all these years, but he was recently diagnosed with an inoperable cancer, and he started to collapse emotionally. Then, Lester's remains resurfaced. Plus, seeing Nita at Reader's Retreat shook him up."

"Well, he sure didn't say anything to me." Nita folded her arms.

"No, but he started wrestling with his conscience. First, he returned the mail sack. Then, he wanted to confess to killing Lester, and the whole scheme, and Bonnie was desperate to shut him up."

"So she did." Mabel got up with a grimace. Her back was as stiff as a British upper lip. She crossed to the coffee table, picked up her tea mug, and finding it empty, set it back down.

"Right," John said. "They argued about it, and then *A Christmas Carol* finally did him in—Bud Bender should be proud. Ricky couldn't face that third spirit, knowing he was facing the end of his own misspent life. When Bonnie couldn't convince him to honor his promise to her, she did what she'd done with her previous problems and killed him."

"I'm glad she confessed anyway." Nita sighed. "After all this. If she'd done that sixty years ago, she could've saved a lot of people a lot of misery."

Chapter Forty-Three

MABEL, SITTING ALONE ON A CHAIR near the organ, sweated in her flowing red polyester choir robe. Hot air poured from the heating system and rose to settle in the loft where the choir and organist melted slowly away during the lengthy prelude.

Mabel wouldn't be singing any of the special music with the choir, but in theory would stick around and join them for the hymns. Privately, she figured she could escape down the back stairs if *O, Holy Night* went too far wrong.

Looking out over the railing, Mabel felt a catch in her throat at the scent of the tree and evergreen swags, the flickering candles on the altar, the massed red and white poinsettias. She remembered other Christmases with her family. With Grandma and Grandpa, God rest their souls. A homesick longing filled her chest.

Mabel wouldn't be home with her family for Christmas till breakfast tomorrow morning—because of this. Tonight, she had to sing.

Afterward, if she survived, John had invited her to his parents' Christmas Eve reception. Lisa would be with Tim and his family, but Nita had also invited her to join the Bedfords for midnight supper.

Mabel hadn't committed to anything, because she wasn't sure whether she'd feel relieved and happy after this…or want to cry. At least, Lisa, the only one of her friends who belonged to Mabel's church, was at Tim's tonight. None would be here to witness whatever happened when Mabel stood up to sing.

She hadn't told her parents about her solo, for fear they'd come. She'd just said she wouldn't be able to leave till morning.

The organ prelude ended, and Janet looked at Mabel and nodded. Mabel rose, hoping her wobbling knees would hold her. A hush filled the sanctuary.

A few people below looked up. Mabel swallowed.

Janet launched into the intro. Mabel heard her pickup notes and opened her mouth, but nothing came out. It was like missing the brass ring on a merry-go-round. She looked over at Janet in terror. She'd already blown it.

Janet smiled and smoothly repeated the intro.

On a silent prayer, Mabel opened her mouth once more and sang. Her first few notes quavered, and she had to gulp for breath. This was awful.

Focus on the words.

Was that Grandma in her head again? The voice of God? Or maybe just what Amanda and Janet had been telling her?

Mabel focused. She wasn't here. She was on a wintry plain thousands of years ago. Those were sheep grazing below her, a few of the shepherds looking up in wonder.

Mabel sang on, still struggling to fit in enough good breaths, but her voice felt stronger as she went. Finally, she reached the blessed last couple of measures and managed to hold the last note nearly as long as she was supposed to.

Her knees gave out and Mabel sank into her seat, as the choir and congregation rose for the opening hymn, *O, Come, All Ye Faithful.* Amanda and several choir members smiled at her. Nanette even gave a covert thumbs-up.

Thank you, Mabel mouthed. Finally, it felt like Christmas.

She stayed for the entire service, all the way through the final *Silent Night,* when all the lights were dimmed. One by one, hand to hand, candles were lit, till their wavering light made bright spots in the darkness.

After the service, Mabel returned to the choir room to hang up her robe and retrieve her coat. She threaded through the crowd in the hallway, collecting several "well dones," more than a few "beautifuls," and a chorus of "Merry Christmases."

When she'd managed to work her way to the choir room door, she stopped in stunned silence, staring at the smiling faces waiting for her in a cluster at the back corner. John came over and pulled her into a hug. "I'm so proud of you. Merry Christmas."

Lisa and Tim were there, along with Nita. They all crowded around Mabel for a group hug.

"Wait. I didn't expect any of you here. Why didn't you tell me you were coming?"

Lisa and Nita simultaneously gave Mabel a hilariously similar raised eyebrow. "You're kidding, right?" Nita asked. "You'd have freaked out if you knew we were going to be here."

"You were great, Mabes," Lisa said. "I knew you'd nail it."

Mabel turned to hang up her robe. "Well, I'm retiring at the top of my career as a tenor, so be glad you all got to hear my farewell performance."

"You're coming over—right, Mabel?" Nita asked. "Everybody wants to see you."

Mabel hesitated. She hated to turn Nita down, but she didn't think she could face a big dinner with all those people, however wonderful they all were. And she definitely didn't want to stay for a midnight supper and then have to drive all the way home afterward.

"Sorry, Nita." John put his arm around Mabel's shoulders. "You *will* come along to my folks'—won't you? I'll drive, so you don't have to do anything but come and enjoy."

Again, Mabel hesitated. She wasn't certain she was ready to meet John's family, but John's smile was so encouraging, she heard her voice say, "Sure."

Nita grinned. "I understand—but walk out this way, okay? I want you to see who else came with me."

At the turn for the side doors, Lisa and Tim hugged everyone and wished them a Merry Christmas before heading out into the night. Mabel and John continued with Nita to the front entry, where people milled around, talking and laughing. Nita nodded toward a bench in the corner, where an older couple sat in their winter coats and grinned at Mabel.

"Merry Christmas, baby," Miss Birdie said. "You sang like an angel tonight. I'm sure your grandma was listening from heaven. She'd be so proud of you."

Mabel stammered a thank-you. "Merry Christmas to you both. Are you going to midnight supper, Miss Birdie?"

Miss Birdie exchanged a fond look with Uncle Charles. "Appears I am, since this gentleman invited me."

John squeezed Mabel's shoulder. "This beautiful lady and I need to get on the road to my parents', but we have to drop off Mabel's car first, so we'd better get going. Have a lovely evening."

"You young people do the same," Miss Birdie said. "Be sure you don't stay out too late, or Santa won't come."

Mabel laughed as she exchanged hugs with Miss Birdie and Nita, then shook Uncle Charles's hand. "Take good care of this lady," she told him.

"You know I will," he promised.

As they stepped out into the night, hand in hand, flurries danced under the parking lot lights. "What a beautiful Christmas Eve." Mabel sighed. "A beautiful Holy Night."

AUTHOR NOTE

I hope you've enjoyed spending Christmas with Mabel and her friends as much as I've enjoyed sharing this holiday adventure with you. Christmas was always a favorite season for me, growing up in snow country in a simpler time. We gathered our own greens from the woods and decorated with WWII-era glass ornaments, a dime-store nativity, and cardboard putz houses sprinkled with mica snow beneath the tree.

Mabel's memories of Christmas at Grandma's strongly echo my own childhood, and I had so much fun recreating a snowy Christmas—with a side of mayhem.

A favorite part of my childhood Christmas season was the flurry of baking and candy-making that led up to Christmas Eve. My mom and grandma were fabulous bakers, each with her own repertoire of cookies and homemade fruitcake. Both made candy. My mother's favorite was hard tack, a traditional holiday hard candy flavored with tiny vials of spicy oils she bought from the pharmacy. Grandma loved no-fail Fantasy Fudge, made from the recipe on the jar of marshmallow crème. The easy fudge recipe can still be readily found. Just check your jar of marshmallow crème, or search online for "original fantasy fudge recipe."

Hard tack is less common, but fun to make. Unless you have a very old-fashioned drugstore near you, your best bet for the flavorings is to look online. Search for "candy oils" or "candy flavoring oils." My mom used LorAnn oils, which are still available, but there are other suppliers. Don't like spice flavors? You'll find a world of others, including fruit and fanciful choices like bubblegum, cotton candy, and butter rum. Cheap food coloring makes for pretty candy, as well as helping you color-code your flavors.

Recipes are available online, but I do recommend you adopt Ms. Kathryn Ann's cooking method, using a candy thermometer, unless you're an experienced candy maker like Miss Birdie's mother (or mine). Temperature precision is essential when it comes to making candy that cracks correctly and doesn't end up soft, sticky, or shattered.

A beautiful glass bowl or jar of hard tack looks like a handful of precious gems. It makes a dandy homemade Christmas gift, or just a sweet, fat-free holiday treat for yourself and your family.

Warning! Handle the hot candy mixture with care—it can stick to your skin and produce a nasty burn. If children want to help, it's best to let them help smash the sheet of cooled candy or shake it in the bag of powdered sugar.

Merry Christmas, Happy Holidays, and a Most Blessed New Year from all of us here in Medicine Spring!

9 781953 957504